I Could Be You

Sheila Bugler grew up in a small town in the west of Ireland. After studying Psychology at University College Galway (now called NUI Galway) she left Ireland and worked as an EFL teacher, travelling to Italy, Spain, Germany, Holland and Argentina.

She is the author of a series of crime novels featuring DI Ellen Kelly. The novels are set in South East London, an area she knows and loves.

She now lives in Eastbourne, on the beautiful East Sussex coast. Eastbourne is the location for her series of crime novels featuring investigative journalist Dee Doran.

When she's not writing, Sheila does corporate writing and storytelling, she runs creative writing courses, is a tutor for the Writers Bureau and is a mentor on the WoMentoring programme. She reviews crime fiction for crimesquad.com and she is a regular guest on BBC Radio Sussex.

She is married with two children.

Also by Sheila Bugler

I Could Be You
When the Dead Speak
Before You Were Gone
The Lucky Eight
You Were Always Mine

I COULD BE YOU

SHEILA BUGLER

CANELO CRIME

First published in the United Kingdom in 2020 by Canelo

This edition published in the United Kingdom in 2022 by

Canelo
Unit 9, 5th Floor
Cargo Works, 1–2 Hatfields
London, SE1 9PG
United Kingdom

A CIP catalogue record for this book is available from the British Library.

Print ISBN 978 1 80436 179 5
Ebook ISBN 978 1 78863 770 1

Look for more great books at www.canelo.co

Printed and bound in Great Britain by Clays Ltd, Elcograf S.p.A.

1

To Sheila Gleeson, Clodagh Curran, Alex Gander and Fiona Walker. You women have got me through a rough few years. I love you all.

A Note on Sovereign Harbour

In this book, Dee doesn't like Sovereign Harbour. In fact, the harbour is a vibrant, bustling marina with lots of bars and restaurants. It's well worth a visit if you're ever in Eastbourne!

Part One

One

Dee

The dead woman lay across the narrow road, speckles of sunlight spotted across her head and shoulders. The lower half of the body was twisted away from the upper half, as if someone had deliberately tried to split her in two. Her dark hair, glossy and shiny in the afternoon sunshine, spread out like an oil slick across the dust track and the sun-scorched tufts of yellow grass beneath her.

Her legs were destroyed. A mess of dirty denim, torn flesh and blood. Lots of blood. A single indented tyre mark where her thighs had once been. A pale blue sandal, the same colour as her T-shirt, lay on the ground beside her. There was no sign of the other sandal.

The position of the body, face down in the dirt, made it impossible for Dee Doran to see her face. She didn't need to. She'd recognised the woman immediately. Katie Hope, her neighbour and friend, and single mother to two-year-old Jake.

She couldn't tell how long Katie had been lying here. A combination of heat and hangover meant Dee hadn't left her house all morning. She tried to remember if she'd heard a car, but her sitting room was at the back of the house, facing the beach. And she'd been listening to music. Leonard Cohen's final album blasting through her speakers, blocking out whatever had been happening out there.

Three words skittered around her head. Hit and run. Someone had driven into Katie, mowed her down and left her to die. Here on this empty stretch of shingle coast on the outskirts of Eastbourne, where days passed without Dee ever seeing a car or another human being.

Her stomach contracted, and she swung away from the body as a stream of puke shot up her throat and out of her mouth. Memories of the dead woman fast-forwarded through her head. Katie heavily pregnant in the weeks leading up to the birth of her son. Pushing the buggy along the bumpy track in winter, the baby bundled up so that all Dee could see of him was a pair of pale brown eyes and a cold-reddened nose. Katie's smile, pure and perfect, when Dee said what a beautiful baby he was.

What's his name? she had asked, not interested but not knowing what else to say. Jake, Katie had told her. His name is Jake.

Dee spat the last bit of vomit out, wiped her mouth with the back of her hand and stood up. She'd tried so hard not to get close to them. Cocooned in her own bubble of self-pity and grief, she hadn't wanted to let anyone into her life. In the end, keeping her distance hadn't been an option. It was obvious to anyone with a pair of eyes that Katie was lonely. And Dee had always been a sucker for a lost soul.

Her chest ached thinking of Jake. Wondering where he was right now, and who would have the terrible task of telling him his mummy wouldn't be coming to collect him.

That was when she saw the buggy. A few feet further along the road, folded in on itself. Its metal frame twisted into awkward angles, reminding her of the dead woman. Two wheels missing. She could see one of them in the ditch. Beside the buggy was a shopping bag, which Dee guessed had been hanging on the handles of the buggy. Its contents were scattered across the path. A bunch of burst bananas; a carton of milk, split open, its contents soaked into the dusty surface of the road; a book, lying open, face down, the title in blue writing across the cover – *What Every Parent Needs to Know*.

At the side of the road, something white, blinding under the cloudless blue sky. One of those parasols you attach onto a buggy to protect your child from the sun. Except the buggy was empty.

Dee ran to the beach, slipping and skidding over the shingle, eyes scanning every inch of stone and sea and sky, her heart pounding so loud and fast it drowned out the sound of the waves rolling over the stones. Nothing. Midweek, not many people came out here, so far away from shops and other amenities.

He was only two years old. He never went anywhere on his own. Either Dee or Katie was always with him. Over the last two months, Dee had taken him swimming two or three times a week. The thought that he might have gone into the sea alone, without an adult to stop him falling face first into the waves, was unbearable.

She clambered back up the stones to the road, thinking she must have missed him. But like the beach, there was no one here. She held her breath, believing in some deep part of her that if she stayed completely still and silent, she would be able to hear him. She imagined him hiding behind the wall of her house, crouched down out of sight, too scared to come out.

But nothing moved, and when she finally released her breath and checked behind the wall, he wasn't there either. She walked back to Katie, calling Jake's name over and over.

But there was no child. Jake was gone.

–

Heat rose in waves from the dusty road, blurring the body and the white-coated men and women milling around it. Dee sat sideways in the back of a navy-blue car. Feet and legs outside the car, arms clasped tight around herself in a useless attempt to stall the violent shivers shaking her body. The car was parked across the lane, giving her an unobstructed view of everything happening a few feet further along.

She had no idea how long she'd been sitting here. Hours, minutes meant nothing. She tried to make sense of what had happened, but the facts kept slipping and sliding around her head. Some part of her brain recognised that she was in shock, and she hated herself for it. She should be stronger than this. Better able to separate herself from the tragedy unfolding in front of her. She'd always been disdainful of people who hung onto someone else's misfortune and used it to bring drama into their own empty lives.

And let's face it, Dee's life was pretty empty right now. Divorced, unemployed and living alone in the house that had belonged to her parents. If you'd told her twenty-five years ago, as a young, ambitious journalist living in London, that she'd end up back here in Eastbourne one day, washed up, worn out and jaded, she would have laughed. Her growing friendship with Katie and Jake had been the only thing that made her want to get up in the mornings. Now Katie was dead and Jake had disappeared.

'Ms Doran?'

A pair of feet on the ground in front of her own. Brown brogues, mud-coloured chinos. Dee lifted her eyes, up and up, all the way to his face. Eyes the same colour as his shoes, and a crooked nose.

'Dee,' she said. 'My name's Dee.'

He smiled and held his hand out.

'Detective Inspector Ed Mitchell. Ed.'

'Have you found him?' Dee asked.

'You got time to answer a few questions?' he asked.

'I'll tell you anything you want,' Dee said, standing up so she didn't have to crane her neck to look at him. 'But I truthfully don't know what happened here, and you need to understand that, because you shouldn't be wasting time with me. You need to be doing all you can to find Jake.'

She had a hard lump in her chest that made it difficult to breathe. Jake was so little. It was late afternoon already. He wouldn't survive a night outside by himself.

'It must have been a shock,' Ed said. 'Finding her like that. How are you holding up?'

'I'm fine. Completely fine. Please. Tell me about Jake. What are you doing to find him?'

'We're coordinating the search right now. If Jake is out here somewhere, we'll find him. I promise. Right now, the best way you can help is by telling me everything you know about the victim. Do you think you can do that, Dee?'

Dee took a deep, shuddering breath. The lump in her chest shifted but didn't disappear.

'Katie's my neighbour,' she said. '*Was* my neighbour. She lived in the mobile home a little further along the beach from my house.'

'Anyone else live there with her?' Ed asked.

A rush of memories. Jake and Katie playing on the beach outside Dee's house. Dee and Jake holding hands as they braced themselves against the icy shock of waves splashing against their ankles. Jake playing with his plastic trains. Fast asleep in his bed, lying on his side with his thumb in his mouth. Running along the shingle on a sunny spring morning, slipping and sliding on the stones. Jake. Jake. Jake.

'It was just the two of them,' she said, forcing herself to focus on the detective's questions. 'No partner or anything like that. Her parents are both dead, and she doesn't have any brothers or sisters. They were always together. He must have been with her when she was run over. He had to have been with her because you've seen the buggy and she would never leave him on his own. Sometimes, if she was going to the shops, I'd look after him for her. But he wasn't with me today, which means he was with Katie. He was in the buggy and…' Her voice trailed off, unable to finish the sentence. She looked at Ed. 'Where could he be?'

'What time was it when you first saw her?' Ed asked.

Dee paused before answering, wanting to be as exact as possible.

'Three? Ten past, maybe? I remember checking the clock in the kitchen before I left. It was just after three then. I was on my way to Asda at the harbour and she

7

was… well, like she is now. I saw the buggy and I realised Jake was missing. I went down to the sea. I thought maybe he'd run off, you know? Do you think that's what happened? I looked but I couldn't see anything, but that doesn't mean he didn't go down there, right? And then I ran back to her house. It was locked, but I banged on all the doors and looked through the windows. I could see into his bedroom but there was no sign of Jake.'

Ed had an A5 spiral-bound notebook and was taking notes with a silver fountain pen while Dee spoke.

'You didn't call the emergency services until three thirty-five,' he said. 'Why the long delay?'

'I told you. I was looking for Jake.'

A white tent had been constructed around Katie's body. Dee wanted to ask how they'd got it up so quickly, but was afraid of sounding flippant, so she shut up and waited for the next question.

'You were at home beforehand?'

'That's right,' she said.

The physical effects of drinking two bottles of wine the previous night meant she'd spent the morning in bed. When she finally dragged herself up, a peek through the curtains confirmed the worst. Another blisteringly hot summer's day. The hottest summer since God only knew when. Even without a hangover, Dee had struggled to cope with the sweltering heat of the past two months. Day after endless day of sunshine that bleached all colour from the grey and white shingle coast and turned the sea so blue it hurt her eyes to look at it.

'You don't work?' Ed asked.

'No.'

Along with the house, Dee had inherited enough money from her parents to live comfortably for the next two years at least. She was still paying the mortgage on the London home she'd shared with her ex-husband, but hopefully those payments wouldn't continue for much longer. The house was on the market; once it sold, her finances would improve even further.

'I didn't hear anything,' she said. 'No car. No screeching brakes, nothing.'

Ed raised his eyebrows. 'What makes you think it was a car?'

'Tyre mark across her leg. More tyre marks on the ground beside her. What else could it be?'

'You drive?'

She nodded. 'My car's parked around the side of my house. Battered old Volvo. It used to belong to my mother and I haven't got around to replacing it yet.'

She didn't tell him she hadn't replaced it because the Volvo, like so much else, held precious memories of her mother, and she was scared to change anything in case the memories changed too.

'We'll need to take a look at it at some point,' Ed said. 'You okay with that?'

'Of course. How long had Katie been there before I found her?'

'We're not sure yet. Does it matter?'

Dee said no, but she was lying. She couldn't stop thinking how different things might have been if she'd exercised a bit of self-control last night. She wouldn't be hung-over, for starters. And she wouldn't have to endure the repeated flashes of excruciating shame every time she remembered what she'd done. Worst of all, though, was

9

the knowledge that if she'd left the house earlier today, Katie might still be alive and Jake would be safe.

'What can you tell me about her?' Ed asked.

'She'd been living here about two and a half years,' Dee said. 'She was in Bristol before that. She told me she'd always wanted to live by the sea, so when she fell pregnant, she decided it was now or never. She's a single mum. I don't know who Jake's father is. Katie never mentioned him, and I never asked her about him.'

She paused, distracted by the things she wasn't telling Ed Mitchell. Like how pretty Katie was, especially when she smiled. How brave she was to have had a baby alone. The rush of love each time Dee saw that little boy with his hazel eyes and a smile that could cut you in two.

'You were friends?' Ed said.

'I'm her landlady. The mobile home belongs to my family. And yes, she was my friend. We're the only two households out this way; it made sense that we tried to get along as best we could. She was on her own with Jake and I felt sorry for her. So I helped out sometimes.'

It was more than helping out, but there was no need to tell him that. Spending time with Jake had become a central part of Dee's life. She adored him and felt privileged to share the experience of watching him grow up.

'You're her landlady but you don't have a key to her house?' Ed said. Then, when Dee frowned to show she didn't understand the question: 'You told me you couldn't get into her house because the front door was locked.'

'It never occurred to me. I've never had to use the key since Katie's been living here.'

'What about other friends, visitors, that sort of thing?'

'I never noticed anyone. Apart from her students. She taught the piano. But I didn't see anyone else call to see her.'

'You sure?' Ed said. 'Seems strange, don't you think?'

Dee thought of her own life, hiding out here on the edge of nowhere, not speaking to anyone for days at a time.

'Not really. She chose to move here. She must have done that for a reason.'

'What sort of reason?'

'Maybe she wanted to be alone,' Dee said. 'Some people do, you know. It doesn't make them weird or strange.'

Ed smiled. 'I never said it did. One more question, and then I think we're done for now. Can you tell me exactly what went through your mind when you first saw the body?'

She didn't answer immediately. Closed her eyes, breathed in and out, trying to slow the racing images. Katie's body. The waves of heat rising around it. Damp patches of sweat gathering in Dee's armpits. The physical and mental pain from her hangover making it difficult to concentrate on anything else. The stomach-churning shock as she realised who it was.

'Her T-shirt,' she said. 'I recognised her T-shirt. I gave it to her, you see.'

That was the start of their friendship. Dee had been sorting through her clothes, because she'd put on some weight since moving back and nothing fitted her any longer. She'd gathered up all the things that were too small, throwing everything into a black refuse bag that she planned to bring to the charity shop. Getting rid of her previous life, item by item.

Pausing when she picked up the blue T-shirt, because she'd loved that top so much. Thinking – out of nowhere – how it would suit the young woman down the road because it was the same colour as her eyes. Seeing Katie and her boy playing down by the water later that evening and wandering out to them. Asking Katie if she'd like the top but not to worry if she didn't, because the charity shop would love it. Vivienne Westwood, you see. And Katie had smiled and said wow, thanks so much.

Ed asked when Dee had given Katie the T-shirt, but she couldn't answer him, because she was remembering how Katie had asked her if she'd like to come over for dinner sometime, and Dee had said yes, thanks, that would be lovely.

She nearly hadn't gone. But a few days later, half mad with loneliness and grief, she'd taken a bottle of Pinot from the fridge and wandered along the beach as the sun was going down. The two women sat on the bench outside the mobile home, watching Jake play on the shingle while they chatted about everything and nothing.

Remembering that evening now, Dee realised she was the one who'd done most of the talking. Telling Katie about her divorce, the deaths of both her parents and her regret at never having had children of her own. Katie had been a sympathetic listener and it ended up being the first of many nights when the two women had shared a bottle of wine together while night crept in across the wide-open sky.

Before she could stop herself, Dee was crying. Big, gulping sobs that shook her body. As she tears rolled down her cheeks, she thought how she was every bit as pathetic as those people who'd cried when Princess Diana died, and every time there was a terrorist attack in London. But it made no difference. She couldn't stop crying for the beautiful young woman with the lovely smile and the little boy who would never see his mother again.

Two

Dee

Dee barely slept. Her mind refused to shut down. All she could think of was Jake. Obsessively wondering where he was and who could have taken him. She kept her phone by her bed and checked the news sites throughout the night, desperate to read that he had been found.

Ed Mitchell and his team had done a good job getting the story out quickly. The hit and run was covered by all the major sites, although the information they had to work with was pretty sketchy. The police hadn't formally identified the victim yet, but they asked anyone with information on Katie Hope or her son Jake to contact them immediately. A photo of Katie and Jake was used with the stories, and Dee found herself looking at this repeatedly.

It was a recent photo. Mother and son posing by the water, both of them smiling. A splash of blue sea behind them. They looked so happy. Over the last few months, Dee, Katie and Jake had spent so much time on the beach together – having picnics, building stone sculptures that collapsed within seconds of being constructed, splashing about in the sea, and generally having the sort of silly fun you could only have with young kids. But Dee hadn't taken this photo, and she'd never seen it before. She tried to think of anyone else who could have taken it, but she'd always thought she was Katie's only friend.

At 7.30, she was still in bed, flicking through the internet and social media, when she heard guitar chords playing and the low, gravelly growl of a man singing about love. She grabbed her phone and checked the caller ID before answering, even though she already had a good idea who it would be.

'You took your time,' she said.

'I was at a charity event at the Winter Garden last night,' Louise replied. 'By the time I got away, it was after midnight. I figured you might be asleep by then.'

'Very considerate of you.'

Dee got out of bed and pulled open the curtains, blinking against the bright sunlight. Her house was in the curve of a bay that stretched along the coast from Hastings in the east to the white chalk cliffs at the southern edge of the South Downs in the west. From her bedroom, she was able to see the buildings lining Hastings seafront on her left. To her right, she got an unwanted view of the sprawling complex of apartments and town houses that made up Sovereign Harbour.

The area had been wasteland when Dee was a child. Now, alongside the houses and apartments, the harbour was home to a busy marina, a selection of bars, restaurants, shops, a cinema and a gym. Dee hated it for no reason other than the sheer fact that it existed. As far as she was concerned, the only good thing you could say about it was that its sprawl didn't stretch as far as the quiet road where she lived.

'So,' Louise said. 'I was wondering if you fancied meeting up this evening? Go for a drink and a bite to eat. I haven't seen you properly in ages.'

The thought of sitting in a restaurant eating good food and drinking wine while Jake was out there somewhere, scared and traumatised and missing his mummy, was unthinkable.

'I don't know, Lou. I'm not sure I can face something like that.'

'It might cheer you up. And dinner's on me, by the way. Come on, Dee. I miss you.'

'You don't have to work so hard at pretending. I know the real reason you're calling. And it's okay. I'd probably do the same in your shoes.'

'I have no idea what you're talking about,' Louise said, the outrage in her voice making Dee smile. 'All right.' Louise tried again. 'I heard what happened. And I want to make sure you're okay, that's all.'

'What have you heard exactly?' Dee said.

'I know they haven't formally identified the body. That's usually because they haven't been able to track down any next of kin.'

'She had nobody,' Dee said. 'I never thought about it while she was alive. But looking back, it seems odd. I mean, everyone has somebody, right? The only people who ever visited were her students. Apart from them, it was always just the two of them, Katie and Jake.'

'She had you. I know how much you helped with Jake. That must have meant so much to her. I keep thinking, if one of my kids was missing like that, how would I feel? I couldn't bear it.'

'He was with her,' Dee said. 'When the car hit her. But by the time I arrived, the buggy was empty. It's awful, Lou. Someone ran her over and took her child. It has to be the father, doesn't it? He's found her and he's killed her and taken his son. And if he's killed Katie, that means he's a bad person. Jake can't be with a man like that. He'll be scared and missing his mum. He's never been separated from her before.'

'Hey,' Louise said. 'Try to stay calm, Dee. You can't know for sure that's what happened. Maybe Jake was on a play date or something when it happened.'

'She had his buggy. Why would she have the buggy if she didn't have Jake?'

'I don't know, Dee. I'm sorry.'

'Do you remember that story I covered a while back?' Dee said. 'Casey Hall – the boy who disappeared from his front garden in south London?'

'I remember. His stepdad killed him.'

'It was the last big story I did before Mum got sick. Casey was missing for three weeks before they found his body. Everyone knew it was the stepdad. They just couldn't prove it.'

'I remember how much it upset you. This must feel as if history's repeating itself.'

She was right. That was exactly how it felt. Only a million times worse, because Dee had never met Casey Hall, whereas she loved Jake as much as it was possible to love a child that wasn't your own.

On the beach, a man was walking along the shoreline. His body was silhouetted in the sun, still low against the water. Dee's stomach lurched as she realised who it was.

As if sensing her eyes on him, Alex Mackey looked up to where she was standing and waved.

Dee's face flushed hot and she turned away quickly without waving back, hoping he'd get the hint. Her mind flashed back to two nights ago. The look on his face when she leaned into him and whispered that she'd like him to stay the night.

'Listen,' Louise said. 'I've got to go. Spin class in ten minutes. I'll be working on this story most of the day. The police are putting a call out for volunteers later this morning. We're pushing it on our website and social media. I think a lot of people will volunteer. Everyone wants to help find the missing boy. You should come along.'

'I'll see.' Dee knew she wouldn't be there. The truth was, she couldn't face the idea of being amongst a group of strangers who'd never met Katie or Jake, all pretending they cared.

'Come to dinner with me this evening, at least,' Louise said. 'Even if you don't feel like it, it'll do you good. You shouldn't be alone at a time like this. I'll spend as much time as I can today trying to find out what's going on with the investigation. I promise I'll tell you everything I know.' She had Dee, and she knew it.

'Where do you want to go?'

'The new sushi place on Grove Road. I'll book a table. Seven o'clock. Okay, gotta rush. See you later. And try not to worry, Dee. Chances are Jake will be found soon.'

'Let's hope so,' Dee said. 'Enjoy your class.'

She risked a glance out the window. The beach was empty, no sign of Alex. She breathed out a sigh of relief, grateful he'd decided not to try to talk to her about what had – or, more accurately, hadn't – happened between them.

–

Dee spent the rest of the morning watching the news channels and checking for updates online. Nothing had changed since the story first appeared late last night. Even the local newspaper, the *Eastbourne Recorder*, was light on detail.

> Woman killed in hit-and-run accident. Victim believed to be local piano teacher Katie Hope. Police hunt under way to find victim's two-year-old son, Jake.

Underneath, details of how to volunteer in the search, and a phone number for people to call if they had information on Katie or Jake.

As editor-in-chief of the *Recorder*, Louise could have included a bit more detail, Dee thought. Her cousin needed to spend more time at her computer and less time on a stationary bicycle in the company of similarly skinny and body-obsessed airheads. The fact that Dee herself had been one of those body-obsessed airheads for many years was beside the point. Louise was a journalist, and surely the only thing that mattered now was doing every single thing she could to make sure every single person in East Sussex knew a little boy was missing.

By the afternoon, Dee had to get out of the house. The relentless switching between TV channels and scrolling through her phone. The suffocating sense of helplessness. Her skin itched with the need to be doing something. To be out there on the beach and in the town, searching for Jake.

A wave of heat hit her as she slid back the bifold doors and stepped outside. She stood on the deck, blinking as her eyes adjusted to the bright sunshine. Gradually the world around her came into focus – sun-bleached shingle, a still blue sea dotted with the crisp white sails of the dinghies from the sailing club in Pevensey. Further along the beach she could see a group of forty or fifty people moving slowly along the shoreline, and guessed these were the volunteers searching for Jake.

She stepped off the deck and walked across the shingle to the edge of the water, and along the strip of sand that only appeared when the tide was out. She walked as far as the Martello tower at Normans Bay, scanning every bit of sea and beach. Even by the water, the air was so thick and heavy it felt like she was walking through soup. When she couldn't stand the heat any longer, she turned around and retraced her steps.

She hadn't expected to find him, but even so, the sense of despair increased the closer she got to her house. She left the beach, clambering over the shingle onto the road. Narrow, with no proper surface, it was more of a track than a road. A track that led from Pevensey Bay Road to the only two houses on this quiet stretch of beach – Dee's house, and the mobile home where Katie and Jake had lived.

The entrance to the road was cordoned off. Police tape and a row of traffic cones prevented any vehicles from coming through. The white tent was still there too, although Dee knew they would have taken Katie's body to the morgue by now. She wondered when the post-mortem would be done and whether it would reveal any useful information.

As she walked towards the tent, she saw a car approach and pull up alongside the row of cones. The driver's door opened and Ed Mitchell got out. A small, round woman with short dark hair pushed open the passenger door and stood beside him.

'Mind if we ask you a few more questions?' Ed said. 'This is my colleague, Detective Constable Rachel Lewis.'

'Is this to do with Jake?' Dee asked, trying to read his face. 'Have you found him yet?'

'Could we go inside for a few minutes?' DC Lewis said. Dee didn't know why she bothered. Ed was already pushing open the front door and stepping into the house.

'And if we could have some coffee,' he added, 'that would be great. We've been out all day and we're in need of a caffeine hit.'

Downstairs, the house was open-plan. Kitchen, sitting room and dining area all merged into one big space. Along the south side, large windows gave uninterrupted views of the coast. Dee made coffee while Ed settled himself on the sofa in the living area. Rachel Lewis perched beside him, looking decidedly uncomfortable.

'Beautiful house,' Ed said. 'I remember my mother telling me about it.'

'Your mother?' Dee carried a tray – cafetière, cups, jug of milk, sugar bowl and spoons – across to the low table in front of him, setting it down and telling him to help himself.

'She was in the same book club as your mum,' Ed said. 'You would have met her at the funeral, I'm sure.'

'Possibly. That day's all a bit of a blur, to be honest.'

'Of course.' Ed leaned forward and poured coffee for all three of them.

'I'll let you help yourselves to milk and sugar,' he said, as if he was the host, not her.

'How kind,' Dee said.

If he noticed the sarcasm, he didn't show it.

'Your dad built this place?' he asked.

'Designed it. He was an architect. But you probably know that. I'd forgotten what it's like, you know. Being back here and realising everyone knows everything about you. I definitely didn't miss that when I lived in London.'

Ed smiled, and his face was suddenly shockingly handsome.

'It's not always a bad thing,' he said. 'There's a sense of community in a town like this. You don't get that so much in London, I'm guessing.'

'You're wrong about that.' Dee thought of Greenwich and all the friends she'd had there. 'The only difference in London is that you can choose your own community. I preferred that.'

Ed took a sip of his coffee.

'Ah, that's good. You planning on going back to the big smoke any time soon, or are you going to settle here?'

The truth was, Dee had no idea what she was doing with her life, but she wasn't about to share this with Ed Mitchell.

'Why are you here?' she asked. 'If it's Jake, tell me. I need to know.'

'We haven't found Jake,' Ed said. 'Not yet. We're here to ask you some more questions about Katie.'

'I've already told you everything I know.' Dee wanted to scream at him. Or hit him. What the hell was he thinking, sitting here drinking coffee and looking like he had all the time in the world when there was a child missing? 'You should be out looking for Jake, not wasting your time asking me questions I've already answered.'

'You were Katie's landlady,' DC Lewis said. 'Is that right?'

Dee forced herself to concentrate. The sooner she answered their questions, the sooner they'd be back out there trying to find Jake.

'Mum set up the initial rental agreement. Then when she died, I took that over along with everything else.'

'And Katie had been living here for about two years?' Lewis asked.

'Closer to two and a half. Like I told Ed yesterday. I wasn't living here then, but I remember seeing her when I came to visit. She was pregnant when she moved in. Mum was a bit worried about whether she'd be able to pay the rent. If she wasn't working, you know. But she felt sorry for her and was willing to risk it. And there's never been any problem with that. I mean, it's a mobile home so we don't charge much. She pays on time every month.'

'Cash?'

'Standing order from her bank account to mine. I closed all Mum's accounts after she died. Katie transferred the standing order to me when I asked her to.'

'You said she was pregnant,' Ed said. 'You're sure about that?'

'One hundred per cent.'

'How far gone when she moved in?' Lewis asked.

'Six or seven months, maybe. Does it matter?'

'Bear with us for now,' Ed said. 'So she moved in and had the baby. Did she ever mention the father?'

'I knew it,' Dee said. 'It's him, isn't it? He killed her and now he's taken Jake.'

'Where was she before she came here?' Lewis asked.

'Bristol. Although I don't think that's where she was from originally. Her accent... she sounded London, maybe. She wasn't a northerner, anyway. Apart from that, I really couldn't say. Is it the father? Because if it is, I can't help you. I've no idea who he is. Katie never mentioned him. When I asked her about him, she said Jake was the product of a one-night stand. She didn't like to talk about it, so I never asked about it again.'

'Would she have had to give references?' Lewis asked. 'Is that something your mother would have asked for? From previous landlords or an employer, for instance.'

'Maybe.' Dee stood up, that sense of needing to do something back stronger than ever now she knew the police still hadn't found Jake. 'We can check,' she said. 'Mum's office is through here. Let's take a look.'

The office was a small room at the side of the house. It was this room, more than any other in the house, that reminded Dee of her mother. This was where she used to sit every day, working on her cases, reading the newspaper and doing the *Times* crossword.

A grey filing cabinet stood in one corner of the room. Dee knew that any files relating to work or finances would be in the bottom drawer. The other drawers were set aside for family matters: photo albums, old school reports, out-of-date passports, all the memories of the life their little family shared before Dee grew up and her father died, followed by her mother a year later.

As expected, Katie's file was in the bottom drawer. It contained a copy of her tenancy agreement, a reference from her previous landlord in Bristol stating that she had been an ideal tenant, and a letter from a software development company in Shoreditch confirming her employment record.

'I thought you said she moved here from Bristol?' Ed said, reading the employer's recommendation. 'This is from a company based in London.'

'I hadn't noticed,' Dee said.

'She must have stopped working for them when she moved here,' Ed said. 'Didn't you tell me she was a piano teacher?'

'Maybe she wanted a change of scene,' Dee said. 'New life, new job.'

'Maybe. All she needed was this letter so she could secure the property. Once she had the house, I'm guessing no one cared very much how she paid her rent, as long as she was on time with it each month.'

'Are you really going to start looking into all that now that she's dead?' Dee asked. 'Does it matter? Oh. Unless… Is that why she was killed? Was she doing something illegal? Sorry, stupid question. Of course she wasn't. So what are you looking for, if it's not that?'

'We need you to come to the mortuary,' Ed said. 'We haven't been able to trace any family, and we need someone to identify the body.'

'But I've already told you who she is.'

'That's right,' Ed said. 'You told me the dead woman is your neighbour, Katie.'

'And?'

'And that's why I need you to take another look at her. Right now, if that's all right?'

She opened her mouth to tell him it wasn't all right. The dead woman was Katie Hope, and her son, Jake, was missing, and surely that was the only thing that mattered right now. But the words caught in her throat.

'What?' she said. 'What is it you're not telling me?'

'You said you were a hundred per cent certain that Katie was pregnant. And that she was Jake's mother. You don't want to change your mind about any of that?'

'She *was* his mother,' Dee said. 'She fed him and looked after him and had parties when it was his birthday. Which is the eleventh of January, by the way. We had a little party in the mobile home. Me, Katie and Jake. I baked a cake.'

A lopsided chocolate cake with ready-made icing. The first time Dee had ever baked a cake in her life. Two thick blue candles, which Jake blew out on the first attempt. Dee took a load of photos and printed them into a collage that she framed and gave to Katie a few weeks later. She had wanted to make a copy for herself as well, but she worried Katie might think that was a bit strange.

'Well then,' Ed said. 'Here's our problem, Dee. According to the post-mortem, our hit-and-run victim has never had a baby. So either you're lying to me, or the woman in the mortuary right now isn't Katie Hope.'

Three

Katie
Eleven years earlier

I've been here two weeks and I've hated every moment so far. I keep my head down, try not to make eye contact, but it makes no difference. Yesterday, a girl shoved her elbow into me as I passed her. She said she was sorry, but her friends all laughed and I know it was deliberate. Today, in class, two geeky-looking losers in the row behind me were whispering about fat people. Not so loudly the teacher could hear, but enough so I knew it was me they were talking about. I had to sit there and do nothing, shame and anger burning my skin while I imagined turning around and stabbing them in the eyes with my pen.

Stupidly, I thought things would be different when I started college. I anticipated a great new life opening up to me. Friends and nights out and invitations to sleepovers. All the things other girls did. I spent the whole summer dieting. Okay, trying to diet. It sort of worked too, because I lost seven pounds. I've put four back on over the last fortnight. Stress weight. I've been stressed since I started here because it's nothing like it's meant to be.

Generally, though, it's not the geeks who are the problem. It's the rest. The long, skinny guys with Converse trainers, ripped jeans and eyes you could drown in. The girls, all tight jeans and perfect eyebrows and straightened hair, who look right through me as if I didn't exist. When they're not elbowing me in the gut, that is.

They act like I'm nothing to them. Someone to ignore or laugh at or stick your elbow into. I've already had five years of that in school. I came here to get away from those people, but they're all around me. Flat stomachs, cat-cold eyes and sharp elbows.

I'm standing at the entrance to the canteen, trying to work up the courage to go inside. The door is closed but I can see through the glass panels that the place is packed. A group of people shove past me, a blur of faces and faded denim. Someone pushes open the door and a cacophony of sound escapes, voices and laugher, the clatter of cutlery on plates. All of it bouncing off the floor and the walls out to where I'm standing.

Two girls notice me, whisper to one another and start laughing. I turn away quickly, heat creeping up my neck and face.

'Hey.'

I've bumped into someone. I take a step back, the fire inside me raging bigger and brighter. My mouth's already open, ready to shout at him to watch where he's going, when my brain registers who he is.

'Katie, right?'

Eyes the colour of the sea on a hot summer's day. Black hair hanging over his face in a perfect messy mass of curls and waves. Shane Gilbert. If my life was a high-school rom com, Shane would be the guy I ended up with. The jock with a heart, clever enough to see through the artifice of the shallow world we live in. Except this is real life, not a movie, and guys like Shane Gilbert never end up with girls like me.

We went to school together. Lee Manor primary school in Hither Green, then Northbrook for secondary. We've known each other more than half our lives, but we've never been friends. We've always moved in different circles. The main difference being that Shane's circle included other people, while mine has always consisted of me and no one else.

This is the first time he's ever spoken to me.

I want to say something back, but I can't think of a single intelligent thing. My brain has turned to sludge. There's a low buzzing sound inside my head and my heart is jumping so hard against my chest I'm worried he'll be able to hear it.

He puts his hand out, touches my arm, and I jump back. My skin, where he's touched me, fizzing.

'Are you okay?' he says.

'Fine.'

He looks like he wants to ask me something else. I hold my breath, thinking that whatever he wants to know, I'll tell him. All the thoughts and feelings I've never told anyone else, and now, right this moment, I understand why. It's because all this time, I've been waiting for him.

But the question never comes, He grins instead and the world stops moving, and if everything were to end right now, I wouldn't care. He says something I think must be 'bye' or 'see you later', because suddenly he's moved past me and disappeared through the doors into the noise and bright lights and clattering cutlery of the college canteen, and I'm alone again.

It's nearly midnight, but I can't sleep. I'm sitting at my computer, looking at Shane's Facebook wall. Trying to get back that connection I felt with him. Wondering if he's in his own room thinking about me too. There was something between us, an understanding. I felt it and so did he. The question I saw in his eyes, I didn't make that up. He wants to know the girl inside me, who's been waiting her entire life for someone who'll listen to her.

He's got a moody black-and-white photo as his profile picture – hollow shadows beneath cheekbones that are so perfect they don't look real. I trace my finger along the picture and wonder what his skin feels like.

We've been Facebook friends for a while now. It's not difficult to get people to accept friend requests, because the more Facebook friends you have, the better. Shane was one of the first to accept me as a friend, and I wonder now if that was a sign that he wanted to get to know me better. He's never liked any of my posts, but that doesn't mean anything. Maybe, underneath all that confidence, he's shy.

Anyway, it's not like I post that much. I stopped using Facebook after all that cyber-stalking bullshit Marsha Carmen spread about me.

Shane's photos are great. Atmospheric black-and-white shots of landscapes and London skyscrapers; group photos of him and his friends, all of them grinning like idiots. Marsha Carmen's in a few of them. I find one that's just of her. She's half turned away from the camera, looking back over her shoulder. Smiling. For a moment, I imagine she's looking right at me, and I get that tingly tightness between my legs. I touch her face with my thumb, remembering the tiny freckles she used to get across her nose and cheeks in the summer. I scroll down the page, and her face is replaced by a shot of another skyscraper. I wonder if Marsha's told Shane about me. I hope she's had the sense to keep her mouth shut.

There are more photos, and I looked at each one in forensic detail, searching through the binge-drinking and dope-smoking for some sign of the soulful person I know is hiding underneath. But Shane's like me. Good at concealing who he really is.

As I lie in bed, muffled sounds from the pub creep through the floorboards, loud enough so I can't forget it's there. I think maybe Marsha's right and I'm deluded after all. Shane probably only spoke to me because he felt sorry for me.

But Marsha is wrong, completely and totally, because the very next day, Shane speaks to me again. He's studying computers too. It's the end of a class in which we've been doing an assignment on programming concepts. I finished it within half an hour and spent the rest of the lesson searching for an elegant way to hack Facebook accounts without being caught. I know there's a way to do it; I just need time to work it out. Suddenly the class is over, and I've been so caught up in what I'm doing I don't notice until everyone's scraping their chairs back and the chitchat of bullshit starts up all around me.

'Hey.' He catches me as I'm walking out. A light tap on my shoulder that sends darts of electricity racing down my arm.

I breathe in slowly and turn around to face him. I try to think of something clever or meaningful or funny, but

I seriously have no idea how you're meant to respond to a 'hey'.

In the end, all I can manage is a feeble 'hey' right back. The smile turns into a grin and he asks me how I'm finding things so far.

'It's okay,' I mumble, my stupid brain refusing to do what I need it to. I'm so busy trying to think of something to tell him, something he'll remember and smile about later, that it takes a moment for me to realise he's talking again.

'Bit different from Northbrook, right? I mean, that place was like a prison. I think it should be against the law to treat kids like that. At sixteen, we're old enough to join the army if we want to. So in theory, right, it's okay for us to, like, *kill* somebody, but we're still not allowed to hang out in the park at lunchtime.'

'Crazy,' I say. 'Yeah.'

He looks like he's thinking about how to respond to that priceless nugget. I'm half expecting him to ask me if I've sought medical help for my mental problems, but instead he says he's heading to the canteen to hang with 'some of the gang', and do I fancy joining him?

I can feel my face burning when I say thanks but no thanks, I have to get home. It's not true. More than anything in the world, I want to stay with him, but I know what it'll be like in the canteen with 'the gang'. They'll all be sitting around talking and laughing, hanging on every word Shane says, and not one person will notice me or speak to me and I'll sit there wishing I was dead.

'No problem,' Shane says. 'Guess your old man's got you working behind the bar these days. Maybe I'll pop in sometime to say hi.'

He says bye then and heads off towards the canteen with that loping walk of his, hoisting his bag across his shoulders, while I stand there unable to move or breathe or speak.

Maybe I'll pop in sometime to say hi.

And I know this is it. The moment it all begins.

Four

Dee

'How sure are you that Katie was Jake's biological mother?' Ed asked.

'It never occurred to me that she might not be,' Dee said. 'I mean, I *saw* her when she was pregnant. You can't fake that, can you? And presumably you've already checked the hospital, her medical records, stuff like that?'

'Someone called Katie Hope certainly gave birth to a baby boy called Jake on the eleventh of January 2016,' Ed said. 'Eight pounds three ounces. Healthy child. No complications. Baby was born in the maternity unit at the Conquest in Hastings. We're still trying to find out whether she gave birth alone, or if she had a birth partner. If she did, that might help us find out where she is.'

They were in Ed's car, driving along the seafront en route to the hospital. He had dropped Rachel Lewis off along the way. She was going to help coordinate the volunteers searching every bit of coast and land for the missing boy. Now, it was just Dee and Ed in the car.

The French market was in full flow – stalls selling cheese and cured meats and crêpes with chocolate sauce. Tourists eating fish and chips and ice cream; seagulls hovering overhead, waiting to dive in and scoop up any scraps of food they could. The pier stretched out over the turquoise sea, white and gold and magnificent.

Dee barely saw any of it. In her mind, she was back on the road outside her house yesterday afternoon. The sweltering sunshine, waves of heat rising from the dusty ground, blurring the outlines of the body. The sudden sharp shock of recognition when she saw the T-shirt and realised who the dead woman was.

'If it's not Katie,' she said, 'who is it? And why was she wearing Katie's clothes?'

'That's why I need you,' Ed said.

At the Cavendish Hotel, he swung right, away from the seafront and along the wide avenue that led into town.

'Why didn't you simply show me a photo?' she asked.

'What do you mean?'

'You know exactly what I mean. You could have got a photo of the dead woman's face and shown that to me instead of dragging me across to the mortuary.'

'I want to make sure this time,' Ed said.

'You think I lied?'

'I think you made a mistake,' he said. 'Not the same thing.'

Dee stayed silent, knowing there was no point trying to argue with him until she'd seen the body again. In her heart, she knew she'd been right the first time. The dead woman *was* Katie, no matter what the pathologist or Ed Mitchell said. If anyone had made a mistake, it wasn't her.

Ed started humming under his breath. Dee paid no attention at first. Until she recognised the tune.

'Are you doing that on purpose?' she asked.

Ed smiled. 'Sorry, it got inside my head and I can't get rid of it.'

'You have no idea how much I hate that song,' Dee said.

'You don't like Tom Jones? Seriously?'

'Seriously.'

'Why do you call yourself Dee, anyway?' Ed asked.

'What sort of question is that?'

'Delilah's such a pretty name,' he said. 'I don't understand why you'd shorten it.'

'If you don't shut up right now,' she said, 'I'll jump out of this car and you'll have to find someone else to identify the body.'

Her father had named her Delilah after the Tom Jones song that was number two in the UK charts the month she was born. Dee had spent most of her childhood and far too much of her adult life enduring stupid people singing the song to her. She'd loved her father very much, but there was a part of her that would never forgive him for that.

The mortuary was located at the back of Eastbourne's District General Hospital.

'Ready?' Ed asked, after he'd parked the car.

She wanted to tell him she'd changed her mind. Her mother had died here in the DGH twenty-two months ago. Dee hadn't been back since and didn't want to go inside now to look at another dead person. But Ed was already getting out of the car and walking towards the swinging glass doors that led into the mortuary. Hating him for taking it for granted that she was okay with this, Dee followed him.

Their footsteps clattered and echoed around them, bouncing off the tiled floor and the concrete walls that seemed to crawl closer to Dee the further she went. The corridor was too long and too brightly lit, reminding her of a recurring dream she had. In it, she was running down a corridor like this one, trying to reach a door at the end. Except no matter how fast she ran, it was never fast enough, because the door never got any closer and whoever was behind her, chasing her, was about to catch her and there was nothing she could do to stop it happening.

And then, different to the dream, they'd arrived at the end of the corridor and were standing outside a blue door with a window panel and a metal handle.

'Okay?' Ed asked. He touched her shoulder, and just for a moment, she wanted him to wrap his arms around her and hold her tight.

'I'm fine,' she said, taking a step back to put a bit of distance between them.

Ed knocked on the door, and it was opened a moment later by a fresh-faced man who looked too young to be a qualified doctor but who seemed, as far as Dee could work out, to be the pathologist.

There was a bit of back-slapping and how-you-doing between the two men, but it didn't go on long enough for Dee to get irritated.

'This is Dee Doran,' Ed said, nodding at her.

'Peter Sweeney,' Babyface said, holding out a hand, which Dee dutifully shook. 'Pathologist,' he added, in case she hadn't worked that out yet. 'I understand you want another look at our victim?'

'I've asked Dee if she wouldn't mind,' Ed said, before she could tell Peter Sweeney that what she really wanted was a large glass of wine somewhere far away from here.

'In here.' The pathologist gestured to a door on her left, one she hadn't noticed until now.

He opened it and stood back to let Dee and Ed go ahead of him into a small room that under other circumstances might be described as cosy. Muted lighting, a comfortable-looking sofa and a low table with a fresh bunch of flowers in a vase. One wall was covered with a grey curtain, which Peter pulled back, revealing a large window.

'She's on the other side of this glass,' he said.

Dee stepped forward, her heart thudding so loudly she was sure the other two must be able to hear it. She held her breath, dreading the moment she would reach the glass. But when she did, all she could see was darkness on the other side. No gurney with a body lying on top of it, nothing.

She looked at Peter, frowning.

'When you're ready,' he said, 'I turn the light on. The switch is here, see? There's no rush. Sometimes people like to wait a few moments.'

'I don't want to wait,' Dee said.

Peter flicked the switch, and the room on the other side of the glass exploded in a flash of light so bright Dee couldn't see anything at first. Then, gradually, as her eyes adjusted, the details became clear.

Off-white walls, a single strip light along the ceiling. And directly beneath the light, a dead woman lying on a gurney. The woman's body was covered with a white sheet, all the way up to her neck, hiding the damage from the car and whatever further butchery the baby-faced pathologist had inflicted on her.

She was beautiful. That was the first thing Dee thought when she saw her. Rich blue-black hair that spread out from her face like a blanket of silk. Her skin was white and unblemished; eyes closed so that her long dark lashes rested on her white skin like strokes from a delicate paintbrush.

'Dee?' Ed Mitchell's voice, sounding as if he was speaking to her from somewhere far away.

Dee shook her head, unable to answer him, unable to drag her eyes away from the body. Trying to work it out.

The dead woman on the road. She'd been pushing Jake's buggy, wearing Katie's clothes. And yet…

'It's not her,' she whispered. 'It's not Katie. I have no idea who this woman is. I've never seen her before.'

Five

Dee

Louise was already seated in the restaurant when Dee got there. Even though Dee had arrived five minutes early, hoping to order a glass of wine and relax before her cousin turned up.

'Darling!' Louise rushed towards her, grabbing her in a hug that felt too powerful for her tiny body. 'Sooooo good to see you. Wow. You look great. Love your hair like that. Come and sit down. I've ordered you a glass of Pinot. You're not driving, I assume?'

'No,' Dee said, extricating herself from her cousin's grip. 'Not driving. You smell lovely, by the way. Jo Malone?'

'Martin keeps me well stocked.' Louise sat down and gestured for Dee to do the same. 'He gets it at the airport, of course. Although I don't think it's any cheaper there than anywhere else.'

'How is he?' Dee asked, not really caring. Martin, Louise's husband, was a pilot with BA. As far as Dee was concerned, his job was the single interesting thing about him.

'He's good,' Louise said. 'Has his ups and downs, you know what they're like.'

'Men?' Dee thought of Alex, flirting with her one second then retreating like a hunted hound when she dared to suggest taking things a step further. 'Not sure I do know what they're like, to be honest,' she said. 'Did you speak to him about helping out a bit more?'

'I didn't say anything in the end,' Louise said. 'It's not his fault really. I mean, he's a pilot. Of course he's going to be away a lot. I knew that when I married him.'

Dee chose not to point out that the problem with Martin wasn't just when he was away for his job. From what she could see, he spent more time on the golf course when he wasn't flying than he did with his family. But she was tired of telling Louise that her husband needed to do more to help with the kids and the house. Besides, it wasn't as if Louise seemed to struggle with any of it. In fact, she seemed to be able to juggle a full-time job with full-time parenting without ever finding it all too much.

'Tell me about the kids,' Dee said instead. 'How are they?'

'They're great,' Louise said. 'Daisy said hi, by the way. Asked if she can come and see you soon. I said maybe we'd pop over at the weekend. What do you think? We could have a picnic on the beach. She'd love it. They both would. You know how much Ben loves being at yours. They could play together and we could chat. Sorry. I didn't mean... It was only an idea, that's all.' She trailed off, looking crestfallen.

'What's wrong?' Dee said.

'You frowned,' Louise said. 'When I suggested coming over at the weekend. Don't worry. We wouldn't like to put you out.'

'Oh Lou.' Dee reached out and took her cousin's perfectly manicured hand in hers. 'It wasn't because I don't want you to come over. When you mentioned Daisy, I thought of Jake, that's all.'

'Of course,' Louise said. 'How insensitive of me. The police have released details of the car, by the way. A red Peugeot 208. Isn't it amazing what they can work out from a few flakes of paint and some tyre marks?'

Dee went back over the last few days, trying to remember if she'd seen a red car anywhere near Katie's house, but her mind drew a blank. She wanted desperately to talk about the dead woman, tell Louise what she'd discovered today. But Ed had made it very clear she wasn't to tell a single soul about it.

'I need to work out what this means for the investigation,' he'd said, after they'd left the morgue and he was driving her home. 'And how it impacts on our search for Jake. If the victim isn't Katie, then we have to consider the possibility that it was Katie driving the car that killed that poor girl.'

'Katie doesn't have a car,' Dee said. 'And she wouldn't... She's a lovely young woman, Ed. There's no way she could have done something like that.'

'Your mother took a copy of her driver's licence,' Ed said. 'Just because she doesn't have a car doesn't mean she can't drive.'

Before he'd dropped her off, Ed had repeated his warning to keep quiet about the dead woman.

'Finding Jake is still our number one priority,' he said. 'Until we do that, I want to make sure we are in complete control of what information we release to the public and what we keep to ourselves. You understand that, don't you?'

Dee got out of the car without answering, slamming the door as hard as she could. She hated him for thinking he could tell her what she could and couldn't do. Hated him even more for his easy assumption that she might do something that would hinder the search for Jake.

She'd spent the rest of the afternoon stewing inside the house, trying, and failing, to make sense of what she'd learned that afternoon. Trying to picture Katie – sweet, smiley Katie – pressing her foot on the accelerator and driving into the woman with the blue-black hair.

'Dee?' Louise's voice dragged her back. 'If you want to talk…'

'Let's order first,' Dee said, pulling her hand away so she could pick up her menu. 'I'm starving.'

They chose their food and talked about inconsequential things until it arrived. As soon as their plates were laid in front of them, Louise got started.

'How are you holding up?' she said. 'I know this must be horrendous for you. What can I do to help?'

'I don't know, Lou,' Dee said. 'This isn't just some story to get an exclusive on. Katie's my… Katie *was* my friend. And you know how much I care about Jake. It doesn't feel right talking to you about it. I'm sorry.'

'Listen to me,' Louise said. 'I'm not here to pump you for information. I wouldn't do that. I'm here as your friend. Of course the paper has to cover the story. That's my job and I'll make sure we get every detail right before we report it. But this conversation right now? This is strictly off the record. I swear.'

Dee had ordered sushi, which she'd barely touched. The raw fish was a mistake. Something about the texture reminded her of the dead woman's face under the too-bright strip light.

'What do you know about it?' she asked.

'I know it's being treated as a hit and run,' Louise said. 'And the police don't know who did it, or where Jake is.'

Dee nodded, relieved that her cousin's resourcefulness hadn't stretched to working out that the dead woman wasn't Katie.

'The police have coordinated a huge search party,' Louise continued. 'They're going back out tomorrow. Further east along the beach this time. The investigation's being led by Ed Mitchell. Remember him?'

Dee shook her head.

'Oh. My. God.' Louise's eyes widened. 'Eddie Mitchell. I had the craziest crush on him for years. How could you not remember?'

'Of course.' Dee smiled, relieved. She'd felt a tug of familiarity with Ed Mitchell that she hadn't been entirely comfortable about. Now she understood why. It was nothing to do with being attracted to him, and everything to do with the fact that they'd known each other when they were younger. She remembered him singing the song in the car earlier, and realised now he'd already worked out that they were in school together. Although it was difficult to reconcile the man she'd been with earlier with the rugby-playing jock Louise had wasted two years of her teenage years mooning over.

'Is it true that Katie was hit on purpose?' Louise said.

'Looks that way,' Dee said. 'You know that road, Louise. Who the hell drives out there?'

'Could be joy-riders,' Louise said. 'That's a growing problem at the moment.'

Dee rolled her eyes. Her cousin's ongoing attempts to make out that the town's morals were in a downward decline never impressed her.

'Do you want me to continue or not?' Louise said.

'Sorry.' Dee waved her fork, indicating that she should carry on.

'My guess is the father,' Louise said. 'She's been hiding from him ever since she had the boy. Probably why she moved here in the first place. She was running away from him. He's found her and killed her and taken his son.'

Dee pierced a piece of raw tuna with her fork and put it in her mouth. But the taste of the fish made her gag and she had to spit it into her napkin.

Louise's nose wrinkled. 'Are you okay, Dee?'

Dee nodded, although she wasn't okay. Images churned around inside her head: Katie and Jake; the dead woman, the black imprint of a car tyre across the pale flesh of her leg. The underlying, pervasive sense of guilt. Knowing that if she hadn't got so drunk the night before, she might have left the house earlier and been able to prevent what had happened.

'I feel so helpless,' she said. 'Like I need to be doing something to find them.'

'Them?' Louise said.

'Sorry,' Dee said, realising her mistake. Ever since discovering that the dead woman wasn't Katie, she knew in her heart of hearts that Jake was with his mum. And that was good, because whatever else Katie might have done, Dee knew she'd never harm her son.

'I meant Jake,' she said. 'And whoever's taken him.'

45

'What can you do that the police aren't already doing?' Louise asked.

'Do you remember the phone-hacking scandal?' Dee said. In 2011, one of the UK's most successful weekly papers had closed down when it was revealed that some of its journalists had been hacking people's phones for information. The scandal was a huge story. As well as big-name celebrities, the victims had included a missing teenage girl. A journalist had hacked into her mobile phone, deleting her voicemail messages once he'd listened to them. The deleted messages gave the family hope that their daughter was still alive and listening to them herself. The sense of false hope seemed unbearably cruel when the family later discovered that she had been murdered on the day she disappeared.

'I remember how angry you were about it,' Louise said.

'I still am,' Dee said. 'But the thing is, Louise, I know so many other journalists who did that and got away with it. And if it helps find Jake, why not do it?'

'You cannot be thinking of hacking into Katie's phone,' Louise said. She leaned forward, lowering her voice as if she was scared of being overheard. 'Even if she's dead, I'm pretty sure it's still illegal. You could get into real trouble for doing something like that.'

Except Katie wasn't dead. Which meant hacking her phone might actually give Dee something useful. Something that would help her find Katie and Jake. She'd called Katie's phone several times earlier. Ed Mitchell hadn't told her she couldn't do that. But each call went directly to voicemail. Dee had left a few messages, but so far Katie hadn't called her back.

'What else am I meant to do?' she said. 'Just sit around waiting for Jake to turn up safe and sound?'

'There's lots you can do. Volunteer to join the search, help with the social media stuff. We're setting up a Facebook page and pushing for information on Twitter.'

'It's not enough.'

'Listen to me,' Louise said. 'I know how awful this must be. I've seen how much happiness Katie and Jake brought you over the last few months. I can't begin to imagine what you're going through at the moment.'

A pain in Dee's throat prevented her from saying anything. Even if she could speak, what would she say? Louise was right. After the break-up of her marriage and the deaths of both her parents, Dee had slipped into a dark depression that had seemed impossible to shake off. Until she'd let Katie and Jake into her life.

Katie had had a child in her twenties and to hell with the consequences. Doing it alone, without anyone to help her or tell her that she was doing a great job, or to share the simple joy of loving their child more than anything else in the world. Unlike Dee, who'd also fallen pregnant in her twenties and terminated it within a week of finding out, believing that a child would be nothing but a huge pain-in-the-arse inconvenience. Back then, she'd assumed there'd be plenty of time to become a mother.

She had avoided them at first, certain that seeing Katie and Jake every day would only intensify her own feelings of loss and failure. As it turned out, the opposite was true. Finding a new friend and sharing the pure pleasure of watching a little boy grow up had brought her more joy than she could have imagined.

'There's something odd about the way the police are handling this,' Louise said. 'They keep saying they want to speak to anyone with information on Katie or Jake. Why won't they simply come out with it and tell people that she's the victim and her son is missing?'

'They must have their reasons,' Dee said. 'But how would I know what they're up to? I found the body. That's it. There's nothing else I can tell you.'

'Of course,' Louise said. 'And I can see how much this has affected you. Is there anything I can do?'

Dee shook her head. She knew the offer of help was genuine, but Ed's warning to keep quiet was echoing round her head. For now, she must keep her cousin in the dark.

–

Dee walked home after dinner, refusing Louise's offer of a lift. They might go back a long way, but Dee was old enough and wise enough to know that the differences in their personalities meant they should limit the time they spent together. After an extended session of hugging and air-kissing and promises to chat soon, she made her escape.

She walked through the town, bars and restaurants buzzing with people and life, exaggerating her sense of being an outsider. There was no one, with the exception of Louise, that Dee could just call and ask to meet for a drink. Apart from Alex, of course, but after the other evening, she doubted she would see him any time soon. Which was just as well, given the fact that he was married and still living with his wife.

Night was drawing in fast by the time she reached the seafront. Strings of lights had come on along the promenade, reminding her – as they always did – of Christmas. The pier, lit up too, stretched like an ocean liner into the black, empty sea. Lots of people were out and about. Couples walking hand in hand, groups of teenagers on the beach, smoking and drinking and God knew what else.

Dee had always loved walking at night-time. In London, she'd never tired of the thrill of being out in the city late; of the little slices of insight into other people's lives, captured in the lit-up windows of their homes. But walking by the sea with the moon low over the water, the waves crashing on the shingle and the blinking and twinkling stars dotted across the sky, was special.

Even the harbour didn't seem so bad at night. The boats bobbing quietly on the water, the sounds of laughter and voices drifting out from the bars and restaurants, and – finally – the peace as she reached the empty stretch of beach between the end of the harbour and her house. Except tonight, for the first time since moving back, she didn't feel safe here. The darkness swallowed her up as she left the bright lights of the harbour behind her. Her footsteps seemed too loud, echoing back to her across the stillness of the night, so that she kept thinking they belonged to someone coming up behind her.

She walked fast, keen to get inside, lock the door and block out the memory of the dead woman lying on the road. Down on the beach, something moved. A dark flash streaking across the shingle. She stopped, heart thumping, breathing too fast, eyes scanning the beach. There it was again, coming towards her.

'Who's there?' she called.

No one answered, and as her eyes adjusted, she realised that what she'd seen was a pair of foxes. A mother and cub. The two animals stopped dead when she shouted, staring at her.

Dee hurried towards the house, averting her eyes from the spot where the body had been. As she fumbled to get her keys out of her bag, she heard a noise behind her, making her jump. The keys fell from her hand, clattering too loudly as they hit the ground so she couldn't hear who or what had made the sound that had startled her.

'Hello?'

When no one answered, she bent down to search for the keys, cursing herself for not replacing the bulb in the motion-sensitive light over the porch. She had to get down on her knees, patting the ground all around her with both hands, until she eventually found them. Breathing a sigh of relief, she stood up.

But when she turned back to unlock the front door, there was someone standing directly in front of her, blocking the way.

Six

Katie
Eleven years earlier

Ella Tate. Pale-skinned, blue-eyed, long-limbed and elegant. I should have hated her the moment I set eyes on her. In fact, I barely noticed her at first. Big mistake.

She's not brash or loud or anything like the usual type my dad hires to work behind the bar. Less 'in your face'. Some of them, I get a feeling for them right away – the sort of person who'll ignore me or take the piss, depending on their mood. Only they can't do that while they're being paid by my dad, so they're forced to be nice to me instead. Smiles as fake as their lipsticked mouths and jiggly pushed-up breasts. I see right through them.

It's different with Ella. She acts as if she barely notices me. Which is a joke, because with a backside as big as mine, I'm pretty hard to miss. Dad says she's shy, but he's wrong. Shyness has nothing to do with it. She's too self-obsessed for that. You see, the simple fact about Ella Tate is this: she doesn't care about anyone else except herself.

The first time I saw her, a week before I started college, I was having dinner in the bar with Dad.

'Who's the new girl?' I asked.

It was the end of the summer holidays and Dad was treating me. Dinner is normally a ready meal by myself in front of the TV. Volume turned up louder than is good for me to cover up the sounds from the pub below. The fact that we live over the pub has always given Dad the excuse he needs not to spend any actual time with me. He's able to convince himself that because we're both in the same building, that's good enough.

'Ella,' he said. 'Started last week. Mark Tate's kid. Remember poor old Mark?'

I nodded. Mark Tate, Dad's golfing buddy, who died of cancer the same year Mum left us.

'Any good?'

Dad finished chewing his mouthful of steak before answering.

'A bit quiet, maybe. But the punters like her. Obviously. She's doing A levels. Same as you. Different subjects, though. Music and something else.'

It was the 'obviously' that made me take a second look. Until then, all I'd been doing was trying to keep the conversation going. He can be a bit quiet himself, my dad, and I hate the silence that hangs between us sometimes. Without my mum, it's like we can't find anything to talk about any more.

Ella must have felt me watching her, because she glanced up from the pint she was pulling. Her face turned a bit pink when I carried on staring, but she managed a sort of half-smile before looking away again.

I could see, especially with a bit of colour in her pale cheeks, that there was something about her. She didn't seem the sort of person who tried very hard or cared very much about how they looked. But girls like that don't need to, do they?

I noted her figure – thin, bordering on skinny – and her dark hair, plaited into a long braid that hung down over one shoulder. She wasn't wearing any make-up, and maybe that's one of the reasons I didn't see her for what she was right away. Alongside Cathy and Rachel, the other girls working that evening, she seemed a bit bland.

But the more I've watched her since then, the more I can see what Dad meant. There's an elegance about her that I've spent the last few days carefully copying. She moves gracefully, like a professional dancer, and when she's tired or hot or bored, she stretches her head back, turning it slowly from side to side, the pale skin at her neck glowing under the soft lighting over the bar.

I kept the dinner going for as long as I could, knowing Dad would make me go upstairs right afterwards. But there's a limit to how long anyone can spend eating a plate of beer-battered fish with hand-cut chips and mushy peas, especially when it's gone cold and lumps of fat are starting to congeal on the sides of the plate. I ate more than I needed to, telling myself I'd skip breakfast in the morning to make up for it.

As always, Dad wolfed down his steak and fries, pausing only to answer the questions I could think of to ask him. When he'd finished, he made a point of looking at his watch every few seconds while I ate the rest of my food as slowly as I could. Eventually, when there was nothing left, I put my knife and fork together the way Mum taught me and asked Dad if I could have a pudding.

'No you bloody can't,' he said. 'There's a tub of Ben and Jerry's in the freezer upstairs. You can have some of

that if you're still hungry. Although,' he looked meaning-
fully at my plate, 'I can't see how you could be after all
that.'

Tears pricked my eyes and I blinked them away quickly
so he wouldn't see. He didn't mean to upset me, and it
wasn't exactly his fault if I was a greedy pig who couldn't
control her appetite.

Dad nodded at Ella, who came over and cleared our
plates away. I wanted to ask him if I could stay down
here for a while, but he'd already stood up, hitching
his trousers over the big ball of his stomach, and said
something to Ella that I didn't catch. It must have been
funny, because she laughed. And there was something
about watching them like that – heads closer together than
they should have been, the light, breathy sound of her
laughter – that sent a surge of hot rage burning through
me.

'Dad.'

I must have sounded sharper than I meant to, because
when he looked away from her to me, he was frowning.

'Can I stay for a bit?'

The frown deepened, and I knew there was no point
arguing. I could feel Ella's eyes on both of us, probably
trying to work out what was going on. Not wanting to
give her the satisfaction of knowing more about us than
she should, I told Dad it was fine, I'd go upstairs if that
was what he wanted, then swung around and left without
another word.

Upstairs, I put the TV on, trying out Ella's way of
moving – back straight, head held high like a puppet's
with the string pulled tight. I turned the volume up, but
no matter how loud I made it, I could still hear the sounds

coming from downstairs. The clink of glasses, the low rumble of conversation, and every few minutes, the light, bright, tinkling sound of Ella Tate's pretty little laugh.

Seven

Dee

The man moved towards her. Dee screamed. As her eyes adjusted, she was able to make out his features. When she realised who it was, she shoved his shoulder, causing him to stagger back.

'What was that for?'

'For scaring me half to death,' she said. 'Jesus, Alex, what were you thinking, creeping up on me like that?'

'Listening to Garth Brooks,' he said, pulling the flex of a white earphone out of the top of his jacket. 'I never heard you.'

'Why are you here?' Dee asked, choosing not to comment on Alex's choice of music. She despised Garth Brooks every bit as much as she loved Johnny Cash. Johnny, who sang every word of every song as if it was the truest thing he'd ever felt. How anyone thought it was okay to put the two men in the same category called 'country' and assume it meant they were similar was a mystery she would never solve.

'I wanted to see if you were okay,' Alex said.

'Why wouldn't I be?'

'I heard about Katie.' He gestured in the direction of the road. 'Is it true, Dee? Is she really dead?'

'Come inside,' Dee said. 'I don't want to talk about it out here. It's too close to where it happened.'

Alex followed her into the house and produced the bottle of wine he'd brought, insisting they open that first. Dee clocked the 'first', but didn't comment. If she had any shred of self-respect, she'd tell him to go home. At fifty-one, she was too old to be sitting up late at night drinking too much wine with another woman's husband. Even if, as Alex claimed, he and his wife were practically estranged.

Alex worked at a boatyard on the beach at Normans Bay, a short walk from Dee's house. She'd met him soon after she'd moved back home. He was on his own, working on the hollowed-out hull of a boat that had seen better days. Unlike Alex, who was one of the most beautiful men Dee had ever laid eyes on – tanned skin, sun-bleached hair and a tight, wiry body.

He was standing on the deck, scrubbing the wood with some sort of carpenter's tool. He must have heard her coming, because he looked up, using his hand to shield his eyes from the sun. The sight of him, bathed in sunshine so it looked like there was a ring of fire around him, made the breath catch in her throat. She was almost past the boat when he jumped down, wiped his hands on the front of his jeans and introduced himself.

Over time, they'd become friends of sorts. Alex was there for Dee after her mother died, dropping into her house on his way home from work to see how she was doing. Gradually, the frequency and length of these visits increased, until he had become a semi-permanent fixture. Dee knew he was married, and she knew it wasn't normal for a married man to spend so much time with a woman who wasn't his wife. But she was lonely, and Alex was there. Someone she could talk to, drink wine with, and who made her feel a little bit less crap about everything.

'It was me who found her,' she said, waiting until the wine had been poured and they were sitting outside on the deck. 'She was just lying there, in the middle of the road. It was horrible.'

'Jesus.' Alex rubbed a hand across his face before downing half the contents of his glass. 'Such a terrible thing. Do they have any idea who did it?'

'I don't think so,' Dee said.

Alex pulled out a packet of tobacco and started rolling a cigarette.

'I was hoping you'd tell me there'd been some sort of mistake,' he said. 'I'm having a hard time getting my head around this. You don't expect something like this to happen to someone you know.'

'I didn't realise you knew her,' Dee said.

'I didn't really. But the little fella – Jake – he loved the boats, see? Remember that big trawler we were working on at the beginning of the summer?'

Jake would have loved the excitement of exploring an old boat, Dee thought. And Alex would have been good with him too. Patient and fun, showing the boy around and sharing interesting facts about the boat he was working on, hamming up his Glasgow accent to make Jake laugh.

'When I knew she was on her own,' he said. 'I took Jake with me the odd time. To give her a break, you know.'

'She never said anything,' Dee said.

'No reason she would. It was no big deal.'

'If you say so.' Dee felt unaccountably disappointed that Katie had never mentioned that she knew Alex. Until she realised that she herself had avoided talking about Alex to Katie as well. She'd felt ashamed that she was spending so much time with a married man, and hadn't wanted Katie to think less of her. Now, she wondered what Katie's reasons had been for omitting to mention Alex's name in any of their conversations.

'He's a lovely wee kid,' Alex said. 'I helped out with the search earlier. It was totally depressing. All of these people out looking for him and not a sign of him anywhere.'

'I haven't been able to think of anything else since I found her,' Dee said. 'And when I saw the buggy... I keep going over it, trying to work out if I could have done something.'

'What could you have done?' Alex said. 'She'd already been run over by the time you found her, hadn't she?'

'It's not her.' The words blurted out of her before she could stop them.

'Who's not her?' Alex said.

'The dead girl,' Dee said. 'It's not Katie. I thought it was when I saw her. She was wearing Katie's T-shirt and she looked like her. But I was wrong. It's not her and no one knows who she is or where Katie and Jake are. And the police think Katie killed her, but I can't believe that.'

'Whoa.' Alex held up a hand, stopping the flow of words tumbling from Dee's mouth. 'Way too fast, Dee. Start again. From the beginning.'

She told him everything – from finding Katie's body and searching for Jake, through to the trip to the morgue earlier today and seeing the dead woman lying on the gurney.

'And it wasn't Katie,' she said. 'The woman who was killed, I've never seen her before.'

Alex opened his mouth, as if he was going to say something, but he stayed silent. Dee understood. He was trying to make sense of something that didn't make sense. A woman wearing Katie's clothes, pushing Jake's buggy, had been killed outside Katie's house. But she wasn't Katie.

'Did she have, like, a sister or something?' Alex said eventually.

'Not that I know of.'

'And you're sure?' Alex said. 'That it's not her, I mean.'

'Positive.'

He lifted the bottle to refill their glasses, but it was already empty.

'Okay if I open another?' he asked.

'Sure,' Dee said.

She watched him moving around inside her kitchen, as familiar with the place as if he lived here.

'My ex-husband's an alcoholic,' Dee said when Alex came back with the open bottle of wine.

'Okay,' Alex said, leaning over her to refill her glass. 'Any reason you're telling me that now?'

'I'm starting to wonder if I might be one too.'

'It's my fault,' Alex said. 'I'm a bad influence. Tell you what, Dee. We'll have this wee glass and then I'll be on my way, okay?'

'Sure.'

She was confused. Had he thought she was asking for help? If so, he was a more arrogant sod than she'd realised.

'If this girl's not Katie,' Alex said, 'at least it means she's okay. And it means Jake's okay too. Because he'll be with her, right?'

'I guess so,' Dee said.

'So where is she, then?' Alex asked.

'I have no idea.'

'You don't think…' Alex paused, then shook his head. 'No. Course not. Sorry, Dee. It's just… I don't know what to think.'

'Katie wouldn't do something like that,' Dee said.

'I know. There must be another reason why she's done a runner. In fact, I thought she was acting a bit funny the last time I saw her. I didn't pay much attention, but now I'm wondering, you know, if something was worrying her.'

'When was that?' Dee said. She questioned how she had missed it. Alex and Katie. It had never occurred to her they could be friends. If that was all they were.

'The day before it happened,' Alex said. 'I dropped by on my way home from work to see if she wanted me to take Jake for a few hours the following morning. She acted funny when she answered the door. Usually she'd invite me in, offer me a drink, and I'd play with the wee fella for a bit. But that evening, it was like she couldn't wait to get rid of me.'

'So you came here instead,' Dee said.

'That's right.' He grinned. 'I was on my way to yours anyway. Like I said, I'd only planned to drop into Katie's for a few minutes.'

When he'd turned up that evening, with a bottle of wine and a supermarket bouquet of flowers, Dee had actually been flattered. It hadn't crossed her mind that they had been intended for someone else.

'The photo,' she said, remembering the image on her TV screen – Katie and Jake on the beach together. 'The one the police are using. Was that you?'

'Yeah.' Alex nodded. 'That's my handiwork. I took it a few weeks ago, gave it to her as a present. She didn't seem to have many photos of the pair of them together.'

Dee drained her glass and stood up. 'I've got a headache,' she said. 'I'm going to take some painkillers and go to bed.'

She picked up his half-full glass, along with her empty one, and carried them into the kitchen. She heard Alex following her but didn't turn around to look at him when he spoke.

'Have I done something wrong, Dee?'

'Nothing,' she said. 'I'm feeling a bit rubbish, that's all. Are you okay to see yourself out?'

She stood with her back to him, waiting for him to leave. He didn't move at first, and she thought she'd have to turn around and scream at him before he got the message. But then he left, shutting the front door so hard Dee felt the vibrations all the way to where she was standing.

Her hands were curled into fists, nails digging so hard into her skin that she had four half-moon indentations on each palm when she unfolded her fingers. The glass he'd been drinking from still had wine in it. Shimmering green and gold under the too-bright kitchen lights.

She slammed the back of her hand into it, and watched as it flew across the worktop, a spray of liquid soaring out of it as it fell and shattered into tiny pieces.

Eight

Dee

Someone was calling Dee's name. She could hear the voice but couldn't see anyone. She was standing on a long, empty road. Nothing moved, there was no sound except the haunting echo of the woman's voice. And then she saw her. Lying on the road in front of her. She was wearing a blue T-shirt. Her feet were bare. One blue sandal lay on the ground beside her. There was no sign of the other sandal.

The woman wasn't moving, and Dee thought she was dead. Until she lifted her head and looked right at her.

'Help me, Dee.'

She'd thought the woman was Katie, but she was wrong. It was her mother lying on the dusty ground, legs destroyed, arms reaching out, calling for her daughter. Dee started to run towards her, but a blinding white light appeared from nowhere, consuming everything, until there was nothing but her mother's voice calling her name and the white light burning her skin, sucking all the air into it until she couldn't breathe.

A screeching sound jolted her out of the dream and she was suddenly awake. Curled uncomfortably in the wicker chair on the deck, an empty bottle of wine on the table.

A pair of squawking seagulls were fighting over a piece of shellfish on the shingle a few feet away.

The sun was coming up, low and white and blindingly bright against the still sea. The last traces of the dream faded as she sat up and vomited over the side of the chair. The stench of sick filled the air; the bitter, burning taste of it lingered in her mouth and throat, chunks of regurgitated food sticking between her teeth.

A wave of sadness washed over her, suffocating in its intensity. The thought of going inside, showering and getting dressed to face another day filled her with dread. She couldn't do it. She wouldn't do it. In a moment, when she was able to dredge up some energy, she was going to go inside, crawl into bed, pull the duvet over her head and stay like that until this long day passed.

Except going to bed would do nothing to ease the tightness across her chest, or the gnawing anxiety eating its way through the lining of her stomach. The only thing that would make her feel better was finding out that Jake was okay.

With immense effort, she dragged herself out of the chair and poured herself a pint of water, which she drank slowly, afraid to glug it too fast in case she threw up again. The water made her feel slightly better, and she was contemplating a shower when the opening chords of 'Ring of Fire' blasted from her phone.

She answered it, knowing there was only one person who'd call this early.

'The dead woman's not Katie,' Louise said, rushing past the hellos and how-are-yous and getting straight to the point.

'How did you find out?' Dee asked.

'How did I find *out*?' Louise's voice rose with that self-righteous tone Dee knew so well. 'You mean you *knew* and you didn't *tell* me?'

'Ed asked me not to tell anyone,' Dee said.

'*Ed*? I didn't realise you were on first-name terms.'

'I would call him Eddie,' Dee said. 'Only he told me he doesn't like it.'

'You can be a real cow sometimes,' Louise said. 'You know that?'

'Lou,' Dee said, checking the time on the microwave. 'It's five past seven in the morning. I'm allowed to be anything I want this early. So tell me, how did you find out?'

'It's all over the bloody news,' Louise said. 'National, as well as local. Switch on your TV. They think Katie was driving the car that killed the woman. Did she own a red Peugeot?'

Holding the phone to her ear, Dee turned on her TV. Katie and Jake smiling on the screen, the sea burning blue and bright behind them. A line of text beneath saying that police wanted to speak to Katie urgently in relation to a hit-and-run incident.

Overnight, she'd gone from victim to suspect.

'You *told* me it was Katie,' Louise said. 'Why would you lie to me, Dee? Don't you trust me?'

Dee closed her eyes so she wouldn't have to look at Katie and Jake while she answered.

'I thought it was Katie,' she said. 'At first. Then yesterday afternoon, Ed asked me if I'd take another look at the body.'

'Why?'

65

'The post-mortem showed something unexpected,' Dee said. 'I was so sure he was wrong. But I went with him, thinking it was some silly mistake. And then I saw her and I realised it wasn't Katie.'

'What did they find in the post-mortem?' Louise asked.

'I don't know,' Dee said. 'Ed didn't tell me and I didn't ask.'

'Bullshit,' Louise said. 'You're a journalist. Of course you bloody asked.'

'I'm a journalist who's taking a career break,' Dee said, although they both knew this wasn't strictly true. The real reason she wasn't working was because no one wanted to employ her. After the break-up of her marriage, she'd come back to Eastbourne to look after her dying mother. It had never occurred to her that she'd have problems finding another job. It was only later, after her mother was dead and Dee started looking for work, that she realised if you were a woman the wrong side of forty-five, no one was interested in employing you.

'Yadda yadda yadda,' Louise said. 'Listen to me, Dee. This is important. You know how tough things are for local papers like the *Recorder* at the moment. If we could get an exclusive on this, before the nationals get involved, imagine what it could do for our readership. What about the red Peugeot? Is it hers?'

'She doesn't have a car,' Dee said.

On Dee's TV, the news had moved on to another story. Brexit negotiations in Brussels had hit another rocky patch. When Dee opened her eyes, Katie and Jake had been replaced by a shot of the prime minister giving a press conference.

'I'm sorry,' she said. 'I'd like to help, Louise. Really. But there's nothing I can tell you.'

'Swear?'

'Swear.'

Louise sighed. 'I don't believe you, but if you're not going to be straight with me, there's nothing I can do. Promise me you'll think about it, at least?'

'Think about what?'

'Being straight with me.'

'I promise,' Dee said.

She hung up, but kept the phone in her hand, wishing there was someone she could call to talk about what was happening. But the only person she could think of was Alex. And right now, he'd probably still be in bed, tucked up beside his wife.

—

Dee spent the rest of the morning holed up inside the house, nursing her hangover and obsessively watching the news. When she saw a journalist being filmed on the stretch of beach near her house, she went to the window. A crowd was gathered at the end of the road. TV vans with satellites on their roofs, journalists milling around on the beach, bright flashes of light from the many cameras taking photos. The journalists were a noisy lot; their voices and laughter carried across the beach to Dee's house, a stark reminder that she was no longer part of all that.

The police were back as well. Two uniformed officers guarding a line of blue-and-yellow police tape that had been put up to block the journalists from coming down the road. Not that it put them off. They came onto the beach instead, peering rudely through the windows of

Dee's house as they passed. Twice someone rang her doorbell. Both times she ignored it.

By mid afternoon, the story hadn't changed. The police were looking for Katie Hope, twenty-seven-year-old single mother, and her son Jake. They wanted to speak with Katie urgently about a hit-and-run incident in Eastbourne on Tuesday afternoon. They were urging anyone with information about Katie, her two-year-old son or the victim to get in touch.

When she couldn't stand being indoors a second longer, Dee slipped out the back of the house and walked along the beach to the extended mobile home where Katie and Jake had lived until two days ago. The journalists had obviously given up on finding anything and there was no one out this far now. When she looked back, she could see them – a greedy pack on the other side of the police tape, waiting to pounce.

This place had been Dee's first home. She'd lived here with her parents until she was six years old. Her father had bought the plot of land, installed the mobile home and built an extension so it was big enough for them to live in comfortably while his grand masterpiece was being constructed a few hundred yards further up the beach.

Today, the entrance was cordoned off by another line of police tape. Dee wandered around to the side of the house that faced the beach. There was more tape here, drawn all the way across the land around the house. She was contemplating whether to dip under it when she heard footsteps on the road outside. She ran back to the beach side of the property, slipped under the tape and walked up to the road as if she was coming from the beach.

The footsteps belonged to a woman – young and slender with glossy blonde hair and the sort of glowing skin Dee could only dream of.

'Hello.' The woman waved and smiled, greeting Dee as if they were old friends, although Dee had never set eyes on her before.

'Melissa Hall. You're Dee, right?' She held her hand out for Dee to shake.

'I don't want to talk to anyone,' Dee said, ignoring the outstretched hand. 'And you can tell the rest of them the same thing.' She nodded at the huddle of journalists at the end of the road. 'I won't be giving any statements or answering any questions. Nothing.'

The woman withdrew her hand, blushing slightly. The colour, Dee noted sourly, enhanced the glow and made her seem even prettier.

'I'm a friend of Billy's.'

The mention of her ex-husband's name was so unexpected, Dee was momentarily lost for words.

'He's the one working on this story. Not me.'

'So you're not a journalist?' Dee said.

'Sort of. At least, I'm trying to become one. It's a very competitive industry these days. Completely different to when you started out.'

That did it.

'You need to leave,' Dee said. 'The last time I checked, this was my property. You're trespassing.'

'Oh.' The woman looked confused. 'Sorry. I thought this was where Katie lived.'

Alarm bells, loud and clanging, started up inside Dee's head.

'It's my house,' she said. 'My land too. I'm Katie's land-lady. Listen, whatever-your-name-is…' The girl wouldn't last more than a few weeks. Remembering her name required more effort than Dee was willing to put into it. 'I have no idea why Billy sent you here. But you can go running back to him now, tell him you've met me and I have nothing to say to you or him or anyone else.'

'He doesn't know I'm here. He's in trouble, Dee. That's why I came.'

'Billy's always in trouble. Luckily for me, that's not my problem any more.'

'No, wait!' Melissa took a step forward. 'This was my idea, I swear. I need to talk to you for a few minutes, Dee. That's all.'

Dee shook her head.

'Please,' Melissa said. 'He needs a good story. He's about to lose his job, and if that happens, he'll lose the house too. And surely you don't want that. Because I know it still belongs to both of you, right?'

'Only because he won't move out,' Dee said.

A knot of tension was forming in the pit of her stomach. Billy Morrison, her ex-husband, was a complete and utter waste of space. He was still living in the Green-wich town house they'd bought together soon after they got married, refusing to move out and refusing to pay more than his share of the mortgage. Leaving Dee stuck with paying for a house she no longer lived in.

'The thing is,' Melissa said, 'if the house is repossessed, you could lose all of this too.' She threw her arm out in a sweeping gesture that took in Dee's house further along the beach, circling back to the mobile home. 'That's what Billy says, and that's why he needs your help.'

The knot in Dee's stomach tightened, tension turning to a white-hot burning rage that coursed through her body until she was sure Melissa Hall must be able to see it rising out of her like the heat waves around that poor dead woman the other day.

'We saw it on the news,' Melissa said. 'Billy recognised the place right away, and he was interested. Then this morning, when it turned out the police don't know who the victim is… You know what he's like – can't pass up the promise of a story. He's done a bit of research on Katie Hope and he thinks he's found something interesting. It would be so good if you'd talk to him – maybe help him fill in the bits he hasn't been able to find out for himself? Poor Billy – he didn't want to ask because he didn't want to upset you.'

Bullshit, Dee thought.

'So,' Melissa said, cracking a smile so wide and bright it couldn't possibly be genuine. 'I thought, why don't I do it – drive down here myself and see if you'll speak to me? I know you were a journalist back in the day, and I thought maybe the two of you could work together on this. If he can get a scoop, think what it could do for him. And you, of course. Because the last thing he wants, Dee, is to see you get hurt. He's still terribly fond of you.'

The rage exploded out of her and all around her. She took a step towards Melissa Hall. And then another one. Saw fear flash across the woman's perfect face and it felt good. Too good. Dee saw her own hand reaching out and grabbing the collar of Melissa's figure-hugging pale-pink T-shirt.

'This isn't some story for Billy,' she hissed, pushing her face too close to Melissa's. 'A young woman and her little boy are missing. Has he paused for more than a second to consider that? Or is he so obsessed with his failing career that all he can think about is how to turn this tragedy into a story?'

A tear rolled down Melissa's cheek. Dee let her go and stepped back, appalled.

'I'm sorry,' she said.

Melissa brushed the tear away, but more tears replaced it. Sorrow and shame replaced the rage, both intensified when Dee put her hand on Melissa's arm and the woman flinched.

'Don't let him drag you down to his level,' Dee said. 'I know you think you're helping him, but it won't make any difference. Even if he finds a good story, he'll drink away any money he makes from it. He's an alcoholic who doesn't want to stop drinking. There's nothing you can do to change that.'

'It's your fault he drinks,' Melissa said. 'He's told me all about you.' Her fingers went up to her neck, straightening the material that had been crumpled by Dee's hand. 'You're a psycho, you know that?'

'Go,' Dee said. 'Please. Go back to London and tell my lowlife ex to keep his nose out of this. If he wants a big story, he'll have to find it somewhere else.'

She turned away, suffused with sadness. This beautiful young woman, who could probably have any man she set her heart on, had hooked up with someone who could never make her happy. A long time ago, so far back it was like remembering a different person, Dee had been like Melissa Hall. Young and full of hope. She'd known Billy Morrison was trouble from the moment she laid eyes on him. But she'd been young enough and foolish enough to believe she could save him. It had taken her sixteen years to realise that you could only save someone who wanted to be saved.

Nine

Katie
Eleven years earlier

I'm not allowed to work behind the bar. Dad justifies this by saying he wants better for me than that. Which is bullshit. We both know the real reason he won't let me work in the pub: he's worried I'll end up like Mum.

But I like the pub and I spend as much time there as I can. This is easier than it sounds, because my dad's not there as much as he probably should be. He prefers to leave things to Roxanne, who basically runs the place as if it's her own. A situation that seems to suit both of them.

Sunday nights are my favourite time to be there. Dad goes out every Sunday and doesn't come home until late, which means I never have to worry that he'll catch me. I come downstairs as soon as I know he's gone and sit in a corner with my book, pretending to read while all the time checking the door in case Shane turns up. I never drink alcohol. Even if Roxanne let me – which she never would because she knows my dad would freak – I've no intention of touching the stuff. Every time I see a drunk person it reminds me of Mum, and I know I'm never, ever going to end up the way she did.

The pub's called the Railway Tavern. It's in Hither Green, on the corner of Ennersdale Road and Leahurst

Road. The average age of most of our regulars is probably around fifty-five. Some younger people drink there too, but they're couples mostly, looking for somewhere they can actually have a conversation without being deafened by the pounding music you get in most pubs.

It's not exactly rocking or cool, but it's my home and I like it. I've lived over the pub my entire life. Until Mum left us, I spent nearly as much time downstairs as I did in the apartment. We ate dinner in the bar two or three times a week. On weekend mornings, I was allowed to help – setting out beer mats, polishing the glasses that hung down over the counter so that the lights reflected off them, creating a golden glow over the whole bar area.

I loved it all and used to imagine growing up and getting married and taking over the pub from Mum and Dad. My whole life planned out, neat and tidy the way I like things to be. And then Mum left and nothing has been neat and tidy since.

Tonight is Sunday, so I'm downstairs. Ella and Roxanne are working, but there's not much for them to do because it's quiet, like it always is on a Sunday night. The two of them are having a right giggle together. Every time one of them laughs, it's like something sharp stabbing me. Roxanne has been the closest thing I've had to a mum these last few years. She should be talking to me, not Ella Tate, who she barely even knows.

Roxanne must have seen me looking over, because she comes out from behind the bar and asks if I'm okay. She tops up my Diet Coke and passes me a chocolate fudge pudding.

'Don't tell your dad,' she says, winking at me.

Ella ignores me and I ignore her right back, not that she notices.

I'm worried Roxanne will send me upstairs soon. I need to be down here. Shane told me he might 'pop in sometime to say hi', and how can he do that if I'm being held prisoner upstairs, like some modern-day Rapunzel without the long hair and the looks? Every time the door opens, my heart jumps so hard it hurts my chest. I know it's stupid to hope, but I can't help it. After all, he was the one who said he might drop in.

I see him nearly every day, but we haven't spoken since that time at the end of class. He always smiles when he sees me, but it never goes beyond that, and there's no way I'm making the first move.

I torment myself imagining he's already called in some other night when I've been locked away upstairs. The problem is, I've no way of finding out. I can't ask Roxanne. She'd want to know who he is and why I'm asking about him, and she'd tease me about him and it would be awful. And there's no way I'm asking Ella. The less she knows about my life, the better.

I'm scooping the last chunk of fudge cake into my mouth when I hear the door opening. I look up, anticipating disappointment, and there he is. Standing in the doorway, looking around like he's not sure what he's doing here.

It's such a shock, seeing him just as I've imagined for so long, that I drop the spoon. It lands on my plate, clattering too loudly so that everyone – including Shane – turns to look at me. He sees me and smiles. I try to smile back, but my lips and jaw refuse to move. It feels as if someone has screwed my face into place.

'Hey.'

He walks towards me, and I wipe my mouth, praying there are no traces of chocolate on my face or lips.

I ate the cake too quickly and my stomach feels bloated and heavy. Cursing myself for being such a greedy cow, I push the plate away and sit like an oversized lemon waiting for him to reach my table. A strand of hair is tickling my face, but I'm too scared to brush it back in case he sees how badly my hand is trembling.

'Nice place you've got here,' Shane says. He's standing in front of me now, so close I have to crane my neck to look up at him.

'Get you a drink?' he asks, like it's the most natural thing in the world. I can barely hear him through the pounding inside my head, blood pumping too fast, making me light-headed and dizzy.

I must have replied, because by the time my head's stopped spinning, he's already at the bar. I watch him wait his turn, gesturing to a woman who's also waiting to go ahead of him. It's kind of him and I don't understand why Ella frowns when she sees him do it. She's in the middle of serving someone else, so Shane has to wait until she's finished to order.

He's up there for ages, talking to Ella while she gets our drinks, and afterwards too, leaning forward while he speaks to her. When he picks up the glasses, I see her face. She looks different. Her eyes are bright and wide open, and she has an angry patch of pink on each cheek, like she's been slapped.

I watch her watching him as he crosses the bar and puts our drinks on the table. He pulls out a stool and sits opposite me, blocking her. But even if I can't see her, I know she's looking at us, her eyes boring into the back of Shane's head like she wants to see right inside him.

I realise this isn't the first time they've met. There's a history there, something between them that I'm not a part of. And I know with a heavy certainty that Shane didn't come here tonight to see me. He's here because of her.

Ten

Dee

Dee had invited Louise and her kids over for lunch on Saturday. She wanted to find out everything her cousin had discovered about the dead woman. Because she had made a decision. She was going to use all the skills and knowledge she'd acquired in her twenty years as a journalist to find Katie and Jake. And once she found them, she was going to protect them from predatory hacks like her ex-husband.

It was another blisteringly hot day. A cloudless blue sky and an ocean as smooth and still as a sheet of glass. When she'd finished preparing lunch, she sat on the deck, going over the notes she'd made on her laptop earlier that morning.

After Melissa's visit, she had tried to find the 'something interesting' the woman had claimed Billy had uncovered. An internet search for Katie Hope yielded 44,400,000 results. She tried to narrow this down by cross-referencing the results against the information she already had from her mother's filing cabinet. The only definite match she got was with the software company in Shoreditch who had given Katie a reference when she moved to Eastbourne. When she visited the company's website, though, all she got was a link to a page that no longer existed, naming Katie as one of the employees.

The company was called Hexagon Consultancy. According to their website, they created 'digital solutions that people want to use'. They were also involved in something called 'the internet of things'. Which as far as Dee could work out was about getting household appliances like your fridge and TV and cooker connected to the internet. The website didn't give her any information that was actually useful, like how big the company was, what job Katie had done when she worked there, or why she'd given up her job when she moved to Eastbourne.

The doorbell rang. At the same time, Dee heard the sound of little feet running around the side of the house towards the back.

'Auntie Dee!' Daisy, Louise's elder child, threw herself at Dee.

'How's my favourite niece?' Dee said, lifting the girl in her arms and swinging her around.

'I'm not your niece,' Daisy said. 'I'm your first cousin once removed.'

'If we're cousins,' Dee said, 'why do you call me Auntie Dee. It should be plain old Dee, right?'

Daisy rolled her head in the direction of her mother, who was trotting carefully over the shingle after Daisy's younger brother Ben.

'*She* says it's rude not to.'

'And what do you think?' Dee asked.

'What does she think about what?' Louise asked.

But Dee couldn't answer, because Ben was demanding her attention now, pulling at her top until she bent down and gave him a hug.

'How you doing, little man?' she asked.

Ben frowned, and Dee's heart juddered as she wondered what was wrong with him.

'Not little,' he said. 'I'm four now. That's big.'

'Not as big as me,' Daisy said. 'Five is bigger than four.'

'You're both big,' Louise broke in. 'Now then, who wants to go for a swim before lunch?'

From the shouting and laughing that followed, it was clear the kids couldn't wait to get into the sea.

'I'll take them,' Dee said. 'Why don't you grab a chair and relax in the sun for a bit?'

While Louise set about getting the children ready, Dee went inside to change into her swimming costume. It was an old one and, like everything else she owned, about two sizes too small for her. She stuffed her flabby bits into as much of it as she could, yanking it down over the tufts of pubic hair that pushed out from the bottom, then wrapped a towel around herself and ran back outside.

'Thanks so much for this,' Louise said. She held up her phone. 'I've got a ton of emails to work through.'

'Still working on the hit and run?' Dee asked.

'No one's come forward to identify her yet,' Louise said. 'How can a woman die like that without anyone missing her?'

'Auntie Dee.' Ben pulled Dee's towel. 'I want to go swimming.'

'Tell you what,' Dee said to Louise, as if the thought had just occurred to her. 'Why don't you pick my brains over lunch? We can eat out here and I'll set up a picnic blanket on the beach for the kids so we can talk without any interruptions. And afterwards,' she looked at Ben and

Daisy, 'you can get an ice cream from the freezer and watch a movie if you like.'

Louise smiled and her whole face lit up. Not for the first time, Dee thought there must be plenty of men who'd do pretty much anything to feel the warmth of that smile.

'That would be great,' Louise said. 'Thanks, Dee.'

'Can we go swimming now?' Ben said. 'Please?'

'Try and stop me,' Dee said.

She took one of their hands in each of hers and the three of them ran to the water. At the last moment, she dropped her towel and tiptoed into the icy-cold sea, marvelling at the children's ability not to notice how bloody freezing it was. She stayed in for as long as she could, lifting each child in turn, swinging them up and out of the water then dropping them down again, taking care to hold onto them so their heads didn't go under. She remembered all the times she'd done the same thing with Jake, the sound of the little boy's laughter all around her. It was impossible to think she'd never do that with him again.

–

After lunch, Louise sent the children inside to watch a film. She kept the living room door open so she could keep an eye on them.

'I'm working on the theory that someone is helping Katie,' she said, tucking her feet under her body, the way she did when she was settling in for a long chat.

'What makes you think that?' Dee asked.

'They haven't vanished into thin air. Someone has to be hiding them.' She paused, chewing her lip as though she was thinking about saying something but was unsure whether it was a good idea or not.

'Spit it out,' Dee said. 'Whatever you want to say, I doubt it will shock me.'

'I was thinking about what you said that night we met for dinner,' Louise said.

Dee frowned, unsure what her cousin was referring to.

'About hacking Katie's phone?' Louise said. 'I mean, I know I was really against it, but at the time, I thought Katie was dead, remember?'

'Ah.' Dee shook her head. 'I've already looked into it, and I don't think it's an option. After the phone-hacking scandal, things changed. It's almost impossible to access someone's voicemail these days.'

'I guess if it was that easy, some other journalist would have already done it by now. You've tried calling her, I assume?'

'Every day,' Dee said. 'But all I get is her voicemail. I've lost count of how many messages I've left. You said you think someone is helping her. Any ideas who that could be?'

'Not so far,' Louise said.

'I've been thinking about the relationship between Katie and the dead woman,' Dee said. 'They must have been close. She was wearing Katie's top. But it was more than that. It was... everything. Her hair was the same, she was dressed like Katie – not just the T-shirt, but the jeans were the type Katie wears. She even had a pair of Birken-stock sandals that I've seen Katie wearing. I know this sounds mad, Lou, but it's almost as if she was pretending to *be* Katie.'

'She borrowed some of Katie's clothes,' Louise said. 'Which means they must have known each other. Stop that, Ben! He's started picking his nose. It's disgusting, but I can't get him to stop. Isn't it more likely that the dead woman was a friend or a sister or something? Ben, I said STOP IT!'

'I guess,' Dee said. 'Except if she had a sister or a friend coming to visit, why didn't she tell me?'

'Maybe she didn't know. It could have been a surprise visit.'

Dee thought of how hung-over she'd been that afternoon. No wonder she'd made such a stupid mistake.

'I should have paid more attention,' she said.

'You were in shock,' Louise said. She leaned down, reached into her bucket-sized handbag and pulled out an iPad. 'Did you know Katie's father was murdered?'

'God, no,' Dee said. 'I knew her parents were dead because I asked her about them once. But she never told me that. Poor Katie. Are you sure about this, Lou?'

'I think so,' Louise said. 'She worked at a software company in London before she moved here.'

'Hexagon Consultancy,' Dee said. 'They wrote a reference for her.'

'I managed to track down the CEO this morning. He didn't want to speak to me at first, but I worked my charm on him. He gave me some background information on Katie – where she went to college, her qualifications, previous work experience. Enough to narrow things down a bit. Katie was a remote worker. The company's based in London but she was living in Bristol when she worked for them. She grew up in Hither Green, in London. A man called Gus Hope was murdered in a

London pub in 2008. He had a daughter called Katie. I've checked it all out and the dates match. I'm pretty sure it's the same woman. Do you remember what you told me one time about coincidences?'

Unbidden, Dee heard Billy's voice. *You say coincidence, Dee, but I say there's a pattern. You can't see it yet, but that doesn't mean it's not there.*

'I remember,' she said. 'How was he murdered?'

'He owned a pub,' Louise said. 'A fight broke out between a punter and one of the bar staff. Katie's dad stepped in, tried to stop things escalating and ended up getting killed.'

'How awful,' Dee said. She thought of poor Katie, living a semi-reclusive life out here by the sea, and wondered if the tragedy had been one of the reasons she'd moved here.

Louise typed something on the iPad, and handed it to Dee.

'Here,' she said. 'See for yourself.'

It was an archived piece on the website of the *South London Press*. Short and factual, the piece stated that a local man had been given an eight-year prison sentence for the manslaughter of Gus Hope. According to the article, Gus Hope was a widower and father to eighteen-year-old Katie. The story was dated May 2009.

'I wonder why she never told me,' Dee said, although she already knew the answer. Katie was a very private person. Any questions Dee asked about her life before Eastbourne were politely rebutted. In the end, she had given up asking because it was clear to her that Katie didn't want to talk about her past.

'It happened a long time ago,' Louise said. 'I know it's terrible, but people move on, don't they?'

'I guess.'

'She must have had other family,' Louise said. 'And friends. I mean, she got pregnant, so she was clearly living some sort of life.'

'She left it all behind her when she moved here,' Dee said. 'Whatever friends and family she had, she never mentioned them and no one ever came to visit her. Did the Hexagon guy tell you why Katie left? I wonder why she stopped working with computers and started teaching piano instead.'

'She handed her notice in,' Louise said. 'Crispin didn't know why she decided to leave.'

'Crispin?'

'Hexagon's CEO,' Louise said. 'I'm meant to be meeting him on Monday, in fact. I'd arranged it all and then, right after it was sorted, Martin called from the golf course to tell me he's taken on an extra shift. Flying out tomorrow evening and won't be home until Wednesday morning. I've told him before not to do that without checking with me first, but it's like speaking to a brick wall. Why is it that he thinks my job is less important than his?'

Dee could think of plenty of ways to answer that question, but she knew Louise wouldn't like any of them, so she kept quiet.

'I've tried to reschedule things with Cris,' Louise said. 'But he's going to India on Monday evening for a week. It's such a pain. Jen's covering an emergency town council meeting on Monday, so she can't go, and Daisy's got a hospital appointment and I can't change it.'

'There's nothing wrong, is there?' Dee asked.

'Something not quite right with her hearing,' Louise said. 'She's having some tests to see if she'll need grommets. I told you about it a few weeks ago.'

'Yes, of course you did,' Dee said. 'Why not let me take Daisy to the hospital? I'd be more than happy to do it, you know that.'

'That's really kind.' Louise shook her head. 'But it should be me or Martin.'

'Well how about I go to London and speak to Katie's old boss?'

'You?'

'Why not? If he's got any information that will help us find out what's happened to Katie and Jake, we need to speak to him as soon as possible.'

'*We?*' Louise said.

'Katie's my friend,' Dee said. 'I can't sit around twiddling my thumbs and waiting for the police to find them. Going to London, knowing I'm helping you at the same time, it makes sense, doesn't it?'

'I thought you wanted to put the journalism part of your life behind you.'

'I never said that,' Dee replied. 'And even if I had, that's not what this is about. I get that it's your job to write about this. And I respect that because I respect you. But it's not like that for me. I need to know I'm doing all I can to find them. Let me do this, Lou. Please?'

'If I say yes,' Louise said, 'do you promise to tell me *everything* you find out. Not just on Monday, but after that as well. No more keeping things from me, even if Ed Mitchell tells you to.'

'I promise.'

Louise nodded. 'Okay then. Cris is a real sweetie. I'll send him an email later. Let him know someone else is coming in my place. I'm sure it will be fine.'

Dee reached across the table and squeezed her cousin's hand. 'Thank you,' she said.

Crispin Marsden. Her first real lead. Dee could feel it. That familiar fizzing inside her body, synapses snapping and connections being made, her mind already starting to build the narrative of Katie's life, leading up to the murder of a young woman who looked just like her.

Eleven

That night was the start of something. Maybe his first visit to the pub was because of Ella, but it's me he keeps coming back for. There's a connection between us; one of those things you can't make up. It's either there or it's not.

Roxanne's been so lovely. I can tell she's happy for me by the way she keeps smiling over and winking at me when he's not looking. And the way she teases me about him when he's not around. I don't mind. It's kind of nice, to be honest; makes me feel like someone else, almost.

Ella doesn't like us hanging out together. She's jealous. Shane says she's too uptight for any bloke to be interested. We spend hours bitching about her. Right after that first night, he told me about her. They used to go out with each other. He's said it was nothing serious, and I want to believe him. Which is why I don't ask for any details. He says it's in the past and he doesn't want to talk about it. But that's a lie, because most of the time, Ella's the only thing he *does* want to talk about.

'She thinks she's better than everyone else,' he says. 'See the way she won't even smile at that poor bloke who's chatting to her? Like it would hurt her face if she tried.'

It's Sunday night and we're in our usual corner. Whispering, heads close together, because the pub is quiet and we don't want anyone to overhear what we're talking about.

'My dad only hired her because he felt sorry for her,' I tell him. 'Her father died a while back and I think her family's struggling a bit. Money stuff, you know.'

'Really?'

He seems to find that interesting and doesn't say anything else for a bit. While I'm waiting for him to speak, I ask him if he wants another drink.

'Sure.' He smiles, and the knot in my stomach melts away, relieved that he's okay and *we're* okay. He gets like this sometimes, quiet and a bit moody. It freaks me out, because every time it happens, it reminds me of Mum. Her moods shifted and changed all the time. You never really knew where you were with her. The sick feeling I used to get when I realised I'd got it wrong, that's what it's like when Shane goes into one of his dark places.

'I'll get them.' He jumps up and takes my glass before I can say anything. I watch him as he bounces across to the bar. He does that thing again, letting other people get served before him, and I can't help smiling even though it sort of drives me mad. He doesn't have to be so thoughtful all the time!

'How's it going?' Roxanne asks as she passes.

'Fine.' I shrug, pretending it's no big deal that I'm sitting here with a guy.

'He's a good-looking fella,' she says. 'A girl could lose herself in those blue eyes of his. You going to tell your dad about him any time soon?'

'It's not like that,' I say, my face burning. The last thing I need is for Roxanne to tell Dad about Shane. There's no way he'll let me see someone without insisting on meeting him and asking all sorts of embarrassing questions and basically being a complete nightmare.

'You shouldn't keep secrets from him, Katie,' Roxanne says. 'He's your dad.'

'There's nothing to tell,' I say.

I can see she doesn't believe me and I think she's about to say something else. But before she can, there's a huge crash from the bar, making me and everyone else jump.

'What the heck?' Roxanne swings around. 'Ella? Are you okay?'

Roxanne's a big woman – not fat like me, but tall and big-boned – and she's blocking my view. I stand up, slide around the table and see Shane. Liquid dripping from his hair and nose and a dark stain across the front of his yellow sweatshirt. An expression on his face that I've never seen before – anger mixed with something else. He looks more alive than any time I've been with him.

Behind him, her face white apart from two patches of pink on her cheeks, Ella looks as if someone's just told her the world's most shocking secret.

'Shane?' I step past Roxanne and go over to him. He's looking right at me but it's like I'm invisible. When I put my hand on his arm, he doesn't move or seem to notice I've touched him. I step back, not knowing what I should do.

'You need to leave.'

Roxanne pushes herself between us, putting her face close to his. He sees her all right.

'I'll leave when I'm ready,' he says.

'You'll leave now.' She grabs his arm and shoves him towards the door. When she lets him go, he swings around, his fist out, and for one awful moment I think he's going to punch her.

'No!'

I don't even realise I've shouted it until his fist drops and he turns to look at me. There's something awful in his face, a darkness I've never seen before. I want him to smile, like he did earlier, tell me it's all okay, but he doesn't.

I try to go to him, but Roxanne puts a hand on my arm, stopping me. I expect her to be angry, but she seems sad, which seems worse somehow although I don't know why. And when she speaks, her voice is soft and gentle, the way she spoke to me in the weeks after my mum died.

'Katie, love, I need you to go upstairs now, okay?'

It's not okay. Nothing about this is okay. I look at Shane again and I know the expression on my face must be pathetically pleading, but I can't help it.

He uses the sleeve of his sweatshirt to wipe his face. When he's finished, I think maybe he'll say something, but he doesn't even look at me. He's looking at her.

'See you around, Ella.'

He stares at her for a second that drags into two seconds and might drag on forever except Roxanne steps towards him and tells him again to leave.

'Keep your knickers on,' he says. 'I'm going.'

He straightens his sweatshirt, gives Ella a final once-over, and then he's gone, without a goodbye or a see-you-tomorrow or anything.

I look at Ella, pale-faced and pink-cheeked, her eyes like two big holes in her face. My fingers twitch and something hot and dark flickers deep inside me. I want to grab her by the hair, drag her across the bar, slap her and punch her and kick her and push her to the ground until she knows what it feels like to hurt this bad.

Twelve

Dee

Monday morning, Dee was on a train to London by 8.30. She had a busy day planned. A trip to the software company in Shoreditch where Katie had worked, followed by a catch-up in Soho with an ex-colleague.

Her train was full of commuters, men in suits and smartly dressed women who probably made this journey five days a week, forty-seven weeks of the year. Dee sat amongst them feeling like an imposter.

As a concession to the sort of people she imagined she'd be meeting at the software company, she was wearing a new pair of jeans with a black linen shirt, one of the few things from her previous life that still fitted her. She'd brought a book, but she couldn't concentrate on it. Her brain was buzzing, ideas forming, making connections all the time. Her mind was brighter, sharper, more focused than it had been at any time since her mother had died. She was going to find Katie and Jake.

Occasionally, moments of doubt crept in. A nagging voice whispering that all of this was a waste of time. She was a washed-up, past-it has-been. What made her think she could solve the mystery of the dead woman before the police or Billy or any of the many journalists chasing the same story? But each time her thoughts started going in that direction, she would picture the dead woman and knew with absolute certainty that she had to do this. She might not be a journalist any more, but she was every bit as good as all those hacks trying to turn this tragedy into a story they could sell. And that included her deadbeat drunk of an ex-husband.

–

Hexagon Consultancy occupied the ground floor of a converted warehouse on the corner of a quiet square near Old Street station. Using the map on her phone, Dee found it easily and was ten minutes early for her appointment.

Inside, the office was a single open-plan space with exposed brick walls. Men and women who didn't look old enough to be working sat in groups or alone, all facing a computer screen. The sound of fingers tapping on keyboards seemed to permeate every corner of the room, digging into Dee's head like the persistent buzzing of a dying insect.

A row of oversized Apple computers stood in a line along one wall. More boys and girls, all wearing white headphones, sat at these. The aroma of fresh coffee filled the air, making Dee's mouth water as she approached the reception desk.

'Hello.' A girl with cropped black hair and a nose ring greeted her with a smile.

'Hi,' Dee said, returning the smile. 'I've got an appointment with Crispin Marsden? Dee Doran.'

'Sure.' The girl checked a screen on the desk in front of her, then pointed to the spiral iron staircase situated in the middle of the room.

'Up there,' she said. 'I'll let Cris know you're on your way.'

She tapped something onto the keyboard, presumably a message to 'Cris', while Dee thanked her and headed across to the staircase. Her feet echoed loudly off the metal steps as she made her way up. When she reached the top, she was met by a tall, skinny guy with a ginger beard, heavy-rimmed glasses and a completely bald head.

'Cris Marsden,' he said. 'Can I help you?'

'I'm Dee Doran. You spoke with my colleague, Louise, on Saturday.'

'Dee?' Cris frowned. 'Oh yeah, of course. Hi.'

'Louise did email and tell you she couldn't make today's meeting?' Dee said.

'Sure. Yeah, it's cool. Hey, how about we grab a coffee before you begin your interrogation?'

He gave her a wolfish grin that set Dee's teeth on edge. She hoped she would get the information she needed from him as quickly as possible so she could get out of there.

She followed him across another open-plan space to a kitchen area with a blue Smeg fridge and the most complicated-looking coffee machine she'd ever seen.

'Take a seat.' Cris gestured at a selection of brightly coloured low sofas and armchairs scattered around the place. 'How do you like your coffee?'

'Black, no sugar,' Dee said.

'Coming right up,' he said. 'You're in for a treat, Dee. The coffee from this machine is banging.'

Assuming that 'banging' was a good thing, Dee smiled politely and settled into an orange armchair that turned out to be far more comfortable than it looked. While Cris prepared the coffee, she looked around. This floor was obviously the meeting area. The chairs and sofas were grouped round a selection of Scandi-style coffee tables. A few people were sitting on some of them, speaking in low voices. She couldn't hear what they were saying, but it was clear from their ages and the way they were dressed that they weren't all employees of Hexagon Consultancy.

'Clients,' Cris said when he saw her looking. 'We've got some big projects in the pipeline.' He placed a cup of delicious-smelling coffee on the table.

'Thanks.' Dee lifted it, holding it with both hands while she breathed in the rich, smooth aroma.

'What is it you do exactly?' she said. 'I'm afraid I'm a bit of a Luddite, so you'll have to give me the dummies' version.'

'We design lots of different things,' Cris said. 'But our speciality is the internet of things. Basically, this involves taking advantage of the unused sections of the radio spectrum to get household devices communicating with each other.'

'So my fridge could talk to my cooker?'

'Or send a message to your mobile phone telling you to order more milk. That sort of thing.'

'Fascinating,' Dee said, because Crispin – Cris – was looking at her as if he clearly expected her to say something.

She took a sip of the coffee.

'You were right,' she said. 'This is good.'

'It never disappoints,' Cris said. 'So then, Dee.' He put his elbows on his knees and leaned forward. 'What's your story?'

'What do you mean?' Dee said.

'I don't like journalists generally. But I made an exception for Louise. She was so passionate when we spoke, telling me all about the paper she runs and how hard it is for local press like hers to stay afloat these days. She made me want to help her. Sunday's my digital detox day – no internet, no email, I don't even switch my phone on – so I didn't get her email until this morning, telling me she couldn't make it and was sending you instead. Such a pity she had to change her plans. I was so curious to meet her. But then I looked you up and realised maybe you'd be just as interesting.'

'Ah.' Dee wasn't sure what else to say.

'I read some of the pieces you wrote for the *Daily Post*,' he said. 'You're a good journalist.'

'Um,' Dee managed. 'Thanks, I guess. The thing is, Cris, this is more than a story for me. Katie's my friend. I'm worried about her.'

'Sure.' He nodded his head and looked very serious. 'I can understand that. Unfortunately, I don't think there's much I can tell you. If I'd known Louise wasn't able to make it, I'd have cancelled this meeting and saved us both some time. I hadn't heard of Katie before she called. I've read up on the story since, of course, but I'm not sure how I can help, to be honest.'

'You hadn't heard of her?' Dee was confused. 'I thought she used to work here?'

'In theory, yes,' Cris said. 'But the truth is, I never actually met her. A lot of our developers work remotely. Katie was one of those.'

'But someone here must have known her,' Dee said. 'I mean, wouldn't she have had to do a job interview and stuff?'

'I checked her HR file,' Cris said. 'Her interview was done over Skype. She came highly recommended from an agency in Bristol, which is where she lived when she worked for us. The interview was little more than a formality, really. The person who interviewed her left the company soon afterwards. Katie was a freelancer. A lot of our programmers work with us on a freelance basis. They like the freedom. Katie started in April 2014 and quit a year later. During her time with us, no one ever met her.'

'Even if you didn't meet her,' Dee said, 'you must have had some idea of the sort of person she was.'

'Not really,' Cris said. 'I asked around this morning. She did her job well enough, apparently, but she wasn't friends with anyone. We organise regular team-building nights. They're a chance for our freelancers to meet the team here and feel part of the Hexagon family. Katie was always invited, but she never came to any of them.'

It was like trying to hold water in the palm of her hand. Just when Dee felt she was getting close to understanding who Katie was, the image faded and changed, trickling through the gaps in her fingers until there was nothing left.

'There must be something else you can tell me,' she said.

'There really isn't.' Cris made a point of looking at his watch. 'I'm afraid I've got another appointment in a few minutes.'

Dee took the hint and stood up.

'Thanks for your time,' she said.

Cris pulled a slim leather wallet from the back pocket of his jeans, took out a business card and handed it to Dee.

'Would you pass this on to Louise?' he said. 'It's got my personal email and phone number on it. If she's ever in London, she might like to get in touch. I checked her profile online. She's every bit as pretty as I imagined. I'd love to take her for a drink sometime.'

'She's married,' Dee said. 'And even if she wasn't, she'd never date someone with a beard as ridiculous as that.'

She left before he could say anything else, her footsteps clattering loudly off the iron, bouncing off the brick walls. The noise stayed in her head as she stepped outside into the bright heat of another scorching summer's day, the clanging echo of her footsteps taunting her as she crossed the dusty yellowed grass square back to Old Street Underground station.

Thirteen

Katie
Eleven years earlier

It's horrible. Roxanne's made it clear that Shane's not allowed back in the pub. If he steps inside the door, she says she'll speak to Dad about it. I've tried reasoning with her because it's so unfair, but she refuses to listen.

'He's bad news,' she said when I pleaded with her. 'Seriously, you're better off without someone like that.'

'Someone like what?' I asked.

'Ella's told me about him,' she said. 'He's not a good bloke, Katie. You deserve someone who'll treat you right and wants to be with you because he likes you, not because…'

She trailed off then and refused to say any more. Even though we both knew what she meant. He's using me to get close to Ella, but I know it's what Roxanne thinks. Because she's like everyone else and she can't imagine that someone like Shane would ever want to be with someone like me.

Roxanne and I haven't spoken since then, even though she's tried a few times. The problem is that she doesn't seem to realise she's not my mum. She's always sticking her nose into my business. She says she's got my best interests at heart, but that's bullshit. If she really cared about me, she'd believe my version of what happened that night, not Ella's.

'She poured me a Coke instead of a Diet Coke like you wanted,' Shane tells me when I ask him what happened. 'I asked her to change it and she lost it. Picked up the glass and threw the drink into my face. She's not right up here, Katie.' He taps his head when he says this, hate twisting his face into something horrible.

We're in the park. It's where we mostly go these days. Shane has a bottle of cider that I sneaked from the pub earlier. He keeps trying to get me to drink some, but I'm scared.

'I don't want to end up like my mum,' I tell him.

'You never talk about her,' Shane says. 'What was she like?'

I don't answer, because what is there to say? She was an alcoholic who went on a drinking spree one afternoon and has never been seen since.

I take the bottle to avoid speaking, and drink some of the cider. I don't like it very much. It's too sweet, and the fizziness bloats my stomach. When I take a second sip, I swear I can feel the waistband of my jeans growing tighter.

Shane says something else, but I can't hear him. My head is too full of the noises and images. Mum's voice, high-pitched, the way it got when she'd had too much to drink. Shouting and calling my dad all sorts of names. Then the sound of the front door slamming, the click-clack of her heels running along the pavement, and my dad, shouting now too, telling her to come back and not be stupid. Telling her she was too pissed to be behind the wheel of a car.

'Doesn't it make you angry?' Shane says.

'What?'

'The way your dad and everyone else makes such a fuss of her?'

I think he's talking about Mum and I don't know how to explain to him what happens when someone disappears like that. The way it leaves this big vacuum in your life that's worse than the worst sort of hunger because nothing you ever do can fix it.

'But you're the one who's lost your mother,' he says. 'Not her. It's not fair, Katie. Makes me angry on your behalf. Like, why does she get to work behind the bar but you're not allowed?' He's almost shouting now. Cider and anger making his voice too loud and his words stumble over each other. 'Why should you have to sit upstairs on your own every night while she's downstairs getting all his attention. We should do something about it.'

'What?' I say, angry now too. Why does he have to bring Ella into everything? I wish he'd shut up about her and talk about something or someone else. Me, for instance. Why can't we talk about me for once? 'You don't know my dad. He's not going to suddenly let me start working in the bar. He'll never do that. My mum was a drunk and he's going to do everything he can to stop the same thing happening to me.'

'Hey.' He nudges the bottle, still in my hand. 'Have another drink. Go on.'

I hold the bottle to my lips and drink as much as I can without throwing up. When I finish, my face is wet and there's cider running down my chin and along my neck, soaking the collar of my Gap sweatshirt.

There's a brightness in his eyes that I recognise from that night in the pub. His pupils are huge and dark. I know that if I look at him for too long, I'll lose myself in that darkness.

'Better?' he says.

'Better.' I try to smile, but the cider is swishing around inside my stomach and I wish I was at home, on my own.

And then the weirdest and loveliest moment of my life happens: Shane Gilbert leans in and kisses me.

Fourteen

Dee

Dee walked through Shoreditch as far as Brick Lane, with its rows of curry shops, hipster fashion stores and grunge-inspired coffee shops. She'd bought her first property in this area. A tiny one-bed ex-council flat in a 1950s low-rise block on a narrow side street. Back in the early nineties, there had been no hipster stores or posh coffee shops; the area was unrecognisable today.

Things had already been changing when she had moved south of the river to Greenwich. Artists and musicians and other 'creatives' had started to flood in, attracted by the low rents and the authenticity already gentrified out of so many other parts of the city. At the same time, the sudden growth and prosperity of the newly developed Docklands area was starting to spread. Eventually, this little area of east London, caught between the City on one hand and the Docklands on the other, found its character and identity washed away by the relentless flow of prosperity and vulgar money inundating it from all sides.

Digital companies like Hexagon Consultancy moved in. The artists, musicians and creatives were pushed out by the sudden hike in rents, moving further east to places like Stepney, Stratford and Clacton. Property prices rocketed, and suddenly no one apart from the super-rich could afford to live here. Walking around the area today, Dee felt like a stranger.

Passing her old local, the Pride of Spitalfields, she had a sudden urge to step inside for a pint. Peering through the door, she could see that this place, at least, had avoided any outward signs of gentrification.

Inside, she opted for a coffee instead of London Pride. She drank it at a table in the corner while she planned out the rest of her day. She was meeting Trevor Dubber, an ex-colleague, at his Soho club later that afternoon. Trevor had started his career on the *South London Press*, the paper that had covered the murder of Gus Hope. Dee was hoping he might know someone there she could speak to.

Revived by coffee and thirty minutes' respite from the gentrification, she walked to Aldgate Underground station with a spring in her step. The meeting with Hexagon hadn't been a success, but the rest of the day stretched ahead of her, and for the first time in ages, it seemed full of possibility.

She felt alive again. Being back in the buzz of the city, meeting old contacts and trying to uncover the facts before anyone else. For so long, being a journalist had been her lifeblood, the way religion, nature or exotic yoga were for other people. She was under no illusions about that part of her life. It was over. But right now, using what she'd learned to help her find Katie and Jake felt good. More than good; it felt right.

–

Trevor's club was on Dean Street, in a tall Georgian town house. After Dee had given her name, a willowy girl with sun-kissed skin and feathery blonde hair led her up several staircases. She caught teasing glimpses of groups of people and bursts of conversations on each floor before she was whisked on to the next one.

Trevor was waiting for her in a booth on the top floor. 'Dee Doran.' He stood up, smiling as he grabbed her in a bear hug and held her tight. 'How the hell are you?' he asked, letting her go but keeping his hands on her shoulders. 'Come on. Let's sit down. I've got a bottle of New Zealand Pinot on ice in your honour. Do you want something to eat?'

Without waiting for an answer, he beamed his thousand-watt smile at the willowy blonde and asked her to bring them a selection of sharing plates.

'You're looking good,' he said, pouring a glass of green-tinted wine and handing it to Dee. 'Life by the seaside obviously suits you.'

'There's nothing in my life that suits me right now,' Dee said, taking the glass and sitting opposite him on a matching chesterfield-style sofa. 'Both my parents are dead, I can't get any work, and one of the few friends I have has gone missing. I spend my days comfort-eating and watching *Ramsay's Kitchen Nightmares* and my evenings drinking too much wine and feeling sorry for myself.'

Trevor grinned. 'Glad to hear everything's going so well. I did notice the extra few pounds, but they suit you. You were always too skinny.'

'You look better than you do on TV,' Dee said. 'What do they do with your hair? It always looks as if someone's glued it to your head.'

'Some sort of gel.' Trevor pulled a face. 'I've never cared enough to ask.'

He was as handsome as ever. A few more streaks of silver in his black hair, but they only added to the silver-fox vibe that turned so many women into gibbering fools around him.

Every heterosexual woman and gay man at the *Post* had fancied Trevor Dubber at one time or another. Dee guessed many of them still did. With his olive skin, melting brown eyes, lean, muscled body and voice as rich and smooth as the finest cappuccino, he had a sex appeal that was on a different level to most of the other men Dee worked with. He was also a hard-nosed hack with a reputation for not taking shit from anyone. Like all of his admirers, Dee respected him, fancied him and was scared of him in equal measure. These days, he was chief presenter on Channel 4's nightly current affairs programme, *Sixty Minutes*.

'I was sorry to hear about you and Billy,' he said.

'Not your fault,' Dee mumbled, embarrassed.

'Still, thought I'd better get it out of the way at the beginning. I felt like a real shit for not getting in touch after it happened.'

'It's okay,' Dee said. 'You were friends with both of us. I guessed you didn't want to get involved, and that's fine.'

She took a sip of wine and felt some of the tension drain from her body. She'd been nervous about meeting Trevor. He'd been one of her closest friends when she was living in London. They'd worked together and drunk together, and there'd been a heady period during the early nineties when Billy Morrison and Trevor Dubber were two of the most successful journalists in the country.

Dee had lied when she said it was okay that he hadn't called. At the time, his silence had hurt. She'd assumed, as you did when you were going through a separation, that Trevor had taken Billy's side. That somehow he blamed Dee for not sticking with the marriage.

'It's not fine,' he said. 'The truth is, Dee, I've been so busy, so focused on the next thing, I lost sight for a bit of what was important to me.'

'You've worked that out now, then?' Dee asked.

'Maybe,' Trevor said. 'Anyway, what about you? What are you up to these days?'

'Nothing,' Dee said, finding it easier than she'd imagined to be straight with him. She'd missed this. Being back in London, hanging out with a friend, catching up on gossip. It felt good.

'After Billy and I split up,' she said, 'everything fell apart really quickly. My dad died, my mum got sick. I felt as if I'd had enough of everything. London, work, that whole little world that was our lives for so long, I needed a clean break. So I got pissed one night and emailed Rob Harvey telling him exactly what I thought of him. It seemed like a good idea at the time. The next morning I already regretted it, but it was too late by then.'

'No one,' Trevor said, leaning forward and boring into Dee with those brown eyes, 'should regret sending an email like that. It's a classic.'

'You've seen it?' Dee asked.

'*Everyone's* seen it,' Trevor said. 'I thought you knew. He forwarded it to someone who forwarded it to someone else and so on, and so on. You're a bloody legend, Dee!'

Rob Harvey had been Dee's boss at the *Daily Post*. He'd only been in the job two months and was already universally hated by all the journalists who worked for him. An ex-politician with a relentless drive for self-promotion and no idea how journalism really worked, he'd been hired to 'make a difference', which basically meant cutting costs in whatever way he could. Dee's email gave him the perfect excuse to get rid of one more 'over-paid hack'.

'After that,' she said. 'I moved home and watched my mum get sicker and sicker. When she finally died, suddenly I was alone, with no idea what to do with the rest of my life.' She tried to smile to lighten the impact of what she was saying, but her mouth wobbled so she took a swig of wine instead.

'You need to start working again,' Trevor said.

'No one wants to hire me. Rob made sure of that.'

'That's bullshit. Is that why you wanted to see me today? Because if it is, then I'd be only too happy to throw some ideas about and see what we can come up with.'

Dee's eyes pricked with unexpected tears, touched by Trevor's faith in her abilities.

'I did look into freelance work,' she said. 'Features, lifestyle pieces, that sort of thing. But that market's already pretty saturated. And it's not me, Trevor. I'm an investigative journalist. It's who I am. But I couldn't work out what I wanted to write about.'

'And now you have?' Trevor asked.

'I'm not sure. In the meantime, a friend of mine is in trouble and I'm trying to help her. That's sort of why I wanted to see you – not the only reason, of course. You started out on the *South London Press*, didn't you?'

'I sure did,' Trevor said.

'In 2008, there was a murder in Hither Green,' Dee said. 'I've been reading up about it and it seems the story was mostly covered by the *South London Press*.'

'I was long gone by then,' Trevor said. He refilled their glasses, sat back on the sofa and crossed his legs. 'But I'm still mates with some of the guys I used to work with at the paper. Tell me what you want. I'm all ears.'

Dee told him about Katie and the dead woman who looked like Katie but wasn't. She told him she thought there could be a connection between the murder of Katie's father and this new death, although she hadn't worked out what it was. And she told him the thing she'd been thinking about for the last two days but hadn't told anyone else. Until now.

As she spoke, she pictured the dead woman. Dressed in Katie's clothes, wearing her hair the same way as Katie's. Pushing the buggy that Katie used for her son. Looking so like Katie, it was the easiest thing in the world to think she *was* Katie.

'Whenever I go back over it,' she said, 'I keep coming back to the same thing. What if the person driving the car made a mistake? What if he hit the wrong girl?'

Fifteen

Dee sat on the deck scrolling through the latest news updates on Katie and Jake. Louise and her colleagues had been busy. A Facebook page and a Twitter account had been set up, both appealing for anyone with information to come forward. On Twitter, the hashtag #findKatieandJake the Facebook page when her phone rang.

'Dee Doran?' A man's voice. South London accent, gravelly timbre, as if he'd spent too many years smoking too many cigarettes.

'That's right,' Dee said. 'Who's this?'

'Leonard Mann.' He stopped speaking to cough.

'Thanks for calling me back,' Dee said when the coughing ended.

She'd got Leonard's name from Trevor, who'd thought he might be a good person to speak to about the death of Katie's father. She'd called him on the way back from London and left a message telling him she had some questions about Gus Hope's murder.

'My pleasure,' Leonard said. 'You're a friend of Trev's, right?'

'He said you'd be happy to speak to me,' Dee said.

'Happy might be pushing it,' Leonard said. 'How's he doing, anyway? Last time I saw him, he was fronting some poncey discussion show on Channel 4. A bunch of self-satisfied wankers talking a load of shite. He still doing that?'

'I doubt he'd describe it as that,' Dee said, smiling. 'But he's still doing it, yeah.'

'He's got the face for it,' Leonard said. 'I'll give him that. My face, on the other hand, well… let's just say I'm destined to remain a print journalist. You're in the business too, I see. I remember reading that piece you did on Casey Hall – the kid killed by his stepfather? You did a bloody good job with that.'

'Thanks,' Dee said, enjoying the warm flush of pleasure his praise gave her.

'So.' Leonard's sentence was cut off by another bout of coughing. 'Gus Hope,' he said, when he was able to speak again. 'Why do you want to dig around in that old story?'

'It's actually his daughter I'm interested in,' Dee said.

She went on to explain her connection with Katie. Leonard told her he'd already seen the news pieces about the police hunt for Katie and Jake.

'Brought it all back,' he told Dee. 'Poor kid. I felt bloody sorry for her. No mum, you know. She'd disappeared years earlier. Had a reputation as a bit of a lush. General consensus was she'd got pissed and fallen into the Thames, although her body was never found, so I guess we'll never know what happened to her.'

'I read that he was killed breaking up a fight,' Dee said, realising Leonard would need a bit of steering to keep the conversation on track.

'Something like that,' Leonard said.

In the background, a woman shouted something.

'Pint and a chaser,' Leonard said. Then, to Dee: 'Listen, love. I have to go. Give me your email address and I'll dig out anything I still have on the story. I'll get it across to you right away. Can't say fairer than that, can you?'

Dee agreed you could not say fairer. She gave Leonard her email address, thanked him several times and promised to buy him a pint the next time she was in London.

True to his word, Leonard's email arrived ten minutes later. There were several attachments. Definitely worth a couple of pints, Dee thought as she scanned the information.

Most of it simply confirmed what she already knew. Katie's father, Gus Hope, had been the landlord of a popular pub in Hither Green called the Railway Tavern. His death seemed to be a straightforward case of manslaughter. He had got into a row with a young man named Shane Gilbert, who had attacked him with a broken bottle, cutting through his carotid artery and causing him to bleed to death. Two women working in the pub had witnessed the attack and both gave testimony in court. The witnesses' names were Roxanne Reed and Ella Tate. In his email, Leonard said that Roxanne had died soon after the trial. The only information he had on Ella Tate was that she'd gone to study at Bristol University a few months after the trial ended. Bristol was where Katie had lived too. Dee wondered if the two women had been there at the same time.

No idea where she is now, Leonard had written. *Not that either of them would be much use to you. The case was clear-cut. Whatever Katie's done, I doubt it's got anything to do with her poor old dad.*

A few of the stories carried a blurred black-and-white photo of Katie, nineteen years old at the time of the murder trial. Dee tried to enlarge the photo, curious to see what Katie looked like back then. But enlarging it made the pixels bigger, so it was even harder to see the details of her face.

A photo of the killer accompanied all the articles. Shane Gilbert had dark floppy hair and strong features. At the time of the murder, he'd been seventeen – the same age as Katie. It wasn't clear whether the two of them had been in a relationship or not. The view on this varied from news story to news story. One piece suggested that Katie had encouraged the young man to kill her father on purpose, although most were more balanced than that.

Dee thought it seemed likely that Katie and Gilbert had been dating. Katie's father, overprotective and overbearing according to several witnesses, hadn't liked it. There'd been a fight, and it had ended tragically.

The whole thing sounded like a terrible accident.

When she'd finished reading everything, she felt deflated. She hadn't found a single thing connecting the dead woman with the pub murder ten years ago. Which meant Leonard was right: the two events were unconnected. Or was the connection right there in front of her and she simply couldn't see it? She scanned the documents again, eyes flitting over the names of all the people involved. The witnesses, the victim, the killer...

The killer.

One of the stories Leonard had sent was an op-ed piece speculating on why a middle-class boy had turned to violence. It was the sort of faux-intellectual right-wing crap that Dee hated. Full of sweeping statements about the lazy, wayward youth of today and calling for the return of compulsory military service to 'show these young men and women what it's like to do a real job'. According to the article, Shane Gilbert had been a 'computer whizz', obsessed with programming and video games. The journalist seemed to be making a direct link between the increase in young people using computers and the rise in violent crime across the UK.

Even though she hated the story, there was something in it that kept drawing Dee back. Finally, as she was scanning it for the third time, it hit her. The length of the sentence.

Nine years ago, the man who had killed Katie's father was given an eight-year prison sentence. He probably wouldn't have served the full amount. With good behaviour, and taking into consideration the time he'd spent incarcerated before the trial, he could have got out in five or six years. Which meant there was every chance he left prison at more or less the same time that Katie moved to Eastbourne.

Dee wasn't deflated any longer. The different strands of Katie's life, which hadn't made any sense until now, were finally coming together to form a pattern that had been there all along, waiting for her to see it.

She typed Shane Gilbert's name into Google, scanning the thousands of results. A few references to the murder trial, and lots of other Shane Gilberts – company directors, self-published authors, an orthodontist in New York City – but none of them the one she was looking for.

There were plenty of Shane Gilberts on Instagram and Twitter, but as far as she could tell, none of them was the one she wanted. She logged into Facebook and typed his name again. Another list. She scrolled through it, a quick glance at each photo to see if any of them could be him.

And then, suddenly, there he was.

He was older, of course. His hair was shorter and he'd filled out quite a bit. But the eyes were the same dark blue, and so intense it seemed as if he was staring into her soul. Dee shivered. No wonder poor Katie had fallen for him.

His privacy settings were locked down, which meant she wasn't able to see any details of what he posted or who his friends were. She could send him a friend request, but if he checked her profile, he'd see she'd spent most of her adult life as a journalist. Chances were he wouldn't want anything to do with her. She needed to find some other way of contacting him. There had to be a way. All she had to do was work it out.

But it had been a long day, and she was tired. She needed to take a break. Her body told her it was wine o'clock and her mind told her that if she was going to think this through, she'd need something to unlock the tight knot of tension in the centre of her body.

It was still warm, traces of the day's heat lingering long after the sun was gone. Her skin was damp and sticky. She used a sheet of paper to fan herself, wondering how much of her body heat was down to the weather and how much was caused by early menopause. Her periods had stopped, abruptly and without warning, nine months earlier. The final confirmation that she would never be a mother.

Living next door to Katie and Jake had helped with that too. Dee had fooled herself into thinking she could be some sort of surrogate mother to the boy. She'd let her imagination take her places it should never have gone – helping get him ready for his first day at school, waiting up with Katie for him to come home after his first date, waving him off to college, watching him get married to the love of his life, holding his first child in her arms. Trying to live her life vicariously through a young woman and her son she had nothing in common with apart from the fact that they were neighbours. Stupid, stupid, stupid.

The regrets swooped in across the dark sea, wrapping themselves around her until she knew the only way out of this black depression was to pour herself some wine and to keep drinking until the pain became bearable.

She was on her third glass when the doorbell rang. She thought it might be Louise. They'd left several messages for each other throughout the day, but so far they hadn't actually spoken. When she opened the door, however, she was greeted by Alex Mackey.

'Hey.' He grinned and held up a bottle of Pinot Grigio. 'This is for you. It's not too late to call, is it? I was hoping we could chat.'

She should probably tell him this wasn't a good time, but the wine she'd already drunk meant her mind wasn't working as quickly as it should have been.

'Sure.' She stepped back, turning her head sideways when he passed so he wouldn't smell the alcohol on her breath.

She poured him a glass of wine and told him to sit on the deck while she made herself a coffee. She couldn't risk drinking any more while he was here. Didn't trust herself not to do something foolish again.

'I wanted to see you,' he said when she came out and sat down.

'Well, now you have.'

'Don't be like that. I care about you, Dee. You know that, don't you?'

Dee took a slurp of coffee. It was too hot, and it burned her tongue and throat. She barely noticed, every bit of her willing Alex not to say anything else. Clearly he was rubbish at reading her body language, because he carried on regardless.

'Do you remember the other night?' he said. 'Not the last time I was here. The time before?'

Dee groaned. 'I wondered how long it would be before you brought that up,' she said. 'Listen, Alex. I'd had too much wine and I made a pass at you. It was bloody stupid of me and I've regretted it ever since. I'm really sorry. It won't happen again.'

'I can't think about anything else,' Alex said. 'I mean, I *know* how I feel about you, Dee. I never for a second imagined you'd feel the same way. I was happy being friends because I didn't think you wanted anything more than that. But if you do...'

'Even if I wanted to sleep with you – and I don't, by the way – you're married. Maybe you're okay to forget that fact, but I can't.'

'You don't want to sleep with me?'

'I really don't,' Dee said.

'Thanks for breaking it to me gently.'

'My pleasure. And Alex?'

'Yeah?'

'You can stay and have a glass of wine, because I'm bored. But I don't want to have sex with you. Not now, not any time in the future. Is that clear?'

'Crystal.'

'One more thing,' Dee said.

'Can't wait to hear it.'

'If you ever – and I mean ever – try to tell me your wife doesn't understand you, I will kick you off this deck and forbid you from ever coming back here again.'

That made him laugh, and the tension eased between them.

'So,' he said. 'You want to tell me what you've been up to?'

And because she'd already had three quarters of a bottle of wine, and she was lonely and missing someone to talk to, Dee put down her cup of coffee, took the bottle from the wine cooler to refill her empty glass, and told Alex about her trip to London and why she was increasingly convinced the wrong girl had been killed.

Sixteen

Dee

Streaks of golden sunshine filtered through the gaps in the curtains. Dee turned her head away, trying to go back to sleep. Random moments from the previous day drifted to the surface of her mind. The green glow of Pinot Grigio under the lighting in the Soho club. Trevor's smile, teeth white against his dark skin, and the warmth of his body as he held her when they said goodbye. Leonard Mann coughing down the phone. Alex standing in her doorway, a bottle of wine in his hand and a self-satisfied grin on his face.

Alex!

She shot up, wide awake now, searching the bed for another body. But there was no one else here. She raced back through her memories, trying to recall how the night had ended. She remembered sharing her theory about Katie being the intended victim. To her surprise, Alex had seemed to take the idea seriously. So seriously that she'd let herself relax, drink some more wine. Until… nothing. The last thing she remembered was standing in the kitchen unscrewing the lid off another bottle.

She fell back on the pillows, hot with shame as the moral hangover took control of her mind and body.

She was drinking too much, doing things she never would have done when she was younger. Practically throwing herself at a married man, prancing up to London pretending she was someone special; someone better able than the police to solve the mystery of the dead girl.

She heard someone moving around the other side of the bedroom door. Her stomach contracted. Glancing at the clock on the bedside cabinet, she saw that it was only 6.45. Either she had an early-morning burglar, or Alex bloody Mackey had spent the night.

The smell of fresh coffee filtered into the room, and she pulled the quilt over her head, thinking she would lie here until he left. He had a job and a family and a life. It was only a matter of time before he'd remember one or all of them and realise he couldn't sit here in her house drinking coffee all bloody day.

'Dee?' A knock on her bedroom door and the creak of an unoiled hinge as he pushed the door open.

'I'm asleep,' she said, keeping the quilt over her head.

'Doesn't sound like it,' he said. 'I've made coffee if you fancy it?'

She threw the quilt off, anger making her forget how embarrassed she was.

'Jesus, Alex. It's not even seven o'clock. I know you have to go to work, but I don't. Can't you leave me to sleep on?'

He grinned, and her heart did that stupid flip-flop-fluttery thing.

'You didn't get enough sleep last night?' he said.

'What do you mean?'

'You fell asleep in the sitting room mid rant,' he said. 'Something about your ex-husband and how you were going to show him.'

'Show him what?'

'You fell asleep before you could enlighten me,' Alex said.

Another memory then. Dim, more a dream than a memory, but real. Waking up in the armchair, her neck stiff and sore. Alex lying on the sofa, arms crossed over his flat stomach, fast asleep.

'Your snoring woke me,' she said. 'A right bloody racket. How does Sandra put up with that noise every night?'

'She doesn't.' He grinned again. 'Why do you think I spent the night here?'

Dee's throat was dry and scratchy. Her body craved liquid, and the smell of coffee was impossible to ignore a moment longer. She told Alex to leave, said she'd be out in a moment. It was only when she got out of bed and went to look for her clothes that she realised there was no need. She'd fallen into bed last night fully dressed.

They sat outside, drinking coffee and watching the sea and sky change colour as day crept in, pushing the night further west until it disappeared altogether.

'So how does it work?' Dee asked.

Two cups of coffee and a pint of water later, the effects of the hangover were receding. Hydration coupled with the realisation that they hadn't slept together meant that she was starting to feel pretty good about herself.

'How does what work?' Alex asked. He was rolling a cigarette on his lap, not looking at her. Which maybe was why she found it so easy to ask the question.

'You and Sandra,' she said. 'When Billy stayed out all night, it drove me crazy. I would literally lose my mind, obsessing over who he was with, why he hadn't bothered to call and tell me he wouldn't be home. I hated it, hated him too for putting me through it.'

Alex put the finished cigarette in his mouth and lit it. Held the smoke in for several seconds before exhaling slowly.

'I sent her a text,' he said. 'Told her I was staying over at Ian's.'

'Who's Ian?'

'My brother.'

'I didn't know you had a brother.'

'There's lots you don't know about me.'

'He lives in Eastbourne as well?' Dee asked. Alex was from Glasgow. His rich, lilting accent was one of the reasons she found him attractive.

'Brighton,' he said. 'Runs a bar in the Laines. I go and see him quite a bit. He and Sandra don't exactly see eye to eye, so she's never bothered if I go see him without her.'

Dee doubted that was true but didn't challenge him on it, deciding to save her energy for the early-morning visitor who'd announced themselves by ringing her doorbell.

She thought it would be Louise, but when she opened the door, she found Ed Mitchell standing in her porch, telling her the coffee smelled good and asking if she had time to answer a few questions.

'This early?' Dee said. 'I hope it's important.'

'It's a murder investigation,' Ed said. 'I've got one dead woman, one missing woman and a missing child. Is that important enough for you?'

Up yours too, Dee thought, following him into the living area.

'I see you already have a visitor,' Ed said. 'Sorry to break up your morning date.'

At the sound of their voices, Alex stood up and came inside.

'You okay?' he asked Dee.

'Fine,' she said. 'Alex, this is Ed Mitchell. He's leading the investigation into the hit and run. Says he's got a few more questions for me.'

'We've already met,' Alex said. He looked at Dee. 'You want me to stay?'

'No. It's probably better if you leave. If that's okay?'

'Sure.'

He came over to her, seemed about to kiss her or give her a hug, but in the end simply patted her awkwardly on the shoulder. A moment later, the front door opened and closed and Dee was alone with Ed Mitchell.

'A bit early for a visitor,' Ed said as she handed him a cup. 'Unless he stayed the night, of course.'

'Coffee, milk and sugar on the table outside,' she said.

'Boyfriend?' Ed asked. 'Or a one-night stand?'

'That's none of your business. I didn't realise you two knew each other.'

'Alex Mackey works in a boatyard a few hundred yards along the beach from Katie's home.'

'And?'

'So of course we've spoken to him as part of our investigation.'

Dee didn't ask Ed what Alex had told him; she wasn't sure she wanted to hear the answer. She went and sat outside, wanting to get her thoughts in order before she spoke again. Predictably, Ed followed her, sitting in the chair recently vacated by Alex.

'I know Mackey's wife.' He poured himself some coffee, then sat back and crossed his legs, cradling the mug in his huge hands. He looked so smug and comfortable that Dee wanted to reach across the table and slap him – hard. 'Sandra. Lovely woman. Paediatric nurse at the Conquest hospital. She a friend of yours too?'

Dee wanted to tell him she hadn't done anything wrong. That Alex was nothing to her and the last thing, the very last thing, she wanted to be was someone who broke up another person's marriage. Because she knew better than anyone how painful it was to be at the other end of that situation. But she kept quiet, because it was none of his business and if he wanted to judge her based on something he didn't know the first thing about, well then, let him judge her to hell. It wasn't like she gave a damn what Ed Mitchell thought of her, anyway.

'I assume you're not here to ask questions about my personal life?' she said.

'What were you doing in London yesterday?'

'Sorry?'

'Rachel spoke to Crispin Marsden,' Ed said. 'Name sound familiar to you?'

Dee couldn't think of anything smart to say, so she kept quiet.

'What did you think you were doing? According to Rachel, you told him you work with Louise. That's bull-shit, Dee.'

'Why would he tell Rachel I was in London?' Dee asked. 'He told me he didn't know Katie. And he certainly didn't seem to care where she was or what had happened to her. As far as I could work out, the only thing he was interested in was getting a date with Louise.'

'Rachel called him yesterday afternoon,' Ed said. 'As Katie's ex-boss, he's a person of interest. He mentioned that an Eastbourne journalist had been asking questions earlier in the day. He couldn't remember your name, but he told Rachel what you looked like. When I heard the description, I knew right away who he was talking about.'

'And that's why you're here?' Dee said. 'Because I went to London pretending to work with Louise? I was doing her a favour because she wasn't able to go herself. What's the big deal? Shouldn't you be spending your time trying to find Katie and Jake, instead of driving out here and asking me pointless questions?'

'What did Crispin tell you about Katie?' Ed asked.

'Nothing,' Dee said. 'Like I already said, he told me he'd never even met her. Why?'

'That's what he told Rachel,' Ed said. 'She believed him, I think. It seems odd, doesn't it? Apart from you and her piano students, we can't find anyone who knows Katie. What do you make of it?'

'I think she did a good job of keeping a low profile.'

Apart from you and her piano students. Dee hoped the omission had been a mistake on Ed's part. She could ask him outright if he knew Alex had also been a friend of Katie's, but she wasn't sure she wanted to hear the answer.

'Could I take another look at the paperwork your mother kept?' Ed asked.

Dee stood up. 'Why not? If you really think it will help.'

Again she was hit with a rush of memories as she pushed open the office door and walked over to the grey filing cabinet. She imagined she could smell her mother's perfume, even though there was no way the scent would have lingered after all this time. And when she leaned down to pull out the drawer, she caught a fleeting glimpse of her mother sitting at her desk working on her computer, fingers moving fast across the laptop keyboard.

'You okay?' Ed asked as she handed him the file.

'Fine. There's a photocopier over there. Copy whatever you need and leave the file on the desk. I'll put it away later.'

She told him she would be in the kitchen if he needed her, and got out of there as quickly as possible. Memories of her dead mother chasing after her along the corridor, fizzling away until suddenly there was nothing left except the burning bright sunshine and the endless sound of the waves rolling in and out across the shingle beach. When she started to wash up, she noticed her hands was shaking and knew the tremors had nothing to do with the wine she'd drunk the night before.

She had cleaned the kitchen and was making a fresh pot of coffee when Ed joined her.

'Any chance of another cup before I go?' he asked.

The deck was already hot from the morning sun. Dee wanted him to leave. All she could think of was a swim in the sea – diving into the icy-cold water, letting it cool her hot, hung-over body.

'Did you find what you were looking for?' she asked.

'I'm not sure I know what I'm looking for,' Ed said. 'I've gone through everything again and I can't find anything new.'

'What about the other girl? The victim. Do you know who she is yet?'

'I have a theory,' Ed said. He patted the pile of photo-copied papers on the table beside his cup of coffee. 'That's why I needed to take another look. To see if there was anything in here that backs up what I'm thinking.'

'Is there?'

'Maybe.' He lifted the papers and shuffled through them, pulled one from the pile and handed it to Dee. 'What do you think?'

It was a grainy photocopied image of Katie's driving licence. Dee was just able to make out the name and some of the digits from the licence number. The photo was so blurred, it was impossible to make out any of her features clearly.

'It's a copy of a copy,' Ed said. 'Your mother obvi-ously photocopied a *copy* of Katie's licence rather than the licence itself.'

'I'm not sure about that,' Dee said. 'Mum liked to do everything properly. Any tenant would have had to provide ID, bank account records, references and so on. It's standard practice.'

'You don't think she'd have accepted a copy of the licence?' Ed asked.

'I don't know. She liked Katie and she probably didn't want to make things difficult. Especially as she was pregnant.'

She examined the photocopy again. The licence had another seven years before it expired. Nothing stood out as unusual or wrong.

Ed left soon after that. He thanked Dee for the coffee, gathered his photocopied papers and told her he'd be in touch if he had any other questions. After he'd gone, Dee went into her mother's office and sat in the chair reading through the various pieces of papers in Katie's file, trying to find something unusual. But everything seemed exactly as it should be, and eventually she gave up.

Putting the file back, she again felt her mother's presence in the room. She closed her eyes, waited for something to happen – a hand on her shoulder, her mother's voice telling her how much she loved her, the soft smell of citrus perfume. But there was nothing.

She slammed the drawer shut, the clanging sound pushing the ghosts away, back into the dark corners of her mind.

Seventeen

Katie
Eleven years earlier

It's three days later, and we haven't spoken. Three days that seemed to drag out forever while I waited to hear from him. I've seen him around college, but he's always surrounded by his other friends, and there's no way I'm going to talk to him with all of them listening.

His silence is like torture. I keep thinking about what we did, wondering if I was okay at it. I don't want to send him too many texts because I know how he feels about needy girls who are so insecure they can't give a guy some space. But I don't know what else to do.

I'm walking home from the station, wondering if I should message him again later this evening, when I see him. He's outside the pub, leaning against the wall like before. He gives a little half-wave as I walk towards him. He's smoking, the cigarette hanging from his lower lip. My neck aches from the memory of that same lip pressed against it, his breath coming hot and fast.

'Hey, stranger.' He throws the cigarette to the ground and pushes himself away from the wall.

'Hey.' I'm dying inside, my entire body curling in on itself, waiting for him to tell me it was a terrible mistake and we can't do anything like that again.

'I thought you might let me buy you a drink,' he says.

'A drink?' I think I must have misheard him.

'It's okay,' he says, misinterpreting my confusion for refusal. 'I know it's Roxanne's day off. And your dad will be at the golf course for another hour at least, won't he?'

'How do you know all this?' I ask.

'I make it my business to find out what's going on,' he says. He pulls open the door, then steps back and motions for me to go in before him, and it feels good to have a guy smile at me and open a door for me.

Inside, I feel self-conscious at first, but Shane makes it easy, acting the way he always does. As if nothing's happened between us. That's what makes this special; everything is so natural, with none of that awkwardness I might have with someone else.

The pub's quiet. Janet, one of the part-time girls, is behind the bar. I don't think she even notices me. We sit at a table near the bar, bold as anything now there's no one here to tell us what we can or can't do. When our drinks are finished, Shane offers to get us some more, but I'm not sure it's a good idea.

'My dad will be back soon,' I tell him. 'He'll go mad if he sees us here. He's seriously overprotective since Mum left. I know it's really boring, but I don't want to upset him.'

The door from the kitchen swings open and Ella comes into the bar, stopping dead when she sees us.

'Oh God,' I whisper, reaching out and grabbing Shane's arm. 'We have to go, Shane. Please? She'll tell Dad about us and he'll kill me. We could go to the park instead if you want.'

A flash of anger crosses his face and I let go of his arm quickly.

'Sorry,' I say.

But it's okay. He's smiling now.

'Tell you what,' he says. 'We'll have one more drink, then grab a bottle of something and head to the park after that. I don't think you should let her scare you that easily, K. Let's stick it out for another few minutes to show her she can't mess with you, okay?' He leans in, brushes my cheek with his lips, making my body tingle with desire, and I agree, even though it's not what I want. I don't care about Ella. All I want is to be alone with Shane, somewhere we can talk and be ourselves without people watching us.

He insists on getting the drinks, but I have to lend him money as he's run out. Janet has gone outside for a fag break and it's only Ella behind the bar now. She's chatting to some old fella who's drinking a pint of Guinness. Leaning forward so she can hear whatever rubbish he's telling her, smiling at him, pretending she gives one shit what he's talking about.

For a moment, it looks as if she's going to ignore Shane. But then she straightens up and walks over to him. He says something but I can't catch the words, even though I'm straining my ears. I can see her face, though, and I recognise the emotion on it. Anger.

I want to know what he said to make her cross, but if I ask, he won't tell me. Or he'll make something up and turn it into a joke. I wonder why he hates her, even though I know deep down inside me in that place I won't look at that it's not hate that makes him want to keep coming back here.

I think she'll argue or refuse to serve him or do some other sort of drama-queen thing. But she doesn't. He's still speaking, leaning over the bar like he wants to touch her. She doesn't say a single word back to him. She pours the drinks and slides them across the counter to him, those pink spots on her cheeks beaming at me like warning lights.

When he comes back to me, he's buzzed. His eyes glowing like polished stones. He's breathing fast, like he's been running, and he knocks his Coke back in a single swallow puts the glass down and says: 'Grab a bottle. I'll wait outside.'

'You better not say anything to my dad,' I tell Ella as I go behind the bar and take two bottles of cider. 'If you do, I swear to God I'll make sure you pay.'

'I don't care what you do,' she says. 'It's your life.'

Her answer makes me angry, and I realise I wanted her to challenge me. I want a reason to fight her. Pull that perfect hair out of its perfect plait and punch that perfect face until her nose is flattened and bleeding.

'He's only using you,' she says as I start to walk away. 'You know that, don't you?'

I stop walking, my hands tightening around the bottles. There's a buzzing sound inside my head and I know it's my blood, pumping too fast the way it does when I get angry.

A flash of memory. Standing in this same spot three years earlier. My mother sitting at the bar, drunk. Her words slurring as she shouted at me. Telling me she'd cleared all the chocolate and other treats from the kitchen that morning because I was eating too much and no one ever loved a fat girl.

I can hear Ella walking towards me. Again I picture her, battered and bloodied, and I'm about to do it, I'm getting ready to turn around and smash one of the bottles into her face, when she puts her hand on my shoulder.

'Be careful,' she says. 'Please?'

Her voice is softer and kinder than it should be. Without warning, my eyes fill with tears and I want to cry.

There's another reason too for the tears. I know Ella's right. Shane is using me and there's nothing I can do about it. I don't care why he's chosen me. All I care about is knowing it's me he'll spend the rest of the day with, me he'll have sex with, me who'll do anything he wants me to, all he has to do is ask.

Outside, he takes one of the bottles and links arms with me as we walk to the park. He's all over me the moment we reach our secret place behind the bushes. Hands clawing at my clothes, his body pressing against mine like he can't wait a moment longer.

And when it's like this between us, I know there's something stronger and deeper connecting us than a few bottles of free cider. I know that right now, in this moment, I'm the only person he needs.

Eighteen

Dee

Wednesday evening, the weather broke. All through the afternoon, thick grey clouds gathered across the sky, blocking out the sun. At 6 p.m. exactly, the heavens opened. It was exhilarating at first. This onslaught of rain after the relentless heat and sunshine. Dee watched a group of children on the beach, still in their swimsuits, screeching and running in and out of the water. She had a sudden memory from her early days with Billy. A boozy afternoon in some hotel in the south of Spain. A torrent of rain like this, both of them dancing naked in the garden of their holiday villa. Drunk, because the only really good times with Billy always involved alcohol.

Such a waste.

She'd known from the beginning that falling for Billy Morrison was like going on a sky dive. Exciting, unpredictable and, if you weren't careful, extremely dangerous. And Dee had never been careful when it came to her ex-husband.

She spent the morning thinking of ways she could track down Shane Gilbert. She went through the names of people she'd come into contact with during her twenty-plus years working as an investigative journalist. She ended up with a list of five – two former colleagues from the *Post*; a retired detective who'd worked out of Lewisham; a criminal defence solicitor based in Hither Green; and Emma Walker, a HR manager working for the prison service.

Emma and Dee had become friends after Dee ran a story on the treatment of rape victims during court cases. Initially she had been trying to write a balanced piece on rape trials, including examples of men who'd been wrongly accused and the devastating effects that could have. But when she interviewed Emma and heard about her harrowing experience in court, the focus of her story changed. Working alongside Emma, she ended up running a two-year campaign for the *Post* on the need to change the way rape victims were treated by the legal system.

The two women had become close friends, seeing each other several times a month and speaking on the phone more frequently. All of that had ended in the messy aftermath of Dee's divorce. Dee had never returned any of Emma's emails or phone calls. In the end, Emma had stopped trying to contact her. Dee wasn't sure how Emma would react if she got in touch now. There was only one way to find out. She opened a new email and typed Emma's address into the recipient line.

Outside, the rain looked like it would never stop. A ceaseless torrent of water that drummed on the roof of the house and bounced off the sea and the shingle. The noise of it got inside her head, making it impossible to think. She pushed open the door and stepped onto the deck, holding her face up to the sky, letting the water pound down on her. There was something therapeutic about getting wet like this. Almost as if the rain was cleaning away all the anxiety and regret she carried around with her. She would have stayed for longer, but 'Ring of Fire' started to play on her phone, telling her she had a call coming through.

She went inside and realised she was too wet to answer it. Letting it go to voicemail, she went to change her clothes and dry her hair. When she was finished, she checked her call log and saw Emma's name.

'Dee Doran!' Emma said when Dee called her back. 'I nearly fell off my chair when I got your email earlier. How the hell are you? I was starting to worry I'd never hear from you again.'

'Sorry I disappeared,' Dee said. 'A lot's happened since I saw you last, Em.'

'I thought as much,' Emma said. 'When you stopped replying to my texts and emails, I knew something wasn't right. But I also knew that if you wanted to tell me, you would. Are you okay?'

Dee gave a potted history of how her life had fallen apart since they'd last spoken. She spoke quickly, wanting to get to the real reason for her call as quickly as she could.

'Katie and Jake were the only things keeping me going these last few months,' she said. 'That's why I'm so desperate to find out what's happened to them.'

'I can understand that,' Emma said. 'Is there anything I can do to help?'

'Actually,' Dee said, 'that's sort of why I got in touch. Katie's father was killed. I think the person who did it might be the reason she's disappeared. I need to find him.'

'You know I could get fired for giving you information on a prisoner's whereabouts?' Emma said.

'He's not a prisoner any more,' Dee said. 'He was released two or three years ago. I'm just looking for a name. Someone who could tell me where he went after he left prison. Could you do that for me?'

'Ten years ago,' Emma said, 'I felt as if I'd nothing left to live for. I wanted to die, Dee. I'd considered suicide more times than you could imagine. The assault, along with everything that happened afterwards, destroyed me. If it wasn't for you, those stories you wrote and the way you got people talking, the way you got *me* talking, I don't think I'd be here today. So yes, I'll help you. Tell me exactly what you need and I'll see what I can do.'

Dee swallowed the lump in her throat and gave Emma the details. Emma promised she'd get back to her as quickly as she could; Dee, in return, promised to be better at staying in touch.

After she hung up, she felt better than she had in days. Emma was another reminder of what she had given up when she'd fled London and her broken marriage, using her mother's illness as an excuse to hide away from the rest of the world. Speaking to her today, hearing her voice and her affirmation of their friendship, meant so much. She wasn't about to let that friendship slip through her fingers a second time.

Nineteen

Dee

The following morning, the rain had stopped but the memory of it lingered. There was a freshness in the air that Dee had missed over the last few weeks. The drop in temperature – from scorching to hot – was a relief. She needed to buy some groceries, and she decided to make the most of the cooler weather by walking to the supermarket in the harbour.

Outside, by the spot where the woman had been killed, people had left bunches of flowers. Some of these had messages pinned to them. Pointless things like *Taken too young* and *Our prayers are with you*. Dee wondered what sort of person would leave flowers for someone they'd never met. The dead woman still hadn't been identified. Which meant the people who'd come out here to leave the flowers had no idea who they were leaving them for.

She could have understood if it *had* been Katie. Many of Katie's piano students were children. She imagined a parent bringing a child out here to lay flowers as a way of helping them process the tragedy. But no one knew who this woman was, which made the whole thing a bit creepy.

She stepped past the flowers and continued to the harbour. She was almost at the supermarket when Trevor phoned.

'I wanted to check you got what you needed from Leonard.'

'He's been great,' Dee said. 'Thanks so much for the contact.'

'Glad to hear it. He called me after you spoke with him. Seemed a bit put out that I'd given you his number without checking with him first.'

'He was upset about it?' Dee asked.

'I got the feeling he didn't want to talk about the trial,' Trevor said. 'He said it was all in the past and you were wasting your time digging around for clues that weren't there. It was weird.'

'Well he wasn't weird with me,' Dee said. 'He was really helpful, actually. I've promised I'll buy him a pint sometime.'

'Good idea,' Trevor said. 'Listen, Dee, there's another reason I'm calling. Billy called me last night. Did you know he's trying to turn this hit and run into a story?'

'I had an idea he might be.' Dee remembered the pretty blonde who'd turned up claiming to be a friend of Billy's. 'What did he want?' she asked.

'Same as you. Wanted to know if I could put him in touch with anyone who covered the trial. He seems to have this idea that it was a miscarriage of justice. Do you know anything about that?'

'Not a thing,' Dee said. 'Did you give him Leonard's number?'

'Course not. What do you take me for? Besides, I think Leonard would kill me if I asked him to help someone else out on this. I told you, he's a bit funny about it all.'

'Thanks for that,' Dee said. 'And for the tip-off about Billy as well. When he was telling you about the miscarriage of justice, did he mention anyone's name?'

'I don't think so. But I got the impression he had a good source.'

Dee thought about calling Billy later and asking him what he knew about the trial. Before she came to her senses and realised that the last thing she needed was to let her husband think he had information she wanted.

She had reached the entrance to the supermarket, and practically collided with Alex, who was on his way out.

'Time for a coffee?' he whispered.

'Okay,' she mouthed. Then, to Trevor: 'I've got to go. Thanks again for this.'

'You'll keep in touch?' Trevor said.

'Of course I will. The next time I'm in London, I'll take you and Leonard out. How does that sound?'

'Sounds wonderful. Make sure you give me a bit of notice. I'll need to go into training before a night out with you two.'

Dee told him he was a cheeky bugger, promised again that she'd be in touch and hung up.

'Fancy bumping into you like this,' Alex said.

'It's hardly a coincidence. This is the closest supermarket to both of us.'

'Fair point. Come on. I'm on an early lunch break. I'll treat you to a coffee in Seasons. There's something I've been meaning to ask you about.'

Seasons was Dee's favourite bar and cafe in the area. They sat at a table outside and ordered their drinks – coffee for Alex, Diet Coke for Dee.

'I was thinking of popping in to see you later,' Alex said. 'If you're up for a bit of company?'

'Not tonight,' Dee said. 'I've already got plans actually.' Not true, but she didn't want to drink tonight, and an evening with Alex inevitably involved booze.

'Sure.' He shrugged. 'You up to anything exciting?'

'I'm working. And when I'm finished working, I'm going to have a long bath and an early night.'

'You work?' Alex said. 'Since when?'

'It's an idea for a story. Something I've been thinking about, that's all.' She didn't want to tell him how much time and effort she was putting into finding Katie. She didn't want to hear him telling her it was a waste of time. Besides, it was none of his business what she got up to.

'Maybe some other night then,' he said.

'You said you wanted to ask me something,' Dee reminded him.

The waitress who'd taken their order arrived with their drinks. Alex waited until she'd left before speaking.

'There's something been bugging me,' he said. 'On the news, they're saying it was Katie who ran over that poor girl. But it doesn't make sense.'

'Why not?'

'Because Katie can't drive.'

'Yes she can,' Dee said, remembering the photocopied driving licence in her mother's files.

'No.' Alex shook his head. 'She's never learned. She told me one time I was over there. I'd just got my new car – the Audi, remember? I was showing it to Jake. Katie told me she'd grown up in London, where she never needed a car, and since then, she'd never got around to taking lessons. I asked her if it was difficult, you know, living where she did, but it didn't seem to bother her. She said she did fine with public transport. Told me she might learn to drive one day but wasn't in any rush.'

'When was this?' Dee asked.

'Recently,' Alex said. 'Maybe a few weeks before she disappeared?'

'That doesn't make any sense. She has a driving licence, Alex. There's a copy of it with her rental agreement.'

'You're saying she lied to me?' Alex frowned. 'Why would she do that?'

'I have no idea,' Dee said.

They finished their drinks and walked back along the beach together. At Dee's house, Alex said goodbye and continued on to his workshop at Normans Bay. As she watched him walk away, Dee wondered why Katie had lied to him about not being able to drive. She thought about it, picked over the various reasons, before deciding on the most likely explanation: it was the quickest and easiest way she could think of to stop Alex going on about his new car.

Unless she'd been telling the truth and she really couldn't drive. Which meant the photocopied driving licence in the file was a fake. And if Katie had lied about that, what else had she lied about?

Twenty

Katie
Ten years earlier

I've started wearing my hair the way Ella does. A loose plait pulled over one shoulder, like a rope. It's much better than how I used to wear it, scraped back into a high ponytail. It actually hurt my head pulling it back that tight. I only ever wore it that way because of Marsha.

I practise in front of the mirror. Keeping my back and shoulders straight, head up, chin out. I stand sideways, holding in my tummy, trying to make it look flat like hers. Wanting to be her so much it hurts.

People watch Ella. I see them, their eyes following her as she moves around the bar. Slender as a gazelle, poised like a dancer. I see Shane, too. The sheen in his eyes that's only there when he's talking about her. He never looks at me the way I've seen him looking at her. But I can change that. I just need to try harder. I'm clever. According to Dad, I take after my mum that way. I've got her smile too, and her eyes, although he never mentions that. After she left, I used to stare at myself in the mirror for hours at a time, smiling at my reflection, searching out the little pieces of her face in mine.

I've already lost two stone. Roxanne's noticed, but I don't think anyone else has. I want Dad to say something, but he never does. He's so used to me the way I've always been – fat Katie – that he's incapable of seeing me differently.

'You're being sensible on this diet of yours?' Roxanne asked. 'Don't want to lose the weight too quickly or you won't keep it off. And try not to lose too much. Those lovely curves of yours, most fellas would go wild for them.'

She was trying to be kind, but it's a bit patronising. No one looks at Ella Tate and thinks she'd look better with a few curves. I'm sick of being fat, and if Roxanne or anyone else doesn't like it, that's their problem.

Shane hasn't said anything about my weight. He can't have missed it completely, because he gets to see more of my body than anyone. Even if most of what we do is in the park, where we're never completely naked. Plus, it's not like when you read about sex or see it on TV or in a film. The things we do, all that heat and passion and *intimacy*, it's always over so quickly. Too quickly. It's never enough, and all it does is make me crazier for him than I already am.

I've bought loads of new clothes. Things I've never been comfortable wearing before, but now they look good on me. I dress like Ella, but not in such an obvious way that anyone would think I was copying her.

Like I said, I'm clever.

I've started smoking, too. Cigarettes help you to lose weight, and now that I've lost two stone, I only have one more to go to reach my target. If Dad finds out about the cigarettes or the cider, he'll go mental. If he finds out what I do in the park with Shane, he'll probably kill me. Roxanne's the only person who guesses I'm up to something. More than once, she's tried to have a word, but each time I've changed the subject. I can see she's worried about me, but she needs to mind her own business. She's not my mother and she has no right to interfere in my life. Besides, she spends so much time with Ella these days, I'm surprised she can even find the time to talk to me.

I saw them together in the bar earlier, chatting and laughing like they were best friends or something. As soon as Roxanne went to the loo, I grabbed a bottle of cider and came to the park. I've sent Shane a text asking if he wants to join me, but he hasn't replied.

We always come to the same spot. It's a little area at the end of the park, behind the bushes. There's a piece of ground where nothing grows, just a patch of dead grass and clay. You can sit in here and no one else in the park can even see you. It's perfect for what we do when we're together.

I've never been here on my own before and it feels a bit weird. I check my phone to see if there's anything from Shane. Nothing. I want to text again but I know that will give the wrong signals, so I don't. I open the cider and take a sip. I've got used to the taste now and it goes down pretty easy. I keep drinking until the whole bottle's gone.

The more I drink, the angrier I get. Shane still hasn't texted me back and I'm sick of being treated like this. I'm the best girlfriend he'll ever have, but you wouldn't think it. He practically ignores me in college. Hangs around with the same stupid group of friends. At lunchtime, he never comes to chat or asks me to have lunch with him. And I've seen him with those girls. Lily and Livvy and Freya. There's a big gang of them, but those three are the queen bees and he's their precious prince who they spoil with their air kisses and their arms draped around his shoulders on their way to the park or the canteen or wherever the hell he goes to when he's with them instead of me.

I need to wee. I stand up and realise I've drunk more than I should have. The cider's gone to my head and the world feels wobbly as I make my way through the park to the toilets. I splash water on my face, but it doesn't make a difference. All it does is smudge my make-up. I do my best to tidy it up, but my face in the mirror keeps blurring, so in the end I give up. I leave the park, not sure what I'm going to do now, knowing I can't go home until the cider's worn off a bit.

I'm halfway across the road when I see Shane. He's walking ahead of me on the opposite side of the road. I open my mouth to call his name. Then I remember he hasn't responded to my text and I'm meant to be angry with him. So I follow him instead, keeping far enough back so it won't look as if I'm following him if he turns around and sees me.

It's too hot. Sweat is rolling down my face. I wipe it away, but more comes and I give up. The woozy cider buzz make me feel like I'm in a dream. Heat rises in waves from the pavement, blurring Shane's body and adding to the sense that this isn't real.

At the end of the road, Shane turns left, heading towards Hither Green station. I hurry forward, scared now that he's going to catch a train and I'll miss him. It strikes me then that I've no idea where he lives. I wonder how I could know someone the way I know him without being aware of basic things like where he lives or whether he has any brothers and sisters or what his parents do.

When I turn the corner, I see he hasn't gone to the station. He's turned onto Leahurst Road. My heart skitters inside my chest and flutters of excitement tickle across my stomach. He's going to the pub.

I slow down, calm now, knowing it's okay. I get to the corner and he's there. Smoking a cigarette and leaning against the wall outside the pub. Waiting. He must have got my text, and I'm smiling so hard my face hurts, my body light with the knowledge that he's here for me.

The pub door opens and Ella comes out. She crosses the road and walks towards the station, in the opposite direction to where Shane's standing, so I don't think she sees him. He throws his cigarette to the ground, twists it out with the toe of his Converse trainer and starts to follow her.

I don't know what he's doing or what I'm supposed to do. So I just stand there in the blazing sunshine, watching through a haze of summer heat as Ella Tate disappears into the tunnel under the train station. And Shane – long, lean and beautiful – walks after her.

Twenty-One

Dee

Friday morning, Dee was in her car by 6.15. She drove along the seafront as far as Holywell, turning right at Duke's Drive and crawling up the steep hill that wound around the edge of town. Suddenly she was in a different world. A world without houses or buildings. Rolling hills of green fields dotted with sheep. The sun creeping over the edge of the white cliffs at Beachy Head.

She pulled into one of the parking bays near the pub and visitor centre. Despite her constant gnawing anxiety, her mood lifted as she got out of the car and let her mind absorb the breathtaking views that stretched out on every side. These cliffs, the highest chalk cliffs in the UK, marked the southern edge of the South Downs National Park. The ocean lay more than five hundred feet beneath her. If she moved closer to the cliff edge, she would see the Beachy Head lighthouse. White with a thick red stripe across its middle, it had been down there for over a hundred years, built to replace the other lighthouse – the Belle Tout – that stood just west of here, perched on the clifftop. Beyond Belle Tout, the jagged white cliffs continued along the coast, their shape changing year by year as the chalk gradually eroded away.

'Dee!'

She turned away from the view to see Louise jogging over to her. Even at this time in the morning, her cousin was perfectly turned out: body-hugging Lycra, her blonde hair tied back in a neat ponytail, and a pair of designer shades blocking out half her face.

This early-morning walk had been Lou's idea. She'd called Dee last night and suggested they meet for a catch-up and a bit of exercise. In the past, too far back to count the years, the pair of them had gone on regular hikes together. Living on the edge of the South Downs had given both girls a taste for outdoor life when they were younger. During their teenage years, they used to get the bus out here and walk for an entire day, sharing secrets and analysing every aspect of their lives in that forensic way peculiar to teenage girls.

After she left Eastbourne, Dee would always try to fit in a walk with Louise whenever she was in town. Since coming back this time, they'd talked a lot about reinstating their regular outings, but over two years in, this was the first time they'd managed it.

'I thought we could walk to Birling Gap and back,' Louise said.

'Promise me we'll take it easy,' Dee said. 'Especially along the first bit, where it's really hilly.'

'You'll be fine,' Louise said. 'You're fitter than you think you are. Come on. I need to be home by eight. The kids'll be up by then and I don't want them to wake Martin. Don't give me that look, Dee. He had a late flight last night and he needs a lie-in, okay?'

'I didn't give you any look,' Dee lied. She linked arms with Louise. 'Let's get going if you're on a deadline. You can tell me about yesterday's meeting along the way.'

Louise had spent the previous afternoon at a town hall meeting set up to give the press – local and national – an update on the hit–and–run investigation.

'The whole thing was a complete waste of time,' she said as they set off. 'Ed wasn't even there. He left Rachel to handle it all. She claimed they're making progress, but she wasn't very forthcoming.'

'You think they know more than they're letting on?' Dee asked. 'And slow down, for Christ's sake. If we keep going at this pace, I'll collapse.'

'Give yourself a few minutes to get into your stride,' Louise said.

Dee didn't reply, saving her energy for the walk. This first stretch was the hardest. Steep hills that rose and dipped, so one minute they were walking along a high ridge with the rising sun warming their backs, and the next they were plunging down into the cold space between hills, where the sun hadn't yet reached.

'Janet Higgins did most of the speaking,' Louise said, managing to talk without any obvious effort as they worked their way up the next steep curve in the cliffs. 'She's their press person. Useless. I asked if they were any closer to identifying the victim, and she nearly wet herself.'

'You mean they know who she is?' Dee paused for a breath, and to take in this latest information. If the police were able to identify the victim, surely it meant they were a step closer to understanding who might have killed her. And if they could identify the killer, prove once and for all it wasn't Katie, maybe Katie and Jake would feel safe enough to return home.

'Definitely.' Louise looked over her shoulder. 'Keep up. It gets easier after this. Janet mumbled something about no formal identification, but she was looking at Rachel the whole time. In the end, Rachel stepped forward, smooth as anything, and said it would be foolish to speculate about who she might be until they had all the facts.'

'You need to speak to Rachel,' Dee said, hurrying up the hill after Louise. 'Tell her it's off the record and see what she'll tell you.'

'I've tried that before with her,' Louise said. 'It doesn't work. She's only interested in cooperating with the press when she thinks we can help. Clearly, at the moment, she doesn't think we can. Maybe you should try Ed. You're just his type.'

They'd reached the top of the hill. Belle Tout rose up in front of them, the white edges of the Seven Sisters cliffs jutting into the sea behind it. The glitter of sun reflecting off water, the white dash of a seagull chasing across the blue sky.

'Heaven on earth,' Dee said. 'How could I have forgotten what it's like up here? And what do you mean about me being Ed Mitchell's type?'

'You're unconventional,' Louise said. 'He likes that. I'm sure that's why things didn't work out with Catherine. They wanted different things.'

'How do you know all this?' Dee asked.

'I know what people are like. And what attracts them to each other. And I think you and Ed would make a good match.'

'No chance,' Dee said.

'We'll see.' Louise grinned. 'But remember, if you do have sex with him, I want to know everything.'

'You're so immature,' Dee said, but she was smiling too. One of the best things about being back home was seeing more of her cousin again. Even if Louise drove her mad half the time, Dee wouldn't be without her.

Louise had been right about the walk getting easier. Dee barely noticed the hill up to Belle Tout. After that, the ground evened out and the final stretch to Birling Gap was painless.

'We should go down to the beach,' Louise said. 'It's beautiful there in the morning. We've got time.'

'Do you mind if we don't?' Dee said. 'The last time I was there was with Katie and Jake. We took him for a picnic here one evening. I haven't been back since.'

Her chest hurt remembering that April evening. Birling Gap was a special place. A pebbled beach situated at the bottom of the white cliffs. The perfect location to watch the sunset. They'd come here because Katie had heard about it but never visited. They had a picnic on the beach and watched the world change colour as the sun dropped lower and lower. There'd been other people there when they first arrived, but gradually everyone else drifted away until it was just the three of them. When the sun had disappeared below the horizon, they'd walked back to the iron steps you had to climb to get off the beach, their feet crunching over the pebbles, the sound bouncing off the white cliffs and echoing back across the still, silent evening. It had felt magical and mystical, and Dee knew she'd remember the moment forever.

'Ready to go back then?' Louise asked, her voice bringing her back from that evening and other memories.

They turned around, walking into the sunshine this time. As they ascended the last slope, Eastbourne appeared below them, spread out across the flat land at the foot of the Downs. The pier, blazing white and gold in the early-morning sunshine; Sovereign Harbour, spread along the next curve in the bay. And somewhere the other side of that, Dee's and Katie's homes. Dee loved her parents' house, but the thought of going back there this morning and spending the rest of the day alone filled her with dread.

She suggested they sit for ten minutes and take in the view. To her surprise, Louise agreed without any mention of having to get back to Martin and the children.

'I've been doing a bit of reading about Katie's dad,' Dee said. 'The killer was a teenager called Shane Gilbert. I think he was probably Katie's boyfriend. I'd like to speak to him, find out if he might know where she is.'

'Maybe they're still together,' Louise said. 'Is there any chance he could be Jake's dad?'

'I don't think so,' Dee said. 'Shane was still in prison when Katie got pregnant. But she moved to Eastbourne around the same time he left prison. I think she came here to get away from him, not because she was still seeing him.'

A pair of herring gulls flew out from the cliff, shots of white against the blue sky. Dee thought she heard the whisper of their wings in the air as they passed.

'You think she was hiding from him,' Louise said. 'And somehow he found her and tried to kill her.'

'Except it wasn't Katie,' Dee said. 'That poor girl died because Shane Gilbert made a mistake.'

'You can't know that for sure,' Louise said.

Dee didn't answer, because Louise was wrong. Dee knew that was what had happened. Now all she had to do was prove it.

Twenty-Two

Dee

That afternoon, Dee had another visit from Ed Mitchell.

'You got a few minutes?' he asked.

'I've just made coffee,' she said. 'If you fancy a cup?'

'Music to my ears,' Ed said, stepping past her into the house. 'Let's drink it outside. It's too sunny to sit indoors.'

'Go right ahead,' Dee muttered, shutting the front door and following him into the house.

While Ed settled himself on the deck, Dee prepared a tray and carried it outside.

'No biscuits?' Ed asked as she put the tray on the table and sat opposite him. 'Probably just as well. Watching my weight.' He patted his stomach and smiled. Dee bit the inside of her cheek to stop herself smiling back.

'Louise told me you know who the victim is,' she said.

Ed reached for the cafetière, pouring the contents into the two mugs before answering.

'Louise is speculating,' he said.

'Is she right?'

'You know better than to ask a question like that.' He reached for his mug and slugged his coffee. In his hands, the mug looked ridiculously small, like an item from a child's playhouse. Something about his hands triggered a memory. Ed Mitchell, body crouched low, rugby ball cradled in his arm, racing towards the try line.

She wondered if it was a real memory or something conjured up by her too vivid imagination. She didn't think she'd ever watched a rugby match in her life.

'I assume you didn't drive all the way out here just for coffee?' she said.

Ed drained what was left in his mug and held it up. 'Any chance of more?'

'If I say yes, will you tell me why you came out here to speak to me instead of simply picking up the phone?'

'I might be persuaded,' Ed said. 'Depends how good the coffee is, of course.'

Dee knew she should probably tell him to sod off. Instead, she found herself winking and telling him he already knew how good her coffee was, so he should come right out and tell her everything he knew.

'Coffee first,' Ed said. When he winked right back at her, Dee grabbed his cup before either of them did anything else cheesy, and went to make a fresh pot.

'Did Katie ever mention someone called Ella Tate?' Ed asked when she came back outside.

Ella Tate. One of the witnesses at Shane Gilbert's trial.

Dee took a deep breath and made sure to keep all emotion from her voice when she answered.

'I don't think so. Why?'

'She was a friend of Katie's.'

'You think she's the dead woman?' Dee asked. Her mind was racing now. She couldn't remember seeing any photos of Ella Tate in the news stories Leonard had sent her. As soon as Ed left, she'd go online and find out everything she could about the woman. Including what she looked like.

'We're trying to find anyone with any connection to Katie,' Ed said. 'Ella Tate's a bit of a mystery to us.'

'I don't remember Katie ever talking about anyone called Ella,' Dee said. 'You sure they were friends?'

'Pretty sure.'

'And you think she's the victim. Is that why you're here? Do you think I've been lying to you?'

'Stop being so paranoid,' Ed said. 'I'm only doing my job, Dee. As for the identity of the victim, we still don't know who she is.'

Liar, Dee thought. But she kept quiet, waiting to see what he would say next.

'Did you ever get the sense Katie was scared, or hiding from something?' he asked.

Goose bumps prickled across the skin on her arms and stomach.

'I never really thought about it,' she said.

'Really?' Ed said. 'You're a journalist. Doesn't that make you curious about everything? I've always assumed a natural nosiness was a basic requirement in your line of business.' He smiled, and in that moment Dee understood why Louise had found him so attractive. 'Like being a detective. It was one of the things my ex hated. I need to understand people. It's not enough knowing *who* committed a crime. I also want to know *why*. People are endlessly interesting, don't you think?'

Dee tried to picture herself through his eyes, wondered what he made of her life. She'd like to ask him, but wasn't sure she was brave enough to hear his answer.

'Is that why you split up?' she asked instead.

Ed laughed. A rich, throaty sound that sent another shiver through her body. She seriously needed to get a grip.

'My natural curiosity wasn't the only thing she didn't like about me,' he said. 'Turned out there were a whole lot of other things as well. Particularly my inability to commit to a wedding.'

'She wanted to get married and you didn't.' Dee was disappointed by this revelation, although she had no idea why she should care whether or not Ed Mitchell was the marrying kind.

'We weren't right together,' he said. 'I guess I knew that for a while, but I was too much of a coward to do anything about it. When Cath finally finished it between us, I was relieved more than anything.'

'How long ago was that?' Dee asked.

'Two years. Footloose and fancy free since then. How about you?'

'What about me?' Dee said.

'You were married, right?'

'And now I'm not. Can we get back to talking about Katie? You were asking if I thought she was scared.'

'And?'

Dee scanned the beach, as if she might find the right words amongst the sun-bleached shingle or the dried-out patches of sea kale. It was so peaceful here. Maybe that was why she'd never really considered that Katie could have been hiding. How could anyone hide in a place this wide open?

Dee had grown up on this beach, spent her entire childhood on the shingle, swimming in the sea, having picnics. Then later, as a teenager, drinking cider with her friends and smoking cigarettes and joints. She'd lost her virginity on a scrubby patch of land where the beach curved around towards Pevensey Bay.

'She didn't like to talk about her past,' she said. 'Any time I asked about her life before Eastbourne, she clammed up. I never pushed it because I didn't feel it was right to do that. I respected her privacy. She told me she was here because she loved the sea. And I believed her.' She threw her hand out, gesturing at the grey and white shingle, the still sea and the clear blue sky. 'I can't think of a lovelier place to raise a child.'

'I've never had kids,' Ed said. 'So I can't say what I would or wouldn't want. I've got two nephews, though. My sister's kids. I know she was lonely as hell after the first one was born. Her partner was away a lot and she found it really tough trying to do everything by herself.'

'Katie didn't have to do everything by herself,' Dee said. 'She had me.'

'And you never thought it was strange that she didn't confide in you?' Ed asked. 'Didn't you want to know why she'd moved here? Why she'd chosen to have her child in a place where she didn't know a single person?'

'I enjoyed being with them so much, I was afraid to push too hard. She made it clear she didn't want to talk about certain things, and I left it at that. I thought that over time, maybe, she'd be able to tell me more about herself.'

'But she never did.' A statement, not a question.

Ed looked at his watch, said it was time for him to leave. As she showed him out, Dee asked him again if he thought the dead woman might be Ella Tate.

'I thought she could have been,' Ed said. 'But we've checked Ella Tate's dental records. It's not her.'

'So why ask me about her?'

'She's a loose end I can't tie up,' Ed said. 'And I don't like that. We've managed to trace a lot of people who knew Katie before she moved here. But this friend, Ella, we've had no luck with at all. She seems to have completely disappeared.'

'Like Katie,' Dee said.

Ed nodded. 'Exactly.'

Twenty-Three

Katie
Ten years earlier

I haven't seen either of them since that afternoon, and no one will tell me where they are or what's happened. Ella hasn't turned up for work. Roxanne told me she's sick. But Roxanne's lying, because she won't look at me when she says it and she tries to change the subject too quickly, asking me if I know where my dad is, even though I saw them talking half an hour earlier and he told her he was going to the cash and carry.

I didn't follow them that afternoon. I couldn't bear to see them together. Instead, I waited. I already knew where she lived. Dad keeps a file with all the phone numbers and addresses for the staff. I'd been to Ella's house more than once, watching her play with that stupid dog. It was clear how much she loved him, and I wanted to hurt her the way she's hurt me. I thought it would make me feel better, but it hasn't. It's made everything worse. Because somehow she's worked out what I did and she's told Shane. That's why he's been avoiding me and not replying to my texts.

I imagine her sobbing into his chest, telling him what a nasty person I am. Boo hoo hoo. Instead of defending me, he holds her gently and kisses the top of her head, and says he'll buy her another dog and he'll make sure horrible fat Katie never does anything to hurt her ever again.

I hate them both.

I'm so sick with worry, I can't eat. Which is good, I suppose. I'm still on the Atkins diet, and normally all I can think about is what I'm going to have for my lunch. Today, though, even the thought of food twists my stomach, and I know if I try to eat anything I'll throw up.

I have two classes this afternoon, but I can't face them. Sitting in a closed classroom surrounded by the smell of bodies and the heat coming off the computers and the sun burning through the big glass windows, turning the room into a furnace. And the noise of people whispering around me and about me, laughing because they know. I'm sure everyone knows by now, and I can't stand it.

I walk across Blackheath. Hot sun, sweat running into my eyes, thighs rubbing together under my denim skirt. I imagine my skin down there, red and raw. And I think about Ella's long, skinny legs. Pale skin that's smooth when you touch it. I can see his hands on them, his fingers pressing into her flesh as he pulls her legs open. His pupils huge and dark, his breathing uneven. She arches up, pushes her cunt towards him, teasing him, pulling back, making him beg the way he never begs me for anything.

They're inside my head, doing all the things we've done together, only it's better and hotter and faster and different because it's her, not me. His hands on her and in her and she's face down now and he's pushing and grunting and I want him to stop but he doesn't and it hurts but it's okay because it's what he wants and oh God now he's moving so fast and digging deeper, his hand on my head shoving

164

my face into the ground. Dirt in my mouth and I'm suffocating. But then, suddenly, it's over and he's rolling off, but when I turn my head to look at him, it's not my face he sees.

'Ella.' He whispers her name and she stretches out one long, perfect arm and smiles as she points at the fat girl who's standing in the corner, watching them.

I'm in Greenwich Park, walking faster but not fast enough, because I can't get away from them. Their laughter chases after me, following me down the hill all the way to the river, wrapping itself around my throat, choking me.

Across the water, the city spreads away from me as far as I can see. I'll go down into the foot tunnel that runs under the river, come out the other side and walk through that mass of concrete and people and glass and churches and traffic and noise. I'll walk through it all, not stopping even when I reach the far edges of the city where it slows down, fades until there's no city any more and all around are fields and trees and sheep.

But it won't help. Even if I made it that far, it wouldn't change this thing that's building up inside me, bursting through my head and heart and body until it's all I am, and the person I used to be is lost in it, consumed by it.

I can't breathe. My throat and mouth and lungs are so clogged up with the desperate desire to see him and feel him and know he's not with her and he never will be. I lean over the railings. Bits of my face reflected in the water. An eye and a chin. The curve of a cheek. I half close my eyes and imagine it's Ella's face I'm looking at. Our two faces merging into one.

Water swirls past, dark and deep and fast. I lean over further, imagining what it would feel like to drop down, to let go. My feet tipping up and over, the hit of cold water against the top of my head as my body shoots down, disappears. Falling deeper and deeper until I don't know which way is up any more. Carried on the current through the south London suburbs and Essex, all the way out to the North Sea.

The river was one of the places they searched for my mum. Dredging, they called it. I remember trying to picture it. A boat with a big net dragging through water and mud and sand. The tug as it found her body and lifted her up, out of the water.

But it didn't happen like that because they never found her. Which doesn't mean she's not down there. Waiting, maybe. I close my eyes, remember what it felt like when she wrapped her arms around me, telling me I was beautiful. Her voice soft and warm, and there's no way you could believe she didn't love you when she spoke to you like that.

'Don't jump.'

For a split second, I'm angry. I don't want to hear his voice right now, even though he's all I've thought about for the last four days. I want my mum's voice to stay, but she's already gone and he's ruined it for me. But then he puts his hand on my shoulder and electricity shoots through me and I'm alive again. I swing around from the railings to make sure it's really him.

A hand-rolled cigarette hangs from the side of his mouth and he's carrying a bottle of vodka that he waves in the air.

'I'm going back to mine to get pissed,' he says. 'My parents are at some event at my dad's work. They won't be back till late. You coming?'

I want to tell him I saw him. And I know. I know how he feels about Ella Tate and I know he's been following her and I know too that she's the only reason he's ever bothered with me.

But he smiles and moves closer, making my body melt to nothing. I grab the railing, because if I don't hold onto something, there'll be nothing left. And inside my head, his hands between her legs and the smell of her all around us, her voice and his and my head so dizzy the whole world is spinning.

'Come on.'

He tilts his head and starts walking. He doesn't look back to check if I'm coming too, because he knows he doesn't have to. He knows I'll always do what he asks me to.

Twenty-Four

Dee

Dee dreamed about the dead girl. In the dream, the girl spoke to her. Told her who she was and asked her to help the police find her killer. When Dee woke up, the details of the dream were already slipping from her consciousness. The only thing that remained was the dead girl's name. Or rather, the name she'd given herself in Dee's dream. Ella Tate. Except according to Ed, the dead girl wasn't Ella Tate.

During the night, Dee had managed to convince herself there was some mistake. The dead girl had to be Ella Tate, because nothing else made any sense. This morning, as the dream drifted away and fingers of light trickled through the cracks in the blinds, she knew that if something wasn't making any sense, it was because she was asking the wrong questions.

After showering and getting dressed, she selected Johnny Cash's *At Folsom Prison* album from her Spotify playlist and turned the volume up loud. Johnny had got her through some of the best and worst times of her life, and he was exactly what she needed right now.

She made coffee and sat on the deck, keeping the doors open so she could hear the music. Every so often, the gravelly voice and guitar chords were interspersed with whoops and cheers from the prison inmates. Dee flicked through the news sites on her phone while she drank her coffee. Nothing had changed since yesterday. Jake and Katie were still missing, and there was no update on the identity of the missing girl.

When she was finished with the news, she called Leonard. She got his voicemail and left a message asking him to call her back. 'It's about Roxanne Reed,' she added. 'One of the witnesses at the trial. I need to know how she died.'

She hung up and opened her laptop. She'd spent too long the previous evening trying to track down Ella Tate. And coming up with precisely nothing. If Ella Tate was a real person, she was a real person who managed to exist in the twenty-first century without any digital footprint. In Dee's experience, the only people who lived like that were those with something to hide.

She had also searched Facebook for Bristol University graduates. She'd found groups for each graduation year and posted a message on the page of every group from 2011 through to 2015, thinking those years had to cover Ella's time at the university. She said she was trying to contact her old friend Ella Tate, and asked for anyone with information to get in touch.

A few people had replied on the 'Class of 2013' page. Several people remembered Ella, but no one was able to tell Dee where she was now. She shut down the page and opened Facebook Messenger. She had one new message from someone called Brian Higgins.

Ella was my pal Tom Doyle's girlfriend. No idea what happened to her but I can put you in touch with Tom if you'd like? Send me a DM for more details.

Bingo! She sent Brian a message with her phone number and email. Told him it was urgent and asked him to get in touch as quickly as possible. Next, she did a Google search for the Railway Tavern in Hither Green. The pub didn't seem to have its own website, but there were plenty of mentions on sites like TripAdvisor and Londonist.com. *Time Out* gave it a five-star review, calling it one of the last authentic pubs in south-east London. There was no mention anywhere of its tragic history.

When she'd finished reading about the pub, Dee tried Leonard again, but with no luck. She didn't bother leaving a second message. Instead, she sent him an email, telling him she needed to speak to him urgently. She checked Facebook Messenger and her emails, but Brian Higgins hadn't got back to her yet.

The sense of nothing happening made her restless. She needed to talk to someone. When she'd been working as a journalist, she always had people to bounce ideas off – colleagues, her boss, Billy. She had Louise and Alex, she supposed. But Lou was always so busy with her kids and her job, Dee didn't feel she could call her for a chat whenever she needed to. As for Alex, she hadn't seen him since that awkward morning when Ed had practically accused them of having an affair.

The rest of the day dragged past. Dee spoke to Louise around lunchtime, but her cousin had no further news about Katie and Jake. Twice she considered going to see Alex. Both times she talked herself out of it. In the late afternoon, she took the key for the mobile home and walked the short distance along the beach to Katie's house.

The police tape had been removed earlier in the week, but so far, Dee had resisted going inside. It felt wrong somehow. But she couldn't shake off the feeling that there might be some clue that the police had missed.

She turned the key in the lock, pushed open the front door and stepped inside. The memories assailed her as she walked into the living area. Jake's drawings on the fridge; the high chair where he ate his meals; the box in the corner with the toy trains that he loved to play with. Each item a reminder of happier times – helping him with his drawing, cutting his food into slices that he could pick up with his little fingers, sitting on the ground while she connected plastic pieces of train track together.

After a moment, she moved around the small house, searching for the elusive clue that would help her find Katie and Jake. Within five minutes, she knew that coming here had been pointless. The police had already gone through everything and taken anything they considered useful. In Katie's bedroom, drawers had been pulled open, the mattress had been turned over and not turned back, and the bathroom looked like a tornado had ripped through it.

For want of anything better to do, Dee set about tidying up. Katie hated a mess. If she was ever coming back, Dee wanted her to find the house as she'd left it. By the time she'd finished, it had grown dark outside. She'd switched lights on as she'd worked, and now she moved around the house turning them off again before she left. In the sitting room, her gaze fell on the photo Katie kept on the mantelpiece over the gas fire.

It showed Katie and two of her friends standing at the top of a hill somewhere rural. Katie was wearing her hair in a plait that hung down over her left shoulder. Dee had noticed the photo before but never paid it much attention. Now, she found herself crossing the room and picking it up, her eyes drawn to the sweatshirt Katie was wearing. Red, with a hood, and what Dee had always thought was a logo across the front. Only looking at it more closely now, she saw it was text, not a logo. *Property of Bristol University.* The word *Bristol* in bigger typeface than the rest of it.

Bristol University. Katie had been living in Bristol when she worked for Hexagon. So she could have gone to university there too. She'd never mentioned university, but Dee was quickly learning there was a lot about Katie's past that she had never spoken about.

Ella Tate had graduated from Bristol University in 2013. Before that, she had been a witness at the trial of Katie's father's killer. Which meant the two girls knew each other. Maybe even became such close friends that they attended university together.

Dee locked up the mobile home and hurried back to her own house. On her laptop, she opened Facebook Messenger. Still no reply from Brian Higgins. She sent him another message, asking him if he remembered Katie. *She was a friend of Ella's*, she typed. *They're both from London originally. I think they may have been at uni together.* She offered a quick plea to whatever higher power was up there to make Brian Higgins check his messages and get back to her.

Right then, her front doorbell rang. Thinking it was Alex, she hurried to answer it.

'You'd better have brought some wine,' she said as she pulled the door open, the end of her sentence fading to nothing when she saw who was standing in her porch.

'How's it going, Dee?'

She opened her mouth, but no words came out.

'You going to invite me in?' Billy Morrison lifted a bottle of champagne from the plastic carrier bag he was holding. 'Only I've got a bit of news. Thought you'd like to hear it in person.' He grinned. That wide-open smile that had attracted her to him the very first moment she'd met him, and kept her with him longer than she ever should have stayed.

'What news?' she managed.

'Come on, Dee,' Billy said. 'You know me, I love a sense of occasion. It's good news and I want to tell you properly.'

She should have said no. Told him to get lost, get away from here; that she never wanted to see him again. But she'd never been very good at saying no to Billy, so she stood back and invited him in, letting that big grin of his get him what he wanted, just like she'd always done.

Twenty-Five

Dee

'We've had an offer,' Billy said.

He'd already popped open the champagne and poured them each a glass. He knocked back half of his and refilled his glass before handing hers over.

'Means you can finally be free of me.' He smiled, but Dee could see there was no feeling behind it.

'Good.' She took a sip of the champagne so she could avoid having to look at his face and be reminded of all the good times they'd shared before the relationship turned sour.

'Seven fifty,' he said. 'More than we said we'd sell it for. I've accepted. Hope that's okay with you?'

Seven hundred and fifty thousand pounds for an unremarkable two-bed town house in Greenwich. The price was crazy. But London prices were crazy and the two of them were lucky. Buying a house in the right location at the right time was one of the few sensible things they'd done as a couple.

'So.' Billy settled himself in one of the armchairs and crossed his legs. 'How've you been, Dee?'

She should tell him not to get too comfortable, that he wasn't staying, but now he was here, part of her didn't want him to leave. The pathetic part of her that would always be weak when it came to Billy. Besides, once the house was sold, there'd be no reason for them to keep in touch. This might well be the last time she ever saw him.

She sat opposite him, told him she was doing very well, thanks.

'I met your girlfriend last week,' she said. 'Did she tell you?'

'Mel.' Billy smiled. 'She told me you weren't exactly welcoming.'

'She told *me* you were about to get fired from your job.'

Billy flinched, as if she'd slapped him. 'She's exaggerating,' he said. 'Mel's a worrier, that's all. You know me, Dee. I'm a survivor. Whatever happens at the *Post*, things will work out. And now we've got a firm offer on the house, it's not like I'll need that shitty job anyway.'

'You love that job,' Dee said. 'Or you did. What's happened to change your mind?'

He would have an excuse, of course. A whole suitcase full of them, but not one of them would be the truth, which was that Billy Morrison was a drunk, and everything that was wrong in his life always came back to that single, undisputable fact.

Dee remembered the first time she heard the phrase 'functioning alcoholic'. Immediately, she knew it perfectly described the man she'd married. The sort of drinker who covered it with a combination of brains, wit and charm. Everyone knew Billy Morrison liked a drink. But he was a journalist, after all. One of the best. And what true-blooded hack didn't enjoy a good old booze-up?

When Dee started at the *Daily Post*, everyone drank. It was as much a part of the paper's culture as the open misogyny in the newsroom, the easy acceptance of bad behaviour from the established hacks and the long hours every single person put into making the paper the success it was.

It was the perfect environment for Billy. A man who could write copy quicker and better than anyone else. A man who liked to live fast and take risks. A man who, on more days than Dee cared to remember, started his day with a coffee laced with whisky. And continued drinking, on and off, throughout the rest of his waking hours. Day after booze-fuelled day. His body so accustomed to the levels of alcohol he poured into it that only those closest to him noticed he was rarely completely sober.

By the time he had the affair, his drinking had already affected every aspect of their relationship. In some ways, it was a relief. Dee had tried so hard to ignore his drinking and the damage it was doing. Because she was scared. Scared of admitting he had a problem, scared of confronting him, scared of losing him. In the end, she'd lost him anyway, and it was only when it was all over that she realised she had always been the second love in his life. Booze first, everything else after that.

'New editor's a cunt,' he said.

Dee frowned at his choice of words, but he didn't seem to notice. Or if he did, he didn't care.

'On my case the whole time. Some jumped-up *child* who thinks she understands the job because she's got a fucking master's degree. One of Nigel's prodigies. You know the type, right?'

Nigel Blackman was a media mogul who owned a string of TV and radio companies as well as the *Daily Post*, one of the UK's major broadsheets. His company,

Blackman Communications, also owned half the local newspapers in the UK, including the *Eastbourne Recorder* where Louise worked. Until recently, Billy had been one of his golden boys. The edgy, successful journalist who got more front-page exclusives than anyone else. Nigel's affection for Billy, and his seemingly endless tolerance for his excesses, had given Billy a job security that was unheard of in today's newspaper industry.

'I thought you and Nigel were mates,' Dee said.

'Yeah, well,' Billy said. 'Turns out he's no sort of friend after all. I thought it was going to be okay, you know? After Rob left.' He grinned. 'That email you sent was the beginning of the end for Rob. He wasn't able to handle the pressure. But then Nigel got this new editor in, and we've gone from bad to worse. You know, Dee, there are some days I don't know if I can trust anyone any more.'

'I know what that feels like,' Dee said. Pointlessly, because the irony was lost on Billy. His glass was already empty, and when he stood to refill it, he swayed slightly. He'd probably been drinking all day.

Dee watched him empty the bottle, forgetting to ask if she wanted any more.

'So,' he said, voice too loud as he sat back down. 'Are you doing okay, Dee? Only I was a bit worried, you know, that nasty business with your neighbour. Must have been quite a shock. Friend of yours, isn't she?'

The room stank of champagne, the stench making Dee's stomach roll. She put her glass on the floor, but the smell was still too strong. She knew it wasn't real. Her mind was creating it so she would have a valid reason for the nausea.

Of course that was why he'd come to see her. What was wrong with her that she could have thought for a single second that he wanted to be with her to celebrate the sale of their one-time home, or – God forbid – that maybe, after all they'd once shared, he still felt something for her?

'I barely know her,' she said.

'You're a rubbish liar,' Billy said. 'Always have been.'

'One of us has to be,' she said. 'Yes, I know her. She's my friend. And I'd like to keep it that way, which means I'm not going to tell you anything about her.'

Billy drained his glass and belched loudly. 'Wouldn't dream of asking,' he said. 'Guess this business is the last thing you needed. It hasn't been easy for you, I get that. Us, your job, poor old Brenda. A lot of shit in a short amount of time. This place doesn't seem the same without her. We had some good times with your folks, didn't we?'

He looked around the room as if he was only now seeing it. Dee wondered if he was remembering the nights the four of them had sat here playing Scrabble or rummy, drinking wine late into the evening and talking about life, love and the universe. Dee's mother, like her daughter, had always had a soft spot for Billy. Even after they'd split up, she'd wanted her to give the marriage another chance.

'Why are you so interested in Katie?' Dee said.

'She's an interesting kid. Did she tell you what happened to her dad?'

'She never spoke about her family.'

'I was wondering,' Billy said, 'how she came to be living down here. A bit out of the way for a young woman with a child, isn't it?'

'What do you know that you're not telling me?' Dee asked.

'I know her dad was killed. And that the wrong person was convicted. Come on, Dee. Tell me what she was like. I'd already worked out you had to be friends. She has a kiddie, and you bloody love kids. You must be pretty cut up right now, wondering where he is.'

'Why do you think he was the wrong person?' Dee asked.

'When I saw she'd done a runner,' Billy said, 'I got curious. I did a bit of research. Wanted to see if she'd done anything like this before.'

'Anything like what?'

'Killing someone,' Billy said. 'And when I looked her up, I found out about her old man.'

'And?'

'And a whole lot more about what really happened,' Billy said. 'Tell you what, Dee. Let's go over there now, take a look inside the house.'

'Why?'

'Might give me a bit of insight. See, I've got good reason to believe your neighbour was hiding a big secret. But right now, I've got no proof. If I could get that, then I'm on to a big story.'

'Why should I help you?' Dee said.

Billy smiled. Or tried to. His face was lopsided, as if he was struggling to control his facial muscles.

'Old times' sake.' He lifted the empty champagne bottle. 'You got anything else? I was thinking maybe I could crash here for the night. Only I got the train down and it's a bit of a trek back to the station at this time. On the sofa, I mean. Obviously.'

She couldn't bear for him to be here a moment longer. It didn't matter what information he might have on Katie and Jake, or the trial or anything else. Dee didn't care. All she cared about was getting him out of her house and out of her life. For good, this time. With blinding clarity, she saw the years she'd wasted on this self-centred addict. Years when she could have had children, created a family, built a life for herself with someone who loved her the way she loved them.

'You can't stay,' she said. 'And I have nothing else to drink, either.'

Somehow she found the energy to stand up, walk over to him and take the bottle from his hand.

'I know this is only a story to you, Billy. But it means a lot more to me. Katie's little boy is missing and no one knows where he is. Don't you even care about that?'

He frowned, looking confused, as if he couldn't work out what was going on.

'Goodbye, Billy.'

'You're kicking me out?'

'I'm going outside,' she said. 'And I'm taking my phone with me. If you're not gone in two minutes, I'm calling the police.'

He started to say something else, so she spoke again, fast, before he could talk her round.

'I mean it, Billy. Get out. Now.'

She turned her back on him and walked stiffly across the room to the sliding doors.

'Bitch.' His voice low and slurred and thick with anger.

Dee ignored him.

When she heard him move, she tensed. But he was moving away from her, staggering towards the front door, which he managed to open. It slammed shut, and she breathed a sigh of relief. He was gone.

She lifted her face to the cool breeze, looked at the pale moon and the pinpricks of light from the millions of stars that speckled the night sky. It was only when the moon and stars started to blur that Dee noticed her face was wet and realised she was crying.

Twenty-Six

Katie
Ten years earlier

I hate Ella Tate more than I've ever hated anyone or anything in the whole world. She's told Dad about us. Of course, he never said it was her, but I know it was.

Shane had been coming to mine in the evenings. It made perfect sense. Dad never comes upstairs when he's working. He prefers to let me do my own thing, which is Dad-speak for ignoring me. We'd been dead careful, and there's only one possible way Dad could have found out about it. Ella.

Six nights ago, Shane was sneaking downstairs on his way home and Dad was waiting for him at the bottom of the stairs. He went mental. I haven't seen Shane since. College has broken up for the summer, and I'm grounded. Not allowed to leave the flat, even to go to the shops.

I've heard Dad and Roxanne talking. Roxanne's told Dad he shouldn't be too hard on me.

'She's only seventeen, Gus. Poor girl's going to mess up every once in a while. You need to let her make her own mistakes. I know it's not easy for you and I know you're doing what you think is right. But she's not a kid any longer and you can't ignore that. No matter how much you want to.'

Dad told her it was none of her business how he chose to raise his daughter. Roxanne left soon after that. I keep hoping she'll find time to sneak up and see me, but so far that hasn't happened. We used to get on really well. Before Ella took her away from me. When I started college, Roxanne spent an afternoon with me showing me how to put on make-up and giving me suggestions for how to wear my hair. She even took me shopping for clothes once. That was when I was still fat, so it wasn't the best day out. I hated buying clothes then.

I've texted Shane loads of times but he hasn't been in touch. I don't understand what he's playing at. I know my dad was a pig to him, but it's not like that's my fault. I've told him I'm grounded. Maybe that was a mistake. He probably thinks there's no point getting in touch if he can't see me.

I'm really starting to lose it when, out of the blue, I get an idea. It's sort of crazy, but I'm so desperate I'll try pretty much anything. The idea starts with Ella. I'm lying on the sofa, looking at Shane's Facebook, scrolling through his posts and his list of friends, wondering what he's up to right now.

I look for Ella's account as well, but she's either blocked me or deleted her account, because I can't find her anywhere. I know Shane used to be friends with her, but that was ages ago. He told me he'd blocked her because she was hassling him and sending him these really abusive messages. I knew he was lying, but I didn't say anything because he would have got angry with me, and that's the last thing I'd have wanted.

Now, I can't stop thinking about it. How he wouldn't look at me when he was telling me he'd blocked her. The way he talked about her when we were first together, as if he couldn't think about anything else. Her face when she saw him in the pub that first time. I close my eyes and I see her walking into the tunnel beneath Hither Green train station. And I see him trailing after her.

I never asked him what happened that day or why he followed her. He has no idea I saw them together. All I wanted to do was forget about it. But I can't forget. It's like a worm eating through the inside of my head, growing bigger and stronger the more it eats until there's nothing else left except a swirling mess of pictures that are all Ella and Shane. And in that kaleidoscope of images, there's no room for anyone else. Especially not me.

I try to remember all the times I've been with him and all the moments we've shared, but they slither and slide out of reach like tiny shards of ice melting and disappearing to nothing.

In a flash, my head clears and I know exactly what I need to do. The sick feeling in my stomach has gone, replaced by something hard and heavy, and I think this pain – this excruciating agony – will never leave me.

Setting up a fake BBM account is easy. I write down Shane's phone number before I start. Then I reset my BlackBerry to factory settings and start from scratch. I set up a new BBM account, and call myself *EllaT995*. I've lost my other contacts, but I don't care about that. It's not like anyone ever sends me messages anyway.

I send Shane a request to be one of my contacts. While I'm waiting for him to reply, I scroll through the photos of Ella I have on my computer. I've got lots of them. I took them from her Facebook page before she blocked me. Stupid cow. If she didn't want me sending her that stuff, she should have kept away from my boyfriend. I stop at one of the photos. In it, her face is turned sideways, away from the camera, and she's wearing her hair in a long plait over her left shoulder. She could be anyone in that photo. She could even be me.

I'm thinking about this, how alike we look now, when my BlackBerry pings. It's Shane, confirming my request. It's taken him less than five minutes to reply. A bit different to six days of silence. The anger abates, replaced by a giddy, excited feeling. My thumbs start moving.

Hey, Shane. Sorry everything got so heavy between us. Think we can be friends again? X

He replies right away. One word that tells me all I need to know.

Sure.

There's an ache between my legs that reminds me of sex. I have to press my legs tightly together, but that doesn't work, so I put my hand down there. Push it against myself while I think of what Ella's going to tell him next.

Twenty-Seven

Dee

Hate was a powerful motivator. In the days following Billy's visit, Dee wallowed in hatred. She went back obsessively over every single thing he'd done to hurt her, all the missed dates, forgotten special occasions, the nights he'd fallen asleep downstairs instead of coming to bed with her, the nights he hadn't come home at all. The children he'd persuaded her she didn't want. The lies he'd told and the many, many ways he'd hurt her. She hated until her body ached from it and she felt as if something dark and rotten was growing inside her.

'It's not healthy,' Louise said when Dee tried to explain it to her. 'Your marriage is over; your divorce is final. It's time to let it go, Dee.'

Dee knew Louise wouldn't understand. How could she? Louise with her perfect children and her sensible husband who adored her and bought her jewellery and nice holidays and remembered their wedding anniversaries and the children's birthdays and... and...

She looked Billy up on the internet. Everything she read confirmed what she'd already worked out. His star was very much in the descendant. All that promise and talent, thrown away for the sake of one more drink.

Always one more with Billy. One more, one for the road, one last round, until all the drink was gone and all the people who'd ever cared about him were gone too.

Over the last three years, he'd gone from being the *Daily Post*'s number-one journalist, front-page stories week after week, to a hack with the occasional byline in the weekend papers. Nothing solid from him in years. No wonder Nigel had finally lost patience.

And now he thought he could piggyback on this tragedy and use it to turn his failing career around. He wanted the story and thought he could use Dee to get to it. Over her dead body.

Brian Higgins, the guy from the Bristol Uni Facebook group, had finally replied to the messages Dee had sent him.

Sorry, he wrote. *Thought I had Tom's email but I appear to have lost it. I'd prefer it if you didn't contact me again.*

When Dee tried to reply, her message didn't go through. Brian Higgins had blocked her from contacting him. Which made her curious. She wanted to know what could have happened to change his mind so quickly.

As it turned out, she didn't need Brian's help. Ten minutes searching through Facebook profiles and she found a Tom Doyle who'd graduated from Bristol University in 2013. She sent him a friend request and a message, telling him she was a friend of Ella's and needed to speak to her urgently. She gave her email address and phone number and told him he could contact her any time. She didn't mention Katie, thinking she'd wait first to see if he replied to her message. So far, she'd heard nothing from him. Either he didn't go on Facebook very often, or he didn't want to help.

On Monday morning, Leonard called. Finally. Dee had left four messages for him and was starting to think he was trying to avoid her.

'You asked about Roxanne,' he said. 'What's got you so interested in her all of a sudden?' He sounded defensive. And decidedly less friendly than the last time they'd spoken.

'You told me she'd died?' Dee said.

Leonard coughed; a prolonged business that went on for some time.

'And?' he said when he was able to speak again.

'There were two witnesses at Gus Hope's murder trial,' Dee said. 'Ella Tate and Roxanne Reed. I think the dead girl might be Ella. If it is, that means both of the witnesses are dead.'

'What makes you think the dead girl is Ella?'

'A hunch,' Dee admitted. 'A pretty dodgy one at that. The detective leading the investigation has told me it's not her. But I can't shake this feeling that maybe he's wrong.'

'And you're thinking that if it *is* Ella,' Leonard said, 'and if it turns out that Roxanne's death was mysterious as well, then you could be on to something.'

'Exactly.'

'Well I'm sorry to disappoint you, but your theory's all wrong, love. I told you already – Roxanne died years ago. While Shane Gilbert was still locked up.'

'How did she die?' Dee asked. 'Do you know?'

'Cancer.'

'You stayed in touch with her? After the trial?'

'Why would I do that?' Leonard said. 'Nah, I only found out she'd died when I went to write a follow-on piece a few years later. Where are they now? That sort of thing. I tried to track her down and found out she'd died soon after the trial.'

'What about Ella?' Dee asked.

'Didn't bother looking for her. Without Roxanne, my editor decided it wasn't much of a story. I gave up the idea and that was the end of it. Maybe you should think about doing the same, love.'

'What do you mean?'

'I mean you're trying to find connections that aren't there. Someone drove into that poor girl and killed her. End of. It's sad but it's got nothing to do with what happened to Gus Hope.'

'Maybe you're right,' Dee said. 'Thanks, Leonard.'

'Not a problem. And don't forget you still owe me that pint, all right?'

'I won't forget.'

She said goodbye and hung up. Leonard's insistence that there was nothing connecting the dead girl and Gus Hope hadn't worked. All he'd done was make Dee more convinced she was on to something.

She called Ed, said she had something to tell him. Instead of asking her to come to the station, he suggested meeting at the Beach Deck, the closest seafront bar to Dee's house, later that afternoon.

He was already there when she arrived. Sitting at an outside table, a glass of Coke in his hands.

'Coke Zero,' he explained once they'd got the greetings out of the way and he'd offered to get her a drink and she'd said no, she was fine, thanks. 'I'm a bit addicted.'

'There are worse addictions,' Dee said, thinking of Billy.

'So,' Ed said. 'What was it you wanted to talk to me about?'

'My ex-husband came to see me. He was looking for information on Katie.'

'Don't tell me,' Ed said. 'He's a journalist too, and he's hoping for some sort of exclusive.'

'How did you know that?'

'I know your ex is a journalist. Lou mentioned it.'

'Louise?' Dee scowled. 'What was she doing gossiping to you about my private life?'

'Small talk,' Ed said. 'Not gossip. There's a difference. What did your ex have to say about Katie?'

'He said she was hiding something. "A big secret" were his exact words, I think.'

'Don't suppose he told you what that secret happened to be?' Ed said. Then, when Dee shook her head, 'Didn't think so.'

'There is something else, though you probably know this already; it's about Katie's dad.'

'Gus Hope,' Ed said. 'What about him?'

'The guy who was convicted of killing him – Shane Gilbert. I found out that he was released from prison around the same time Katie moved here. Billy – my ex – is full of shit, but he has good reason to believe she was hiding something. I'm sure it's all connected somehow.'

'Is that it?'

'Not quite,' Dee said. 'Billy told me the wrong person was convicted for Gus Hope's murder.'

'He has evidence of this?' Ed asked.

'I think he's been speaking to Shane Gilbert.'

'You wouldn't try anything stupid like that, would you?'

'Of course not,' Dee said. 'What do you take me for?'

'You need to be careful. This is a criminal investigation. If you do anything to mess it up, you could be in serious trouble.'

'All I'm doing is trying to help you find Jake and Katie. That doesn't give you the right to accuse me of interfering with your precious police work.'

Ed took a sip of Coke. 'You're living out here on the coast, all alone in that big house. I'm guessing you're more than a bit bored. Katie was your friend, and you're missing her. I'm sure you're sick with worry about Jake as well. So you've taken it on yourself to try to solve this case before anyone else. You're a clever woman, Dee. I've read some of the stuff you've done in the past. It's good. I don't understand why you haven't gone back to your old job, but that's none of my business. What would upset me, though, is if you somehow thought you're better placed to solve this case than the entire East Sussex police force.'

'That's not what I'm doing,' Dee said. A lie, but his accusation hurt, and it was all too easy to transfer some of her anger at Billy to this arrogant man sitting across from her.

Ed pushed his chair back and stood up. 'Maybe not. And if I'm wrong, I apologise.'

He stared down at her. The sun was behind him, so she couldn't see his face, and she was glad of that.

'But I'm not wrong,' he said. 'Am I?'

She looked away, refusing to answer.

'Don't be stupid,' he said. 'That's all I'm asking, Dee. If you keep going with this, you'll make a fool of yourself. Believe it or not, I really wouldn't want that to happen.'

He stayed where he was, but when she didn't say anything, he sighed and walked away. When she looked up again, he was gone. The empty glass on the table was the only sign he'd ever been there at all.

Twenty-Eight

Katie
Ten years earlier

We've got quite a thing going on BBM, me and Shane. Only of course it's not me really. He thinks I'm Ella and I can't believe the things he's telling me. Telling her, I mean. He never really cared about me. With every single message he sends, I hate him more and more. The feelings I had for him are as strong as they've ever been, but they're the reverse of what they used to be. Love turned to hate.

He's told me the police questioned him about Ella's dog. And he's promised me it wasn't him. He says he'd never do something like that. I tell him it's okay, I believe him, and he's pathetically grateful.

We're on BBM the whole time. He can't stop. Neither can I. This is what it's like to be an addict. My phone pings each time I get a new message. My every waking moment revolves around these pinging sounds until this is the only thing that's real and the gaps between me sending him a message and his reply are an empty agony.

It was his fault they split up the last time, apparently. He two-timed her and she found out about it. He begged her to take him back, but she wouldn't. At least I understand now why she didn't want to see him when he started showing up at the pub. He tells me – her – all the time how sorry he is, how he'll never do anything like that again.

He wants to see her. I've put him off so far, but I can't do that forever. Sooner or later, he's going to want more than a few snatch shots and fake sexy messages. Sooner or later, he's going to want the real thing.

She works two afternoons each week and three evenings, including Sunday. It needs to happen on a Sunday, the only night Dad's not here. He's never back before midnight, and when he does come home, he goes straight upstairs to bed.

I've asked Roxanne where he goes but she says she has no idea.

'It's his business what he gets up to in his spare time,' she said. 'Not mine.'

It makes me sad when I think about my dad having a secret life I know nothing about. But when my phone pings, I realise everyone has a secret life. That's how the world is. People pretending on the surface to be one thing when beneath it they're someone else entirely.

Like Mum. She pretended to be happy with me and Dad, but she wasn't happy at all, was she? She was so miserably *un*happy that she went out drinking with people she didn't even know, and we never saw her again.

Come on, baby. I need to see you.

He's starting to sound like a child. A needy, pathetic child who's used to getting his own way. Which, when you think about it, is pretty much exactly what he is.

I feel the same, I lie-type into my phone. *I need more time. You know what a cow my mum is.*

Truthfully, I have no idea what sort of woman Ella's mother is. She might be the nicest person in the world. But it makes me feel better pretending she's a bitch, because I like putting a bit of misery into Ella's perfect fucking life. Even if it's true and her mother is horrible, at least she still has a mother, which is more than you can say for me.

Maybe I could hook up with you after you finish work some evening? How would she ever find out?

I wonder if he means coming here, to the pub. And if he's given a thought to what that would be like for me.

What about Katie? I type back.

He replies right away. *What about her?*

I watch the words, willing them to change, waiting for him to say something else. But nothing happens. I cross my arms around my body, holding myself tight so I don't fall apart. My ribs feel like bony fingers. I've lost more weight. The other day, Roxanne told me I needed to be careful I didn't get too skinny. I bet no one's ever told Ella Tate she shouldn't let herself get too skinny. People only ever say shit like that to people who are trying to lose weight.

I don't want to do this any more. I want it to stop but I don't know how I can make that happen. I'm like Mum, except my problem isn't drink. My problem is Ella Tate. And Shane Gilbert.

And my dad, because when you think about it, everything that's wrong in my life is his fault. It's his fault my mum left us. It's his fault Ella is working in the pub. And it's his fault we live in this shitty flat when people like Ella Tate and Shane Gilbert live in big bright houses with mothers who love them and cook them healthy meals so they don't get fat.

In my head, I'm back on the street that afternoon watching them. Ella is walking into the tunnel under Hither Green train station and Shane is loping after her. She has no idea he's there, right behind her. I imagine what it would feel like. For him, following her knowing she has no clue he's behind her, anticipating what he's going to do to her. For her, that moment of shock when his hand reaches out and grabs her.

I want to know what it's like to have that power over someone. And I want to see her face when she realises he's there and she can't do a single thing to stop him doing whatever he wants to her.

I send a message telling him I'll think about it. Then I stick the phone between my legs, take a photo and send him that too.

Men are stupid, Katie, remember that. They never think with their heads. Only with this. My mother, her voice slurring, her breath shooting fumes of wine through the fug of cigarette smoke. Pointing to her crotch area, jutting it at me. *Only with this.*

Maybe she wasn't so good at pretending.

We message back and forward a bit more. The photo's made him even more desperate, like I knew it would.

And suddenly we have a plan.

Next Sunday evening, when Dad's out and after Roxanne has gone home, he's going to call over. Ella has told him Katie won't be there to mess things up.

I wait for him to say something nice about me. To tell her we were friends, at least, and he didn't mind if I was there. Maybe even that he'd like to see me and say hi.

Gr8, he says instead. *C u then. Can't wait xxxx*

Twenty-Nine

Dee

First thing Tuesday, Dee called Emma Walker.

'I was going to call you later today,' Emma said. 'It's taken me a bit longer than I expected to find what you needed.'

'What did you get?' Dee asked.

'You got a pen and paper?' Emma asked. 'Only I don't want any email trail on any of this.'

'Of course.' Dee grabbed the pen and notepad she kept in the kitchen and balanced the pad on her lap. 'Ready.'

'Shane Gilbert is living and working in Maidstone, Kent,' Emma said. 'He served his sentence in Brixton prison before being released in May 2015.'

'You sure about that date?' Dee asked.

'That's what it says on his file. Why?'

'No reason,' she lied.

May 2015 was six months before Katie moved to Eastbourne. Dee didn't think for one second the two events were unconnected.

'He's been in the same place since being released,' Emma said. 'He's one of the lucky ones who was able to find a job. A lot of ex-offenders can't get anything.'

'What's he doing?' Dee asked.

'Works for a computer company. Software design. According to his file, he studied computers while he was inside. Got a degree in computer science. Clever boy.'

Katie had worked for a computer software company as well. Did that mean something? Dee couldn't focus on whether it did or not, because Emma was speaking again.

'I can't give you an address,' she said. 'That sort of information isn't kept in the public part of his file. But I can give you the address of where he works if that's any good?'

'It's more than good,' Dee said. 'It's bloody brilliant.'

She noted the address Emma gave her, checking the location on her laptop as she ended the call.

'I can't thank you enough, Em,' she said. 'I owe you for this. Big time.'

'I already told you,' Emma said. 'I'm only too happy to help. Just promise me you'll stay in touch. And contact me the next time you're in London.'

'You can hold me to that.'

They said goodbye and ended the call. According to Dee's laptop, it would take her one hour and forty minutes to drive from her house to the software company where Shane Gilbert worked. She checked the time. Five to eight. If she left by eight thirty, she could be speaking to him by ten o'clock.

–

Even the best-laid plans could go wrong. And there was nothing well laid about Dee's plan to confront Shane Gilbert. Traffic on the outward journey was slow. It took her half an hour longer than it should have to simply get to the other side of Eastbourne. And another two hours

199

before she arrived at the business park on the outskirts of Maidstone where Shane's employer, Tec Twenty-One, was located.

The company was based in a flat-roofed Portakabin building, one of several built around a concrete courtyard. Dee parked up, climbed out of her car and looked around. The contrast between Hexagon Consultancy's slick City office and this bleak outpost in the middle of nowhere was impossible to ignore. Shane Gilbert might have been lucky enough to get a job, but one look at this place told her it wasn't some high-end tech company like Hexagon.

The Portakabin door was ajar. Through the gap, she could see a reception area, with a woman about her own age sitting behind a desk. She pushed the door open further and stepped inside, into a wall of heat. The place was more like an oven than somewhere people could reasonably be expected to work.

Up close, she could see the woman was older than she'd first thought. Early to late sixties, she guessed. Her hair was dyed a startling yellow-blonde colour and done up in an oversized sixties-style beehive that made it difficult to judge her age more accurately.

'Wonder Wok Catering's the other side of the business park,' she informed Dee without looking up from her computer screen. 'Go back the way you came and take a left before the entrance.'

'I'm not looking for catering,' Dee said.

There was a fan on the desk, blowing out noisy puffs of air that made little impact on the suffocating heat. Dee wafted her hands in front of her face as she waited for the receptionist to look up and acknowledge her.

'This is a tech company,' the woman finally said, eyes scanning Dee before dropping back down again. 'We don't trade directly with consumers. And you're sure as hell not one of our usual contacts.'

'How can you be so certain?' Dee asked.

This time the woman looked at her properly and smiled. 'Lady, we've got three people working in this place. Mick Stafford, that's the boss. Our software developer, Shane, and yours truly. Besides, if you don't mind me saying so, you're a bit long in the tooth to be working in tech.'

Dee didn't mind. Not if the woman was going to lead her to Shane Gilbert.

'Is Shane here at the moment?' she asked, peering into the gloomy, indistinct space behind the reception area.

'Have you noticed how hot it is in here?' the woman replied. 'How do you think anyone's going to get any work done in this?'

'You're here,' Dee pointed out.

'I don't exactly work,' the woman said. 'I mean, I answer the telephone, which hardly ever rings, and I reply to queries that come in by email. But there aren't that many of them, truth be told. Most of the time I sit here planning my next holiday. Cruises, mainly. You ever been on a cruise?'

'Never,' Dee said.

'You should try one,' the woman said. 'Free food, sunshine, lots of interesting people to talk to, entertainment every evening. The best part of a cruise is you don't have to do anything. It's all done, see. You don't need to cook, or shop, or clean up after yourself. I went on my first one five years ago and haven't looked back. Wouldn't have any other sort of holiday now.'

'Sounds lovely,' Dee lied. She couldn't think of anything she'd enjoy less than being trapped on a boat in the middle of the ocean with hordes of people she'd have nothing in common with and no way of escape.

'What you want with Muscle Man?' the woman asked.

'Shane?'

'I call him Muscle Man,' the woman said. 'On account of his unhealthy obsession with his own body. He's not in any trouble, is he?'

'What makes you ask that?'

'He's not been himself recently,' the woman replied. 'Edgy, anxious, like something bad has happened. I know he's had his problems in the past, but I thought all that was behind him.'

'I'm an old friend of his mum's,' Dee said. 'When she heard I was going to be in Maidstone this week, she asked me to drop in and say hi.'

'She didn't give you his address?'

'She texted it to me,' Dee said. 'But I deleted the text by mistake. I've tried calling her back, but she's not picking up. Luckily I remembered the name of the company he works for, so I thought I'd try here. The problem is, I'm only in the area this morning. If I can't get to see him, she'll be really disappointed. I don't suppose you could tell me where he lives?'

'It's not company policy to give out personal details for our employees,' the woman said.

Dee doubted a cowboy outfit like Tec Twenty-One had any policies at all, but she refrained from saying this.

'You could do it as a favour,' she said instead. 'It would mean so much to his mother, you see.'

The woman looked back at her computer screen. 'I'm thinking of the Caribbean next summer. Only problem with a cruise like that is the money. I mean, I'm good at saving, but a holiday like that, it's going to cost me.'

Going to cost *me* more like, Dee thought. Luckily, her years as a journalist had trained her to never go anywhere without an emergency supply of cash. She extracted a twenty from the wad of notes in her purse and laid it on the counter.

'All I need is an address,' she said. 'He doesn't need to know how I got it.'

'Another thirty and you've got a deal.'

'Fifty quid!' Dee exclaimed. 'You've got to be kidding me.'

The woman shrugged. 'You're the one who wants the information.'

'Another thirty and I get a phone number as well.'

The woman nodded, and Dee handed over the remaining money.

Two minutes later, she was back in her car, holding a piece of paper with Shane Gilbert's address and telephone number. It hardly seemed important that it had cost her fifty pounds to get it. Especially not if he turned out to be the key to finding Katie and Jake.

Shane's home turned out to be located in an ugly row of modern buildings in the town centre. The ground floor was taken up with shops and cafes while the three floors above were given over to flats. There was a door midway along the block that appeared to be the entrance to the flats. The lock on it was broken and Dee was able to push it open and enter.

A plastic sign on the wall showed the layout of the building. Four flats on each floor. Dee checked her piece of paper. Shane lived in Flat 12, which was on the top floor. There was a lift, but when she pressed the button, nothing happened. After trying several times, she gave up and took the stairs.

Flat 12 was at the end of a narrow corridor. It was easy to find: of the four flats on this floor, it was the only one with a number visible. Dee pressed her ear against the door and heard the muted sound of voices she guessed were coming from a TV or radio.

She knocked on the door. Inside the flat, the voices stopped. She knocked again.

'Post,' she called. 'Got a package for Mr Gilbert that needs signing for.'

'Mr Gilbert's not in,' a man replied from the other side of the door.

'Anyone can sign for it,' Dee said. 'Doesn't have to be him.'

A moment later, she heard a bolt being pulled back. The door opened and she found herself face to face with the man from Shane Gilbert's Facebook profile. Up close, she could see how he'd earned his nickname. He had the build and bulk of a professional bodybuilder.

'Where's the package?' he asked.

'There isn't one,' Dee said. Then, as he started to push the door closed, 'Shane, wait. I'm a friend of Katie's. She's my neighbour and I'm worried about her. I'm not police or press; I'm just someone who's worried about my friend.'

'I can't help you.'

The door slammed shut and stayed shut, despite Dee's repeated knocking and requests for him to reconsider. She only gave up when a man from one of the neighbouring flats came out and threatened to call the police if she didn't 'pack in that racket right now'.

Frustrated, she slammed her fist against the door one final time, before rooting around in her bag for her pen and notebook. She scribbled down her name, phone number and email address, then tore the page from the notebook and slipped it under the door of Flat 12.

She'd give him a couple of days to get in touch. If she didn't hear from him, she would come back. Now that she'd found him, there was no way she was letting him go without learning everything he knew about Katie and Jake.

Thirty

Katie
Ten years earlier

'What do you want?'

Ella's looking at me as if there's a bad smell coming off me. She's had her hair cut. Long layers that frame her face and make her look softer, rounding the hard edges of her jaw and cheekbones. It's dead straight and proper shiny. When she moves, streaks of copper and gold flicker and shimmer beneath the pub lighting.

My own hair, plaited so carefully less than an hour ago, feels heavy and tight. The plait is like a snake hanging over my left shoulder. I shake my head, flick back the plait, but it doesn't help.

'I wanted to tell you that I'm sorry,' I say.

She doesn't reply. This is going to be harder than I imagined. I thought she'd want to tell me why she hates him so much. But she's not interested in speaking to me or becoming my friend. Her face has shut down, like she wants to hide every piece of herself from me. Like she doesn't think I'm worth the effort.

'What for?' she asks. She's turned away from me and has started collecting glasses from across the top of the bar. The question catches me by surprise.

'For bringing Shane here,' I say. 'And for those stupid messages I sent you.'

She stops what's she doing and turns back so she's looking at me properly. Not hiding now. All sorts of emotions flickering behind her blue eyes. It's too intimate, as if she's literally lifted a mask away to reveal all the feelings and emotions she's been carrying around for weeks. Hate and anger and… sadness. I see it even though I don't want to. She looks sad.

'You don't need to apologise for him,' she says. 'It's not like he's your responsibility. Shane made you send those messages, didn't he?'

'Yeah,' I say, even though it's a lie. Shane doesn't know anything about them.

'Don't let his problems become your problems. He's not worth it, Katie.' The way she says it, sincere and kind, makes my eyes hurt. If I'm not careful, I'll cry.

'What did he do?'

I already know the answer, of course, but I want to hear her tell me herself. She flinches and takes a step back, but recovers quickly, and when she speaks again, there's nothing in her voice to let me know what she's thinking or feeling.

'It doesn't matter,' she says. 'He has to keep away from me now.'

I think of the little whimpering noises her dog made after it ate the poison. It's hard not to smile, wondering what she'd do if I told her it was me, not Shane, who did that.

'How can you make someone keep away from you if they don't want to?' I ask, because this is something I really want to know. I'm thinking of the messages he's sent me/her. All the things he's told us. He's crazy about us. I have over sixty messages on my phone to prove it.

'I got an injunction against him,' Ella says. 'If he comes anywhere near me, he'll be arrested.'

My stomach fizzes and there's something tight and hard pressing against my chest. My mother's voice, inside my head. *Men are stupid, Katie, remember that.*

Ella clears away the rest of the glasses and wipes the top of the bar until it's as clean and shiny as her hair. She must feel me staring, because she looks up suddenly, her eyes blue and bright.

'You know what's weird?' she says. 'I never really thought Shane was that bad. I mean, he two-timed me, yeah. But I put it down to immaturity more than anything else. I had no idea of the sort of person he really was. I guess he had us both fooled. Not just us, either. Most of the girls he's gone out with still seem to adore him. Maybe that's what happens to guys when they've got so much going for them. They think they can get away with anything.'

She's beautiful. I see her the way Shane must. Gold and copper and blue. Skin the colour of sand and all of her moving as smoothly as water.

The punters like her. Obviously.

In a flash, I understand why she's here. He pretended it was because of Mark Tate, his old golfing buddy. But my dad's not the sort of person who does favours. Not for my mum when she was still here, and not for me. Certainly not for some dead person who won't be around to return the favour any time soon.

She smiles, and I know she's seeing inside me the same way I've seen inside her. Because there's something between us. I can feel it and I know she can too. We're two halves of the same person. A two-sided coin, or mirror images of each other. Ella and Katie. Us.

Except her smile tells me it's not that simple. Because she is slender and graceful and beautiful. She's all the things I'll never be, no matter how hard I try. And I've tried, God knows. I've tried harder than anyone should ever have to try. I've starved myself and spent hours shaping my face and my hair and my clothes and my entire body, but it's never good enough. I will never, ever be like her.

She's still smiling, and when she turns to open the fridge, I'm sure it's to hide the fact that she's laughing at me.

'We should have a drink,' she says. She pulls out two beers, opens them and slides one across the bar to me. 'It's okay. Gus always lets me have one at the end of a shift.'

Gus.

The way she says his name, like they're friends. Or more than friends. An image inside my head. Ella Tate on her back on the shiny bar. My dad moving on top of her, grunting like a pig. I shake my head, but the image is stuck.

'Cheers.' She clinks her bottle against mine.

I take a sip of beer. It's bitter and cold and I have to force myself to swallow it down instead of spitting it out.

She leans forward, elbows on the bar, chin in her hands.

'Gus says you're studying computers,' she says. 'You're at Christ the King, right? What's it like?'

I shrug, thinking of the tall, slim girls with the straight hair who all remind me of her. 'It's okay. Can't wait to leave, though. I want to start working, get a place of my own.' I look around, see Ella and my dad humping on the bar, and shiver. 'I can't bear living here.'

I don't know why I said that. I didn't even know it was how I felt until the words were out.

'It's hard,' Ella says. 'When there's only one parent left. I feel a bit smothered by my mum right now.' She smiles. Again. I don't think I've ever known someone to smile as much as she does. 'That's why this job is so great. It gets me out of the house, away from all that. Plus I get to earn my own money, and that gives me a bit of freedom too.'

'Lucky you.' I don't bother to hide the bitterness in my voice, and she winces before smiling again. A softer, more sympathetic smile that makes me want to smash my fist into her face.

'I can see how protective Gus is,' she says. 'I'm guessing that can't be too easy either.'

I'm about to tell her she doesn't know the first thing about it when my phone vibrates in the pocket of my jeans.

'Need the loo,' I say, moving away from the bar. 'Back in a sec.'

I go into the ladies' and check my phone. A text from Shane.

It's me. I'm outside.

There's still time to turn back. There are lots of things I can do to stop whatever is going to happen next. I could tell him I'm sick or I've changed my mind, or that Gus is back early or fat, stupid Katie with the crush on you has come downstairs and won't leave me alone. I could run back to the bar, warn Ella that he's here.

I could do any one of those things. The fizzing in my stomach has started up again, joined by a buzzing in my head. I have to reach out, touch the wall to steady myself, afraid that if I don't, I might float up and up and away.

I'm going to watch. I don't know exactly what he'll do, but I have a good idea. I've given him enough hints about what I/she/we want. I think how angry he'll be when he finds out she's changed her mind. I remember the times he was angry with me and the ways he hurt me. I want to see him hurting her like that. I want to see him and film him doing it so I can think about it again and again, any time I want to.

Come on in, I type. *Back door's open.*

Thirty-One

Dee

A good night's sleep was becoming a distant memory. Every night was spent tossing and turning, anxious thoughts about Jake bouncing around inside her head. She tried to tell herself he was okay. Katie was with him, and no matter what else she'd done, there was no way she would ever harm her son. But lying in bed alone, unable to sleep, Dee couldn't prevent her mind travelling to the dark places it had no right to go to.

Each morning she crawled out of bed exhausted. The endless worrying, pushing against the sides of her brain, was wearing her down. As time passed, her confidence about finding Jake and his mother diminished. Until she reached the point where she couldn't remember why it had ever seemed like a good idea. What had possessed her to think she was capable of uncovering Katie's secrets when the police, with all of their resources, hadn't been able to find anything?

She was stupid. Stupid and deluded and bloody depressed. She tried not to think about the future, but it loomed before her each night as she lay awake in her bed. A bleak, black hole of a place without light or hope.

The day after her trip to Maidstone, she was up early following another restless night. Her brain felt sluggish, her limbs heavy when she moved them. Too nauseous to eat, she sat outside drinking coffee and checking her emails every few minutes in case Shane Gilbert made contact.

When her phone started ringing, she grabbed it, hoping it might be him. But it was Billy's number on the screen. The last person in the world Dee felt like speaking to, but she answered anyway, curious to find out what he wanted.

'Hey, Dee,' Billy said. 'You okay to chat for a sec?' He sounded upbeat. And sober, which wasn't always a given, even at this time in the morning. 'I wanted to apologise,' he continued. 'For the other night.'

'Which bit of the other night?' Dee asked. 'Turning up pissed or calling me a bitch?'

'Both.' Billy sighed. 'I'm really sorry, Dee. This whole business with work is getting to me, you know? If I lose this job, I don't know what I'll do.'

Dee could hazard a guess at what he'd do. He'd spend his time drinking and feeling sorry for himself. Not much different, in fact, to how he spent it now. Except without a salary coming into his bank account each month.

'I can't help with that,' she said.

'I know. We're divorced and my problems aren't your problems any more.'

Dee didn't say anything. She knew him well enough to know he hadn't simply called just to apologise.

'There was something else,' he said.

'Spit it out.'

'Shane Gilbert.'

'What about him?'

'He told me you paid him a visit yesterday,' Billy said.

Dee held the phone away from her ear and looked at it, not sure she could trust what she'd just heard.

'Hello?' Billy said. 'You still there, Dee?'

'When did he tell you this?' she asked, putting the phone back.

'He called me last night,' Billy said. 'I already told you I was looking into what happened to Katie's old man. One of the first things I did was find out what had happened to Shane. I got an old contact to help me find him. But Dee, you're wasting your time if you think he'll talk to you. Poor bloke's a bloody mess. Took me ages to get him to trust me enough to speak to me.'

'Billy, if he knows anything about where Katie might be, I need you to tell me.'

'I would,' Billy said. 'Swear to you, Dee. But he's as much in the dark as you are.'

'Did he kill her?' Dee asked. 'Because if he did, and you're hiding that from the police, you know that's a crime?'

'I already told you. Shane's a mess. I'm the only person he's got and I'm doing all I can to stop him falling apart.'

'When you were here,' Dee said, 'you implied you'd found out something about how Katie's dad was murdered. What did you mean exactly?'

'I can't tell you that. But I can tell you Shane doesn't know anything about Katie and Jake. You need to leave him alone, Dee.'

'You can't tell me what to do,' Dee said.

'I'm not trying to tell you what to do.'

'How has he managed it?' she asked.

'Managed what?'

'To persuade you he didn't kill Gus Hope. Two witnesses saw him doing it, Billy.'

'I can't say any more than I've already told you. But I promise you Shane can't tell you anything that will help you find your friend.'

'Your promises don't mean anything,' Dee said. 'I learned that the hard way. I'm going to hang up now, Billy. Thanks for the call. And tell Shane I'll be in touch.'

–

She spent the rest of the day mulling over the phone call. By the time evening came, she would have welcomed any distraction from her unhealthy inability to stop obsessing about what Billy was up to.

When Alex turned up with a bottle of wine, she had to stop herself throwing her arms around him. Alex was exactly the distraction she needed right now.

'Did you tell the police you knew Katie?' she asked, once the wine was poured and they were settled on the deck.

'Course I did,' Alex said. 'Why wouldn't I?'

'Do you think she did it, Alex?'

He sighed. 'Truthfully? I don't know. I mean, she seemed like a lovely girl to me. Sweet, funny and a good mum to the little fella. But who knows what someone's really like? I mean, how much do either of us really know about her life before she moved here?'

'Most of what I know is from her file,' Dee said.

'File?'

'To rent the mobile home, she needed references, bank statements, stuff like that. There's a file in Mum's office.'

'Anything interesting in there?' Alex asked.

Dee shook her head. 'Nothing that would explain why she'd kill someone. Did she ever talk to you about Ella Tate?'

'Never heard of her,' Alex said.

'Yes you have,' Dee reminded him. 'She was one of the witnesses at the trial into the killing of Katie's dad. I told you about her.' When Alex nodded, she continued, 'Ed asked me about her the other day. Which makes me think there's a connection, somehow, between the trial and the dead woman.'

'Or maybe Ed thinks you're hiding something from him.'

'No,' Dee said. 'He knows how desperate I am to find Katie and Jake. He must know I'd tell him if I knew anything.'

'If you say so. What about the other witness? Did he ask about her as well?'

'She's dead,' Dee said.

'You think someone's going around killing off the witnesses?'

'According to Leonard, she died of cancer. But I don't know if he's telling the truth. The last time I spoke to him, it felt like he was trying to warn me off. Maybe I should call him again. Push a bit harder to find out what he knows. Yes, that's exactly what I'm going to do. Right now.'

She stood up, looked around for her phone. Alex stood up too, came over and put his hands on her shoulders.

'It's late,' he said. 'You can't call him now. Wait until the morning, Dee.' He was still holding her shoulders, and somehow his face had got closer to hers. 'Now, do you think we can forget about all of this for a while and concentrate on something else?'

The heat radiated off every part of his body as he pulled her close, so close she couldn't see him, but she could feel him. Heat and solid strength. And when he placed his lips on hers and kissed her, her whole body seemed to lift and spin until she was floating, higher and higher, Alex's arms tight around her body so she didn't fall.

Thirty-Two

Katie
Nine years earlier

The courtroom is crowded. The mass of bodies adds to the suffocating heat that the electric fans either side of the judge's bench do nothing to alleviate. The atmosphere is unbearable, the air thick and tight, and I'm struggling to breathe. I look around, searching the crowd for someone – anyone – who can help. But there's no one.

I'm sitting in the top row of the public gallery. Ella is a few rows below me. Of course, she's not alone. She's got her mother with her. And Roxanne. Each time I see them together like that, I get a pain in my chest. Roxanne was my friend first. She's tried to contact me, lots of times, but I won't have anything to do with her. She thinks I don't know what she's done. They both do. They're wrong.

It's nine months since it happened, but I remember it like it's yesterday. I dream about it every night, and when I wake up in the morning, it's the first thing I think about. Shapes and sounds and colours inside my head. A broken bottle, the jagged edges stained and dripping. Screaming. Red blood and green glass and a dark hole in the side of my father's neck. And his voice, calling my name one last time before he dies. I still can't believe I'll never see him again. Maybe it's something you never get used to. At least with Mum, I can pretend she might come back one day. I can never do that with Dad.

Shane's family are here too. His mother and father, and his older brother. His mother has barely stopped crying since the trial began. Boo hoo hoo. I can't stand it. If I can control my tears, surely she should be able to? I'm the one who's lost everything, not her.

The strange thing is, I thought I hated my dad. I blamed him for the way my mum drank and for the way she left without ever saying goodbye. But the truth is, he did his best. It's just that his best wasn't good enough. I miss him. I wouldn't say we had the best relationship or anything, but it's lonely without him.

'All rise.'

This is it. Four hours and thirty-five minutes is all it took for the jury to decide if Shane is innocent or guilty. My eyes bore into the back of Ella's head. I wonder what she's thinking right now. She must be scared. Because if the jury come back with a 'not guilty' verdict, then the investigation will remain open.

There's a different feeling in the room now. Excitement. People shifting and shuffling and whispering to each other. But it all stops when the judge starts to speak. She's spent three days sitting up there listening to evidence in the Crown v. Shane Gilbert. Three days hearing three people's versions of what happened the night my father was killed.

'Please bring the jury back in.'

A door opens, and the seven women and five men walk in, one after the other. I scan their faces, searching for something that will tell me what their verdict is going to be. I know what I want them to say. I want them to say he's guilty. I want him to go to prison. He hurt me and he deserves to pay for what he's done.

'Ladies and gentlemen of the jury,' the judge said. 'Have you reached a verdict?'

My heart is beating fast. There's a buzzing sound in my head and my legs feel too weak to hold up my body. I look at Shane, sitting in the dock waiting to hear his fate. I keep watching him as the foreman – who's actually a woman – stands up.

'On the charge of murder,' the judge says, 'what is your verdict?'

'Not guilty.'

No!

Shane's face lights up. He looks around the room, searching for someone. I hold my breath, but his eyes move past me. The words dance around the room, taunting me. *Not guilty. Not guilty. Not guilty.*

A rush of memories, all hazed in pain and shame. He treated me so badly, and I let him do it. I am pathetic and weak, and everything I planned so carefully has fallen through. He's going to get away with it. People are speaking again, muffled whispers that are still too loud for the judge, who slams her gavel and shouts for silence.

'And on the second charge, of manslaughter,' she says, 'what is your verdict?'

The silence stretches out forever. I close my eyes, breathe in and out slowly, waiting.

'Guilty.'

I open my eyes, scared I haven't heard it right. But then I see his face, the shock and fear and confusion, and my spirits soar. It's over. Ella and her mum are hugging. When they stop, Ella turns around and looks up at me. Our eyes meet, and she looks like she wants to say something.

Bile rises up my throat. I can't bear being here. It's hot and packed and noisy and I need to get out. I try to push my way towards the exit, but there are too many people in my way.

'Let me out!' I don't mean to scream, but it works. The crowd parts and I'm able to get through. As soon as I'm outside, I start running. Down the courtroom steps, past the groups of reporters and onlookers, across the road and down the hill towards the river where my mother may or may not have drowned.

I run until I can't run any further, and when I stop, I have no idea where I am. But it's okay, because I'm alone. I know now that Shane was a mistake. Trying to get close to anyone is a mistake. When you get close to someone, you give them the power to hurt you. And no one is ever going to hurt me again.

Thirty-Three

Dee

The sun was low on the horizon, moving gradually closer to the surface of the still sea. Light reflected across the water, turquoise shot with slices of silver. The air was still and warm and muggy. Dee wanted water, but drank more wine instead, as if somehow that would have the same effect.

Louise sat across the table from her. When she lifted her glass, the Pinot Grigio sparkled gold and yellow in the evening sunlight.

'I heard back from Emma,' Dee said.

'And?' Louise sat forward in her chair.

'And I was right. Shane served his sentence in Brixton prison. He was released in May 2015. Six months before Katie moved to Eastbourne. She came here to hide, Lou.'

'Where is he now?' Louise asked.

'Maidstone. I got an address, but he refused to talk to me when I went to see him.' She paused, wondering whether to mention Billy, before deciding against it. 'Emma told me Shane did a degree in computer programming while he was inside. There must be loads of ways for someone with that sort of expertise to find someone who doesn't want to be found. Katie had a bank account. I'm sure there's a way to find that information online, if you know how to do it. I think he used her online information to trace her to Eastbourne.'

Louise frowned. 'But why would Katie need to hide from him? She didn't give evidence at his trial. And even if she was hiding from him, it still doesn't explain why someone else was killed. The dead girl isn't Katie, remember?'

'I know,' Dee said. She had so much information, but none of it quite fitted together. The facts kept slipping and sliding through her hands, as impossible to hold onto as bubbles. 'But there are simply too many coincidences to ignore. Shane Gilbert killed Katie's father. Six months after he was released from prison, Katie cut all ties with whatever life she had until then and moved to Eastbourne, a place where she doesn't know a single soul, to raise her child alone. Why would she do that if she wasn't hiding from someone?'

'I still think it's more likely she was hiding from Jake's dad,' Louise said. 'Besides, none of what you've found so far gets us any closer to working out who the dead girl is, or why she was killed.'

'I thought it was Ella Tate,' Dee said. 'One of the witnesses at the trial. But Ed told me it's not her.'

'Maybe Ed's lying.'

'Maybe,' she conceded. Truth was, she didn't know what to think any longer. She was tired of chasing dead ends, never seeming to get any closer to finding Katie and Jake.

Apparently Louise felt the same way, because she abruptly changed the subject.

'Are you going to tell me what's happening with you and Alex Mackey?' she asked. 'Or do I have to speculate?'

'You'll have to speculate,' Dee said. 'Because there is nothing going on between us.'

'That's not what his wife thinks.'

'How the hell do you know what Sandra does or doesn't think?'

Louise's right eyebrow shot up. 'You know her name?'

'Of course I know her name. Jesus, Lou, what is this? Alex is a mate. *Was* a mate. I'm not sure he's even that any more.'

'Why not?'

Dee closed her eyes, then wished she hadn't, because instantly she was back to last night. The physical contact had felt so good. How could she explain to Louise what it felt like not to have been held or touched or kissed for so long? How you reached a point where you stopped believing anyone would ever hold you or kiss you ever again.

'Okay,' she said. She leaned over and refilled her glass, needing the Dutch courage before she told Louise how stupid she'd been. Sprinkles of melted ice danced off the bottle, sun–bright and glistening, evaporating to nothing in the sticky heat of the early evening. 'Alex was here the night before the hit and run. We drank too much wine and… Oh God, Louise, I practically threw myself at him. I asked him if he'd like to spend the night, and he said no.'

'He said no?'

Dee covered her face with her hands and groaned. 'It was mortifying. Well, mortifying and sort of funny as well, if I'm honest. He looked like I'd told him something really shocking.' A sudden snort of laughter at the memory startled her. When she took her hands away from her face, she could see that Louise was struggling to understand what could be funny about this.

'You propositioned a married man,' Louise said. 'After everything Billy put you through. That's not funny, Dee.'

'There's more.'

Louise rolled her eyes. 'Please don't tell me you've slept with him.'

'We kissed,' Dee said. 'Last night. But that's all, Lou. I swear.'

'What about the next time?'

'There won't be a next time.'

'How can you be so sure?'

'Because I slapped him,' she said.

This time, Louise smiled. 'Scarlett quality?'

'Scarlett would have been proud of me.' Dee returned the smile. As young teenagers, *Gone with the Wind* had been one of the cousins' favourite films. They'd watched it together countless times, both girls relentless in their support of Scarlett O'Hara. No matter how badly she behaved, they were able to forgive her and find a justi-fication for her actions.

'Well then,' Louise said. 'Good for you.'

'Can we talk about something else now?' Dee asked.

'You'd never have kissed him if you weren't missing Katie and Jake so much,' Louise said.

'It's the not knowing that's killing me. Every single day, I wake up thinking that surely today I'll hear something. But I never do. It's unbearable, Lou.'

'I know Katie's your friend, and I understand you don't want to think she's capable of running someone over. But why else would she disappear right after it happened?'

225

'She couldn't drive,' Dee said. 'She gave Mum a photo-copy of her driving licence when she started renting the mobile home. But it was a fake.'

'How do you know?'

'It was a copy of a copy. Not a copy of the real thing. Plus, she told Alex she couldn't drive.'

'Alex knew her?'

'Alex knows everyone,' Dee said. 'It's no big deal.'

'If you say so.' Louise stood up. 'I need to be heading off. Martin's cooking tonight. A rare treat. I don't want to be late. Promise you'll let me know if you find out anything else?'

'Promise,' Dee said.

After Louise left, Dee fetched her laptop. There was still no email from Shane, and no message on Facebook from Tom Doyle. She sent Tom another message, telling him she needed to speak to him urgently.

Unable to relax, she went into her mother's office and took a sheet of A3 paper from the printer. In the sitting room, she laid the paper out on the floor and got to work. Thirty minutes later, she had a mind map, Katie's name in the centre, linked by a series of lines, scribbled writing and messy bubbles with more writing inside to all the events and people who were connected to her.

She'd written everything she could think of. The disap-pearance of Katie's mother. Her father's murder. Shane Gilbert. Ella Tate. Roxanne Reed. She'd drawn a line from Ella's name in the bottom right-hand corner of the page to Katie's name in the middle. Now, looking at the two names, she drew another line – dotted to show the link was less clear – from Ella to Shane.

Shane Gilbert, Ella Tate, Katie Hope.

Shane had killed Katie's father. Ella had witnessed the murder and given evidence during the trial. How were those events from ten years ago connected to what had happened so recently outside Dee's house?

Again Dee was transported back to that afternoon. Heat rising from the dusty path, the girl's body face down and unmoving. The tyre track across the pale skin of her thighs. Someone had killed that poor woman on purpose. Someone – Shane Gilbert? – had put their foot on the accelerator and driven into her, throwing her body forward and up into the air. Then, as the body hit the ground, they had reversed back over her.

Dee looked at the dotted line joining Ella Tate's name to Shane's. If the dead girl was Ella, it all made sense. Ella had been a witness at the trial that put Shane Gilbert behind bars. He'd come out of prison wanting revenge, and he'd killed her. It was the only logical explanation, except for one thing. According to Ed, the dead girl *wasn't* Ella Tate.

The words on the A3 sheet of paper were starting to blur when Dee heard her phone ringing. She picked it up: caller ID withheld.

'Hello?'

She told herself it would be a cold caller, someone selling something she didn't want. But when there was silence at the other end, she knew who it was.

'Shane?'

Another long silence before he spoke.

'Is this Dee?'

'Yes,' she said. 'I'm so glad you called. Thank you.'

'There's something I need to tell you,' he said. 'But not over the phone. Can you meet me tomorrow?'

'Of course.' Dee grabbed a pen and notepad. 'Just tell me where and when.'

'Manor House Gardens,' he said. 'Hither Green. Two o'clock. And don't be late, because I won't wait around.'

He hung up before she could ask him anything else. It didn't matter. In less than twenty-four hours, she'd be meeting him. Any questions she had could wait until then.

Thirty-Four

Dee

An internet search told Dee that Manor House Gardens was a public park in Hither Green, south London. Katie had grown up in Hither Green. The pub where her father had been killed was a short walk from the park.

Dee left home at 10 a.m. and was in Hither Green by 11.45. Once she had parked, she spent the next hour exploring the area. She found the Railway Tavern, the pub where Gus Hope had been killed. It looked like the sort of pub she liked – an old-style Victorian boozer situated on a residential street. Inside, it was clean but not too fancy. No loud music to distract the lunchtime drinkers and – best of all – no TV screens. Stained-glass windows that looked original, sunlight refracted through the green and red glass, adding to the cosy atmosphere.

She sat at the bar, taking her time over the prawn sandwich she'd ordered, trying to get a feel for the place. Wondering how much it had changed since Katie's father was the landlord.

'This is a really nice pub,' she said to the chirpy Australian barman when she paid her bill.

'We've got a great landlady,' he said, dazzling her with a huge, sunshine-filled Aussie grin. 'Hey, Roxanne!' he shouted to the woman working the other side of the long bar. 'Someone here wants to tell you how much she likes your pub.'

Dee put her glass of water down and stared at the woman he was talking to – tall and broad, in her late fifties, with shoulder-length hair so black it had to be dyed.

Roxanne Reed. Leonard said she had died of cancer. It could be another Roxanne, of course, but the chances of two women called Roxanne working in the same pub were slim to zero.

The woman nodded at Dee. 'Glad you like it.'

'Unusual name,' Dee said. 'I don't think I've ever met a Roxanne before.'

'It's Greek,' Roxanne explained. 'Means dawn, apparently. At least that's what my dad used to say. He had a bit of a thing about the Greeks.'

'You're lucky,' Dee said.

'Oh yeah?' Roxanne eyed her with a bit more interest.

'My dad had a bit of a thing for Tom Jones. Thought calling me Delilah was a good idea.'

Roxanne threw her head back and laughed. 'You poor cow,' she said. 'Named after a woman stabbed to death by her jealous lover. That Philip Larkin was dead right, wasn't he?'

'They fuck you up.' Dee smiled. 'I don't think mine did, actually.' Then, changing the subject, 'It's not easy, is it? Running a pub, I mean.'

'You got that right. Long hours, back-breaking work and sod-all money at the end of it.'

'My dad used to run pubs,' Dee said. A lie, but one she'd used in the past. Nothing pub owners liked better than a kindred spirit. Someone who understood what a shitty job they had.

'It's not an easy life for a kid.' Roxanne shrugged. 'I'm lucky. Never had any myself. The previous landlord lived with his daughter in the apartment upstairs. They found it tough, I think. Although it was worse for her than it was for him.'

'I loved it,' Dee said. 'Dad and Mum let me help out, evenings and weekends, and they paid me. Not much, but it seemed like a fortune to a skint teenager.'

'Maybe that was Gus's problem. He never let his girl anywhere near the bar. A bit overprotective. Not surprising, I suppose, given their history.'

'What do you mean?'

'Wife left him,' Roxanne said. 'He was never the same after that. Anyway, love, glad you like the Railway. Remember to tell your friends about it.'

There was a clock on the wall of the bar. One thirty. Dee estimated she had at least an hour and a half before she'd have to drive back to Eastbourne. Enough time for a small glass of wine to work its way through her system.

'You know what?' she said. 'It's so nice here, I'm going to treat myself. Glass of dry white wine, please. Can I get you a drink as well, Roxanne?'

'I'm all right, thanks.'

Roxanne turned away to open the bottle of wine and Dee got the sense the woman wanted the conversation to be over. But she wasn't ready to give up.

'How long have you been landlady here?' she asked, handing across a ten-pound note.

'A long time now,' Roxanne said. 'I worked here before I took over as landlady too. All in, I've been serving drinks behind this bar for the best part of thirty years.'

No doubt about it, then. This was the same Roxanne who'd been a witness at Shane Gilbert's trial. The same Roxanne that Leonard claimed had died of cancer. Leonard the liar. Lying because there was something he didn't want Dee to discover. Her body tingled with the sense that she was on to something. The big secret about Katie. This woman standing in front of her had the answers she was looking for. All she had to do was take things slowly.

'Must feel like home to you,' she said.

Roxanne shrugged again. 'Home's where your heart is. My heart's not in this place. It's a living for me. Nothing more than that. I was lucky enough to be able to buy the freehold, but I'll sell up when I'm done with it. Let some other bugger do all the hard work while I enjoy the money from the sale.'

'Oh no,' Dee said. 'You need to make sure it stays the way it is. What if they sell it and it's turned into some horrible modern gastropub?'

'Won't matter to me either way. I'll be here until I can't do the job any more. After that, I've got a little villa out in the Canaries, and when I move there, I won't give a fiddler's jig what happens to this place.'

'Seems a shame,' Dee said. 'All the hard work you've put into it.'

'Hard work's overrated. Now, love, I don't mean to be rude, but I've got a bar to run and you're not the first journalist that's turned up here pretending to be a regular punter and giving me all sorts of compliments as if that'll get me to talk to you. I'll tell you the same as I've told the ones before you and the ones who'll come after you. Katie Hope was a lovely girl when she lived here. Poor little thing has already suffered more than anyone ought to. Whatever the police are saying she did, I don't believe it. And that is all I'm prepared to say on the matter.'

She paused for breath, nodded at the untouched glass of wine in front of Dee.

'Enjoy your drink.'

'How did you know?' Dee asked. She lifted the glass and took a sip. Not bad for a pub wine. Roxanne clearly knew what she was doing.

'Easy. You say your old man was a pub landlord? Maybe he was, maybe he wasn't. My dad, he was a hack, see? Proper Fleet Street. Worked for the *Sun* his entire life.' She touched the side of her nose. 'I grew up surrounded by journalists. Can spot one a mile away.'

And with that, she turned her back on Dee and walked away. Dee noticed the woman's shoulders were shaking slightly. Almost, she thought, as if Roxanne was laughing.

–

Manor House Gardens was a lovely park. The sort of place that would make a family want to move to this part of London, Dee thought. Assuming they could afford the inflated house prices that seemed to have affected every corner of the city over the last few years.

Today, it was full of families. Groups of yummy mummies sitting on picnic blankets in the grassy area. Gangs of children racing up and down the paths that wound gently around the park. More of them in the playground, clambering up climbing frames, flying high

233

into the air on swings, hanging from monkey bars. Dee watched them playing, until she realised she was obsessively scanning every child's face hoping to see Jake.

Shane hadn't given any indication of what part of the park he'd be in. Dee walked around it several times, but there was no sign of him anywhere.

There were plenty of places he could hide. Lots of areas planted with mature trees and bushes where someone could watch everything that was happening without being noticed. A paedophile's dream, she thought, revising her initial impression of the park as a family idyll.

In the cafe beside the playground, she ordered a coffee and sat at one of the tables outside. From here, she had a good view of the park. Although she was starting to suspect Shane had changed his mind.

She waited for over an hour. As she sipped her second coffee, she wondered what it would be like to grow up in an urban environment like this. When she herself was a teenager, there were so many places she could hang out with her friends away from the judgemental eyes of adults. All they'd had to do was go a few hundred yards further along the beach and there would be no one to watch what they got up to.

Growing up here would be a different matter entirely. Looking around, Dee realised there were almost no teenagers in the park. It was all hipster parents and kids no older than eleven. Where did the older children go to drink illicit cans of cider or smoke cigarettes and dope and do whatever else teenagers got up to these days?

Right then, as if they'd staged it just for her, a teenage boy and girl emerged from behind some bushes at the far end of the park. Dressed entirely in black, faces caked with white make-up, the pair of wannabe goths wandered away holding hands, oblivious to everyone else around them.

Of course!

Dee pushed her chair back and ran to where the teenagers had come from. It was overgrown here. A sign beside the shrubbery said that the park keepers deliberately let this section grow wild for the local bee population. She shoved her way through the bushes and weeds and found herself in another section of park, invisible from the other side. Not a large area, but big enough for four or five people to sit. Empty lager cans and cigarette and roach butts littered the ground. Clearly a favourite hideout for local teenagers.

Except now, the place was empty. Frustrated, Dee kicked an empty can, which rose a few inches into the air and landed less than a foot away. She couldn't even kick a can properly.

In her jeans pocket, her phone started to ring. She checked the screen, saw a mobile number she didn't recognise and answered, half hoping it might be him.

'Dee?' A woman, not Shane.

'That's right,' Dee said.

'This is DC Rachel Lewis,' the woman said. 'Where are you?'

'I'm in London visiting a friend,' Dee said. 'Why?'

'I'm at your house,' Rachel said. 'How quickly can you get here?'

Thirty-Five

Katie
Five years earlier

We're living in Bristol. Same city, very different lives. The main difference being she has a life and I don't. I made two lists last night. Drew a line down the middle of a sheet of paper and wrote my name on one side, Ella's on the other. Underneath our names, I wrote all the things we have in our lives right now. In my list I wrote: job, money, a place to live. Here's her list: job, money, a place to live, friends, mother, boyfriend. I underlined 'boyfriend' three times, pushing the pen so hard that I ripped the paper.

His name is Tom and he's cute in a geeky kind of way. Not in Shane's league, but maybe that experience has scared her off the soulful, sexy type and she's gone for something a bit safer. It's clear he's crazy about her. You can see it in the way he follows her around the place like a devoted puppy. She clearly likes that devotion, though I think it's a bit sad really that she's decided to go for a Tom when she could have anyone she wants.

We've started hanging out together. Not too often, but enough for her to think we're becoming friends. Tom doesn't like it. More to the point, Tom doesn't like me. He suspects I've got an ulterior motive for wanting to spend time with his girlfriend. Clever old Tom.

Ella, on the other hand, hasn't got a clue. She thinks it's a wonderful coincidence that we've both ended up in Bristol. 'What are the chances?' she gushed the first time we bumped into each other. Hardly a coincidence given that I've moved here to be close to her. And our bumping into each other only happened after I'd been following her for weeks and knew her routine inside out.

She graduated last week, and now she's trying to work out what she wants to do next. She's been offered a music scholarship in Australia, but isn't sure if she's going to accept it. She doesn't want to be too far away from her mum. I'm doing my best to persuade her that moving to Australia is a seriously bad idea. I've told her how much I regret not spending more time with my parents, and that if they were still alive, I'd do everything I could to see them as much as possible. I think it's having an effect, but I'm not stupid enough to think I've got more influence over her than Tom. Not yet, anyway.

She's invited me for dinner this evening. I've spent ages getting ready, but I'm still not sure what to wear or what to do with my hair. I've straightened it, but now I've remembered that she doesn't bother doing that any more. Maybe I should stop too. I don't want Tom to notice I'm copying his girlfriend, but I'd like to look my best. In the end, I leave it as it is. It's not like Tom's going to notice. Beside Ella, I'm always going to be invisible.

Their flat is small and untidy and not really how I imagined. But they seem actually pleased to see me, even Tom. He takes my coat and pours me a glass of wine and steers me to the sofa, where we sit and chat while Ella prepares the food.

The more I talk to Tom, the more I can see why Ella likes him. He's funny, and he listens when I speak, instead of talking over me like most guys do. I'm so relaxed, my wine goes down faster than I expect. When I'm finished, Tom offers to top me up right away.

'Only if you're having one too,' I say.

'Try and stop me,' he says. Then, leaning forward, he mock-whispers, 'We'll need something strong to block out the taste of Ella's cooking.' He grins, and I can't help smiling back.

'Don't listen to him,' Ella shouts from the kitchen area. 'He loves my Moroccan chicken.'

Tom reaches for my glass, and when our hands touch, a shot of electricity tingles up my arm. He's still smiling, and I know he's felt it too. Something is happening. Fate, destiny, call it what you want. Tom Doyle and I are meant to be together.

Ella thinks she's been so clever. She has no idea that the only reason she's got away with what she did is because I let her. I've stood back and watched her build a shiny new life for herself, knowing I can make it all come crashing down any time I want to.

Thirty-Six

Dee

The drive to London that morning had taken Dee an hour and forty-five minutes. She made it back in sixty-five minutes. True to her word, Rachel had called Ed, who was standing outside Dee's house when she pulled up.

'How bad is it?' she asked, jumping out of the car.

'Your mum's office got the worst of it,' Ed said. 'I'm sorry. I know how much that space means to you.'

Dee pushed past him into the house, not bothering to ask Ed how he knew that about the office.

'I'm sorry,' he said again, following her inside.

She went as far as the doorway of the office and stopped. The whole place had been ripped apart. The drawers of the filing cabinet had been pulled out, their contents emptied onto the ground. A mess of files and papers was scattered around the room. The desktop computer her mother used to work on was gone.

When Rachel had called earlier, she'd told Dee she'd gone to her house because she had some more questions. When she got there, she saw the front door had been prised open. Her first thought was for Dee's safety. After calling her to make sure she was okay, she went inside to see how bad the damage was. Then she called Ed and told him what had happened.

'I got our guys out here right away,' Ed said. 'We've taken fingerprints from the door frame and in here. But they could belong to anyone who's been in those rooms. Nothing else seems to have been disturbed. Although I'll need you to confirm that, of course.'

The thought of all these strangers inside her house when she wasn't here made Dee want to throw up. Or hit someone.

'There's been a spate of burglaries in the area recently,' Ed added. 'Looks like you're the latest victim. We'll check all the fingerprints we've got from here with those from the other burglaries. I wouldn't get your hopes up, though. We've had no matches so far.'

But Dee knew who'd done this, and it wasn't some random lowlife criminal. Shane Gilbert had known she wouldn't be here today. He'd lured her up to London, and as soon as she was out of the way, he'd broken into her house.

'What about the mobile home?' she asked. 'Have you checked there too?'

'I didn't think of that.'

Ed pulled out his phone and made a call. While he issued instructions to whoever was on the other end of the line, Dee went into the office and got down on her knees, searching through the files and papers. Even though she already knew what was missing.

'Hey,' Ed said, turning around. 'You shouldn't be in there yet.'

Dee ignored him. 'Katie's file is gone. All of it. There's nothing left. This is to do with her. You said it yourself, this is the only room that's been disturbed. He hasn't taken the TV or my jewellery or any of the paintings.'

'They took the computer,' Ed said.

'That was an ancient heap of shit. The only reason he took it was in case there was something about Katie on there. Thank God I took my laptop with me. I wasn't going to, but I threw it in the boot of the car in case I needed it.'

'He?' Ed said. 'You've said that twice now, as if you know who it was.'

Dee was still on the floor; her knees were starting to hurt. She stood up, painfully aware of how creaky her body was these days.

'Am I allowed into the kitchen to make some coffee?' she asked.

'Afraid not. Why don't you let me take you somewhere? We can leave the guys to get on with things here. I'll make sure they let me know when they're finished. I can drive you home after they're gone.'

She thought he'd take her into town somewhere. Instead, he drove to Pevensey Bay, where they bought takeaway coffees from the bakery and drank them on the beach. Sitting on the shingle like a pair of old mates, instead of a detective investigating a murder and one of the victim's only friends.

'You were right about the mobile home,' Ed said. 'I got a call while I was ordering the coffees. The whole place has been turned over. Much worse than yours.'

'I knew it. That bastard.'

'Why are you so sure you know who did this?'

Dee blew on her coffee to cool it and took a sip before answering, making sure she didn't tell him anything she shouldn't. Like how she'd arranged to meet Shane Gilbert in London today.

'What did Rachel want to speak to me about?' she said. 'That's why she was at my house. Because there was something she wanted to ask me.'

'She wanted to ask you about your ex-husband. He's been in touch, asking a lot of questions about the case.'

'What's that got to do with me?'

'We thought he might have confided in you. When I spoke to him, I got the distinct impression he wasn't telling me everything he knows.'

'I'm the last person he'd confide in,' Dee said.

Ed rubbed his hands down his face, and when he looked at her, she could see how exhausted he was. She had always been a sucker for a troubled man. It had been the undoing of her marriage and it looked like being her undoing now too.

'Ed—' she started.

'I know.' He held up a hand. 'You've already told me everything he knows. Sorry. It's been a rough week. No excuse.' He smiled. 'But it's the only one I've got. Forgive me?'

'Nothing to forgive,' she said.

She finished her coffee and crunched the paper cup in her hand. The tide was out, leaving a stretch of rose-gold sand. A couple were walking hand in hand along the edge of the water, a black-and-white border collie bouncing around them. The air was so still that Dee could hear the splashing of their bare feet in the shallow water and the murmur of their voices.

Exhaustion and rage made her body ache. She was so tired she wanted to lie down and never get up again.

So angry she wanted to punch someone until they bled. Shane Gilbert, Alex Mackey, Billy Morrison. Any one of them, or all of them.

Ed's phone started to ring. When he answered it, he listened for a moment before giving Dee the thumbs-up.

'Your house is clear. SOCO have got everything they need. I'll drive you home as soon as you're ready.'

She didn't want to go back. She wanted to stay here, watching the tide come in and talking with Ed Mitchell about nothing and everything.

'We can stay out a bit longer if you want,' he said. 'I'd understand if you didn't want to be there after what's happened.'

'It's okay.' Dee stood up quickly before she changed her mind. 'I'm tired. I feel like a bath and an early night.'

On their way back to her house, Ed asked Dee if she thought Katie and the dead woman could have been in a relationship.

'It's possible,' Dee said. 'Except if they were a couple, I'd have seen her around, right? I assumed Katie was straight. Maybe because of Jake. But she could be gay, I guess. Although I find it difficult to think she wouldn't have told me if she was.'

'Maybe that's not as unlikely as you think. From what you've told me, she was a very private person.'

'Yeah, but you still get an impression of what someone's like. No matter how private they are.'

'What impression would Katie have had about you?' Ed asked.

'What sort of question is that?'

'I'm curious, I guess. I remember you from school. You were always so... out there. Different to the other girls. I wasn't surprised when I heard you were in London making a name for yourself.'

Something in his voice, a hint of pity, made Dee want to smack him. Or cry.

'You'll need to get someone to fix your front door,' he said. 'We've boarded it up, so you're secure for now. But you should get it sorted as soon as you can. Ah, your boyfriend's here.'

He had pulled up outside Dee's house and pointed at Alex, standing by Dee's broken front door. Dee's spirits sank even further. Alex was the last person she wanted to see right now.

She didn't want Ed to go. She wanted to explain that she wasn't the loser he clearly thought she was. To rip that trace of pity from his voice, replacing it with admiration instead. Get him to see that all this – living here in her childhood home without a job or any real prospect of one – was an interlude. She was having a career break, that was all.

But the look on his face told her there was no point. He'd made his mind up about her and there was nothing she could do about it.

'He's not my boyfriend,' she said, her voice sharper than she'd meant. 'He's a friend, nothing more than that.'

'And his wife knows this is where he comes every evening when he's finished work?'

'That is none of your bloody business.'

Ed shrugged, like he didn't care one way or the other what she got up to. Somehow, that made her even angrier. What right did he have to criticise her for living her life the way she wanted to?

She opened the door and got out of the car.

'Thanks for the coffee,' she said. But she doubted he heard. He was already driving off, the passenger door slamming shut as he turned the car around and sped away.

–

'I came to see how you're doing,' Alex said. 'Figured I'd let enough time pass so you wouldn't whack me again. Then I saw the door all boarded up and I didn't know what to think. What the hell happened, Dee?'

'A break-in,' Dee said. 'Apparently there's been a few of them over the last few months. I'm sorry about hitting you, by the way. Even if you deserved it.'

Alex smiled. 'Can't blame me for trying. But don't worry, message received loud and clear. It won't happen again. Did the burglars take much?'

They were in the kitchen. Dee was making coffee while Alex paced around the place like someone with too much energy and not enough space.

'Mum's computer,' she said. 'Nothing else as far as I can make out.' She didn't tell him that Katie's file had been taken as well. After the last time, she wasn't sure she wanted to talk to him about Katie at all.

'You were lucky,' he said.

'I don't feel particularly lucky. But I guess you're right. It could have been a lot worse.'

'At least you're okay.' He stopped pacing, came and sat beside her at the island in the middle of the kitchen. 'I'm so sorry about the other night. I was a right dick.'

'I'm sorry too. I probably should have responded with a little less violence.'

'Friends?' He held out his hand.

'Friends,' Dee said, but she didn't shake his outstretched hand. 'Listen, Alex, it's been a really long day and I'm knackered. All I want to do is have an early night. Thanks for coming over. Maybe we can get together another time?'

'Do you want a hand tidying up the office before I go?' he said.

She shook her head. 'I need a bit of time to get my head around what's happened. Mum's office is a kind of special place for me. It's where I feel closer to her than anywhere else. Knowing someone else was in there, going through her stuff, messing it all up, it makes me feel sick.'

'Okay.' Alex drained his coffee and stood up. 'Not a problem. I'll leave you to your early night, but only if you promise to give me a ring when you feel up to a bit of company.'

'Sure.' She forced herself to smile, not wanting him to see how desperate she was for him to leave. When he leaned in for a hug, she stepped back and he put his hands awkwardly on her shoulders instead.

'You take care, Dee.' He let himself out through the door that led onto the deck.

The sun had started to set, flooding the house with red and orange light. Dee watched the colours shift and change as it dropped lower in the sky. She kept thinking about the conversation they'd had the last night he was here. When she'd told him about the file in her mother's office full of information about Katie. Right before he'd kissed her.

Thirty-Seven

Katie
Five years earlier

I leave it a week. Then I send her a text saying I need to see her urgently. I know this will freak her out, and sure enough, she calls me back right away.

'Hey, Katie, is everything okay?'

'Not really,' I say. 'I don't suppose you're free any time today or tomorrow?'

'I'm not around today,' she says. 'But I'm home tomorrow evening if you'd like to pop over?'

'Will Tom be there?' I ask.

There's a pause. Then, 'Is that a problem?'.

'Not for me. But I'm worried you won't want him hearing what I have to say.'

That does it. She agrees to meet me at Beanz coffee shop in an hour. Which, by the way, goes to show. She could have just said yes straight away, instead of deliberately trying to make it difficult for us to meet.

Beanz is a hip coffee shop in Clifton. It's full of arty, studenty types and I hate it immediately. I deliberately arrive ten minutes late and I'm glad to see she's already here. Sitting at a table by the window, hands wrapped around a white mug, looking miserable.

I swallow down my anger and force myself to smile as I walk over and say hi. I ask if she wants anything, but she nods at the mug and says no thanks, she's fine.

'Thanks for seeing me,' I say, once I've ordered my own coffee and am sitting opposite her. The table wobbles and coffee spills onto it when I put my mug down. It's annoying, but nothing like as annoying as the look on her face right now. I want to grab her by the shoulders and shake her and tell her that I know what she did. But it's not the right time for that. 'And thanks for the lovely evening last week,' I continue. 'I meant to write you a proper thank-you note, but I never got around to it. I hope you don't think I'm rude?'

'Katie,' she says. 'I don't care about that. Cooking you a meal is the least I could do.'

'What do you mean?' I ask, knowing exactly what she means.

'Nothing.' She shakes her head. 'You said you had something to tell me?'

I take a sip of coffee. It's bitter and strong and the kick of caffeine hits the back of my throat.

'It's about Shane,' I say.

Her mouth drops open, but she doesn't speak. I wait a moment, and there they are: perfect pink circles on each of her cheeks.

'What about him?'

'I'm sorry,' I say. 'I've been thinking about the best way to tell you, but I don't know how, so I'm going to come right out with it. Is that okay?'

She nods, mouth clamped tight.

'I've been to see him,' I say.

She looks proper shit-scared now, and the anger I've been carrying around with me starts to recede, replaced by something else. The sweet taste of revenge. You ruined my life, I think. You destroyed my family. Now it's my turn.

'Why would you do that?' she asks.

'The family liaison officer said it might help. It's all part of his rehabilitation, apparently.'

I don't tell her how I hard I made him beg before I agreed to see him. Or how long it took him to convince me he was innocent. There was no need for him to put so much effort into it. Because I already knew, didn't I? I was there that night and I saw everything that happened.

'What did he say?'

I stare at her, letting the silence drag out, knowing how freaked out she must be.

'He told me the truth,' I say.

'Oh God,' she whispers.

I take another sip of coffee, wait for her to speak, but nothing happens. Fine, I think. I've given you your chance and you've messed it up.

'He told me it was an accident,' I say. 'That he never meant for Dad to die and he was sorry. He wanted me to forgive him.'

She frowns, clearly struggling to understand what I'm telling her.

'It was good. I think I needed to hear him tell me he was sorry. I lost my dad, Ella. He was the only family I had. Now that he's gone, I've got no one.'

She reaches out, takes my hand, but I pull away from her. Her skin feels like damp plastic. I can't bear to touch it.

'Can you imagine what that's like?' I say. 'To have someone take away the only person you've got left? His apology meant so much.'

I'm laying it on a bit thick, but it's working. Her eyes have welled up and her chin has that crumpled look you see right before someone's about to cry.

'In fact,' I say, 'it was so good, I've been back to see him a few more times. That's why I wanted to talk to you.'

She uses the sleeve of her jumper to wipe her eyes. 'You wanted to tell me you've been visiting Shane?'

'I wanted to tell you what he said about you.'

'You know you can't trust him,' Ella says. 'He's dangerous, Katie. What does your family liaison officer think about you continuing to visit him?'

It's the wrong thing to say and she knows it. 'I'm sorry. It's none of my business. But you know what he's like, what he's done to both of us. Wouldn't it be better if you kept away from him?'

'I don't have anyone else,' I say. 'And you're right. It's none of your business.'

'So why are you here?' There's an edge of anger to her voice now, as if *I'm* the one who's in the wrong. It would be funny if it wasn't so awful.

'Because he knows about you,' I tell her.

'What do you mean?

'He knows everything about your life. He knows you've recently graduated, he knows where you live and who you live with. He even told me about Tom. He knows where you met and how long you've been dating. Everything, Ella.'

She puts her hand over her mouth, holding it there as if she's afraid of what will happen if she takes it away.

'I wasn't sure whether or not to tell you,' I say. 'But I thought you should know.'

The hand drops away, and when she finally speaks, her voice is so low I have to lean forward to hear what she's saying.

'He killed Oscar,' she says.

She looks at me as if I'm meant to know what that means. It takes a few seconds, but then I get it. The greedy Labrador that couldn't get that piece of steak into its mouth quickly enough.

'He followed me home one afternoon. He was on my train and got off when I did. It freaked me out, so I walked around Bromley for hours until I thought I'd lost him. Only I hadn't, because the next morning, when I left to go to college, I found Oscar lying dead in our front garden. The vet said he'd been poisoned.'

She looks so sad, and I have to bite down on my lip to stop myself shouting in her stupid face. Doesn't she know how unimportant a dead dog is compared to everything I've gone through?

'I could never prove it was Shane,' she says. 'But I knew. I told Mum about the way he'd acted after we broke up. All the messages and texts he sent me, and the way he kept turning up at the pub, like he wasn't going to leave me alone no matter how many times I told him I wanted nothing to do with him. Mum insisted we go to the police and make a statement, accusing him of harassment. But it wasn't enough, was it? And now it's happening all over again. I've had this feeling for a while now, as if someone's been watching me. I thought it was my imagination, but it's not. He's got someone following me, watching my every move.'

I reach out and take her hand, ignore the shudder of revulsion that runs through me as I squeeze it.

'It'll be fine,' I tell her. 'We'll sort it together. Trust me.'

Thirty-Eight

Dee

Despite the burglary, Dee slept better than she had in weeks and woke early the next morning feeling refreshed. She reached for her phone, charging on the bedside table, and checked her news feeds. Nothing new on the police search for Katie Hope. In the days following the hit and run, Katie's disappearance had been front-page news. Now, Dee had to scroll down the list of other stories until she found it. Soon it would be gone altogether, disappearing as effectively as Katie and Jake themselves.

There was an unread text message on her phone, which must have come through last night while she was sleeping. It was from Ed.

Will drop by tomorrow to check you're okay.

Dee started to reply, then stopped herself and deleted his message. The less contact she had with him, the better off she would be. She went back to the news site. One of the stories included a photo of Ed. It had been taken at the press conference the day after the police realised the dead woman wasn't Katie. He looked crumpled and tired in the photo, and old. But when Dee looked at it, all she could remember was how his smile transformed his face and made him look ten years younger.

'Arsehole,' she muttered, putting the phone back on the bedside table and throwing back the duvet. She needed coffee and breakfast.

It was a grey, overcast day but she ate her breakfast outside anyway. She loved this view, no matter what the weather was like. The sea was rough this morning. Big, frothy waves growling across the shingle. A wind whipped in from the east, making her shiver.

After breakfast, she called Billy.

'I want you to tell me why the hell Shane Gilbert broke into my house yesterday afternoon,' she said.

'He did what?'

'You heard me. And I think you know why he did it.'

'Shit,' Billy said. 'Are you sure it was him?'

'He called me the day before yesterday. We arranged to meet, but he never turned up. Coincidentally, my house got burgled at the same time as I was sitting in a London park waiting for him.'

'I haven't seen or heard from him recently,' Billy said. 'I've left him messages and emails but he's not getting back to me.'

'Is he on some sort of revenge trip? Is that what this is about? I know he's convinced you he didn't kill Gus Hope. If that's true, it means Roxanne Reed and Ella Tate lied at the trial. Which also means one or both of them killed Gus and framed Shane for the murder. How am I doing so far, Billy?'

'He didn't kill Gus,' Billy said. 'I can't tell you any more than that.'

'Not even if it helps me find Katie?'

'The best thing you can do is stop worrying about Katie. She's not who you think she is.'

'What do you mean by that?' Dee asked.

'Have you told the police you think it was Shane who broke into your house?'

'No.'

'Well maybe you should. If he's done that, who knows what the hell he'll do next? The guy's really messed up, Dee. I'm pretty sure he takes steroids. And I know for a fact he's got a coke habit. That's a lethal combination. You need to be careful.'

Dee's phone beeped to tell her someone else was trying to call her.

'I've got another call coming in,' she said. 'Can we talk later?'

'This evening,' Billy agreed. 'Call me then and we'll chat. I'll try to track Shane down today and find out what he's up to. In the meantime, promise me you'll be careful? Shane's got a lot of problems. I'm not sure how stable he is.'

By the time she'd hung up, the other call had been diverted to voicemail. She could see the message icon flashing on her screen. She dialled her voicemail and listened to it.

'Hi. This is Tom Doyle. You sent me a message asking about Ella. Call me back on this number whenever you can. I'd like to speak to you.'

His voice was a surprise. Low, lilting, Irish. He sounded like Dee's dad. Her father had come from Galway, in the west of Ireland. Despite living in the UK for all his adult life, he'd never lost his Irish accent. Tom's was similar. Which meant Dee was already inclined to like him, even before she'd met him.

'I'm sorry I didn't get in touch earlier,' he said when she called him back. 'I've been travelling for the last three weeks. I finished a big job recently and I needed a complete break. No internet, no phone. Three weeks of sightseeing, reading and chilling out.'

'Sounds lovely,' Dee said.

'It was. Until I came back and heard about Katie. I've spent the last two days reading everything I can find about what happened. You said you were a friend of Ella's?'

'Not exactly,' Dee said. 'I'm Katie's landlady. I've got a mobile home that I rent out. Katie and Jake have been living there for two and a half years now. We're neighbours, in fact. My house is next door to the mobile home.'

'Why did you tell me you knew Ella, then?' Tom asked.

'I wasn't sure you'd get back to me otherwise. I'm sorry.'

Tom was silent for so long, Dee worried he had hung up. She was about to ask if he was still there when he finally spoke.

'So you know Katie,' he said. 'Not Ella. Is that right?'

'Katie's my friend. I've looked out for her since she's been living here. I'm worried about her, Tom. I know she and Ella were friends and I know they were in Bristol at the same time. I thought maybe you'd be able to tell me something that could help me find her.'

'You're sure it's her?' Tom said.

'Who?'

'The woman the police are looking for. It's definitely Katie?'

'Who else would it be?'

He paused. 'Are you free to meet? Today, ideally.'

'Where?'

'I flew into Gatwick this morning. I'm here now. Waiting to catch a train to Eastbourne. I've got an appointment with the police later this afternoon. They think I can help with their investigation.'

Finally, a lead. Someone who knew Katie and Ella and might be able to tell Dee what had really happened the night Gus Hope was killed.

'I can meet you at the station,' she said. 'Text me your train times and I'll see you there.'

After hanging up, Dee went to have a shower. There were regular trains from Gatwick to Eastbourne; Tom would be here soon. The combination of a good night's sleep, a pot of coffee and the prospect of new information was the buzz she needed right now. Today was going to be a good day.

Thirty-Nine

Katie
Four years earlier

Something big has happened. I followed them tonight. All the way through town up to Clifton. They walked onto the bridge, then stopped halfway across. It was like something in a film. It was late, and they were the only two people there. Captured in the milky glow of the fat full moon. He turned towards her, put his hands on her shoulders and started to speak. When he'd finished, there was this moment where nothing happened, and then she came alive like I've never seen her before. She threw her arms around him and he lifted her off the ground and held her as he leaned in and kissed her on the lips.

I held my breath the whole time and didn't start breathing again until he'd let her go and they were walking towards me, wrapped around each other so you could almost believe they were one person, not two. In that moment, I could have gone right up to them and I don't think they would have seen me. I didn't do that, of course. I stepped back into the shadows, watched them pass, my heart beating so fast and hard inside my chest it was the strangest thing that no one apart from me could hear it.

He's proposed. It's all I can think of. A hard, aching lump sits in my throat. I tried to imagine what it would be like, having someone hold me the way he held her, kiss me like that and tell me they love me so much they want to spend the rest of their life with me. It should have been me, not her, on the bridge tonight. It could have been me too. Because that connection I felt when I was in their flat, that was real. He's trying to ignore it, but you can't ignore something forever.

I stand on the street across the road from their flat, watching the shadows of their bodies moving around inside. The curtains are closed. She's kept them like that ever since I told her about Shane. It's not ideal. I used to like being able to see inside at night. Knowing they had no idea I was here, just across the road, watching.

I wait until the lights are turned out before making my move. Tom answers the door, and he doesn't look too happy to see me.

'Katie,' he says. 'It's almost midnight. Is everything okay?'

I burst into tears and he looks horrified.

'Jesus, Katie,' he says. 'Come on in.'

He wraps his arm around my shoulders and guides me into the sitting room. He's so kind and gentle, I don't want him to let me go. But as soon as he's lowered me onto the couch, he's off to get Ella, and all I'm left with is the memory of him.

'I'm sorry,' I sob when she appears. 'I'm so sorry for barging in like this. I didn't know where else to go.'

I tell her that today was my parents' wedding anniversary and I'd tried so hard to get through the day as normal.

'But I couldn't do it,' I wail. 'I keep thinking about how much I miss them. And how I wish more than anything that they were still here.'

She goes into overdrive then. Hugging me and telling me how brave I've been and how she doesn't have any clue how I've managed to cope with so much.

'I'm glad you came here,' she says. 'You absolutely shouldn't be alone tonight.'

She insists I stay the night in their flat.

'Please,' she says. 'I'd feel so much better if you were here.'

'I don't want to be a burden,' I say. 'I shouldn't have come at all. I just didn't know what else to do.'

'You're staying,' she says, standing up. 'It's decided.'

Tom has gone back to bed, so it's just the two of us. Ella makes us cups of cocoa and we snuggle under the quilt she's brought out for me. It's nice. This is what it's like when you have friends.

'So,' I say, after I've gone on about my parents' happy marriage for a bit. 'How are things with you?'

'I'm not sure really,' she says. 'Freaked out, I guess. I've spoken to Victim Support, but I don't know whether it's made any difference. What can they do? Shane's still in prison. I don't know how I can prove he's got someone watching me.'

'Have you told Tom what's going on?' I ask.

She looks horrified. 'God, no. He doesn't know about what happened. I should have told him, I know. But I never got around to it, and the longer it went on…' She shrugs. 'I was never able to find the right time. You think that's bad of me?'

'Of course not,' I tell her. 'But are you sure he's right for you? I mean, if you're not able to talk to him about something like that?'

'Oh, Tom is absolutely right for me,' she says, smiling in that smug way people do when they're one half of a happy couple.

Usually this would annoy the crap out of me. But right now I'm too busy thinking about what I can do with the information she's just given me.

'In fact,' she continues, leaning in and lowering her voice, 'can I tell you a secret?'

This is it. She's going to tell me they're getting married.

'Sure.'

'We're going to Australia.'

I'm so shocked, I don't know what to say.

'Not right away,' she says. 'But soon. I'm going to take up the scholarship. It's a once-in-a-lifetime opportunity. I'd be mad not to do it.'

'Wow,' I manage eventually. 'Australia. So… what? You go there and start a new life?'

'I need to get away,' she says. 'I don't want to leave Mum, but it's not like we'll be gone forever. And she can visit while we're out there. All that stuff with Shane, everything you've told me, it's made me realise I can't stay. It's not good for us. We need a fresh start.'

For one ridiculous moment, I think she's talking about me and her. Until she says:

'We row too much and it's all my fault. I can't talk to him. Can't open up to him the way he deserves. I think moving away will help. I want to be with him, Katie, and I don't think I can do that if we stay here.'

'A fresh start,' I say. 'Where no one knows who you are or what's happened to you. That sounds wonderful, Ella. Really.'

She's still holding my hand, and she squeezes it again. She's smiling and she looks so happy, and I think this is it. She's going to suggest I come with them. Because she knows it's every bit as difficult for me as it is for her.

'I can't wait,' she says. 'And we'll stay in touch, won't we? I mean, we can email and stuff. You could even come visit maybe?'

'Of course,' I say.

I pull my hand away and tell her I'm tired. She slips out from under the quilt and stands up.

'Sleep tight,' she says. 'See you in the morning.'

After she's gone, I lie on their sofa, thinking about what she's told me and how she's made me feel. I can't let her go to Australia, that's for sure. There's at least another year before Shane is released, and I need Ella here, in the UK, when that happens.

Her relationship with Tom is built on a pack of lies. I bet he wouldn't stay with her if he knew the truth. He sure as hell wouldn't give up everything and follow her all the way to the other side of the world.

She'll never tell him, of course. But I wonder: what would happen if I did?

Forty

Dee

Dee picked Tom up from Eastbourne station. She stood near the ticket barriers scanning the faces of the people coming off the train until she saw him. Tall and lanky with light brown hair, hazel eyes and a smattering of freckles across a nose that was slightly crooked. He came through the barrier and stopped, looking around as if he wasn't sure where he was meant to go next.

'Tom?' She stepped towards him and he smiled.

'Dee.' He held his hand out for her to shake. 'Good to meet you. Thanks so much for coming to pick me up.'

'My pleasure,' Dee said. 'My car's outside. This way.'

As they walked to the car, she tried not to stare at him. Struggling to get over the shock of recognition when she'd seen his face for the first time. She wondered if he knew, and if not, how she was going to tell him.

She drove along the coast back to her house. Tom, who told her he'd never been to Eastbourne before, raved about the bits of it he could see from the car. The raving continued when he saw where she lived.

'This house is amazing,' he said as he followed her inside. They had to enter through the back door. The front was still boarded up following the burglary. 'Was it like this when you bought it? Or did you commission the work yourself?'

'I didn't build it,' Dee said, unwilling to talk about her parents to someone she barely knew. 'Milk with your coffee?'

'Black for me. You don't know the name of the architect, do you?'

Dee, midway through plunging the cafetière, paused to look at him. 'What's it to you?'

'I studied architecture at uni,' he said. 'Never worked as an architect, mind. I mean, I loved it at the time, but I moved back to Ireland soon after graduating and ended up working as a production designer. Movies, TV, stuff like that. How about yourself?'

Dee put the cafetière, cups and a plate of biscuits on a tray. 'Here. Make yourself useful and carry this outside for me.'

More gushing when they were on the deck, but at least the view had taken his mind off the house.

'I don't know this part of the world at all,' he said. 'And this place… Look at the view. It's incredible.'

'Won't you sit down and have some coffee? All that hopping around is making me uncomfortable.'

'Sorry.' He sat as instructed. 'I'll pour, will I?'

'Thanks,' Dee said. 'And when you're done, you can tell me all about you and Katie.'

He frowned, a look that didn't suit him. He had a face made for smiling.

'Have a biscuit,' Dee said. She selected a chocolate chip cookie for herself and slid the plate towards him.

'You weren't the only person who's been trying to get in touch with me,' Tom said. 'My pal Brian – I think you contacted him as well? – sent me a link to the story. It said a woman had been killed in a hit and run and the police wanted to speak to Katie about the incident. There was a photo with it. That's why Brian sent it. He thought I'd be interested.'

'Why?'

'The way the story was written implied Katie was driving the car that ran the poor woman over.'

'That's what the police seem to think. Although they have no proof of that. It's true someone was killed. And it's also true that Katie hasn't been seen since it happened, but that doesn't necessarily mean she was the driver. You and Katie are friends – is that why you're here?'

'Not exactly,' Tom said. 'Maybe. I don't know. Yes, Katie's a friend. Was a friend. An ex-girlfriend. Although we only dated a few times. We both worked out pretty quickly that we were better suited as friends than anything else.'

'I knew it.' Dee spoke before she could stop herself. 'You're Jake's dad.'

'Jesus, no. We split up years ago. We kept in touch for a bit. She was in Australia by then, but we exchanged emails. She never said anything about a baby. And she would have, right? I mean, if she was pregnant and about to have a baby, surely she wouldn't have kept that from me?'

'I never knew she lived in Australia,' Dee said. 'But I didn't know much about her, I guess. You're the first friend of hers I've met.'

'She can be a bit difficult to get to know. Apart from me and Ella, I'm not sure she had many other friends.'

'Katie and Ella are friends then?' Another piece of the puzzle fitting into place. 'I've been wondering about that.'

'They *were* friends,' Tom corrected. 'It was Ella who introduced me to Katie. But that was ages ago. Ella and I split up and I started dating Katie soon after that. It caused a rift between them.'

Dee refilled both their cups before speaking.

'Let me make sure I understand this properly. You're a friend of Katie's.'

Tom nodded his head.

'And when she moved to Australia, the two of you stayed in email contact.'

'That's right.'

'And after she moved to Eastbourne?'

'That's the thing,' Tom said. 'Katie never moved to Eastbourne.'

'You've lost me.'

'It's not Katie. The woman in that news story. The one the police are looking for. She's not Katie Hope.'

'Bullshit,' Dee said. 'She rents that house from me. We've lived next door to each other for over two years. I've seen her almost every day. I sometimes get her post by mistake. I've got copies of her bank statements, a driving licence, employer references. If she's not Katie, then who the hell is she?'

'She's Ella,' Tom said. 'That's why Brian got in touch. He saw the photo and he knew it wasn't Katie. The woman the police are looking for is Ella Tate.'

Forty-One

Katie
Three years earlier

She's pregnant. The bump's not that big, but I noticed it right away. We haven't seen that much of each other recently. She didn't like it when Tom and I got together. She would have liked it a lot less if she'd known I was the reason they split up. I told him about my dad. Not everything, of course. All I had to do was tell him that Dad was killed and Ella was a witness at the trial. I acted as if I assumed he knew all about it. He played along as best he could, but he didn't fool me. I knew he'd ask her about it. And I knew she wouldn't be able to lie to him. She told him the truth and, unsurprisingly, he couldn't handle hearing what his perfect Ella was really like.

I thought Tom and I were meant to be, but things didn't work out the way I wanted. He wasn't ready for another relationship. We're still friends, and I pretend I'm okay with that. I never let on that he meant a lot more to me than I clearly did to him.

But we're not here today to talk about Tom. He's part of our shared history, but not part of our future. Shane's out of prison, and that's changed everything. Ella called me yesterday and we arranged to meet this morning for, in her words, 'a coffee and a catch-up'.

She's already there when I arrive. Sitting down, so I don't notice the bump until she stands up. When she sees me looking at it, she blushes and puts her hands over her stomach.

'Congratulations,' I say, doing my best to keep the tension out of my voice. 'Who's the lucky father?'

Tom swore they'd never get back together, but that was a year ago, and people can change. Besides, it was clear – even when he was with me – that he was still crazy about her. Despite everything she'd done, he wanted to be with her, not me.

'It was a one-night stand,' she says. 'I don't even know the guy's name.'

She doesn't say anything else, but she doesn't have to. It's enough. I couldn't bear it if she'd said it was Tom's. The two of them getting back together in spite of my best efforts. Tom choosing her over me, like everyone else has always done.

'I heard he's moving back to Ireland,' I say.

'Tom?' She shrugs like she doesn't care, but I know her better than that. Those red patches on her cheeks appear, and when she changes the subject, asking me if I want a coffee, there's a definite tremor in her voice.

'I'll go and order the drinks,' I tell her. 'You stay here. What would you like?'

By the time I come back a few minutes later, she's composed herself. She sips her lemon and ginger tea and smiles.

'The morning sickness is terrible,' she says. 'This is about the only thing I can drink without throwing it straight back up again.'

Too much information, but I smile and pretend I give a shit while I wait for her to get to the real reason she's contacted me. I don't have to wait long.

'Have you heard from Shane?' she asks.

'Shane?' I frown, pretending to look confused. 'Why would I hear from him?'

'Because you were visiting him when he was in prison. I sort of assumed you'd carry on seeing him when he got out.'

She's right, but no need to tell her that. We're seeing quite a bit of each other, as it happens. Prison's changed him. He's not the cocky, confident arsehole he used to be. If anything, he's a bit of a loser now. He keeps telling me he loves me, and maybe that's true. All I know for sure is that actions speak louder than words, and if he really loves me, he knows what he needs to do to prove it to me.

'I just want to get on with my life,' I tell her. 'Put all that behind me and look to the future. You can do that too, can't you? I mean, you've got a baby to look forward to. That's pretty exciting.'

'I'm scared,' she says.

'Oh Ella.' I reach across the table and take her hand. 'What's happened?'

She tells me, but there's no need. A week ago, she received a letter from someone who didn't sign their name. Naturally, she skips over the details, only saying that the content was 'threatening'. Which isn't quite true. I know exactly what the letter says because I typed it and hand-delivered it myself. It lays out exactly what Ella did, and ends by telling her she isn't going to get away with it. She's also had a series of text messages – also threatening – from a withheld number, and ten phone calls where, each time she answers, the person at the other end doesn't say anything.

Shane doesn't know about any of this. It's been harder than I thought, getting him to understand what needs to be done. Last night, he told me that all he wanted was to put the past behind him and get on with what's left of his life. Or 'our life', as he insists on calling it. As if I'm still that stupid fat seventeen-year-old girl who'll do anything he wants.

'I hope you've told the police all this,' I say, knowing she wouldn't dare.

'You think I should?' she says.

'Yes.' I squeeze her hand. 'You have to tell them. He sounds unhinged. You could be putting yourself and your baby in danger.'

She chews her lip. 'I don't know,' she says eventually. 'Maybe I should just leave. Go somewhere he'll never find me.'

'He'll find you wherever you go,' I say. 'If that's what he wants. But maybe it isn't. Look, he's only just got out, right? There's every chance he'll get bored with this and move on with his life. He must know if he keeps harassing you like this he'll end up back in prison.'

'I guess,' she says. 'Sorry, Katie. I just feel so confused and alone. My mum died a few months ago and I haven't been coping too well. I can't seem to get any perspective on things.'

'I'm sorry to hear about your mum,' I tell her. 'I didn't realise she'd passed away.'

'Cancer,' Ella says. 'It's been a horrible time. But you know better than anyone what it's like to lose both your parents.'

'It can feel very lonely,' I say. 'And I get how that loneliness can make you lose perspective. But I really think you need to stop worrying so much about Shane. Wait and see what happens over the next few weeks. If things get worse, we'll come up with a plan. Chances are nothing else will happen. He's had his fun and that's the end of it.'

'Okay.' She nods. 'Maybe you're right. I'm so glad I called you, Katie. I really don't know what I'd do without you.'

Forty-Two

Dee

'There must be some mistake,' Dee said.

'No mistake,' Tom said. 'I lived with her for three years. I'd know her anywhere.'

They were walking east along the beach, towards Normans Bay. They stayed on the stretch of sand that appeared when the tide was out. It made for an easier walk than clumping across the shingle higher up the beach.

Dee's mind was racing, chasing different pieces of information and trying to put them together into something coherent. But she couldn't get her mind past the fact that Katie – lovely, funny, kind Katie – was someone else entirely.

'You need to tell the police,' she said.

'I'm going to do that later today. I wanted to come here before speaking to them.'

'Why?'

'I'm not sure. Maybe I thought I'd find something that would explain what's going on. Or something that would help me find her. The police think it was Ella who killed that woman, don't they?'

'They think the woman who lived next door to me and called herself Katie Hope killed her,' Dee said. 'If she's really Ella, then yeah, they think she killed her.'

She didn't mention Shane Gilbert, but she couldn't stop thinking about him. If Billy was right, Shane had gone to prison for something he didn't do. Which meant Ella Tate and Roxanne Reed framed him. Which meant one of them had killed Katie's dad. If it was Ella, if she'd killed once before, would that make it easier for her to kill a second time? Dee had no idea, because there wasn't one part of her that could believe her friend – Katie or Ella or whatever her real name was – capable of something like that.

Waves lapped at her feet. Any minute now the tide would turn, and before long the sand would be covered over.

'We should turn back,' she said.

'You said the detective leading the investigation is called Ed Mitchell,' Tom said. 'But the person who contacted me was someone else. Lewis, I think?'

'Rachel Lewis. She works with Ed. We'll call her when we get back to the house.'

'What do I tell her?' Tom asked.

'You tell her what you told me. That the woman living in my mobile home for the last two and a half years isn't who we all thought she was.'

As it turned out, Ed was standing outside Dee's house when she and Tom got back from their walk. Dee introduced the two men to each other, explaining that Tom was a friend of Katie's who had some news Ed might be interested in.

'My colleague's been trying to contact you,' Ed said. 'You're a hard man to track down.'

'I've been travelling,' Tom said. 'Sorry. I've got a meeting with DC Lewis this afternoon.'

'Good,' Ed said. 'There are a few things we're hoping you can clear up for us.' He looked at Dee. 'Any chance of a coffee before we all start sharing what we know?'

Dee told them to sit on the deck while she made the coffee. Tom did as he was told, but Ed insisted on hovering inside, watching her in the kitchen. His presence irritated her, and the way he kept looking at her was making her feel self-conscious. She ran her fingers through her hair, trying to remember if she'd brushed it when she got up. And when she'd last washed it.

'How did you and this Tom guy hook up?' he asked.

'He's out there,' Dee said. 'Go and ask him your-self instead of interrogating me, okay?' She banged the cafetière onto the tray beside the mugs, milk and sugar. 'Open the back door so I can carry this outside.'

'I'll take it.' He leaned past her and lifted the tray before she could protest. As she watched him place it carefully down on the table and sit opposite Tom, she wondered if Ed Mitchell ever did anything he was told.

He waited until they were all sitting down and the coffee had been poured before asking Tom what he was doing here. Tom told him about the email he'd received from his friend. How he'd seen the photo and realised immediately that the woman the police were looking for was Ella, not Katie.

'I thought it was a mistake,' he said. 'You know, that they'd got the wrong photo. But that's not what's going on, is it?' He looked at Dee. 'You're her neighbour and you think she's Katie too. Which means that all this time, Ella's been pretending to be someone else.'

'How long were you with Ella?' Ed said.

'Three years.'

'Is Jake your son?'

'Jake?' Tom frowned. 'Oh, Katie's kid. No. Katie and I… that was years ago. We… Oh God. Shit.'

He put his cup down and stood up. Walked onto the beach and bent over, his hands on his knees, looking as if he was about to throw up. Dee went after him.

'Are you okay?' She put her hand on his shoulder. His whole body was shaking, and when he looked up at her, his eyes were bloodshot.

'Sorry.' He wiped his face and straightened his back. 'Jesus. It's the shock, you know?'

'Come and sit down,' Dee said. 'I'll get you some water.'

She and Ed waited while Tom sipped water from the glass Dee had filled. Gradually his face regained some colour, and after a few minutes he started to speak.

'Ella and I split up years ago,' he said. 'I was heart-broken at the time. Really devastated. I thought we'd be together forever, you know? We were planning to move to Australia. But she… she was complicated.' He looked at Ed. 'Do you know about Katie's father?'

'Gus Hope was killed in a fight that broke out in his pub one night,' Ed said. 'Ella Tate, your ex, was a prose-cution witness in the trial that found Shane Gilbert guilty of manslaughter.'

'That's right.' Tom nodded. 'Well, the whole thing caused a rift between us.'

'Why?' Ed asked.

Because she'd told him, Dee realised. She'd told Tom she'd lied and he couldn't handle it.

'Lots of reasons,' Tom said. 'Personal stuff that I don't want to talk about. The point is, we split up. Soon after that, I started dating Katie. That was a mistake. Classic rebound stuff. Anyway, things were already pretty bad between me and Ella. When she found out I was seeing Katie, that was the end of anything left between us. I moved to London soon afterwards. She stayed in Bristol.

'We might never have seen each other again, except I had to go to Bristol for a friend's wedding. We bumped into each other and went for a drink. Ended up sleeping together. The timing was crap because I was moving back to Ireland two days later. I thought we'd stay in touch. I begged her to, but she disappeared and I never saw her again.'

'When was that?' Dee asked, already knowing the answer.

'Three years ago,' Tom said. 'It was only one night. Like I said, I never heard from her again. But Jake – the boy – he's about the right age. Do you think… I mean, is there any chance he's mine?'

Dee thought of Jake, with his light brown hair, freckled skin and eyes just like Tom's.

'I think there's a pretty good chance.'

'We've had several people contact us over the last couple of weeks,' Ed said. 'All of them wanting to tell us that the woman in the photo we've been circulating is Ella Tate, not Katie Hope. For reasons we don't yet understand, Ella has been living in Eastbourne for the last two and a half years pretending to be Katie.'

'You already knew?' Tom said. He rubbed his hand up and down his face. 'Jesus. What the hell is she playing at?'

'At the moment, we think we're looking at a very clever case of identity theft.'

Dee waited for Tom to protest, to stand up and insist that the Ella he knew would never do something like that. But he sat silently, his face blank. She guessed it was too much for him to process in one go. Or else he knew more about the sort of person Ella really was than he was letting on.

'Ella was hiding,' she said. 'She was a witness at Shane Gilbert's trial. He was released from prison a few months before she moved here. Something must have happened after that. Something that scared her enough to pretend to be someone else.'

Her body was pumping with adrenaline. She was getting closer to finding them. She could feel it.

'How did she get away with it, though?' she wondered. 'How could she steal Katie's ID without Katie knowing anything about it?'

'I can't answer that,' Ed said. 'But I think that when Katie found out what she had done, she confronted her.'

'And then Ella killed her,' Dee said. 'Oh God. So the dead woman is Katie?'

'That's why we've been trying to contact you,' Ed told Tom. 'You, Roxanne Reed and Shane Gilbert are the only people we can find who knew both girls. Roxanne hasn't seen either of them for years. Shane Gilbert claimed he hadn't been in contact with them either. Which leaves you.'

'I've got a photo,' Tom said. He pulled his phone out of his pocket and started scrolling through it. 'I don't have any photos of Ella. I deleted them all one evening after I'd had too much to drink. But this is Katie. She sometimes sent me photos of herself when she emailed. I think she wanted to prove to me what a great time she was having in Australia. Here.'

He held the phone out so Dee and Ed could both see what was on the screen. The photo showed an attractive young woman standing on a beach in a bikini. Tanned skin, dark hair tied in a single plait that she wore over her left shoulder. Laughing and looking so alive that Dee's stomach hurt. Because she recognised her right away.

'Poor girl,' Ed said.

His voice startled her; she'd forgotten he was here. She'd forgotten everything except that moment she'd first seen the same woman lying face down in the dirt outside her house, the lower half of her body twisted away from the upper half and her glossy hair spread out across the dusty track.

Part Two

Forty-Three

Chugga-chugga-chugga, chugga-chugga-chugga. The sound drilled through Ella's head. She pressed her forehead against the glass, watching the world outside blur into flashes of green and blue as the train sped through the Sussex countryside.

Chugga-chugga-chugga, chugga-chugga-chugga.

'Jake!'

It came out harsher than she'd intended, and he looked up from his toy train, his little face crumpled up, ready to cry.

'Sorry,' she said. 'I'm sorry. Try not to be too noisy. It's not fair on the other passengers.'

She leaned into him, kissed his face and stared into his hazel eyes. He smiled, and Ella's insides somersaulted with love. Protecting him was the only thing that mattered.

'We're on a train, Mamma,' he said.

'Yes we are, darling.'

In the seat behind them, a man coughed. Ella tensed. She imagined Shane, watching her, waiting. No. She knew the man wasn't Shane. Shane wasn't on the train. She'd moved through every carriage when they'd first got on, scanning the faces of all the passengers, checking and double-checking he wasn't amongst them.

But knowing it and feeling it were two different things.

She shouldn't have run. She should have stayed in Eastbourne, faced up to what had happened and to hell with the consequences. Instead, she'd taken one look at Katie's dead body and panicked. Thrown a few things into an overnight bag, grabbed Jake and run. After that, the memories had got mixed up. Jake crying as she carried him out the back door. Sometime later, getting out of a taxi at the train station, handing a ten-pound note to the driver. Holding Jake's hand as the two of them ran across the station forecourt. Jumping on the next train to London. Her only thought to get away.

Because Shane had found her. Three years had passed. Ella had let her guard down, started to believe she was safe. And then two days ago, Katie had turned up out of the blue.

'Surprise, surprise,' she had said. Smiling at Ella like this was all one big adventure, then stepping past her into the house before she could stop her.

As she watched her crouch down to say hello to Jake, Ella knew Katie would have to go. Because she had promised there'd be no contact. They'd both agreed it was the only way to make this thing work. They'd kept in touch by email, which was just about okay. Although if it had been up to Ella, she'd have stopped that too. But she'd always felt sorry for Katie. More than anything, she knew how much she owed her, and if a few emails went some way to repaying that debt, then what right did she have to complain?

Another image. Katie pushing the buggy, wearing Ella's blue T-shirt. The shock on her face as the car hit her, the empty buggy flying out of her grasp and careering down the lane. And even though Jake hadn't been in the buggy, Ella imagined it as if he had been. His voice crying out in shock and fear as his little body crashed into the tree.

Stop it!

But she couldn't stop it. The memories kept coming. More and more of them, until they were the only thing she could see and feel and hear. Shane's face as he stood too close to her in the pub that night. His tongue inside her mouth. A flash of blinding light and the sudden splash of warm liquid on her face and hands and arms. Looking down and seeing blood. Lots of blood.

Chugga-chugga-chugga, chugga-chugga-chugga.

Glastonbury 2014. In the silent-disco tent with Tom. Everyone was listening to music through headphones instead of a traditional speaker system. If you didn't wear headphones, you didn't hear any music. Ella couldn't remember what she'd been listening to, but she could remember Tom dancing to the music playing through his headphones. Different music to Ella's. Dancing to a different beat. His body moving wildly and with abandon. He'd never cared what anyone thought of him. It was one of the many reasons she'd loved him.

Their eyes met. Tom smiled, and Ella, who until then hadn't been sure about Glastonbury, who had found the noise and crowds and dirt and chaos all too much, experienced a moment of such pure, perfect happiness that she would happily have spent the rest of her life in that tent if only she could make that feeling last forever.

Tears burned her eyes. She wiped them away, but more came. Running down her cheeks, pooling in the hollow spot at the bottom of her throat.

'Mamma.' Jake's hand on her arm. His little face scrunched with worry. His voice dragging her away from Tom and everything else. 'Look.'

He pointed a chubby finger at the window. At some point, the Sussex countryside had disappeared, replaced by the suburban edges of south London. Ella looked at the houses and the roads lined with cars and the tiny green parks and the church spires, without really seeing them. Instead, all she could see was Katie's body on the road after she'd been run over. Someone would have found her by now. It was only a matter of time before the police worked out who Ella really was. And when that happened, she would have to face up to what she'd done. Finally.

All these years spent hiding the truth, pretending – even to herself – that she hadn't done a terrible thing. And now here she was, possibly only days away from being arrested anyway. It was almost funny. Except there was nothing funny about two people killed for nothing more than being in the wrong place at the wrong time.

Forty-Four

Dee

When Alex showed up that evening, he was the last person Dee wanted to spend time with.

'Can we take a rain check?' she said. 'I really need an early night.'

Alex ignored her. 'Noticed your pal Ed was here earlier.'

There was no balance in their friendship. Alex knew where she lived, and he came to see her whenever he felt like it. While she didn't have a clue what part of town he lived in, what times he might be at home or when was the best time to visit. The only thing she could control was whether to let him in. And tonight, she was determined not to.

'He's not my pal,' she said.

'Did he have any news on Katie?' Alex asked.

It would be so easy to invite him in. Open the bottle of wine he was carrying and tell him everything over a few drinks. She'd spent the afternoon on her laptop, researching ID theft. It was a growing problem, apparently. Criminals got hold of someone's personal information and used it for their own gain. The many different ways someone could take your name, date of birth and address and pretend to be you was frankly scary as shit.

She might have given in and said he could stay. Except right then he put the bottle of wine on the table and sat down, crossing his legs as if he was settling in for the evening.

'I told you,' she said. 'Not tonight, Alex. Okay?'

'Fine.' He grabbed the bottle and pulled open the back door. 'Thanks for nothing, Dee.'

As he walked away, his feet crunching across the shingle, Dee wasn't sure if she felt relief or disappointment that he was gone. Because now she was on her own, the rest of the evening stretching ahead – an empty space she didn't know how to fill.

Twenty minutes later, her phone rang. When she saw Ed's name on the screen, she didn't pick up. She was still angry with him for withholding so much information from her. It turned out the police had known the victim's identity for over a week. Once they'd discovered the ID fraud, they'd gone back and checked old dental records for Katie Hope, confirming what Tom had told them today. The dead woman was Katie.

So far, they had kept this information to themselves. Unsure who else might be involved in the fraud, they didn't want to reveal what they knew to the wider public. Now that Dee and Tom both knew the victim's real identity, Ed told Dee that the situation had changed and she should keep an eye on the news over the next few days.

When her phone rang again, she answered without checking the caller ID.

'I don't want to speak to you right now,' she said.

'Dee? It's Tom. Ella's ex?' He said it like a question. As if she might not remember who he was.

'Sorry,' Dee said. 'I thought you were someone else. You okay?'

'I'm not sure. I can't stop thinking about Ella and Katie. I didn't know who else I could talk to.'

'It's fine,' Dee said. 'I can't think about anything else either.'

They had talked the whole thing to death earlier and she'd thought there was nothing else to say. Turned out she was wrong.

'Ed said he'd spoken to Roxanne Reed,' Tom said. 'Do you remember that? She told him she hadn't seen Katie or Ella in years. But that doesn't make sense. Ella and Roxanne were really close. They were always emailing and phoning each other.'

Roxanne Reed. The pub landlady who had made a liar out of Leonard Mann.

'You think Roxanne knows where Ella is?' Dee said.

'Maybe. I should be telling this to Ed, not you, I guess.'

'I get the feeling you don't want to. Otherwise you wouldn't have called me.'

'I'd like the chance to see them first,' Tom said. 'Ella and Jake. If he's my son, I need to know. The thing is, all I have is Roxanne's name. I've no idea where she lives or how to find her. Will you help me, Dee?'

'If you agree that we tell the police right after you've spoken to her. And you have to tell them everything, Tom.'

Silence on the other end, stretching out so long, Dee thought maybe he'd hung up.

'Of course,' he said eventually. 'I only want to see them. That's all.'

After she'd hung up, Dee called Trevor. 'I need to speak to you about Leonard Mann,' she said, when she got his voicemail. 'Call me as soon as you get this.'

She was starting to piece together everything that had happened, although there were still too many gaps. She knew who had killed Gus Hope, but she didn't know why. She knew why Ella had pretended to be someone else, but she still had no clue how she had managed to steal Katie's ID and get away with it for so long.

At some point, Katie had found out about the ID theft and had come to Eastbourne to confront Ella. Ed thought Ella had killed Katie to keep her secret safe. But whatever lies Ella had told, Dee couldn't believe that.

Something about the physical similarities between the two girls was still bugging her. It was possible, wasn't it, that Shane Gilbert had also found out where Ella was hiding. He'd come to Eastbourne to kill her, seen Katie and thought she was Ella, and killed her instead.

Except the coincidence of Katie and Shane both turning up in Eastbourne at the same time didn't make any sense. Unless they were working together. The more Dee thought about, the more she realised it was the only possibility that made any sense. Katie and Shane had been dating when Katie's father was killed. Maybe their relationship had continued after he went to prison. Dee couldn't imagine ever wanting to date someone accused of killing her father, but that didn't mean anything. Nowt as queer as folk, and all that.

Her head hurt from trying to make sense of it all. She went into the kitchen to make herself a camomile tea. Midway through filling the kettle, she turned off the tap and poured herself a glass of wine instead. She drank it quickly and refilled the glass. Acid burned her stomach. If she was going to continue drinking, she should eat something. She threw a couple of slices of processed cheese between two pieces of white bread and ate it in the sitting room, watching the sky darken as night drew in.

A sudden smattering of hailstones against the window made her jump. The plate fell off her lap, the remaining bits of sandwich spilling onto the ground. Cursing, she cleared it up and threw the mess into the bin.

As she opened the fridge to get more wine, she saw something flash past outside the window. She tensed, half expecting to see Shane Gilbert's face loom up against the glass. Then she remembered the foxes she'd seen recently and realised that was all it was.

She opened the back door and stepped onto the deck. The hail had stopped but the wood was covered in melting white balls of ice, making it slippery. Carefully, so she didn't fall on her backside, she walked across the deck and onto the shingle.

The beach was vast and dark and silent. And very beautiful. She walked down the slope until she reached the water. She stood very still, her body relaxing as her breathing fell into the same rhythm as the sea as it rolled in and out over the shingle.

Across to her left, the lights of Bexhill and Hastings twinkled on the edge of the black ocean. The silver slice of a new moon curved above the sea. Flashes of white foam crested the surface of the water.

There was no sign of any foxes.

A flash of lightning split open the dark sky. Dee had a snapshot view of sea and shingle before the world was plunged into darkness again. And then the thunder came, a single explosion of sound that shook right through her. It started to rain, sheets of water pouring out of the sky.

Drenched through, pushing her soaking hair back from her face, she ran back towards the house. She'd left the sitting room light on, and she could see the sofa and the TV and the table where she'd been working on her laptop earlier. It was all blurred because of the rain battering the window. Even so, she could make out enough to know that the laptop was gone.

As she ran, she heard something behind her. It sounded like footsteps, but when she swung around, scanning the beach, there was no one there. She strained her ears, but it was impossible to hear anything over the clatter of rain battering the sea and shingle.

She turned back to the house, using the light from the sitting room to guide her. She was almost at the deck when a shape rose up in front of her, blocking out the light. The sudden darkness disoriented her, made her slow to react.

She saw his arm, swiping towards her face. She jerked sideways, but not quickly enough. His fist caught the side of her head, and an explosion of pain burst through her ear. She stumbled and fell, landing on her elbow, then scrabbled forward, shingle shifting and sliding beneath her as she tried to get up. But again she wasn't fast enough. His weight landed on her, knocking the air from her body, pressing her into the cold, hard stones. She screamed and thrashed and bucked against him, trying to knock him off her. She tried to hit him and kick him, but she was on her stomach, and her fists and feet couldn't get near him.

He grabbed a handful of her hair, yanked her head back and smashed her face into the ground. Flashes of white light exploded inside her brain. Blood in her mouth.

Something broken. Teeth or nose or everything. Too much pain to understand what was going on.

His hands wrapped around her neck, and there was a brief moment of relief. Because if he killed her, the pain would be over. He was strong. Hands squeezing the life from her, blocking her airway. She couldn't breathe, pressure building up inside her head, and any moment now it would explode and she would be gone.

Suddenly, she didn't want it to end. Dredging up one final surge of energy, she jerked her head back. Felt it connect with something and heard a howl of pain. The pressure on her neck disappeared and air rushed down her throat, filling her lungs, choking her all over again.

She crawled forward, hands fumbling on the stones. Grabbing the biggest one she could find, she swung around in time to see him lunging for her through the rain. With a scream of pure rage, her arm went up and out and she smashed the stone as hard as she possibly could into the side of his head. He fell forward, his entire weight landing on top of her. Still screaming, she hit him again, and again.

Rain poured down on them, water mixing with the blood on Dee's face. The man lay on top of her, not moving. She tried to push him off, but he was too heavy. She shifted her body, trying to slide out from under him. The stones beneath her moved too. She tried again, and kept trying. It took all she had, but at last she managed to wriggle free.

When she was able to, she struggled upright. It was only when she was standing that the full impact of what had just happened hit her. She started to shake. Her stomach contracted. She twisted away from the body, vomiting onto the stones, the acid stink of her own puke rising through the wet air.

She staggered into the house, closed the bifold doors, locking them so no one could get inside. There was a switch on the wall for the outside light. She pressed it, and the beach and deck were illuminated so she could see him. A dark shape lying on the shingle, about ten feet from the house.

She knew there was something she was meant to do, but her brain couldn't work out what that was. She looked around the room, unsure what she was looking for, until she saw her mobile phone lying on the sofa.

She picked it up, hands shaking so badly it took three attempts to dial the digits she needed.

A woman's voice. 'Emergency services, how can I direct your call?'

'Police,' Dee said.

The woman said something Dee didn't catch, distracted by the drip, drip of blood falling from her face and splashing onto the parquet floor that her mother had loved so much.

There was someone else on the phone now, a man, asking Dee if she was in any immediate danger.

'It's not me,' she said. 'I'm okay. But he's not. I think I've killed him.'

'Who's dead?' The man had a kind voice, but she knew this wasn't who she needed right now.

'I have to speak to Ed Mitchell,' she said. 'Tell him it's Dee Doran. Tell him I've killed someone and the body's lying outside my house and I don't know what to do.'

The man started to say something else, but Dee didn't hear it because she'd already hung up. The blood from her broken nose was still dripping onto the floor. She knew she needed to wipe her face, but she didn't have the energy even to lift her hands.

After a while, the steady rhythm of her blood splashing onto the polished floor became soothing. Her body swayed in time with each drop that hit the ground. She closed her eyes, but he was still there, branded onto the inside of her brain. The dark shape of his body lying ten feet from where she stood.

Forty-Five

Dee

The doorbell was ringing; someone was banging on the front door and a man was shouting her name. The world was moving in slow motion. Every noise took an age to reach her, every movement she made dragged on forever.

She reached the front door, but it was still boarded up, so she had to open the hall window instead.

'Dee! Thank God.'

Ed.

She tried to say his name, but the hard lump in her throat made it impossible to speak. He lifted himself up and through the window and put his arms around her.

'It's okay,' he said. 'Everything's going to be okay.'

He was lying.

Flashes of blue light blinked through the open window. Shadows moved about outside. Dee recognised Rachel Lewis's short, stocky figure amongst them. It wasn't okay. Ed was here to arrest her, because she'd killed someone.

Sometime later, they were in the living room. Dee was sitting on the sofa, a blanket wrapped around her shoulders and a wad of tissues in her hand to soak up the blood still coming out of her broken nose. Ed sat beside her, holding the hand that didn't have the tissues while he spoke to someone on his mobile phone.

'Stay back for now. Let me speak to her first. Have the paramedics on standby. She's going to need medical treatment.'

When he'd finished, he put the phone into his jacket pocket and asked Dee if she was able to tell him what had happened.

The outside light was still on, but she couldn't see the body from where she was sitting. She never wanted to see it again, but she knew that at some point she'd have to take Ed outside and show him where it was.

Her eyes drifted around the room, landing on the empty table. 'My laptop.' When she spoke, her throat felt as if she was rubbing sandpaper across it.

'Here.' Ed held a glass of water to her lips and she took a sip.

'Thanks,' she whispered, pushing the glass away.

'Think you're ready to talk?'

She told him everything, starting from the moment she saw something flash past the window, finishing with the sickening sound of bone crunching when she hit him with the stone. Killing him.

'It must have been terrifying,' Ed said when she stopped talking.

Tears pricked her eyes and she looked away so he wouldn't notice. 'It's my fault.'

'No,' Ed said. 'He attacked you, Dee. You were defending yourself, that's all. From what you've told me, it wasn't like you had a choice. Jesus.' He rubbed a hand down his face. 'Thank God you were able to fight back.'

'I contacted Shane Gilbert.' There. She'd said it.

'Sorry?'

'I found out where he's living and I went to visit him. He wouldn't speak to me. But I left him my name and contact details. The day my house was broken into? I was in London waiting to meet him. Only he never turned up.'

'Jesus Christ.' Ed leapt up, walked to the other side of the room, as if he wanted to put as much distance between them as possible. 'What the *hell* do you think you're playing at, Dee? You promised, remember? I asked you to keep your nose out of this police investigation and you promised me you'd do that.'

'I never promised anything. You issued an order that you expected me to obey whether I liked it or not.'

'Listen to yourself. You sound like some spoilt kid who hasn't got their own way. You could have been killed. Do you understand that? It could be you lying out there right now. From what you've told me you, it almost *was* you. And look at you. You're a mess. Christ only knows what else is broken besides your nose. There could be permanent damage to your vocal cords, broken ribs, concussion, anything.'

'You're saying I should sit back and do nothing?' Dee said, anger making her forget how much pain she was in. 'She was my neighbour, Ed. And that little boy… I love him. I loved that they lived next door. I loved knowing I'd see him grow up, watch him having parties with his friends down on the beach like I used to. It made me feel…'

She stopped, but it was too late. She'd caught the look of pity on his face and hated him even more than she had a moment earlier.

'I can't let them simply disappear,' she said. 'I'm a journalist and I'm going to use everything I've learned as a journalist to find them. This is what I do, whether you like it or not.'

'Bullshit,' Ed said. 'You told me yourself you haven't worked in over two years. If I stopped working, do you think it would be okay for me to go on calling myself a detective two years later? I'd be a *retired* detective, like you're a *retired* journalist who's made the decision to waste your days away with a lowlife like Alex Mackey, who has a wife and should know better.'

'How fucking dare you.'

'Someone needs to tell you the truth,' Ed said. 'And Mackey sure as hell isn't going to do that. Not when he's got you waiting around for him every evening like some sad schoolgirl who doesn't know any better. You do realise you're not the only one? Oh, I forgot. You're a journalist. You'll already have it all worked out, I'm sure.'

Dee was considering the various ways she could tell Ed Mitchell to get out of her house and never come back when his phone started to ring. He turned away from her to answer it, and it took all she had not to leap off the sofa and attack him, screaming and punching every bit of judgemental crap from his body.

'Rachel,' he said. 'You sure about that? Okay, let me speak to her.'

He finished the call and turned back to Dee.

'Dee, can you come outside and show me where the body is?'

Every instinct Dee possessed recoiled at the thought of going back out there, but she wasn't about to let Ed see how she felt. She stood up, waited for the room to stop spinning, and went out to the deck.

'Down there somewhere?' Ed asked.

The outside light gave her a clear view of the scene. The shingle, still wet from the earlier rain, was slick and black under the glaring light. She scanned the beach, trying to locate the exact spot. She knew where it was, because the memory of looking at him from inside the house was seared onto her brain. Except the place where he'd been lying was empty.

The body was gone.

Forty-Six

Ella
Three weeks earlier

Victoria station. A blur of bodies and movement and noise. Ella pushed her way through the crowds, disorientated. She held tight to Jake's hand, terrified that if she let him go for a second, she'd lose him. She saw a row of metal chairs and collapsed into one of them, pulling Jake onto her lap. A pair of police officers walked past, a man and a woman, eyes scanning the crowd as if they were looking for someone.

She buried her face in the top of Jake's head. When she looked up again, the officers were gone. She couldn't stay here. Her every move would be tracked by CCTV. There were probably cameras all over the station, sending her image to a bank of screens. If the cameras didn't catch her, there were so many other ways she could be found. As soon as she took cash out, there'd be a record of that somewhere; they could track her from the GPS signal on her phone as well. She'd switched her phone off on the train, but she wasn't sure if that was enough, or if there was something else she should do to stop it alerting the police to her location.

'Come on, Jakey. Let's go.'

She stood up, but he started to cry when she tried to get him to walk. She tugged his arm, trying to pull him forward, but that only made him cry louder. Aware of faces turning to look at them both, she sat back down again.

She needed help. Balancing Jake on her lap, she took her phone out of her bag and switched it on. She'd already called Roxanne from the train, but had got her voicemail and hadn't bothered leaving a message. She called her again. This time, she left a message.

'It's me. Can you call me as soon as you get this? Something's happened.'

She didn't know how she was going to find the words to tell Roxanne that Katie was dead. Katie, who for so many years had been the closest thing Roxanne had to a daughter of her own. Even if the two of them had drifted apart after the trial and hadn't spoken to each other in years, Ella knew Roxanne would be devastated.

She scrolled through the list of contacts on her phone, wondering who else she would call. Dee was the person she most wanted to speak to. But she didn't think Dee would want anything to do with her when she found out the sort of person Ella really was. A liar. And worse.

Most of the other contacts in her phone were parents of the students she taught. Apart from one name. Someone she hadn't spoken to in years. Phoning him now, asking for help, was a risk. But what choice did she have?

She couldn't focus. Her mind kept racing back to places she didn't want it to go. To the night it happened. Shane and Gus and the bottle breaking and the blood. So much blood. Gus holding his hands to his neck, the look of surprise on his face right before he fell. To all those years later, in Bristol, when Shane got out of prison and came looking for her. To yesterday morning, on the beach with Katie and Jake. Building a sandcastle on the sandy strip that appeared when the tide was out. Waiting for the sea to come back in and wondering how she was going to tell Katie to leave. Watching the castle being slowly erased until there was no sign of it.

Like the sandcastle, the image faded, replaced by Katie again. Being so greedily needy that Ella wanted to scream. When she offered to go to the shops, Ella said okay, because at least that would give her time to think. She gave Katie a list, telling her to take the buggy because it was handy for carrying the shopping...

She wanted to shut her mind down, stop all the images, but her mind was something she could no longer control. The fear was a wave she was drowning under. Her throat closed over, her chest so tight and sore she couldn't bear it. She shut her eyes, tried to breathe slowly and focus. But how could anyone focus when there were so many people, and Jake was wriggling and squirming in her lap, his feet kicking against her shins?

She opened her eyes. And there was Shane. He was on the other side of the concourse, walking towards her. Pushing his way through the crowds in his rush to reach her. She stood up, Jake in her arms, and started running in the opposite direction. People shouted at her as she jostled against them, but she ran on, ignoring them. She ran until her heart was pounding and her breath was burning the back of her throat.

She looked over her shoulder, scanning the faces in the crowd as she stumbled forward. She couldn't see him, but it was impossible to make out any one individual. The sea of faces blurred together, eyes and noses and mouths. The weight of Jake in her arms was too much. She put him down and took his hand in hers, ready to move forward once more.

Someone grabbed her shoulder, the sudden contact making her scream. She jumped sideways. Saw the man she'd thought was Shane stepping back, hands in the air.

'I didn't mean to startle you,' he said. 'You dropped this as you were getting off the train. I tried to shout after you, but you didn't hear me.'

He lowered his right hand and she saw he was holding Jake's toy train. His little blue Thomas the Tank Engine that he would be devastated to lose. She hadn't even noticed it was missing.

'Thank you so much,' she managed, taking the train and handing it to Jake.

'No problem,' the man said. 'I've got a boy about the same age as yours.' He looked as if he was going to say something else, so Ella thanked him once more, said they were late for their next train and hurried away. When she looked behind her again, he was gone.

Holding Jake's hand, she made her way outside the station. There was a hotel across the road. She went inside, located the bar and sat at a table by the window, watching people hurry along on the street outside. In contrast to the hustle and bustle of the station, there were barely any people in the bar. For the first time since arriving in London, she was able to clear her mind enough to think. Roxanne still hadn't called her back, and she couldn't afford to wait until she did. Which left her with only one other option.

He answered after four rings.

'Hello?'

She paused, unsure whether to speak or hang up.

'Ella? Is that you?'

'I'm in trouble,' she said. 'Roxanne's not answering her phone. I didn't know who else to call. Will you help me, Leonard?'

Forty-Seven

Dee

'Got everything?' Louise asked.

'I think so,' Dee said. Except it sounded like *I dink do*. Speaking with a broken nose wasn't easy. 'And I don't care if I've forgotten something. I want to get out of here.'

She'd spent the night in hospital. When she finally got to be examined by the consultant, in the early hours of the morning, she was told she needed to stay in for twelve hours before they'd allow her to go home. An hour ago, she'd been declared fit to leave, on condition she was able to arrange for someone to come and pick her up.

'You look terrible,' Louise said when she saw the damage to Dee's face and neck. 'Will they be able to fix your nose, or are you going to need surgery?'

Dee's nose had been bandaged and held in place with surgical tape. She had two black eyes and a trail of purple bruises around her neck. Her throat was raw and aching, although the consultant said there was no lasting injury.

'It's not as bad as it looks.'

'I should hope not,' Louise said.

'You should see the other guy,' Dee joked, before remembering that was the one thing Louise couldn't do. Because the other guy had disappeared.

The police had searched the beach and the entire area around Dee's house and there was no one out there. On the one hand, this was a good thing, because it meant she hadn't killed him. But it also meant that whoever had attacked her was still out there.

'I went to the supermarket,' Louise said once they were in the car. 'Got you some supplies. I wasn't sure if you'd be well enough to go to the shops. What about painkillers? I didn't think to get any. Sorry. It was only when I saw you that I realised you might need them.'

'I got some at the hospital,' Dee said.

Every part of her body ached. All she wanted to do was curl up on the sofa, switch on the TV and block out everything else.

'Your voice sounds funny,' Louise said.

'I've got a broken nose. What do you expect?'

Home had always been her sanctuary. Now, as Louise turned right after the harbour and Dee's house appeared, the memories from the previous night rushed back.

She didn't want to be here.

'You could always stay at mine for a few days,' Louise said. She pulled up outside the house and switched the engine off. 'Dee?'

'I'm okay.' Dee released her seat belt and opened the door, climbing out of the car before she weakened and changed her mind.

Louise insisted on carrying the shopping inside, telling Dee to get the kettle on. 'I'll have a coffee before I go,' she said. 'It'll give you a chance to tell me what happened last night.'

'You know what happened. Someone broke into my house, stole my laptop and decided to knock fifty shades of shite out of me.' Her head was aching, and her throat was so raw it felt as if it would close up unless she drank something right away.

'Coffee's ready,' Louise said. 'Let's sit down and you can tell me what's really going on here. I want to know who broke in and why they stole your laptop. It's all connected, isn't it? The dead girl and...' she gestured at Dee's face, 'that.'

They took their coffee outside. Dee was working out how much she should tell Louise when the doorbell rang.

'Stay there,' Louise said, standing up. 'If it's that creep Alex Mackey, I'm not letting him inside the house.'

Dee listened as Louise answered the door, the low murmur of voices as she spoke to whoever was there. Then footsteps, and she appeared on the deck with Ed Mitchell trailing behind her.

'I'll get you a cup,' she said. 'There's plenty of coffee left and I'm sure you could do with some after the night you've had.'

'Not for me,' Ed said, speaking to Louise but looking at Dee. There was something in his face Dee didn't like.

'What is it?' she said.

'Mind if I sit down?' He'd never asked before. Always sat down uninvited, like he belonged here. Dee hadn't liked it, but she preferred it to this sudden politeness, which felt so wrong.

'Ed?'

He pulled out one of the wicker chairs and sat down. Crossed his legs and cleared his throat. Doing it all slowly and carefully. Stalling. Putting off whatever he'd come here to tell her.

It was Jake. Had to be. Dee's chest hurt from holding in the grief already building inside her.

'I've got some bad news,' he said.

She shook her head. She didn't want to hear it. But Ed kept going regardless.

'It's your ex-husband,' he said. 'William.'

'Billy,' Dee said. 'He hates being called William.'

'Billy then,' Ed said. 'I'm sorry, Dee. Billy's dead.'

Dee knew she'd misheard him, because Billy couldn't be dead. Billy, with his smile that made you feel good no matter what sort of a day you were having. Smart, clever, funny wild boy Billy raging through life like a fire that would never burn out. Her first love.

'No.' It wasn't true. She felt a surge of hatred for Ed Mitchell.

'There's something else,' Ed said.

Dee's stomach contracted, and she tasted vomit. But she didn't move from her seat, because she needed to hear the rest of it. The words left his lips and travelled across to her in slow motion. As if the sound had to fight its way through a wall of cotton wool.

Her head was full of Billy. Memory after memory. Their wedding day. A pissed-up party in Las Vegas. Twenty of their close friends. Billy in a white tux; an Elvis impersonator crooning love songs in the chapel. Everyone singing along to 'Can't Help Falling in Love'. Dee had cried, like she was crying now, except on that day they were tears of pure joy. Before that. The first time she'd ever seen him. Standing at the bar of the Lamb and Flag surveying the entire pub before his eyes found her and he gave her that big smile. Knowing she was lost right then, and not caring, because he was still smiling as she walked over to him and introduced herself.

'Dee?'

Ed's voice dragged her away from it all, reminding her she could never get that back. That Billy – her beautiful, wild Billy – was dead.

'He had your laptop.'

She heard him, but the words made no sense and she had to repeat them, out loud, twice, before their meaning kicked in. And even then, she didn't understand.

'We're working on the assumption that Billy stole your laptop,' Ed said.

'He wouldn't,' she whispered.

Images of the night before flashed through her head. The rain and the weight of the man's body on top of her, the strength in his hands as they wrapped around her neck, choking the life from her. A bigger, stronger man than Billy.

'We think he had an accomplice,' Ed said.

'I don't understand.'

'His body was found by Maidstone police. At the bottom of the stairs in the block of flats where Shane Gilbert lives.'

He said something else. Dee watched his mouth moving. Heard the words swimming in the air around her. But she couldn't make sense of them. Couldn't make sense of anything. Her head was too full of Billy to speak and her heart was too broken to imagine a world where he no longer existed.

Forty-Eight

Ella
Three weeks earlier

'Tell me again,' Roxanne said. 'From the beginning.'

Ella didn't want to go through it a second time. Telling Roxanne the first time had been a harrowing experience. She'd sat opposite her old friend, watching the confusion on her face turn to disbelief, then grief, as she described what had happened to Katie.

'Shane killed her,' she said. 'He drove straight into her, then reversed and drove over her while she was still on the ground. She didn't stand a chance.'

They were sitting in Roxanne's kitchen. Leonard had picked Ella and Jake up from Victoria and taken them to Roxanne's home in Chislehurst on the southern edges of Greater London. When he heard what had happened to Katie, he wanted to stay to comfort Roxanne, but she wouldn't let him.

'I'll call you tomorrow,' she told him, kissing his cheek before showing him out. 'I promise.'

Ella had put Jake to bed half an hour ago. He'd fallen asleep quickly, and she'd spent the time since then talking with Roxanne.

'Katie turned up two days ago,' she said. 'It was completely out of the blue. I didn't even know she was back in the country. Jake and I had spent the morning on the beach. He was tired, so I'd switched on the TV for him while I did some ironing. When the doorbell rang, I thought it was Alex. Remember the guy I told you about? We'd had a row. I thought he was my friend, but he was just some sleazy married guy looking for a bit on the side. I didn't want to see him, so I didn't answer the door. But it rang again and I thought, he's not going to go away, so I went to answer it. Only it wasn't Alex.'

She paused, remembering the shock, like a punch in the stomach, when she'd opened the front door and seen Katie standing there.

'She seemed to think it was okay, dropping in on me like that, but I wasn't sure how I felt about it.' She paused. 'No,' she said. 'That's not true. I was angry with her.'

'Why?'

'Because she shouldn't have been there.'

How to explain it to someone who couldn't know what it felt like to live almost three years of your life pretending to be someone else?

'When I asked her why she'd come, she said, why not? Like it was the most normal thing in the world. And I thought maybe she was right and it *was* normal, and I was the one with the problem. So I let her stay. Told her it was great to see her.'

Consumed with self-loathing, Ella wondered what was wrong with her. All Katie had wanted was a bit of company, and she had begrudged her even that.

'I should have stayed,' she said. 'But when I saw what he'd done, I panicked. I thought he was going to come for me and Jake next. I grabbed Jake and got the hell out of there. I was in shock, but that's no excuse, is it?'

'No excuse for what?'

'For leaving her. She didn't deserve that.'

Roxanne pushed her chair back and stood up. She went to the sink and refilled the kettle. Her back was to the table, so Ella couldn't see her face. But she could imagine it. Roxanne would never have left Katie like that. No one in their right mind would have done that.

'I'm going to check on Jake,' she said.

Roxanne didn't answer. Ella wished there was something she could say that would make this better, but she knew there were no words for that. So she left Roxanne standing at the worktop and went into the spare bedroom where Jake was sleeping.

He was lying on his back, sprawled across the double bed he was sharing with Ella for as long as they stayed here. Which wouldn't be long, judging by how things were going so far. The steady rhythm of his breathing soothed her. She touched his face, feeling the smooth, warm skin. Marvelling as she so often did at his very existence.

He didn't deserve to be drawn into this mess. His life so far had been free of stress and fear and anxiety. She had to do everything she could to keep it that way. Yet even as she thought this, she knew time was already running out.

Earlier this evening, she'd switched on the TV and seen her own face staring out at her. She'd had to put her hand across her mouth to stop herself crying out with shock. Jake had started laughing, pointing at the TV and shouting, 'Mamma, Mamma!'

It was a photo of the two of them on the beach. Alex had taken it and presented the framed print to her one evening. At the time, she'd thought it was a sweet gesture.

Later, when she knew the sort of person he really was, she thought it was creepy.

On the TV, they were still calling her Katie. But it was only a matter of time before someone from her old life saw the photo and recognised her.

Back in the kitchen, Roxanne had made more tea. She put the teapot on the table, then sat down and gestured for Ella to do the same.

'I need to ask you something,' she said. 'You said it was Shane driving the car that killed her. Are you absolutely certain about that?'

'Positive,' Ella said.

'What if you're mistaken? It wouldn't be the first time, love, would it?'

Three years ago, Ella had gone to the police and accused Shane of stalking her and breaking into her house in Bristol. They'd told her this wasn't possible. Shane was living and working in Maidstone in Kent. He was wearing a security tag that monitored his location. He hadn't left Maidstone any time over the previous two months. Whatever Ella thought Shane had been doing to her, she was wrong.

'That was different,' she said. 'That time, I never actually saw him. But I did today, Roxanne. I know what I saw.'

'So you're telling me that two days ago, Katie turned up at your place in Eastbourne. You weren't too happy about it, but you went along with it. Because you didn't think you had any choice. Because you felt you owed her. Is that right?'

Ella nodded.

'And then this morning, even though you haven't seen or heard from him in all the time you've been living in Eastbourne, Shane Gilbert turns up as well. And he drives into Katie and kills her.'

'I know how it sounds,' Ella said. 'But that's what happened.'

'How did he find you? And why now – exactly at the same time as Katie was visiting you? That's not a coincidence, Ella. That's impossible.'

'Unless she told him how to find me.'

'She wouldn't do that,' Roxanne said. 'She hated him more than you did. She thought he killed her father, remember?'

'Maybe he convinced her he was innocent,' Ella said. 'I know she'd been to see him in prison. What if she carried on seeing him after he came out?'

More memories from that night. She'd tried so hard to put it behind her, to never think about it again. But now she'd started, she couldn't stop.

'Oh God.' She put a hand over her mouth as she realised. 'Katie didn't work it out. She didn't have to. She was there. We were about to have a drink together. I thought it was good that we were finally speaking. I took it as a sign she was getting over Shane.

'When he came into the bar, I forgot about Katie. Afterwards, everything was so messed up, it never occurred to me to wonder where she'd gone. If I thought about her at all, I assumed she'd heard his voice and couldn't face seeing him so she went up to the flat. But I don't think that's what happened. I think she stayed downstairs and saw everything.'

'No way,' Roxanne said. 'Gus was her dad. If she'd known who killed him, she would never have kept quiet about it. She'd have wanted justice.'

'Shane treated her badly. He really hurt her. Maybe it suited her to see him punished like that.'

'Poor Katie.' Roxanne buried her face in her hands. 'She must have hated us so much. No wonder she wanted nothing to do with me after I bought the pub. I really let her down, didn't I?'

'We both did. We thought getting rid of Shane was the answer to everything. Instead, all we did was make things worse.'

'You need to tell the police,' Roxanne said. 'He killed her. We owe it to Katie to make sure he pays for what he did.'

'I know it's what I should do. But I can't tell the police what Shane did without telling them why. And if I do that, they'll arrest me and I'll end up in prison. We both will, Roxanne.'

'It's what we deserve,' Roxanne said.

'It's what *I* deserve. And I wouldn't care if it was just me. But I can't do that to Jake. I'm all he has. I won't leave him. I'll do whatever it takes to make sure that doesn't happen.'

'So we just hide out here and say nothing? We can't do that. Can't you simply tell the police what you saw today? Gus's death doesn't have to come into it.'

'I've spent the last three years pretending to be someone else,' Ella said. 'Do you really think the police won't want to know why I did that?'

'Tell them he's a psycho and you're scared of him,' Roxanne said.

'And he'll tell them I lied in court. He'll tell them we both lied.'

'They won't believe him.'

'But that means more lies. Is that what you want? For us to carry on heaping lies upon lies upon lies? That's not the person I want to be. It's not the sort of mother I want my child to have.'

Ella's eyes were gritty with exhaustion. When she lifted her mug to drink some tea, she was shaking so badly she needed to use both hands.

'I don't know what to do,' she said. 'I can't think of a way out of this that doesn't involve Jake getting hurt.'

'The thing I'm still not getting is why he did it. I can understand if he wanted to hurt you or me. But why Katie?'

The images were back. Jake standing at the window in the sitting room, pointing at something outside and saying, 'Mamma, Mamma.'

But it wasn't Ella. It was Katie. Pushing the buggy along the lane, a shopping bag on either handle and another bag on the seat where Jake normally sat. She was wearing Ella's blue Vivienne Westwood T-shirt. The one Dee had given her. She had taken it from Ella's wardrobe without asking, saying she hadn't brought many clothes with her and she didn't think Ella would mind.

'That's not Mamma,' Ella said. She pointed at her chest. 'This is Mamma. Here.'

'Mamma,' Jake repeated. He ran off to get his train, and that was when it happened. The screech of tyres. The shock on Katie's face as she heard the noise and looked over her shoulder to see the car roaring towards her. Right before it hit her, Ella caught sight of the driver's face through the windscreen. It was over nine years since she'd seen him, but she recognised him instantly.

Shane Gilbert.

'He made a mistake,' she said. 'Our plan worked too well. Shane saw Katie and he thought she was me.'

Forty-Nine

Dee

Dee stood across the road from the building she'd once called home – a characterless town house in a row of identical properties on the eastern edge of Greenwich. She'd loved living here. It wasn't much to look at from the outside, but inside, the house was bright and spacious. The river and Greenwich Park were within walking distance, and there were enough bars and restaurants to keep her and Billy happy when they'd first moved here.

She hadn't been back since the day their marriage ended. This house represented everything that had been both good and bad about their life together. They'd had so much fun when they first moved in. But over the years, as Billy's drinking grew progressively worse, the fun times gave way to long, anxious nights sitting home alone waiting for him to come back from whatever bender he'd been on.

'Dee?'

She turned and saw Trevor walking towards her, his face creased in sympathy and grief. Seeing him took some of the tension from Dee's body, and when he put his arms around her and hugged her, she wanted to stay like that forever.

He stepped back but kept his hands on her shoulders.

'Wow. You told me you'd been in a scuffle. You didn't tell me it was this bad.'

'It's nothing,' Dee said, touching the bandage across her nose. 'Can you believe this, Trev? He's dead.'

Trevor shook his head. 'Have you heard anything else about how it happened?'

'They can't tell if he fell or was pushed. It happened in the building where Shane Gilbert lives. I keep going back over our last conversation, wondering if I missed something. I don't even know how I'm meant to be feeling right now. All I can think about is how good we were together. Before it all went to shit. Remember back then? I thought we were strong enough to get through anything.' She bit back a sob.

'I remember.' Trevor smiled. 'I never thought he'd settle down. Then you turned up that evening in the pub, and it was clear from the moment he clapped eyes on you how wrong I'd been. He was crazy for you, Dee. Even after you split up, I don't think he ever stopped loving you.'

Tears pricked Dee's eyes. None of that mattered now.

'He never had any taste,' she said. 'Poor bastard.'

'He had great taste. You were the best thing that ever happened to him.'

She'd called Trevor last night and they'd arranged to meet here this morning. Trevor was one of the few people left who knew what Billy and Dee had been like together when they first met. He was the only person she wanted to be with right now.

'How's Melissa holding up?' she asked.

'She's a mess,' Trevor said.

Dee wasn't able to dredge up much sympathy for Billy's girlfriend. She didn't care if they'd been living together, didn't care if Melissa was twenty years her junior or twenty times prettier. She knew that whatever sort of relationship Melissa had shared with Billy, it wasn't a patch on what Dee's marriage to him had been like during the good times.

The grief came and went in waves that crashed into her, obliterating everything else, then rolling back for a while to give her enough time to brace herself for the next onslaught. She recognised the cycle, having gone through it after each of her parents died. Disbelief, anger, and then the numbing acceptance that her world had changed forever.

Another wave hit her now. She put her hand over her mouth, blocking the sounds coming out. Trevor said something she didn't hear and took her arm, leading her away from the house. She started to pull back before she realised there was no point. It was just a house, and no matter how much she wanted him to be there, Billy wasn't inside. Billy was gone.

-

They went to a coffee shop around the corner and sat at a table outside.

'Billy and Mel had an argument two days ago,' Trevor said. 'They met for lunch and Billy turned up pissed. Melissa got angry with him and they rowed. She stormed off, leaving him alone in the restaurant. She couldn't face going home, so she went to stay with a friend. The next thing she heard, he was dead. Naturally, she blames herself. She's convinced that if she'd gone home that night, he'd still be alive.'

'She thinks Shane Gilbert killed Billy because she didn't come home?'

'She thinks she could have stopped him going to see Shane,' Trevor said. 'She thought Shane was unstable. She'd warned Billy more than once to keep away from him.'

'My laptop was beside his body,' Dee said. 'I think I disturbed Gilbert stealing it, and that's when he did this to me.' She pointed at her face. 'I wonder if they argued about it. Billy would have been upset if he knew Shane had taken it.'

'Why would Shane Gilbert steal your laptop?' Trevor asked.

'He knows I'm on to him,' Dee said. 'And he wants to know how much I know. I use my laptop for all my notes when I'm working on a story. Billy would have known that. Maybe he told Shane.'

'It's still a jump from stealing your laptop to killing Billy,' Trevor said.

'Maybe.' She thought of Gilbert's physique – the excessive muscles of someone who worked out too often. Billy was tough, but he wouldn't have stood a chance against someone like that. 'I don't know. Did you manage to get hold of Leonard?' She had asked Trevor to contact his old colleague and try to find out why he had lied to her.

'He wasn't answering his phone,' Trevor said. 'So I went around to his flat this morning before I came to meet you.'

'Did he admit lying?'

'Told me he must have made a mistake. Acted like it was no big deal.'

'And you believed him?'

For the first time since they'd met this morning, Trevor smiled. 'What do you take me for? Of course I didn't believe him.'

'And?'

'He was still in bed when I got there,' Trevor said. 'Silly bugger left his laptop in the kitchen while he went and had a shower. It's password-protected, so he probably thought it would be safe. I guess he didn't remember all the times he gave me his password when we worked together so I could log on to the network for him in the morning. He always used the same one – Bermondsey – followed by a number for whatever month it was. I tried Bermondsey08 – for August – and got in right away.'

'You're far too good to be fronting some stupid TV show,' Dee said. 'You do know that?'

'If I had any sense, I'd tell you what I found out and walk away from this. Go back to my stupid TV show and my lovely life. I earn a good living doing that job. I live in a big house in a beautiful part of the city. I have friends. I have girlfriends.' The smile turned into a grin. 'Lots of girlfriends.'

'Sounds boring. Don't you long for a bit of excitement every now and then?'

'You were right about Roxanne,' Trevor said. 'I found a load of emails between her and Leonard. He's clearly mad about her, and the feeling seems to be mutual. I think they've probably been seeing each other since the trial. That's why he lied to you. He doesn't want you to find her.'

'Why not?'

'I have no idea.' Trevor drained his coffee and put his cup down. 'But I was thinking we could go and see her and ask her that ourselves, if you're interested?'

'How?' Dee asked. 'I called the pub this morning. She's not working this week. I spent half the train journey searching for an address for her, but I couldn't find a thing.'

'Roxanne Reed lives in Chislehurst. She sent Leonard her address soon after she moved in. Check your emails. I sent it to you this morning.'

Dee took out her phone. Three new emails. Two spams, and one from Trevor.

'Chislehurst,' she said, reading the email. 'Shouldn't take us too long to get there. That's if you want to tag along?'

'Of course,' Trevor said. 'On one condition.'

'What's that?'

'When all of this is over, you let me interview you.'

'What? For *Sixty Minutes*?' Dee said.

'It's going to be a great story. Everyone will want to talk to you. Promise me I'll get the exclusive?'

'Maybe.' Dee stood up. 'Let's find them first, okay?'

Fifty

Ella

On Monday morning, Ella turned on the TV in Roxanne's sitting room and realised it was finally over. The police knew who she was. Her face was on the screen again. This time, it was her name, not Katie's, running across the bottom, beneath the photo.

It was a shock, even though she'd been expecting it. Although she'd spoken about little else with Roxanne, they hadn't been able to make a decision about what they ought to do. As the days went on, they'd existed in a limbo world of waiting, neither of them knowing when the police would come knocking on Roxanne's door to tell them the game was up.

They'd thought about running away, but there was nowhere to go. They couldn't leave the country. Ella had left Eastbourne without Katie's passport, and she'd never got round to applying for one for Jake. In the end, they'd decided they were as safe here in Roxanne's house as anywhere else. Apart from Leonard, there was no one who knew they were here. And Roxanne assured her that Leonard wouldn't tell a soul.

They'd decided they'd make the most of whatever time they had left. Roxanne cut back her hours at the pub, and the three of them hung out together. Jake had adjusted well to the change of scene, although he missed Dee and kept asking for her. Ella missed Dee as well. Several times she'd thought about calling her friend and telling her not to worry about them, before realising the last thing she should do was involve Dee in any of this.

Her face disappeared from the screen as the news moved on to another story. She hit the remote, switching off the TV. Here it was, then. The reckoning. She'd spent years running from what she'd done, but in the end, the past had caught up with her anyway. All that time and effort pretending to be someone else; all for nothing.

Roxanne was in London. She'd driven up first thing to check the pub and make sure things were ticking along without her. She'd told Ella she'd be home by early afternoon, but Ella didn't think she could wait until then to talk to her. She went into the kitchen, where Roxanne kept her landline, and dialled the mobile number she'd learned by heart.

'I was about to call you,' Roxanne said. 'I've just arrived at the pub and seen the news. Don't do anything until I come back, okay? I'm already on my way.'

'How do you think they found out?' Ella asked.

'We both knew it was only a matter of time. Even if Shane had never found you, you couldn't have carried on being Katie forever. You know that, don't you? Katie hated who she was. She wanted to be you. She thought changing her name would change how she felt about herself. But it was never going to be that simple. That's why she came back. She grew tired of pretending. She wanted to be Katie again.'

Except she never got the chance. Swapping identities had been Katie's idea. Ella should never have let it happen, but when Katie had proposed it, it had seemed like the only way out of the nightmare that her life had become. She'd been so scared back then. Fear and anxiety had distorted her ability to see things clearly.

Katie had been the only person who'd seemed to understand. And Ella had been so pathetically grateful, it had never occurred to her that Katie might have her own reasons for suggesting what she had. But whatever those reasons had been, they hardly mattered now. The only thing that mattered was telling the truth. Finally.

Fifty-One

Katie
Three years earlier

I'm standing outside Ella's house, ringing the doorbell. I can see the shape of her body through the glass. She's scared to open the door because she doesn't know who she'll find standing outside. I've done this to her. Two months is all it's taken. Which just goes to show – this is as much about her own guilty conscience as anything I've done. If she'd never done anything wrong, she wouldn't have any reason to think Shane wanted to hurt her.

I lift the letter box, lean down and shout through the gap. 'Ella, it's okay. It's me, Katie.'

I hear the shuffle of feet, and a moment later she opens the door. She's huge. Bigger than she was three nights ago, if that's possible. Her belly distorts her body and her face is puffed up, giving her a swollen look. I thought she'd be the sort of person who'd look beautiful pregnant. But she doesn't. Apart from the weight, her skin is pale and unhealthy-looking, her hair is greasy and she has thick black rings under her eyes.

Inside the flat, it's obvious she's started packing. I wonder where she thinks she's going or how she thinks it could ever be that easy.

'He'll find you,' I say, pointing at the half-full suitcase on the sofa in the sitting room.

Her hands move to her stomach, and when she looks at me, I see fear. Despite this, she shakes her head. 'He's not going to find me. No one will.' She keeps her hands on her bump, as if she thinks that will protect her child somehow. She hasn't got a clue.

'Hey,' I say. 'The last time we spoke, you said you were going to show me your scan photo. I'd love to see it.' I'm probably pushing things, but it's worth it to see the pain on her face.

'It's gone,' she says.

'What do you mean?'

'I woke up the other night and someone was in the house. It was Shane.'

'You can't know that,' I say. And I'm right, of course. Because it wasn't Shane. He doesn't know about any of this. Ella keeps a spare key in a drawer in the kitchen. I found it the first time I came to visit her. I took it away, made a copy and put the key back the next time I called around. It's made everything so easy.

I've come here a few times now. Mostly I just stand and watch her sleep, thinking about how easy it would be to stick a knife in that big stomach and kill both of them. But I'm not some sort of psycho, so of course I haven't killed her.

The last time was three nights ago. After watching her for a while, I got bored, so I switched on the light in the bathroom and started running the taps. When the noise woke her up, I ran downstairs and left through the back door, making sure to leave it open so that she'd know someone had been in the house. I wasn't planning to take anything. But I saw the scan photo on the fridge and grabbed it on my way out.

'I'm so scared, Katie.' Her voice trembles and she gives me this sad look, like she wants me to feel sorry for her. Like she thinks I actually care about her.

'You look terrible,' I say. 'Why don't you sit down and let me make the tea?'

After the tea is made, we sit in her little sitting room and she tells me what's been going on. The phone calls and the night terrors – waking up convinced Shane is here in her house. Watching her.

'You need to go to the police,' I say, when she pauses for breath.

'They don't believe me,' she says. 'I'm like the boy who cried wolf, except I'm the crazy pregnant lady who keeps calling the police. The other night was the second time I've run out of my house in the middle of the night. Both times, I've knocked on my neighbours' door and they've called the police. But every time it's happened, I've come home and there's no sign the flat's been broken into. The police told me Shane hasn't been anywhere near Bristol. He's still wearing his tag, so they can track his movements. They gave me a lecture on wasting police time, and told me I should make an appointment with my GP to discuss my mental health.'

Her hands go back across her stomach. She's thinking what it would be like to have a baby in prison. How she'd probably have to give it up for adoption or something.

'You said it was a one-night stand.' I look at the balloon. 'What made you decide to keep it?'

'I was over three months before I even realised I was pregnant,' she says. 'Sounds mad, I know, but everything's been so… erratic this last year. My mum passed away soon after Tom and I split up. I sort of lost my way a bit. My periods have never been regular anyway. I was sick a few times, but I've felt sick for most of the last year so I didn't think anything of it. By the time I found out, I had less than a week to make a decision. In the end, it was easy. I wanted to be a mum.'

I can't pretend to understand that, so I don't say anything. After a bit, she starts talking again. Yabbering on in a way that's so unlike how she usually is. Scared I'll go if she doesn't keep talking. Because she can't stand to be alone with her thoughts and her fear.

My mind flashes back to years ago, when she was working in the pub. Smiling and laughing with the regulars, leaning across the bar and sharing a joke with some old drunk. It's sad, in a way, to think how much she's changed since then. Sad for her, I mean. As far as I'm concerned, she deserves everything that's happened to her.

She's talking about her body clock and maternal instincts, and I zone out until I hear Tom's name.

'I don't think I'll ever have that again with anyone else,' she says. 'I know it sounds melodramatic, but that's how it is. I feel so alone, Katie. With Mum gone, I've got no family. I didn't have any uncles or aunts, so I haven't got any cousins. My grandparents both died years ago. There's no one else.'

She's such a self-centred bitch. How can she say that to me of all people? She starts talking about Tom and how she still loves him and how she's sure he still loves her too, and not once – not for a single second – does she consider how shit that might make me feel. How it might make me wonder what's so special about her and so wrong with me.

'Oh Katie.' She reaches out and takes my hand. 'I'm so sorry. I know it's the same for you.'

She means we're the same because we're both without any family. But it's not the same, is it? Because her parents died naturally and it was no one's fault what happened to them. My dad, on the other hand, he'd still be here if it wasn't for her.

I squeeze her hand and smile and tell her we're lucky we have each other. Then I ask if she knows what she's going to do.

'I've deleted all my social media accounts,' she says, 'and I'm leaving Bristol. A friend of mine from uni has an aunt living in Eastbourne. She knows someone who's got a house to rent. It's only a mobile home, but it's right on the beach and the rent isn't too bad. If I move there and keep a low profile, there's no way he'll be able to find me, right?'

'I don't know,' I say, after a moment. 'If he's as desperate as you say he is, who knows what he'll do?'

There's a photo on her mantelpiece. It's Ella with two of her friends. The three of them are in the countryside somewhere. Standing at the top of a hill, rolling fields stretching out behind them. In the photo, she's wearing her hair in a plait that hangs over her left shoulder. The same way I'm wearing my hair today. I did it like this on purpose. When I was in here last week – while she was at the shops – I saw the photo, and that's when I first got this idea.

I've spent a week working it back and forth in my head, looking at every angle for a flaw, but it's really the perfect solution.

I stand up, go over to the mantelpiece and pick up the photo.

'Snowdon,' she says. 'Two years ago. Feels like another life completely.'

'Strange,' I say, running my fingers along my plait. 'When I saw this first, I thought it was me in the photo, not you.'

I look across at her and smile.

'I could be you, couldn't I?'

Fifty-Two

Ella

When Roxanne got back, they agreed it was time to go to the police. Ella asked her to keep an eye on Jake while she went outside to call Dee. Somehow, she had to find a way to persuade Dee to come to Chislehurst and take care of Jake.

'You really think she'll do this for you?' Roxanne asked.

'She'll know by now that I lied to her,' Ella said. 'And I think that will have hurt her. But she'll come. Maybe not for me, but she'll do it for Jake.'

She followed the path that led from the west side of Roxanne's house, past fields of sheep and cattle, through a wooded area that was cool beneath the cover of leafy trees, and onto the ridge of a hill with spectacular views across London.

The city was so huge, so full of promise. It would be easy for Ella and Jake to lose themselves amongst all the millions of other people living there. She imagined the different lives they might lead if they kept running. They could get the train from Chislehurst into the city, melting into that great melting pot along with everyone else. Except she was so tired of running.

The decision to tell the truth was liberating. Finally she could stop pretending. It was a clear, sunny day and it felt good to be out here, feeling the heat of the sun on her face, instead of stuck inside too scared to step outside the house in case someone saw her. She was alive. Unlike Katie.

She wanted to be you.

Had Ella always known? Maybe. More than once, Tom had commented on how Katie copied the way Ella dressed and wore her hair. At the time, Ella had thought he was reading too much into it. Didn't all young women basically dress the same?

Back when she was working in the pub, Gus had noticed it too.

'You and my Katie could be sisters, you know,' he'd told her once.

To her shame, Ella hadn't found the comparison flattering. It was only a few months later that she realised Gus was right. With all the weight Katie had lost and her new hairstyle, Ella could see why some people would think they looked alike.

Had it all been for Shane? she wondered now. Had Katie tried to look like Ella so Shane would notice her? Sadly for Katie, it hadn't worked. If it had, maybe none of the rest of it would have happened. Gus would still be alive, Shane would never have gone to prison and Katie wouldn't have been killed.

At the time, Shane going to prison seemed like the answer to all Ella's problems. Now, she understood that you couldn't fix one bad thing by simply replacing it with another. She should have told the truth about what happened that night and faced the consequences.

She hadn't switched her phone on since leaving London. When she did so now, the voicemail symbol appeared on her screen. She dialled her voicemail, then wished she hadn't. Message after message from Dee, begging her to let her know she was okay.

'I don't care what you've done,' Dee said. 'Just call me, Katie. Please. I need to know you're both all right.'

Dear Dee. By now, she'd know Ella had lied to her. She'd be hurt, but Ella hoped that wouldn't prevent her doing her this one final favour. Even if she didn't want to help Ella – and who could blame her for that? – Ella didn't think she would turn her back on Jake.

She scrolled through her list of contacts until she found Dee's number. As she waited for the call to connect, she pictured her friend sitting on the deck outside her house. A glass of wine in her hand, her mobile phone blasting out Johnny Cash's 'Ring of Fire'. But the phone went straight to voicemail, and Ella got a recorded message of Dee's voice asking her to leave a message. She told Dee she was sorry and asked her to call her back as soon as she could.

She had barely hung up when the phone started to ring. She answered, expecting to hear Dee's voice, but it wasn't Dee.

'Hello, Ella.'

Everything stopped. Her blood froze. Shock and terror made speaking or breathing impossible. She took the phone away from her ear, looked at it as if doing that might help her understand. Saw Roxanne's name on the screen. Thought for a moment it was her mind playing tricks on her. But when she listened again, she knew there was no mistake.

'Aren't you going to ask me how I'm doing?'

His voice was exactly as she remembered it. She opened her mouth to ask him what she wanted. But before she could speak, she heard Jake. Crying and calling her name.

'Mamma, Mamma, Mamma!'

'Shut up!' Shane shouted. Too loud and too angry. Jake's crying intensified, the sound scraping through Ella's insides, splitting her open.

'Please,' she whispered. 'Please don't hurt him.'

In reply, Shane ended the call. The click as the line disconnected echoed in Ella's ear as she turned and ran back towards the house. Running faster than she'd ever run in her life. Knowing her son's life depended on it.

'Jake!'

She shouted his name repeatedly as she ran from the kitchen to his bedroom to the sitting room, searching for her son. But the house was empty. Fear gnawed its way deeper into her soul. He had to be here. She searched the rooms again, looking in wardrobes, behind the sofas and underneath beds.

The wardrobe in Roxanne's room wouldn't open. Ella was about to leave it when she heard something. A shuffling sound coming from inside the wardrobe.

'Jake?'

The wardrobe vibrated, as if someone inside was trying to get out.

'Jake! Is that you, darling?'

Ella grabbed the handle and pulled. Nothing happened. She banged her fist against the door.

'Hang on, Jake,' she said. 'Mummy's here. It's okay. I'm going to get you out now.'

But it wasn't Jake. Because she could hear him outside the house, screaming. She raced out, following the sound until she reached the shed at end of the garden. The door was open. She could see Shane and Jake inside. Shane was holding on to Jake with one hand, using the other to keep the knife pressed against his throat.

A moan rose through Ella's body. Her little boy. His face white, eyes wide open, terrified. Ella ran forward, willing Shane not to hurt him.

'It's okay, Jakey. Mummy's not going to let anything bad happen to you.' Her voice was trembling so badly she could barely get the words out.

She dragged her eyes away from Jake's face to Shane's.

'Let him go. Please, Shane. This is nothing to do with him.'

'This is everything to do with him!' Shane screamed. 'It's his fault. She was pushing his buggy and I thought she was you.' His face was white and damp, sweat rolling down his cheeks. His eyes darted about the place. He looked ill. Or high.

'Let Jake go.' Ella made her voice as calm as she could. 'Let him go and leave him here and we can talk. I don't want to do this in front of him.'

'I don't care what you want,' Shane said. Splatters of spit exploded from his mouth each time he spoke, landing on Jake's hair. Ella had to clench her hands to stop herself reaching out and grabbing him. 'Katie was my only friend. She knew all about you. Does your son know? Mummy's a murderer, Jake. She killed a man. Did you know that?'

Jake started to cry. Fat tears rolling down his cheeks. His little body shaking.

'Six years,' Shane said. 'Six years inside that shitting hellhole for something I didn't do. How old's your boy? Two? Three? Even if I killed him now, that wouldn't make up for it.'

Ella couldn't take her eyes off the knife, willing it not to move, not to press harder.

'Six. Fucking. Years.'

'I'm sorry,' she whispered. 'Let him go, Shane. If you let him go, I'll turn myself in. I'll tell the truth.'

'It's too late for that.'

'I know,' she said. 'I know. If I could turn the clock back, I would. Let Jake go and I'll do anything you want. I swear to you.'

'Anything?'

She nodded her head, not trusting herself to speak.

'Prove it,' Shane said. 'Take your top off. Show me how far you're willing to go to make things up to me.'

'Not in front of Jake,' Ella said.

'Fine.' Shane shoved Jake away and came towards her. He traced the knife along her cheek and down her neck. Used the blade to cut through the thin material of her blouse, slashing until it fell open, revealing her bra underneath.

She could see Jake on the ground behind him, curled up in a ball, sobbing.

'In the house,' she said. 'We'll be more comfortable.'

Shane shoved her, hard. She stumbled backwards and fell out of the door onto the grass. As she scrabbled to stand up, Shane reached down, grabbed her shoulder and dragged her up. With his free hand, he pressed the knife against her throat, then pushed her towards the house.

She told herself it didn't matter what he did to her, or how badly he hurt her. The only thing in the world that mattered right now was keeping Jake safe.

Fifty-Three

Ella

He half pushed, half dragged her across the lawn. She saw Roxanne's car parked in the driveway. Which meant Roxanne had come home earlier than expected. It was Roxanne in the wardrobe. Locked inside, unable to get out.

Shane pushed open the door to the sitting room and shoved her inside. She landed heavily, the air rushing from her body. She tried to get to her knees, but he put his foot on her back, pushing her down until she was lying on her stomach. He pressed harder, so hard she couldn't breathe and she thought her ribs would crack beneath the weight.

Suddenly the pressure was gone. But before she could try to get up again, Shane grabbed her left wrist, then her right, pulling them both behind her back. Kept pulling until she screamed out in pain. He wrapped thick tape around her wrists, and when he was done and she couldn't move her arms, he did the same to her ankles.

'Let me go!' She tried to wriggle forward. He grabbed her right ankle and she screamed, kicking back as hard as she could. He pulled harder and she fell forward, her face smashing into the carpet. Through the pain, she could smell him. The stink of his body all around her. The memories of everything he'd done to her and the terrible thing she'd done too, all of it churning around inside her and around her until she couldn't control the panic that rose up inside her like an explosion.

He grabbed a handful of her hair, pulled her up until she was on her knees. Then he walked around so he was facing her, his crotch centimetres from her face. He moved closer, put his hand on her head. She bit back the scream that rose up her throat. Told herself again that it was okay, it didn't matter. She could do – would do – anything. He leaned down, tore off another strip of tape and wound it around her mouth and the back of her head.

'What did you think?' he said. 'That I'd want to touch you after everything you've done?'

She couldn't speak, could just about breathe through her nose if she stayed calm. But every time she thought of Jake, panic rushed through her, making her heart race and her chest and throat so tight she was unable to drag enough air into her lungs. She heard a whistling sound, knew it was her own breathing. Tried to tell herself that meant she was okay. She was breathing, even if it didn't feel like she was. She wasn't going to die. Not just yet.

'You ruined my life.' Shane took a step back so she could see him properly for the first time. She didn't want to look at him, but she couldn't help it. Her eyes drawn to the face that had haunted her dreams for so many years.

He'd aged. His body was twice the width it had once been, although the bulk was more muscle than fat. Strands of white in his dark hair that he now wore cropped short. His face was gaunt and drawn. There was an unhealthy sheen to his skin and dark rings like pouches beneath his eyes. The left side of his face was bruised and swollen. And he was trembling. His entire body shaking, as if he was cold. But he couldn't be cold, because he was sweating. His face was wet and there were dark patches under the arms of his faded grey T-shirt.

She started struggling, trying to free her hands, because she knew now that he wasn't going to let her go.

'You stitched me up,' he said. 'You and that cow Roxanne. Katie was the only one who believed me. If it wasn't for Katie, I wouldn't have the courage to be here today. She helped me understand how much damage you'd done. And she knew we needed to make you pay. We waited. We wanted you to think you'd got away with it. Then, when you were all happy with your new life, we were going to take it away from you. Only I fucked up, didn't I? I killed Katie instead of you.'

His voice broke, and Ella realised he was crying.

'She left me.' Shane took a few shaky breaths and used his sleeve to wipe his nose. 'She went to Australia and I had nobody and no way of finding you. She was the only one who knew where you were. All the time she was away, I waited like she asked me to. Then three months ago, I get a phone call and it's Katie and she says she's back in the UK. And it was so bloody good to hear her voice again. I thought, this is it. We can punish you for what you did, and afterwards we can be together. Finally. She told me what you'd done. Making her pretend to be you, just so you could get away from me. What kind of sad fuck would do something like that?'

Ella shook her head. It was Katie's idea, not hers. But Shane didn't seem to notice. He'd started pacing, his movements jerky and uncoordinated, spittle flying from his mouth as he continued speaking. He was wired, Ella realised. Coke or speed and something else too, maybe.

'Katie said she'd had enough. She wanted to see you alone first to tell you she wasn't going to pretend any longer. She asked me not to come. She let me drive her to Eastbourne, told me to go home and wait until she called. But I'd already waited too long, hadn't I?

'She never called and I was worried you'd hurt her, so I drove back. I wasn't planning to do anything. Not right then, anyway. But then I saw you pushing the buggy, and something inside me snapped. There you were, walking in the sunshine without a care in the world. With your own child. You had a child, and what did I have? Nothing. It was too much. I didn't even think about what I was doing. I pressed my foot down on the accelerator and I drove straight into you.

'But it wasn't you, and now she's dead and I've lost the only person who really loved me, and everything has got so messed up and it's your fault.'

Ella shook her head again.

'Yes!' Shane screamed. 'You fucked it all up for me, Ella. What did I ever do to you that was so bad?'

Images of that morning danced in front of her. She'd slept badly, her mind going back to the previous afternoon, when she'd spotted him on the train. She realised he must have followed her from the pub, although she hadn't noticed him there when she'd left. She'd pretended to eat breakfast, mumbling monosyllabic answers to her mother's questions, before grabbing her bag and heading out to college. The first thing she'd seen when she stepped outside was Oscar, her beloved dog, lying dead in their front garden. And she knew it wasn't a coincidence. Shane Gilbert had followed her home, and now Oscar was dead.

She stared at him, hoping he'd see the hatred she felt for him burning out of her eyes.

'Why would you do that to someone?' he asked, sounding genuinely confused. 'One minute you're with them and it's all great, the next you're ignoring them and telling them you don't want anything to do with them.'

She wanted to tell him they'd split up because he was a sleaze who had cheated on her during their short time together. But the tape prevented her from saying anything. All she could do was listen to his deluded perspective on their short-lived romance.

'We had a connection,' he said. 'Something special. I wanted to keep the connection alive, but you pushed me away. And then, when I was ready to accept it was really over, you reeled me back in. All those messages telling me how much you wanted me, pretending to feel something for me. It was all a joke, wasn't it?'

Ella had no idea what he was talking about. After Oscar, she'd never wanted to see him again.

Shane leaned forward, grabbed her by the hair, forced her to look out of the window. At the shed.

'Ever seen a shed burn down, Ella?'

No! The word got lost behind the tape.

He pushed her to the ground and walked away, leaving her alone in the room. She struggled to her knees, shuffled across to the door, into the hall. The back door was open. She could see Shane outside, leaning down by the corner of the shed.

Moments later, the bottom edges of the shed lit up. A line of flames moving fast along the sides of the building, creeping up along the walls. Ella threw herself forward, tumbling down the steps that led to the garden. The stink of burnt timber filled her nose and throat. The crackle of flames roared as the fire took hold. And her little boy was trapped inside the shed, unable to get out.

Fifty-Four

Dee

Dee was familiar with Chislehurst from when she'd lived in London. It was a quaint, affluent village on the southern edges of the city. She used to get a train there on Sundays and go walking in the nearby countryside.

She entered the address Trevor gave her into the sat nav. The estimated journey time was forty-three minutes.

'I'm worried about what Shane might have found in my laptop,' she said.

'Did it have a password?' Trevor asked.

'We both know how easy it is to get past a laptop password. I use the same password for my email. If Shane used software to get into my laptop, the first thing he'd have done was try the same password to access my email.'

'But when I sent you the email with Roxanne's address, Shane didn't have your laptop. It was with Billy by then, remember?'

'I use webmail,' Dee said. 'If Shane got my login details, he could access my email from any device.'

'There's a good chance that hasn't happened. You and I know about that sort of stuff because we're journalists. Shane Gilbert's an ex-con. Probably not very well educated. Only a proper techie would know about stuff like that.'

'Shane is a proper techie. He has a degree in computer programming.'

'Well, even if he has been able to access your emails, there's every chance we'll get to Chislehurst before he does. He can't know we're on our way there right now.'

'I hope you're right,' Dee said, but she couldn't shake off the feeling that they were already too late. She looked at the line of cars snaking slowly ahead of her along the A2 and wanted to scream. 'I wish this bloody traffic would shift. How could I have forgotten how clogged up the roads in London can get?'

'It'll clear once we get the other side of Eltham,' Trevor said. 'Try to stay calm until then.'

Dee tapped the steering wheel with the tips of her fingers and took several deep breaths. It made no difference. All she could think about was Jake. Her need to see him was increasing with every slow mile that passed. To distract herself, she told Trevor what she'd worked out so far about Gus Hope's murder.

'Shane didn't kill him,' she said. 'That was Ella or Roxanne. I don't know why he was killed, and maybe that doesn't matter. What's important is this: after the murder, the two women lied to the police, framing Shane for something he didn't do. He served his time in prison, and when he got out, Ella was scared he'd come looking for her. She was pregnant; she panicked and decided to steal Katie's ID. And the plan worked. Until Katie found out what she did and confronted her.'

'And when she did that, Ella killed her,' Trevor said.

'No. That's not what happened. Ella was right to be scared of Shane. He came looking for her. But he had help. I think Shane and Katie were working together. At some point, possibly when he was in prison, Shane convinced Katie he'd been set up. They used to go out with each other. Maybe she still had feelings for him. Either way, my original theory still stands. Katie was killed because someone – Shane Gilbert – thought she was Ella. He made a mistake and killed the wrong girl.'

'Which one of them killed Gus?' Trevor asked. 'Roxanne or Ella?'

As she considered this, Dee remembered something Tom had said. She glanced across at Trevor. 'Get my phone out of my bag. You'll find Tom's number in my call log. Call him and put him on speaker phone.'

Tom answered on the second ring. 'Dee, is everything okay?'

'We may have a lead on Roxanne Reed. But there's something I need to ask you first.'

'Sure,' Tom said. 'Fire ahead.'

'You mentioned something about Gus's murder causing a rift between you and Ella?'

The silence at the other end told her all she needed to know.

'It's going to come out sooner or later,' she said. 'Shane's already telling anyone who'll listen that his trial was a miscarriage of justice. If Ella killed Gus, that might help us understand why Katie was killed.'

'She swore it was an accident,' Tom said. 'I believed her about that. The thing I couldn't get past, the thing that caused us to break up, was that she'd let an innocent man go to prison for something she'd done.'

'How do you kill someone by accident?' Dee asked. 'She sliced his throat open.'

'I don't know. She would never have spoken about it if it wasn't for Katie. We were in a pub one evening, waiting for Ella, and Katie told me her father had been killed. She assumed I already knew about it.'

'Because Ella was a witness.'

'Exactly. When I asked Ella about it later, she told me she didn't speak about it because she was consumed with guilt. And then she told me what she'd done. I couldn't handle it, and we split up.'

'Roxanne perjured herself to protect Ella,' Dee said. 'Why?'

'I never asked. Once I knew the truth, I didn't want anything else to do with her.'

'Didn't stop him sleeping with her a few years later,' Dee said to Trevor after she'd rung off.

'New voicemail on your phone,' Trevor said. 'Someone must have called you while you were speaking to Tom.'

'Stick it back on speaker phone and dial my voicemail, would you?'

'Anything else I can do for you, your ladyship?' Trevor asked.

Dee waved her hand in the air, gesturing for him to hurry up and do what she'd asked.

She listened to the automated voice telling her she had a new message. This was followed by a silence, and then a woman's voice, sounding timid and far away.

'Dee? It's me, Katie. Well, you probably know by now that's not my real name. I'm so sorry I lied about who I was. Can you call me back as soon as possible? I need your help.'

The shock made Dee almost crash the car. She swerved into the hard shoulder, switched the engine off and grabbed the phone from Trevor. A van swung past, horn blasting. Dee barely heard it as she replayed the message twice more.

'Shit,' she said. 'Shit, shit, shit.'

She pressed 3 to return the call, and got Ella's voicemail. 'Ella?' she said. 'I got your message. Call me back. I need to know you're okay, that you're both okay. Nothing else matters. I don't care that you lied, or why you lied. Call me.'

'You don't care that she lied?' Trevor said, after Dee hung up.

'She's my friend and she's in trouble. Right now, that's the only thing I care about.'

She switched the engine back on and checked in the rear-view mirror before pulling away from the kerb.

'Keep calling that number,' she told Trevor. 'Hopefully she'll pick up before too long.'

'Whatever you say, boss,' Trevor said. Then, a few minutes later, 'I think her phone may be switched off. All I'm getting is her voicemail.'

'Keep trying,' Dee told him. 'Jesus, this bloody traffic.'

'It's thinning out a bit. You need to take the next right. After that, I reckon another fifteen minutes and we'll be there.'

'I may be a woman,' Dee said, 'but I'm more than capable of following sat nav directions, thanks.'

–

Roxanne's house was a pretty whitewashed bungalow down a quiet road on the edge of the village.

'What if she's not here?' Trevor asked when Dee pulled up outside.

'We wait.'

Dee opened the door and stepped out of the car. Almost immediately, the smell hit her. Thick and acrid, the stink of something burning in the still summer air.

'Someone's having a barbecue,' Trevor said. He opened the gate and indicated for Dee to pass through before him.

The front door was red, the same colour as the roses planted in the beds lining the path that led up to the house. Normally Dee would have commented on how pretty it all looked. Right now, though, her attention was focused not on the flowers but on the plumes of smoke rising up behind the house.

'You don't get smoke like that from a barbecue,' she said. 'I'm going back there to see what's burning.'

They ran towards the source of the smoke, stopping abruptly when they saw the inferno. At the end of a long, tidy garden, a wooden shed was burning rapidly to the ground. Flames licked up the sides, sending thick plumes of smoke into the air. Heat radiated off the blaze, so hot Dee felt as if her skin might peel off.

Someone was screaming. The sound came from inside the shed. Dee ran forward, but Trevor caught her arm.

'You've got your phone,' he shouted. 'Call 999. I'll get a bit closer and see if I can do anything.'

When Dee hesitated, he pushed her gently back.

'If you go down there, you won't be able to hear when they ask you where you are.'

'Don't get too close,' Dee said, but her voice was lost in the hiss and spit of the flames eating up the sides of the shed.

She pulled her phone out, punched in three nines.

'Fire brigade,' she shouted when someone answered. She gave the address and said the fire engines needed to get here as quickly as possible.

Trevor was nearly at the shed. He stopped running, seemed unsure what to do next. Heat came off the shed in waves, scorching the air and burning the back of Dee's throat each time she breathed in.

'Come back!' she screamed, but Trevor either didn't hear her or chose to ignore her.

She was about to shout again when she heard the smash of glass breaking. The noise came from the house, behind her. She turned round, saw a burst of flame rush through the newly broken window.

She swung back to check on Trevor. Saw him run a few steps forward, then withdraw again, driven back by the smoke and the flames and the unbearable burning heat.

She dialled 999 again, screaming to the emergency operator that the fire was worse than she'd thought. 'It's not just the shed,' she said. 'It's the house too.'

'The fire service is on its way,' the woman told her. 'Estimated arrival time ten minutes. You need to move away from the area, madam. Take yourself out of danger.'

'I can't stand here and do nothing,' Dee said. 'What if someone's inside the house?'

'You can't help them if you're injured too. Get as far away as you can.'

Trevor had disappeared. Dee scanned the area, searching for him. Her eyes were streaming, making it difficult to see. At the end of the garden, the fire blazed brighter, flames rising higher so that she couldn't see the shed any more. All she could see was a burning mass of fire and smoke.

Something shot across the flames. Someone was running towards the fire.

'Trevor!'

'Madam?'

Dee hadn't realised she still had the phone pressed to her ear.

'I need you to confirm you're moving to a safe area.'

She ended the call and ran towards the fire. Heat and smoke and flames. No sign of Trevor. She screamed his name, but her voice was lost in the storm of noise the fire was making.

And then she saw him. He was at the entrance to the shed, his body a black silhouette against the flames. Relief made her want to laugh. He was okay.

'Trevor!' He turned his head and she gestured for him to move back.

He looked like he was about to say something, but Dee never heard it. A deafening sound cracked through the air, drumming through her body. At the same moment, there was a flash of light, white and bright, and an explosion so strong it threw Dee up into the air.

She was flying, weightless and free. Spinning in the air with the flames and the smoke and exploding pieces of wood. And then she was falling.

She hit the ground, hard. Landed on her back, all the air knocked out of her. Unable to move or breathe or speak, she lay on the neatly mown lawn. Above her, thousands of burnt and broken pieces of wood were twisting and turning in the whirling orange and black air, like tiny dancers beneath a setting sun.

Fifty-Five

Ella

Smoke clogged her nose, burning the back of her throat. Choking her. The tape across her mouth meant she couldn't shout for help. She could barely breathe. Flames raced along the edges of the curtains. Red and roaring. She never knew fire could make so much noise.

The hero next door.

Words from a song. Music jingling. Jake pointing at the TV, laughing. Fireman Sam. Jake was here somewhere, in this burning shed, breathing in the same thick smoke. It would kill him quicker than it would kill her. She had to find him before that happened.

She was lying on her side, her hands tied behind her back. Tape cut into the skin on her wrists, blood ran down her hands as she tried to pull them free, desperate to find Jake before it was too late.

Then she remembered. She wasn't in the shed. She was in the house. Shane had caught her in the garden. He'd dragged her up off the ground, punched her in the stomach, knocking all the air from her body. Then he'd pulled her back up the slope, away from the shed. And she couldn't do anything because she couldn't breathe. She was dying.

Except she hadn't died. She'd woken to find herself lying on the floor of the sitting room, watching the curtains dissolve into the flames. She tried to get up, but the smoke meant every breath was a struggle. Standing, the effort it would take to push herself up without using her hands or arms seemed impossible.

Tears of rage and frustration ran down her face. Damn him. He wasn't going to win. Not now. Jake wasn't dead. He couldn't be. Ella was going to get out of here and save him. And when she'd done that, she was going to find Shane Gilbert and she was going to kill him.

Shane's voice, echoing in her head.

Mummy's a murderer.

Not murder. Self-defence. Maybe. A mistake. Yes.

An eye for an eye.

She deserved to die. She had killed, and so she should be killed.

Gus and Katie. Both dead because of her.

Poor Katie. She must have hated us so much.

It didn't matter now. Nothing mattered except not dying.

It was too hot to breathe or think. She had to close her eyes to stop them burning. There was a roaring sound inside her head, matching the noises all around her as the fire moved closer.

A ring of fire. Johnny Cash. Dee's favourite.

Gus and Shane and red, red blood. Jake. There he was. Standing with his back to her, surrounded by a light so bright and white it made her body ache.

Jake! She called his name and he turned slowly, his arms reaching for her. But when she saw his face, it wasn't Jake. It was Gus. Smiling and walking towards her. His mouth was moving but she couldn't hear the words until he was right in front of her.

'What took you so long?'

He reached for her and she tried to resist, because she knew that the moment he touched her, it would be over. She tried to step back, but she couldn't move. And now his hand was on her shoulder, drawing her into the white light and saying her name, his voice so full of love and loss and joy and pain all at the same time.

'Katie. My Katie.'

It's not me, she tried to tell him. I'm not Katie. But he didn't hear, because there was another voice. Katie's. Ella couldn't see her, but she could hear her speaking, soft and close. So close.

I could be you. I could be you.

The words whispering around her and through her until there was nothing except Katie's voice and the bright white light that was love and life and nothing to be scared of. She would never be scared again.

Because the ache was gone. She was free.

Fifty-Six

Dee

There were three fire engines. And lots of people. Firemen
and women and police and paramedics. Someone was
talking to her. A fireman with ears that were too big
for the rest of him. Asking questions about Trevor and
the screams and the fires still burning in the house
and the shed. Was anyone inside the house? Dee didn't
know. She didn't know anything except that Trevor, dear,
lovely Trevor, had gone inside that... thing. That burning
inferno.

'Will he be okay?'

She had asked the same question already, kept asking
it because no one would tell her. They wouldn't tell her,
yet they expected her to answer all their questions. The
fireman – Frasier, his name was Frasier, like the TV show
– told her she should see the paramedics.

'We need to get you checked out,' he said. 'Let me take
you over to one of the ambulances.'

'No.'

She wouldn't go. She had to wait until Trevor came
back out. Four firemen were aiming a hose at the shed,
water pumping out of it. But the water disappeared into
the flames, didn't seem to make any difference. Dee

wanted to tell them they would have to go inside, but she couldn't find the words she needed, so she just stood there like a stupid, useless idiot, holding onto the blanket the fireman – what was his name? – had given her.

It was the second time in the space of a few days that someone had wrapped a blanket around her. She didn't understand why she needed a blanket. It was too hot for one. But she kept it around her shoulders, holding onto the edges so it didn't slip off, because she didn't know what else to do and she was a stupid, useless idiot who had done nothing to help anyone.

'Will he be okay?'

'Frasier!'

That was his name. She remembered now. Frasier, like the TV show that she and Billy used to watch together. Tossed salad and scrambled eggs.

'We've got a body.'

A fireman, his eyes white and huge, the only part of his face not covered in black soot, was running towards them. Coming from the house, not the shed.

A body. Not a person, a body. But it wasn't Trevor. It couldn't be Trevor because the body was inside the house and Trevor was in the shed. Jake. Oh sweet Jesus, please, not the little boy. He was too young to die. He liked ice cream. Chocolate ice cream from Fusciardi's.

Dee remembered one day a few months ago. Walking along the seafront, on her way to meet Louise for lunch. She'd heard someone calling her name and knew it was Jake. Knew because she'd recognise his little-boy voice anywhere. He was coming out of Fusciardi's, clutching a cone that looked bigger than his face. A huge scoop of chocolate ice cream wobbling precariously on top. Katie was wearing the blue T-shirt and she looked so pretty. She took Jake's hand as they crossed the road, and Dee felt such a swell of warmth inside her, knowing they were crossing because of her.

Another shout. This time from inside the house. A flurry of activity, an army of firemen moving around the side of the house. The smash of glass as they broke through a window. A black face appearing in the space where the window had been.

'In here!'

A stretcher was lifted towards the window; two men sliding a body onto it. The body was too big to be a child's. Dee turned back to the shed. The water was still pumping out. Flames not as high now. Nothing left to burn. She ran towards it, thinking she might be able to get in. She had to do something, and if the firemen weren't going to find Trevor, she would do it herself.

A hand on her arm dragged her back. A man – not Fireman Sam or Frasier, younger and harder-looking – shouted at her not to move any closer. She tried to pull her arm free, but he was much stronger than she was.

'We're going in now,' he said. 'But you need to wait here. Okay?'

He didn't give her a choice. Stayed with her, keeping his hand on her arm, his fingers digging into her flesh, hurting her.

Two firemen kicked down what was left of the shed door. Not difficult, as most if it had already burned away. Dee could see now that the fire was almost out. Still the firemen kept the hose trained on it, water pumping out, dousing what was left.

Her mouth and nose and throat were full of the stink of charred wood and roasted metal and something else too. Something bitter and sour and very, very wrong.

Light flooded through the entrance to the shed. Dee didn't understand where it was coming from at first. Until she realised it was sunshine. The back of the shed was gone, burned or broken, or never there in the first place perhaps. She was able to see right through to the fields beyond.

Trevor was safe. She knew it! He had managed to break through the back of the shed and get out.

'He's okay.'

She turned to the man beside her, smiling. He didn't smile back, and she couldn't understand why, because it was okay. Trevor was alive.

'He's okay.' She said it again before she realised he wasn't looking at her. He was looking at the shed behind her.

She turned back to the shed, saw the other fireman standing in the broken-down doorway. Frasier. She remembered his name now. Frasier Crane. A psychiatrist in Seattle. All the facts about Frasier and his life tumbling through her head because it was easier and better to think about that instead of what she was looking at.

Frasier the fireman, looking across the neatly mowed lawn to Dee. She didn't want to meet his gaze, but she knew he was waiting. So she lifted her head and asked the question, even though she knew he was too far away to hear her.

'Is he okay?'

Frasier the fireman shook his head.

No.

Fifty-Seven

Ella
Ten years earlier

Ella took a sip of her beer and checked the time. Eleven thirty. She took her phone out of her pocket and sent a text to her mother.

Working late. Will get a taxi x

Mum hated that she was working in a pub. But there was no way Ella was giving up this job. She'd meant it when she told Katie she felt suffocated at home. She guessed it was worse for Katie because her father was so protective, he wouldn't even let her get a job.

Which was so wrong. Katie was seventeen, and Gus wouldn't be able to keep her locked up forever. Especially the way she looked these days. Ella remembered the first time she'd seen her. Here in the pub. Katie had been having dinner with Gus. Ella had guessed who she was right away. Although if she was being honest, she'd been a bit surprised.

Her parents had been friendly with Gus and his wife, Marianne. The couple had been for dinner at Ella's house a few times and she had vivid memories of Katie's mother. Vivid because Marianne wasn't the sort of woman you forgot in a hurry. Tall and slender, with huge dark eyes, olive skin and long, luxurious black hair. Ella had expected Katie to look like her mum. But she couldn't have been less like her if she'd tried.

After her initial surprise, Ella's next reaction was pity. She liked to think she would never let herself get that fat, but the truth was, she didn't know what she'd do if she had the sort of body that put weight on easily. She tried to imagine what it would be like to have been overweight your entire life. But it was too difficult. Or maybe she just didn't want to imagine it, because that made her feel even worse for Katie.

But now she didn't have to feel bad for Katie at all. Now, Ella admired her, because Katie had clearly put a huge amount of effort into changing her appearance. And that effort had really paid off.

She heard the whoosh of the bar door being pushed open and she smiled. It was good that they were having this chat tonight. She'd wanted to find a way to talk to Katie, explain why she hated Shane so much. She was sure that if she told her what Shane was really like, Katie wouldn't want anything to do with him.

But when she turned around, it wasn't Katie she saw.

He was standing in the doorway, watching her, his pupils dilated so it looked like he had two black holes where his eyes should be.

'Hey.' He smiled like it was the most natural thing in the world for him to be here after closing time, when no one else was around. A surge of rage consumed her, overriding any fear she'd felt. He wasn't meant to be here, and if he took a single step towards her, she would kill him.

'Get out,' she said, her voice trembling with the effort of not screaming. Not wanting to give him the pleasure of knowing he could get inside her head and make her so scared she was literally jumping at the sight of her own shadow.

He looked surprised for a moment, then that stupid grin was back.

'Ah,' he said, walking towards her. 'That's the game, is it?'

She pushed herself off the bar stool so she was standing facing him.

'Don't come any closer.'

'Or what?'

'Or I'll kill you.'

He hesitated. 'I don't get it, Ella. You said this was what you wanted.'

'Bullshit.'

For a moment, she thought it would be okay. Then he took another step forward. She could smell him, his scent filling up the room, making it difficult to breathe. Sweat and cigarette smoke underlaid with something sour that made her retch as he drew closer.

She was still holding the beer bottle. As he reached for her, she smashed it on the corner of the bar. Beer splashed onto her hand and her T-shirt, shards of glass skittering across the mahogany surface of the bar. She swung around, pointing the jagged edge of the broken bottle at his throat.

'Jesus,' he said, putting his hands up. 'Be careful, would you?'

'Get away from me.'

'No. You can't mess me around like that, Ella. Sending me all those messages, telling me how much you want me, and then this? It's not right.'

She hadn't sent him any messages. He was deluded. But before she could tell him that, he pushed his hand into her chest, shoving her hard. She stumbled back, fell. Pain exploded through her shoulder. She screamed, but the sound was blocked off as he threw himself onto her, crushing the air from her body.

She tried to get up, but he was too fast. His hands held her arms over her head, pinning her wrists to the ground, while his other hand stroked her face. The sensation of his finger was like a snail's trail across her skin.

'Ella.'

His breath all over her face. The smell of him stuck at the back of her throat. He leaned in closer, pressed his lips against hers. She swung her head sideways, but he grabbed her chin, forced her face back to his and kissed her a second time, using his tongue to force her mouth open, pushing it deeper.

She retched and screamed and struggled against him, but he was stronger than she was. He slammed her wrists against the ground and she felt the bottle drop from her hand, heard it roll away from her.

He lifted his head and she breathed in gulps of clean air, trying to get rid of the taste of him. He was moving his body against her and she could feel his erection pressing against the inside of her thigh. The light disappeared as his head came back down again.

'No.'

Her voice was cut off by his tongue, shoving deeper inside her mouth until she was gagging. No. She wasn't going to let him do this. She opened her mouth wider, and he pushed into her and against her. And then she bit down, hard, her teeth clamping into his tongue.

Liquid gushed down her throat, choking her. Shane rolled off her, his hand clamped over his mouth, screaming. She saw the blood seeping through his fingers as she scrabbled away from him, eyes scanning the floor for the broken bottle.

She saw it resting against the leg of a chair, just out of reach. She threw herself forward, felt the glass with her fingertips but wasn't able to get a grip on it because Shane was on top of her again, hands grabbing her hair, pulling her head back.

She jerked against him, but he held tight, pulled harder. White dots danced in front of her, the pain too much to bear a second longer. With one final surge of energy, she lunged for the bottle again, rage and pain screaming out of her until her throat was raw.

Her fingers closed round it. Behind her, someone shouted, but she couldn't hear over the churning of the blood pumping inside her head and her own screams. The weight of his body disappeared. Still holding the bottle, she pushed herself off the ground, lunging out and up towards the figure standing over her, aiming for his neck, shoving the bottle into him as hard as she could. Blood erupted out of him, all over her face and arms and body.

His hands flew up to stop the flow of blood, but there was too much of it and he was cut too deeply. He staggered back and away from her.

It was only when the light caught his face, right before he fell to the ground, that she realised what she'd done.

He landed in a heap, his hands still clutching the gaping hole she'd made in his neck.

'Gus?' A woman's voice.

Ella swung around, saw Roxanne standing in the doorway.

'Oh love,' Roxanne said. 'What have you done?'

She wasn't looking at Ella. She was looking past her, at Gus, the blood pooling from his neck.

'Katie.' The word heaved out of him in a whisper. He reached out, as if he was looking for her, and then his hand fell back and hit the ground with a soft thud.

Fifty-Eight

Katie
Six months earlier

It's nothing like I thought it would be. I'm still me, that's the problem. I've done everything I can, but it's not good enough. I'll never be her. It was a stupid idea. Because how can I be her when *she's* still her?

Australia hasn't worked out for me. I don't like the people. They're too loud, too in-your-face, wanting to know all about you and inviting you to their houses for 'barbies' all the time. Sydney is overcrowded and hot. I've been to the beach a few times, but that's as bad. Full of loud-mouthed Aussies drinking lager and cracking bad jokes.

Home is a cramped apartment near the city centre. A forty-five-minute walk from the beach. I can't help comparing it to the pictures Ella has sent me. I don't know Eastbourne, but it looks beautiful. Peaceful and unspoilt and sort of perfect, really.

She's found a house right on the beach. I imagine what it would be like to be able to open your door every morning and step outside to that view. I don't have to imagine very hard, because she never tires of telling me how great her life is. She sends me a lot of emails, and they're always bursting with news and regular updates on Jake. I know when she stopped breastfeeding him, when his first tooth came, when he started to walk and sleep through the night and eat solids and go in the sea for the first time and everything else about his life, because she cannot help herself.

She always asks me how I'm doing and what I'm up to, even though she must know there's never anything to tell. How can there be? All I do is work and sit in this apartment, thinking what my life would be like if it was me who'd got pregnant instead of her.

She thinks I don't know it's Tom's baby. I'd always suspected it, of course. Then I saw the photos and I knew.

When we email, we use our new names. So I'm Ella and she's Katie. Apart from our names, nothing else has changed, though.

I keep thinking back to that afternoon in her Bristol flat. When she was fat with pregnancy and half-mad with paranoia. The power of it all buzzing inside me, bringing everything into sharp focus so it was as if I was seeing the world properly for the first time.

I knew, even before I suggested it, that she'd say yes. And when she did, I thought my life – my real life, the one I'd been waiting to live for so long – was about to begin.

But it didn't last. How could it when she's there, living her perfect life by the sea, and I'm here, three storeys up in a poky little box of a flat with paper-thin walls and no air conditioning?

Shane emails or FaceTimes me almost every day. I'm still Katie to him. I don't want to tell him I'm someone else now. If I do that, he could try to look for Ella before I'm ready. Without me, he has no hope of finding her.

He wants me to move back to England so we can be 'a proper couple'. It's funny, really. Just when he's realised how much he needs me, I start to lose interest. All that endless crap about how much he's suffered, it gets boring after a while. But I reply to his emails and I usually take his calls because I loved him once and that's got to mean something, hasn't it?

It's warm in the apartment this evening. I've opened the windows to try to cool the place. The air outside is every bit as hot and the noise from the street below is deafening. I check the time. It's almost ten o'clock, but you wouldn't think it. The street I live on is lined with bars with tables and chairs outside. When I moved here, I liked the idea of that. Imagined myself spending evenings down there, sitting at a table with my friends drinking glasses of grassy Sauvignon Blanc and sharing gossipy stories. Not stuck up here on my own listening to other people having the time of their lives.

A woman keeps laughing every few seconds, a screechy sound that slices through me like nails dragging down a blackboard. I'm closing the window, thinking I'd rather be too warm than listen to that sound a second longer, when my laptop pings with the sound of an incoming email.

I open the laptop and see the message on my screen: *Email from KHope93@gmail.com.*

I click on it right away, hungry for news of my other life. She's attached a photo. I wait for it to load, resentment seething inside me as I anticipate another snapshot view of her perfect home with her perfect child. When the photo finally loads, I'm confused for a second, because I'm in it.

I'm kneeling on a beach building a stone tower with a boy who's kneeling opposite me holding a stone in his hand and smiling at the camera – a big, gappy grin that tugs at my insides.

Almost immediately, I come to my senses. The woman in the photo isn't me. It's her. She's bending over to pick up a stone and her hair has fallen across her face so you can't see it clearly. It's the first photo she's sent me with her in it. All the others have been just of Jake or the beach. That's what caused my confusion. I haven't seen her in over two years. Somehow, during that time, I forgot how alike we've become.

I stare at the woman in the photo, and all I think is this:

It should be me.

Fifty-Nine

Autumn. Dee's favourite season. She loved the changing colours, the cooler temperature, the way the weather could change in the blink of an eye from fooling you it was still summer to a sudden downpour that left you drenched. She loved the shortening days and the shades of grey at dusk, when the world was somewhere between day and night and everything seemed to slow down and the ocean grew so still it was easy to believe the tide had stopped turning and the world would stay like this forever.

She'd spent most of the afternoon on the deck, drinking tea and watching the shifting colours of the sea and sky as the day gradually turned into night. The sun had set over an hour ago and it was getting cold, but she stayed outside anyway, not wanting to leave in case she missed them.

Of course, there was always a chance they'd changed their plans, but she didn't think so. She was so familiar with the patterns of their life, she would know, surely, if they were doing something different. Tonight was Friday. Pizza and movie night. They provided the pizza and Dee brought dessert. It was something they'd done every Friday for the last two months.

Until tonight.

It was already seven o'clock, and she was starting to feel stupid. She'd clearly misinterpreted the situation. Thinking something was happening when they'd obviously made other plans and not bothered to tell her.

'Idiot,' she muttered, picking up her mug to go inside. No pizza or movie tonight, then. Instead, she'd have to do with a bottle of wine and whatever she could find in the freezer.

She stepped into the sitting room and was closing the door when she heard a noise behind her. She froze. Memories of the attack three months ago flooding back.

'Surprise!'

A burst of noise and voices, shocking her so badly that the empty mug fell from her hand, smashing onto the parquet floor.

'What the...?'

She swung around, angry now, not scared. Four faces beaming at her from various points of the sitting room.

'What the hell are you all doing in my house?'

'It's your birthday,' Louise said, stepping out from behind the sofa to give Dee a hug.

'You were *ages*,' Daisy said.

'Sorry.' Dee bent to hug her niece, holding her until Daisy wriggled away. 'I would have come in earlier if I'd known you were all here.'

'Then it wouldn't have been a surprise,' Ed said. He was grinning like this was the best idea in the world, even though he must know – mustn't he? – how much Dee hated surprises. He kept grinning as he moved across the room and gave her a quick kiss on each cheek.

Dee was torn between wanting to slap him and kiss him back. As always, she ended up doing neither and stepped away from him to hug Ben, who was tugging the bottom of her sweater.

'Hey, Ben boy.' She lifted him in the air and held him tight, breathing in the warm, comforting smell of his little-boy body.

'We got cake!'

Ben jumped out of her arms, took her hand and started dragging her towards the kitchen. She let him pull her, while she looked around the room for the two people she hadn't seen yet.

As she was admiring the cake, a chocolate caterpillar with far too many candles on its back, she spotted Alex Mackey outside on the beach. He was down by the water, walking along the stretch of sand that appeared when the tide was out. He was speaking to someone on the phone, his shoulders hunched up, making him look tense and tired and old.

Even now, three months after the event, Dee felt the familiar mix of anger and shame when she saw him. He had lied to her. He was nothing more than a shallow womaniser who preyed on lonely, vulnerable women. He had been seeing her and Ella at the same time. Pretending to both of them that he was their friend when all along he was only interested in having sex with them.

He'd known that if anyone found out he'd been seeing Ella, he would become a suspect. So he'd pushed to keep Dee close. Using her to find out how the police investigation was going, making sure no one suspected him of doing anything wrong.

At least Dee knew now that it wasn't Alex who had broken into her house and stolen Katie's file. That had been Shane Gilbert.

By the time the emergency services had turned up at Roxanne's house, Shane had disappeared. The police eventually tracked him down to a caravan park in Kent. He was arrested and had been in custody since then, awaiting trial for multiple murders.

Thanks to Ed, Dee had been able to piece together most of Shane's story from his police interviews. He'd admitted breaking into Dee's house and taking Katie's file. But he'd denied coming back the next day and stealing her laptop. Instead, he was claiming it was Billy who'd taken the laptop and attacked Dee.

Dee didn't believe this, and neither did Kent police, who had decided to include Billy Morrison's manslaughter in the list of charges facing Shane Gilbert. Their version of events was that Shane had asked Billy to help him hack into Dee's laptop. When Billy refused, Shane lost his temper and pushed Billy down the stairs, planting the laptop beside his body to make it look as if Billy had stolen it.

Ed had told Dee that when Shane's case came to trial, his defence team might well put forward a plea of not guilty by insanity. While still in prison, he had started using bodybuilding steroids, an addiction that had got worse over the years. At some point, he'd also become a heavy cocaine user. The combination of steroids and cocaine was known to cause psychotic and violent outbursts.

Dee knew Shane's story was tragic. He'd been sentenced for a crime he'd never committed. There was every chance that his subsequent drug habit was a direct consequence of this miscarriage of justice. But he'd killed too many people for her to feel sorry for him.

'Hey.' Ed put his hand on her shoulder. 'You okay?'

'Sure.' Dee forced herself to smile.

'They're here,' he said. 'They got stuck in traffic apparently. Look.' He pointed out of the window at the two people walking along the beach from the mobile home. Dee opened the back door and went out to greet them, smiling so hard her face hurt.

'Dee!'

Jake started to run when he saw her, tripping and slipping over the shingle, a smile lighting up his face.

'We got you a present.' He was carrying a gift-wrapped box, far too big for him, which he thrust into Dee's hands. 'Candles. They smell.'

'I'm sure they'll be lovely,' Dee said. 'That's really thoughtful. Thank you.' She looked over Jake's head at the man standing behind him.

'I wasn't sure what to get you,' Tom said. 'But Jake saw these and said you liked candles.'

'He's right,' Dee said. 'I love them.' She looked back down at Jake. 'We've got cake inside. Chocolate cake.'

'I love cake,' Jake said, already running towards the house.

'How's he doing?' Dee asked.

'Not great today,' Tom said. 'He misses her so much, you know?'

'Of course he does. How about you?'

'This week's been a bit crap,' Tom said. 'But that means next week will be better, right?'

'And you'll see her next week,' Dee said.

'We'll see her next week.' Tom smiled. 'Yeah. That'll be good. She called last night. She sounded okay, actually. Although I never know how much of it she puts on for Jake, you know?'

'I thought she seemed all right the last time I went to visit,' Dee said. 'I know it can't be easy, but I get the feeling she's relieved it's all over. And she knows how lucky she is. How lucky they both are.'

Unlike Trevor and Roxanne, Jake and Ella had survived that terrible afternoon. Inside the burning shed, Trevor had managed to knock down the back wall and push Jake outside to safety. He was following the little boy out when a piece of burning wood fell on him, trapping him.

Ella was barely alive when the firemen found her. In the days following the fire, it had been touch and go whether she would survive. But she was tougher than she looked, and she fought back.

One of the first things she did when she was able to speak was confess to killing Gus Hope in 2008. Roxanne, who had witnessed the tragedy, had come up with the idea of framing Shane for the attack. At the time, Ella had gone along with it, thinking it was the only way she could escape Shane's obsessive attention. But the guilt at what she'd done had never left her. If anything, it had grown worse over the years. It was guilt that had made her maintain her friendship with Katie. Not knowing that Katie had her own agenda for wanting to keep her close.

'She knew,' Ella told Dee. 'All that time when she was pretending to be my friend, she knew what I'd done. She set out to destroy my life. Not that I can blame her. I never should have lied about what happened that night.'

When Shane was released from prison, it was all too easy for Ella to believe he was out to get her. Pregnant, alone and half crazed with guilt, she had never imagined it could be Katie behind the silent phone calls and the break-ins. By the time Katie suggested they swap identities, it seemed like the answer to all her problems.

'Katie orchestrated the whole thing,' she said. 'In my head, I'd turned Shane into this monster. He was never half as powerful as I made him out to be.'

Ella had recounted all of this during Dee's regular visits to her in HMP Bronzefield, where she was being held on remand. After she'd confessed, the Crown Prosecution Service had decided to charge her with manslaughter and perverting the course of justice. Given her history, she was deemed a flight risk and bail was denied.

Once the trial was over – whatever the outcome – Dee would be able to write about it. If that was what she wanted. At its heart, she sensed this was Katie's story. A messed-up, lonely kid so full of self-hatred she'd spent most of her life trying to become someone she wasn't. She wasn't sure this was a story she was ready to tell.

Unlike Katie, Dee had been given a second chance. She was rebuilding her life. A different life to the one she'd had in London, but a life nonetheless. Tom and Jake were living in the mobile home. Dee helped a lot with Jake because the boy needed all the support he could get. He was having counselling following the fire, and he missed his mother every single day. She had been the sole source of everything for the first two years of his life. Learning to live without her wasn't easy. Even with a dad like Tom to help him through.

Dee had started hiking again; long, solitary walks across the South Downs that gave her the space she needed to breathe and the time she needed to think about what she was going to do with the rest of her life. She had a few ideas, but nothing concrete. Not yet.

Then there was Ed. She wasn't sure how she'd define their relationship. If she'd even call it a relationship. Nothing had happened between them. But it felt as if something was about to. And that sense of anticipation was reason enough to get her out of bed most mornings.

On the days she found it harder – the days she was tempted to do nothing except laze about inside waiting until the evening came so she could start drinking – those days, she would think of Trevor Dubber and Billy Morrison. She would think of the life and promise they'd both had, that sense they gave of anything being possible. And she would think how lucky she was, how very lucky, because she was still here.

She was alive, and the sun was shining outside her bedroom window, and she had friends, people she cared about. And maybe, when she had worked out what she was going to do with the rest of her life, she would write a story that would make Billy and Trevor proud.

Acknowledgements

Massive thanks to all my friends who've stuck with me through this writing journey and so much else. Thanks also to: my parents (the Irish sales team); my lovely agent, Laura Longrigg; my writing buddies Chris Curran, Sarah Reed, Alison O'Leary, Louise Phillips, Claire Flynn and Adele O'Neill, for being so generous with your time and support; everyone at Team Canelo, especially Louise Cullen, Francesca Riccardi and Siân Heap. Finally, and most importantly, my family – Luke, Sean, Ruby: we've been through so much and we're still here, stronger and tougher and better than ever. I love you guys more than words can ever say.

CANELOCRIME

Do you love crime fiction and are always on the lookout
for brilliant authors?

Canelo Crime is home to some of the most exciting
novels around. Thousands of readers are already enjoying
our compulsive stories. Are you ready to find your new
favourite writer?

Find out more and sign up to our newsletter at
canelocrime.com